Praise for the novels of
New York Times bestselling author
Jessica Clare

"Blazing hot."   —*USA Today*

"Sexy."   —*Smexy Books*

"Sizzling! Jessica Clare gets everything right in this erotic and sexy
romance. . . . You need to read this book!"   —*Romance Junkies*

Praise for the novels of
USA Today bestselling author
Jen Frederick

"Sexy and sinful."   —*New York Times* bestselling author Katy Evans

"I love these strong characters."   —*Sizzling Pages Romance Reviews*

"Wonderful . . . I wholly recommend you read it."
                                          —*Nocturnal Book Reviews*

OTHER TITLES BY JESSICA CLARE

THE BILLIONAIRE BOYS CLUB

Stranded with a Billionaire
Beauty and the Billionaire
The Wrong Billionaire's Bed
Once Upon a Billionaire

THE GAMES NOVELS

Wicked Games
Playing Games
Ice Games
Bedroom Games

THE BLUEBONNET NOVELS

The Girl's Guide to (Man) Hunting
The Care and Feeding of an Alpha Male
The Expert's Guide to Driving a Man Wild
The Virgin's Guide to Misbehaving

OTHER TITLES BY JEN FREDERICK

WOODLANDS SERIES

Undeclared
Undressed in the anthology Snow Kissed
Unspoken
Unraveled

ALSO BY JESSICA CLARE AND JEN FREDERICK

Last Breath

LAST
HIT

Jessica Clare
Jen Frederick

BERKLEY BOOKS, NEW YORK

The Berkley Publishing Group
Published by the Penguin Group
Penguin Group (USA) LLC
375 Hudson Street, New York, New York 10014

USA • Canada • UK • Ireland • Australia • New Zealand • India • South Africa • China

penguin.com

A Penguin Random House Company

LAST HIT

ISBN: 978-0-425-28150-5

An application to register this book for cataloging has been submitted to the Library of Congress.

PUBLISHING HISTORY
Pear Tree Publishing eBook edition / December 2013
Berkley trade paperback edition / February 2015

PRINTED IN THE UNITED STATES OF AMERICA

10 9 8 7 6 5 4 3 2 1

Cover design by Meljean Brook.
Interior text design by Kelly Lipovich.

To the MGL.

You made this book happen.

To our families.

Your support makes this all possible.

NIKOLAI

I have been a contract killer since I was a boy. For years I savored the fear caused by my name, the trembling at the sight of my tattoos. The stars on my knees, the marks on my fingers, the dagger in my neck, all bespoke of danger. If you saw my eyes, it was the last vision you'd have. I have ever been the hunter, never the prey. With her, I am the mark and I am ready to lie down and let her capture me. Opening my small scarred heart to her brings out my enemies. I will carry out one last hit, but if they hurt her, I will bring the world down around their ears.

DAISY

I've been sheltered from the outside world all my life. Home-schooled and farm-raised, I'm so naïve that my best friend calls me Pollyanna. I like to believe the best in people. Nikolai is part of this new life, and he's terrifying to me. Not because his eyes are cold or my friend warns me away from him, but because he's the only man that has ever seen the real me beneath the awkwardness. With him, my heart is at risk and also, my life.

CHAPTER ONE

DAISY

I have planned for this day in secret for six long years, I think as I wake up and stretch, a giddy burn in my stomach that might be nerves.

Today, I will escape.

The day starts as any other. It's like the world can't see how excited I am inside, but I'm practically vibrating with anticipation. Freedom is so close I can taste it. I get out of bed and dress in a dark, floor-length skirt and matching blouse. I throw a sweater on over it, so every inch of my body is covered. Then I go to my mattress and pull out the disposable cellphone and the small wad of cash I have saved up.

Seven hundred dollars from six years of saving. It has to be enough. I tuck them both into my bra to hide them.

I go to the bathroom and pull my dark hair into a ponytail and then splash water on my face to cleanse it. I stare at my reflection. My face is bleach pale, but there's a flush on my cheeks that betrays me. I don't like it, and I wet a cloth and press it to my cheeks, hoping the color will fade. When I can't delay any longer, I leave the safety of my bathroom.

My father is seated in the living room. The room is a dark cave. No light comes in. There's a chair and a sofa, and a TV. The TV is off, and I know it's only programmed to broadcast happy, chaste channels like religious TV or children's shows. If I'm lucky, I get to watch PBS. I long for something edgier, but my father has removed everything else from the channel list, and I'm not allowed the remote.

As usual, the only light in the room is a small lamp beside his chair. It halos his recliner, and my father is seated in an island of light in the oppressive darkness. He reads a thick hardback—Dickens—and closes it when I enter the room. He's dressed in a button-up shirt and slacks, his hair neatly combed. It is ironic that my father dresses so well, considering he doesn't leave the house and no one will see him but me. If I ask, he will simply say that appearances are important.

Our entire house is like the living room: dark, oppressive, thick with shadow. It's sucking the life out of me, day by day, which is why I must do what I can to escape.

"Sir." I greet my father, and wait. My hands are clasped behind my back, and I'm the picture of a dutiful daughter.

He eyes my clothing, my sweater. "Are you going out today?"

"If the weather is nice today." I don't look at the windows in the living room. Not a shred of light comes through them. It's not possible. Despite my father's pristine appearance, the house looks like a construction zone. The arching windows that once filled the living room with light are boarded up with plywood, the edges smoothed down with yards of duct tape. Father has made the living room into a fortress to protect himself, but I have grown to hate the oppressive feel of it. I feel like a bat trapped in a cave, never to see sunlight.

I can't wait to escape.

He grunts at my words and hands over a small key. I take it from him with a whispered thank-you and go to the computer desk. It has a roll-down top that my father locks every night. He doesn't trust the Internet, of course. It's full of bad things that can corrupt young minds. He has a filter set up on the browsers so I can't browse explicit websites, not that I would. Not when the only computer in the house is ten feet from his chair.

I calmly go to the computer and type in the address for the weather website. Today's forecast? Perfect. Of course it is. "The weather looks good."

"Then you will run errands today." He pulls on a pair of glasses and picks up a notepad, flipping through it. After a moment, he rips off a piece of paper and hands it to me. "This is the grocery list. Go to the post office and get stamps as well."

I take the list with trembling fingers. Two places today. "Can I go to the library, too?"

He frowns at my request.

I hold my breath. I need to go to the library. But I can't look too anxious.

"I'm already sending you to two places, Daisy."

"I know," I tell him. "But I'd like a new book to read."

"What topic?"

"Astronomy," I blurt. I'm only allowed to read nonfiction around my father. It's a harmless topic, outer space. And if he presses, I can say I'm continuing my education despite finishing my homeschooling years ago. Father won't relax his grip enough for me to go to college, so I have to continue my learning as best I can.

He stares at me for a long moment, and I worry he can see right through me, into my plans. "Fine," he says after an eternity. He checks his watch. "It's eight thirty now. You'll be back by ten thirty?"

It's not much time to go to the grocery store, the post office, and the library. I frown. "Can I have until eleven?"

His eyes narrow. "You can have until ten thirty, Daisy. You are to go to those places and nowhere else. It's not safe. Do you understand me?"

"Yes, sir." I close the computer, lock the desk, and hand the key back to him.

As I do, he grabs my arm and frowns. "Daisy, look at me."

Oh no. I force my guilty eyes to his gaze. He knows what I'm doing, doesn't he? Even though I've been so careful, he's figured it out.

"Are you wearing makeup?"

Is that all? "No, Father—"

His hand slaps my cheek in reproach.

We both stare at each other in shock. He's never hit me before. Never.

My father recovers first. "No, *sir*," he says, to correct me. I stare at him for so long that my eyes feel dry with the need to blink. Resentment burns inside of me, and for a long moment, I wonder what my father would do if I slapped back. Or if I marched down to the basement and shot off a few rounds into the wall of phonebooks that acted as the backstop for father's makeshift (and probably illegal) indoor shooting range.

But I can't think like that. Not right now. I'm not yet strong enough. So I swallow my anger.

"No, *sir*," I echo. Calling him "sir" is a new rule. Now that I'm twenty-one, I'm not allowed to call him "Father" anymore. Just "sir." My heart aches at how much he's changed—as if every year the terror in him grows stronger and if I stay here, it will overtake me, too.

He grabs my face with his other hand and examines it closely, though I know it's dark enough that he can't see me all that well. The festering resentment continues to bubble in my stomach, but I permit this. It won't be much longer. After today, I won't have to deal with this ever again.

After a moment, he licks his thumb and rubs it on my flushed cheek, inspecting it under the light. No makeup. He makes a *hmmph* sound. "Fine. You can go."

"Thank you, sir," I tell him. I take the list he hands me, and the cash, and rush to the front door.

There are six locks and four deadbolts on the door, and it takes a moment for my trembling fingers to undo all of them. I get to go out.

I get to leave.

I'm never entering this house again.

Once the door is unbolted, I carefully shut it again and then wait a moment. The sound of my father locking and turning all the bolts again reaches my ears. Good. I stand on the covered porch for a moment and stare out at our yard. Our small house has a rickety fence in the front that is falling down, but we don't repair it. The grass is knee high because Father won't let me mow it but once a month. Surrounding our house are acres and acres of farmland that we let out to neighboring farmers. We don't grow anything ourselves, since that would entail being outside.

And the Millers don't go outside unless they can't help it. I know that when I was eight, he witnessed my mother's murder while shopping. I was too young to remember much about her, just a smiling, happy face with warm brown hair and even warmer eyes that disappeared one day. And I know that my father reported her murder to the police but that the killer was underage. A fluke, a random shooting at a grocery store, and my mother had been the victim. Two years later, the murderer was back out on the streets, and he'd commented in court that he was coming after my father for locking him away.

I think it was bravado, nothing but the bragging of a young boy full of rage. My father took it to heart. He refuses to go outside, believing himself safe and protected in his home.

I can't hate him for it. I want to, but I can't. I know what it's like to live every day in fear.

I head down the road, practically running to the bus stop so I'll have time to do everything. The bus arrives a few minutes later, and I go to the local grocery store. I get my cart as if it's just another day. I shop for the items on the list, taking great care with my selections. When I get to the checkout, they frown at me. They recognize my face. They hate me at this grocery store, but I don't care.

As soon as I have my purchases bagged, I immediately head to the customer service counter. I place two of the items I've bought—vitamins and ibuprofen—on the counter. "I need to exchange these."

The clerk there knows my routine. I'm sure she thinks I'm crazy, but she simply waves a hand. "Get what you need and bring it back."

I do, and five minutes later I have exchanged the expensive, pricey brands for two cheap generics. After years of receipt scanning, I know which ones don't print brand names on the receipt and I always, always switch them out and pocket the change. It's the only way I can save money and not have Father notice it missing.

Now I have seven hundred and fifteen dollars.

I take the groceries with me to the post office, get the stamps, and then head to the library. I should have gone to the library first so the groceries would stay colder, but today, I don't care.

I head to the romance shelf, looking for the book I was reading. It's there, tucked safely behind other books so no one will borrow it until I'm done reading it. I fish it out and read chapter seven while standing up. I wish I could take the book home with me, but Father would never let me keep it. I'm only allowed to read classics. So I come to the library as often as I can and read a chapter at a time.

I close my book with a dreamy sigh a few minutes later. The hero has just kissed the heroine and is sliding his hand into her panties. I want to read on, but I mustn't. There's still so much to do. I will dream about how he touches her, I'm sure. I want to be touched, too.

I want a hero. A big, strong, handsome prince to come rescue me from my miserable life. But since one has not arrived, I must rescue myself.

I soar through the nonfiction and grab a book on astronomy. Then I pause, and I put the book back. I don't know why I'm keeping up the pretense. I'm not going home to Father. Not today. I head back to the romance section and grab my novel.

Then, I move to the computers and pull up the Gmail address I have created for myself. If Father only knew that the library had computers to use that could access the Internet, he'd never let me come here.

There's a response in my email. I dance in my chair, so excited I can barely stand it.

Daisy,

I'm so glad you found my ad! You sure you don't want to see the place before you come here? It's not the greatest, but it's a roof

over the head, and the rent is cheap enough. Come by and say
hello before you decide anything. We'll have lunch.

XOXO
Regan

There's a phone number at the bottom of the email. I print it
out, along with the original Craigslist listing for the apartment in
Minneapolis. Will she get upset if I meet her for lunch and then
just never leave? I hope not.

There is a second email as well. This one is a confirmation of
an appointment. Today, at ten thirty. The timing is perfect.

I also print out the bus schedule. I check out my book and
head home. The bus drops me off on the road fifteen minutes
before the person I've scheduled will arrive. Nerves begin to
gnaw at me. I walk exceedingly slowly, watching for a car to pull
up in front of my father's boarded-up farmhouse.

It shows up right on time, and I rush to meet the man that
emerges from the car. He's big, middle-aged, balding. No-nonsense
looking. He wears dark scrubs and frowns when I come running
out of the bushes, grocery bags in hand.

"I'm Daisy Miller," I say breathlessly and extend my hand
to him.

"John Eton," he says, and glances at our house, taking in the
boarded up windows, the overgrown lawn. "Someone lives here?"

"My father." At his skeptical look, I say, "He's agoraphobic.
He won't leave the house. That's why the windows are boarded
up." I want to tell him so much more about my father's craziness
and his controlling nature, which has gotten worse over the
years, but I can't. I need to leave.

A look of sympathy crosses the man's face. "I see."

"He's going to need an assistant twice a week," I tell him. "That's why I've hired the service—you." I sound so calm, even though I'm dancing inside. "I need you to come by and see what errands he needs to be completed. Check in on him when he needs it. He doesn't use email and won't answer his phone unless you ring once, hang up, and then ring again. That's how he knows who is calling."

John Eton stares at me like I'm the crazy one. "I see."

"When you knock at the door, you have to knock four times," I tell him. "Same reason."

"All right," he says. "Shall we go in and say hello?"

I hold the two grocery bags out to him. "I'm not going in."

"I'm sorry?"

"I'm leaving," I say, and I offer him the grocery bags again. To my relief, he takes them. "Father . . . wants me to stay. And I can't. I can't stay any longer." Tears well up in my eyes, but I blink them away. I love my father, I do. I just can't live with him for one more moment. The entire world is out here, waiting. "I hired you to take care of him. His disability check is direct deposited on the first. I've set up the service to be auto-debited on the fifth of every month. I just need someone to come out and take care of him, since he won't leave the house."

"I see." John doesn't look happy, but he glances at the house and then back to me. "Are you running away?"

I'm twenty-one. Can adults truly run away? But I nod. "I can't take it any longer."

Sympathy crosses his face again. "I understand. Is there a number I can reach you at in case there are any questions? Or if something goes wrong?"

I'm startled at his words, guilt coursing through me. Something . . . goes wrong? I'm leaving my father in the care of this man.

A stranger. A service I've hired that won't care that he has a panic attack if he hears a car backfire, who won't care that my father weeps when he goes to bed every night, who won't care that even a hint of sunlight in the living room will send him into hysterics.

But I can't think about that, because if I do, I'll end up staying. I give him the number of my disposable phone, knowing I won't answer it. There's too much guilt involved. My father will be heartbroken and angry that I have left without so much as a good-bye. But I know my father. I know that if I go in and confront him, he'll overpower me. Not physically, but with guilt.

And I have to leave. I just have to.

So when John steps toward the house, I clutch my wallet close and then run. Tears stream down my face as I go, but they're not tears of sadness.

They're joy.

The sun is bearing down on me, the birds are singing in the trees, and for the first time, the world is wide open.

I'm free.

Clutching the printout close, I head up the dirty stairs to the fifth floor of the apartment building.

I have just gotten off of a six-hour bus ride to Minneapolis, and it feels good to stretch my legs. I should be tired, but I feel invigorated instead. I'm free. I'm free. I'm free.

Earlier, I texted Regan to let her know I was on my way. We set up a meet up at the apartment, and then we're going to go to dinner afterward to hang out and get to know each other and see if we mesh and I want to move in. I don't care if she's the most obnoxious person in the world. I've lived with a difficult, demanding person for twenty-one years. Nothing she says or does can be that bad. I will still want to move in.

The building is dirty, but it's buzzing with life. There are people hanging out in the hallways, chatting, and people out on the streets. I smile at everyone. I can't stop smiling. I'm so excited to be out living a real life. A normal life, like everyone else my age.

I find Regan's apartment—224. It's at the end of the hall. I knock, and a moment later it's answered.

A cheerful blonde opens the door. She's tall, statuesque, and gorgeous. She's wearing tight-fitting clothing and her hair is curled into loose waves. Regan is beautiful. She lights up at the sight of me. "Are you Daisy Miller?"

I smooth a stray lock of brown hair into my ponytail, feeling very plain next to her. "That's me. You must be Regan Porter."

"You're so cute! Not what I imagined at all." She examines me with an excited look on her face. "But . . . I hate to ask. You sure you're not pulling my leg about how old you are?"

"I'm twenty-one," I say, pulling out my identification card. It's not a driver's license; that would have involved Father letting me leave the house for longer than an hour at a time. I make a mental note that I need to learn how to drive in this new life.

She takes the card from me and nods. "Sorry. I just had to ask. You have this . . . I don't know. You look younger than I thought." She squints at me. "Or just sweeter, I guess. Anyhow, how's it going?" Her enthusiasm is back, and she waves a hand at me. "Don't just stand there. Come on in!"

I enter the apartment, clutching my wallet to my chest, and look around. It's a tiny apartment, easily a quarter the size of my father's house. The walls are grimy and there are cracks in the corners, but the back wall has three enormous windows that give a view of the city, and I'm pleased to see that they're wide open. Sunlight pours in, shining on scuffed wooden floors. There are posters of horror movies up on the walls, and a futon for a couch. There's a folding chair off to one side and an ugly coffee table.

I love it.

"I know it's not much to look at, but I'm slowly furnishing by hitting estate sales," Regan says to me with a grin. "It'll get there."

"It's just fine," I say enthusiastically. "I love it."

She laughs. "Well, you're not hard to convince. So Pollyanna of you. I like that. Come on. I'll show you the rest of the place."

The bathroom is little more than a closet with an ancient tub and a toilet. My room isn't much bigger, but there is a bed, an old dresser—courtesy of Regan's last roomie who'd moved out—and a nightstand with a lamp on it. There is also a window. I move to the window and glance out. It faces the street and a building across the way. I don't care what the view is as long as it has one.

"So, what do you think? Like I said, your share of the rent is four hundred, due on the first, and that includes all utilities paid. It's not a great place, but it's pretty central to everything, which is good if you don't have a car. Do you?"

I shake my head. "I don't."

"Like I said in the ad, my boyfriend stays here a lot. If that bothers you, this might not be the apartment for you. My last roomie couldn't handle it, so she left." She shrugs her shoulders, unapologetic. "Just putting that out there up front so there's no misunderstandings."

"I don't mind." I don't care if she has three boyfriends.

"There's a laundry room down in the basement if you want to wash clothes." She eyes me curiously. "If you don't mind me asking, where *are* your clothes?"

I don't have any bags with me. "I . . . left them at the farm." I know I must seem weird to her.

"Fresh start, huh?" She pats me on the shoulder and then rubs my arm. "I know how that goes."

I nod, feeling a lump in my throat. Fresh start, indeed.

CHAPTER **TWO**

DAISY

I move in with Regan and hand over four hundred dollars of my precious cash. Regan seems to accept my story and me, and she's fun to be around. She wants to introduce me to her friends. "You need to come hang out with us, Pollyanna."

She's started to call me Pollyanna, because she's already noticed that I'm a bit naïve. I don't mind. I've seen that movie, and I liked Pollyanna. She's going out for drinks that night with some friends, but I can only take so much stimuli at once. It has been an exhausting day, and I crash into bed, too exhausted to even put sheets on the dirty mattress.

For the next week, I explore the city on my own. It's terrifying and exhilarating all at once. I scour thrift shops, secondhand stores, and a yard sale for clothing. When I pass by a window filled with pretty, lacy under-things, I want to go inside and buy a few pairs for myself. I head immediately for the clearance racks, but everything there is far too expensive. I go to the clearance bins at the shopping center instead and purchase the cheapest items. They're in odd sizes and probably won't fit right, but I don't care. They're clean and they're mine, and if they're not pretty, they'll do.

It doesn't take long to realize that money goes faster than I'd anticipated. After a few days, I count out what I have left. I've spent seventy dollars for clothing. Sixty for bus tickets around town. Ten for dinner with Regan the other night. Four hundred on rent. I have enough for groceries, and then I must find a job.

Any job.

I want to go to college, too. Just the local community college will do, but I need to save up some money first. There are several in the city, and I take a bus to one of the campuses, just to see what it's like. My heart fills with longing as I walk the grounds. There are people my age everywhere, laughing and talking as they head to class or pause to chat. I want to be one of them.

I just need the money first.

I'm still feeling out of sorts after a week of freedom. I feel restless and uneasy. This is a new place, and I'm not used to new places and new things. For twenty-one years, I've been in the same small room at home, with the same four walls. The new apartment is different. My new room is small but pleasant; the view outside the apartment window allows me to see the sky above the buildings.

My room is stuffy, so I use this as an excuse to open the window again and let the cool night air brush against my skin. Now that I can, I sleep with the window open every night. I want to keep it open forever. It feels like defiance and freedom, and I love it.

I return to bed, pleased with the breeze and the night view. Maybe that will take some of the edge off of my nerves. I flick the lights off and strip out of my new jeans and ill-fitting new bra and then climb into bed in nothing but an old T-shirt borrowed from Regan and a pair of panties. After a moment of indecision, I kick the blankets off. Still too warm.

I press a hand to my forehead and sigh.

As if in response to my sigh, I hear a moan come from the other room followed by a loud, "Oh God, almost!"

My hands slide over my face in embarrassment despite the darkness of my room. Regan is having sex with Mike, who stays over quite often, as Regan had said. He's here more nights than he's not, and they have loud, noisy sex every time they get a chance. It's embarrassing and a bit startling for me.

I've been incredibly sheltered, my only exposure to sex what I've read in romance novels. Somehow, I never pictured it sounding so very . . . carnal.

A moment later, music turns on, and it drowns out Regan's cries for more, which is a welcome relief. Now I just hear strains of heavy metal. Not that this is easier to sleep to, but it's less disturbing to hear. The whole interlude makes me more on edge, though.

I know I'm uneasy and out of sorts because of more than just the view outside my window. I think other people would adjust to the change in lifestyle quite well, but I'm just timid Daisy, afraid of her own shadow. This new place is completely foreign, and it feels like I'm in a different country instead of just a different city and state.

It's weird, but I feel lonely despite my happiness.

There are so many people around me now. More than ever. I smile at everyone—the postman, the bus driver, the people at the grocery store. I can't stop smiling. There is a giddy happiness to me, and I think I will never be able to frown again. I love life too much. The world feels so open and full of opportunity.

But at the same time, I think of my father. Does he feel betrayed?

Guilt gnaws at me, and I push the thought away. I left him behind because I wanted to be someone new. Someone different and vibrant.

Yet I still feel like the same, scared little Daisy. Despite being here a week, I feel like I'm adrift. I know only Regan and her boyfriend. I haven't gone out with Regan's friends yet, mindful of my money.

I'm changing, but it's not enough. I need more.

I think of the duo in the other room, having sex. And I think of my romance novel. For some reason, this combination makes my body flush, and the tension I feel takes on a whole new aspect.

My hand slides down my belly, to my new, pink lacy panties. Fingers dip into the sweet warmth between my legs, and I gasp at the sensation. My fingertips brush over my clitoris, and I think of a man doing this to me. I rub teasing circles around my clitoris, imagining him. His hands on my body. His fingers where mine are. Him kissing me sweetly on the brow and pressing my body against his. I rub harder, arching with need.

My dreamy hero leans in and I can almost see his face . . .

Almost.

My fingers stop. Burgeoning desire dissipates like a soap bubble.

I lay back, utterly still.

Utterly frustrated.

All this freedom, and yet I'm still no different than I was before. I can't visualize a man touching me when I haven't even been kissed. My guilt for leaving my father turns into a momentary flash of hatred. He's made me this sheltered freak. Who will date a twenty-one-year-old woman who has never kissed a man? Never seen sex, not even on TV? Only read about it?

For a moment, I want to sneak into Regan's room and watch her and Mike, just so I know, just so I understand.

If I can't experience it myself, the next best thing is watching, right?

I want to clutch at my new life with tight hands, but I don't even know where to begin.

So I sigh, slide my fingers to my panties, and try again.

NIKOLAI

I watch her through my bathroom window. I've placed one of my four rented chairs in here for that express purpose. I tell myself it is not creepy, as the American girls would say, because I watch everyone. But really I watch only her.

I cannot see everything. I've never seen her nude. I've never seen inside her shower. Smartly there is no window there. But I can see her bedroom and her living room and beyond that, with my scope, her kitchen. I know her schedule. When she gets up in the morning, when she returns to her apartment. If she were a mark, I could've killed her a dozen times over by now and been in the wind.

She throws her bag onto her bed and then lies down next to it. It takes many muscles to smile, more to frown, but only a few to pull the trigger. I peer down the scope and place my crosshairs over her forehead. Puff, dead.

She has a roommate. Tall, blond, who brings home one man regularly. He is bad in bed. I can see the roommate masturbating after the man falls asleep. I place the crosshairs over his heart. It would be a mercy killing. A man who goes to sleep without satisfying his woman deserves punishment. He sleeps through her self-pleasure? Death is too kind.

The roommate is not my business, though, and I swing my

scope back to my girl's room. She is still lying on her back. Through my magnified glass, I can see furrows on her brow. I had toyed with the idea of planting listening devices in her apartment but I stopped myself because, stupidly, I thought it would be too invasive. *She is not the mark*, I remind myself but scowl at my lack of audio.

I should know what is causing her to frown so that I can make the cause go away. I watch her until she gets up and leaves the room. She does not reappear in either the living room or her roommate's bedroom. I assume she is using the bathroom. I flip open the foam case at my feet and survey the contents. There are several different devices that I could use. *No, Nikolai*, I tell myself. *This is wrong.*

Then I let out a humorless laugh. Why am I preaching morality, even to myself? I gave up that right many years ago. Before I was a grown man. Perhaps it happened in the womb. I was born a killer, my teeth bared, and I claimed my first victim almost before I had taken my first breath. But that is Ukraine. A boy on the streets without a gun is prey. I have never been prey. Always the hunter.

This girl in room 224 is unprotected, but she is innocent and sweet. I envy her. When she first walked into her apartment, she did not notice the cracked and peeling paint, the cheapness of the mattress on the floor, or the chipped countertops. It all looked wonderful to her. I could see her wide-eyed amazement even through my scope. She is so unaware and so . . . joyful. There is no other word for it. Her every expression is one of anticipation, as if life is just an ongoing present.

I wonder what she would think of me—I am not unlike her apartment. I am cracked and peeling inside. She treats this slum of hers like a palace and every activity within it is a delight, from cooking her own meals to sleeping in her ratty bedroom.

I would like to lie down in her bedroom, pull down her long brown hair around me, and caress my hands over her very adult-like curves. My eyes drift shut as I think about what kind of look she'd give me. The wide-eyed innocent stare? The newly awakened one? The satisfied one? I want them all. My hand strays downward toward the ache that has developed between my legs.

A sharp piercing note fills the room. The phone. A distinct ring tone tells me it is business. Walking out of the bathroom, I move into the second bedroom. It is completely empty except for one table, also rented. I flick a switch and a light hum sounds in the room. No listening devices will be useful here; the frequency released by my sound machine will kill it. I smile grimly, thinking of the painful reverb that anyone who is listening in might suffer.

"Allo." I answer. A series of clicks sound off as my caller attempts to make his call untraceable. No matter, I record the trail anyway. No one is untraceable. Not today.

"*Bonjour, monsieur.* I call on behalf of Neuchâtel."

"*Oui.*" I switch from Russian to French to match my caller. Neuchâtel is a town in Switzerland. This call is on behalf of the Watchmakers. Hence the reference to Neuchâtel, a town renowned for its custom, hand-assembled watches, which take months to complete and sell for six figures. I received one as a gift in addition to payment after a job well done. Either the Watchmakers had no respect for me or were trying to trap me. I threw it into the River Doubs, a waterway that marked the border between Switzerland and France.

"Neuchâtel requires your services. Information will be placed on the Emperor's Palace at 2100."

"*Convenu,*" I say. Agreed. The Emperor's Palace is a marketplace on the deep web, buried so far down that no ordinary search engine can find it. These transactions are said to be not allowed but, couched right, everything from flesh to drugs are traded anonymously.

"You will do the job then?" the voice asks. He is either testing me or is new. Either way, my response is the same.

"*Je ne sais pas.*" I do not know. I always research my targets first. Although killing has been my life since I was old enough to form memories, when I left the Petrovich *Bratva* at age fifteen, I found I could not kill without reasons. Even if they were bad reasons. Each job left its own mark, and while I knew my time here on Earth was short, I bargained with myself. *This man*, I would say, *needs killing.* The inscription on my chest aches. I bring mercy to those around the targets. This is the lie I use so that I can sleep at night and be able to look at myself in the mirror. I must convince myself that the world is a better place with the target dead.

Only the heaving breath of my caller can be heard as he digests my conditions. I wait. The assassin's most powerful weapon is patience. The second, improvisation.

"*D'accord, ça me va.*" Okay, fine, he agrees.

I hang up and set an alarm on my watch for 2095. As I exit the second bedroom, a motion through the bathroom window catches my eye. *She* has returned. I place my eye against the scope. Her bed is cleared of her bag, and her back is resting against the headboard.

Her lithe body is clothed in a thin T-shirt. I can see the faint, dark outline of nipple beneath the cloth. My eyes dip lower. The shadow of her pubic hair is also visible. I can feel my heart rate pick up as I map her body with my eyes.

I feel restless and think perhaps I should review the information I have compiled for the mark or perhaps look at the routing pattern left by the caller from Neuchâtel. I do neither. As I begin to draw back from the scope, her motions arrest me. Her small hand, with the pink-tipped nails, is moving over her belly. One finger traces the tiny lace adorning the top band of her panties. My breath is suspended. Time is suspended.

I have never seen this before. She has never touched herself. Never brought a man home with her. I'd have shot him, maybe. No, I would've caused some disturbance. Something. I thought her maybe an innocent and fantasized about awakening her. But now her small fingers are delving beneath the cotton. I can see the bumps of her knuckles as they press against the pale pink fabric. She is moving her fingers in circles.

I imagine my own fingers, much larger, dark and rough, pressing down upon hers. My fingers flex involuntarily at the thought of her pussy beneath my touch. I'd stroke her lightly and in circles as that is what she appears to like. I'd move my fingers lower, beyond her clit to her hot cunt. It would be wet, dripping wet. My fingers would be soaked, and I would pause so that I could lick her sweet honey off each digit.

My cock is so hard I fear that it will break against the denim of my jeans. I draw a hand over my chest and pinch my own nipple hard, imagining it is her tiny white teeth tugging on it. I've broken out in a light sweat.

Her legs tense, and her hand motions become more frantic. I can see her chest rise and fall rapidly. Her whole body is strained, but when her release comes it is truncated. The look on her face is one of frustration rather than satisfaction. She wets her plump lips and closes her eyes. She begins again, but again she is unfulfilled.

My emotions war against each other. I am unhappy that she cannot find her own fulfillment, but there is also fierce possessiveness that arises from an idea I've tried to suppress. In my mind, only I can bring her to orgasm and release. I can teach her to touch herself in a way that will be pleasurable and satisfying.

I would not start with her pussy. No, the skin is the largest sex organ. I would stroke my hands over every inch, starting from her forehead. My lips and fingers would smooth away any furrows. My hands would encircle her neck and sweep down over her shoulders to her fine wrists.

I'd rub my body over hers so that she smelled of me. When she walked this city, other men would stay away, recognizing she was marked as my own. Belonging to Nikolai. Maybe I would tattoo it around her neck like a collar.

I stroke the homemade tattoo over my chest. The words inscribed there still burn, years after they were applied. I scowl at myself. She would run in fear if she saw me—the stars on my knees, the dagger through my neck, the spiderweb on my shoulder. The epaulets on the other. The inscription. I am tempted to throw my scope at the wall. I would never be allowed to touch her pristine skin, not with my dirty fingers or my tongue. I would defile her.

I do not hurl my weapon. An assassin's tools are his friends; perhaps the only things he owns. But I do leave my seat. She has gone into the kitchen anyway, to eat. We have one thing in common right now. We are both dissatisfied.

The thought of food alerts me to the fact I have not eaten since the morning. This is not good. I must carefully attend to my body as seriously as I treat my SAKO rifle or my HK knife. I slap together a peanut butter sandwich. The protein in the peanut butter and the grain of the wheat bread will provide me enough sustenance to last through a light workout.

I head for the arm bar that I've hung in the doorway to my bedroom. Staring at the stark space, I realize that I could not even bring her here in the dark. I curl up and down repeatedly, but my attention is wholly on the blank walls and nearly empty space of the apartment.

Nothing of value is here other than my tools. I could pack up everything in about two minutes and be gone. This is the life I'm trying to put behind me, but old habits still control me. Tomorrow I will buy a real bed to replace the foam cushion I have on the floor. A solid, wooden bed that will not move, even if an elephant fell upon it.

I do eight sets of ten and stop. My biceps and the muscles in my upper back ache pleasantly. I drop to the floor and begin my routine of one-handed push-ups. Four sets of twenty-five, and then triangle pushups until the sweat is dripping down my forehead and my deltoids, biceps, triceps, and pectoralis muscles are too weak to hold me.

Lying against the wooden floor, I think of her again. Tomorrow, perhaps I will talk to her. I will tell her that she smells of fresh air and wide spaces. That her blue eyes remind me of the sky above the Ural Mountains. I want to drown in them.

The phone rings again, and this time the tone tells me it is Daniel. Daniel is another killer whom I've run into now and again. I've had only a few communications with him because he is a dangerous man. I do not need to bring myself to the attention of people.

I remind myself to call him Daniel, short vowel sound instead of the long *e* sound as we would say it in Russian. Once I called him *Danyeel*, and he cautioned me that my mispronunciation revealed too much if we were enemies and not enough if we should be friends. I was unsure whether that was a warning or an opening. No one in this business has friends, so I never called him *Danyeel* again. Only Dan*yil*.

"Hello," I say, adopting my most American accent.

"Nick," Daniel says. We both use voice modulators. It is possible that *Danyeel* and I could stand next to each other on the street corner and not recognize the other. I would know he was a soldier, perhaps, by the watchfulness in his eyes and the careful way he held his body.

"Daniel," I answer. "What is happening?"

Daniel coughs into the phone, as if he is covering a laugh. I wonder what mistake I have made.

"It's *what's* happening. You're too formal."

This is why I do not socialize with others. Accents are fairly easy for me to adopt, but my language is too stilted to pass as native. It is a major flaw, and one Alexsandr said would be my downfall. I have learned to reduce risk by remaining silent. It is this tool I employ now. I wait for Daniel to continue. He is the one, after all, who has contacted me. The quiet between us stretches out as we wait for the other to give in. I look at my watch. I will give Daniel only sixty more seconds before I hang up.

Daniel gives in first. "I have information on the death of Alexsandr."

I shut my eyes. I am relieved but anxious. This is what I've been waiting for. It is why the man I have dubbed Mr. Brown still lives.

"You?" I ask. Why should Daniel be offering information regarding Alexsandr? I try to be casual and am grateful that Daniel cannot see me. The tenseness of my muscles would give me away. I try to not drum my fingers or pace, worried that Daniel will pick up on my motions even over the telephone.

"You are not the only one who cared about Alexsandr." Daniel's curtness surprises me. He's never exhibited anything but a laconic attitude, even when carrying out a hit. I once overheard him tell a target that he'd have killed him earlier but that he'd had to stop for his morning coffee. Sip. Bang.

"I apologize, Daniel. My selfishness is unbecoming," I say. "How much?"

Daniel sighs. The hiss of breath is irritating with the voice modulator; I pull the phone away from my ear and wait again for Daniel to speak. "This is a freebie, buddy, because I didn't like what happened, either."

"I do not accept." Never owe anyone anything. Lesson number one from Alexsandr.

"Fine, then I'll accept your SAKO rifle," Daniel tells me.

"You are gathering my bullets?" The only way Daniel could know of my kill piece is through examination of the bullet casings and extensive knowledge of barrel markings. Once again, Daniel has shown himself to be a formidable opponent. I clench the phone tighter. If Daniel becomes a problem, then I will use the knowledge I have acquired about him to eliminate the threat. I know that Daniel uses a Barrett M98 bolt-action rifle, and his bullets—.388 Lapua Magnum—contain gunpowder primarily manufactured in the southern United States, likely Texas or Arizona.

It would not take long to listen to all the taped conversations I have of Daniel, examine the trace routes of the phone calls, and track down the manufacturer of the gunpowder. But I have done none of these things because Daniel has been no threat to me in the past. I feel an affinity for him. Perhaps he is a terrible person who has killed thousands of innocents. Perhaps, like me, he was groomed to this career because no other options were available to him. Perhaps his earlier statement was not a warning but an open hand of greeting that I turned away.

"Only a few, man. I didn't want to leave them for the Rambaudis to find." He's returned to his easy manner and now he taunts me.

"Understood. So now I owe you for more than one thing," I say grimly.

"I'll just mark it in my ledger."

I think he is making a joke, but my plan is fixed. I will pinpoint Daniel's location just in case. Insurance, nothing else.

"Thanks, man," I say, trying to adopt a more American slang. I should study some of my neighbors. Many are very young, like puppies, but if I spoke like them, I could be less noticeable. Likely, people would assume I was dumb simply by my usage of their common vernacular.

"Nice try." There is humor in Daniel's voice. Again the thought niggles that perhaps Daniel's overtures are invitations to a shared confidence, but I push it away.

"The information?"

"The revolution can't go forward without an army's backing."

Chills seize me. Alexsandr was the weapon of the Petrovich *Bratva*, one of the most powerful organizations in Russia. He trained many boys to ensure that the *Bratva*'s business was carried out all over the world without interference. Some boys, like me, he pushed out of the nest to stand on our own. Our blood wasn't pure enough for him, unlike Vasily, who stood at his right hand; or our skills weren't sharp enough, unlike Yury, who stood at his left.

Even though I could take Yury when I was fourteen, and even though I carried out every task asked of me—even ones I did not like—it was not enough in the end. One time I deviate from the orders by allowing the little ones to wreak their vengeance on the art curator. The end was messy but, for those boys, necessary so that they could finally rest, knowing that the monster that haunted them during the day and night was gone and would never return.

For that, Alexsandr dismissed me from the ranks and sent me off on my own. At fifteen, all I knew how to do was kill. And so that is what I do. I am a man who kills for money. "Alexsandr would never betray the *Bratva*."

"Maybe not betray. But withdraw support? Make known his disappointment?" Daniel countered. I envisioned him sitting on a chair, leaning back on only two wooden legs, at ease and unconcerned. For a moment, I considered Daniel's words. They weren't what I'd expected. I didn't know what had led to Sergei's actions—but sedition? Alexsandr believed the brotherhood to be more important than anything, which is why I, his brightest protégé, was let go. I had placed my own feelings above the needs of the *Bratva*.

I tell none of this to Daniel. "That's all?" I ask.

"That's it for now," Daniel replies and hangs up.

I wonder why Daniel offers this. His motives are mysterious to me, and it makes him a danger. Did Daniel feel some tender emotion for a master killer? A man who took boys off the street and turned them into machines for hire deserved respect, perhaps, but tender emotion? Love? I did not love Alexsandr. Respect, yes; love, no. But then, I do not know what love is. I know lust and anger. Despair and satisfaction. But love? No. That is not for me.

At 2095 I log in and wait for the private chat room to be created. At 2100, I type the information in, and my contact from the Watchmakers is there. The mark is revealed along with several other details. I copy and paste it into a text document without reading. Before I log out, I see one last message after the cursor.

If you complete this task, the information you seek regarding your compatriot, Alexsandr Krinkov, will be revealed as a bonus.

Gotcha, I reply as if I were Daniel rather than Nikolai. The offer of extra information seems like a trap, as do all the little bonuses these people offer in order to bind you into their families or organizations. But a house hit man has no power, and I've worked only for myself since I left the Petrovich *Bratva* at the age of fifteen.

I was raised by the *Bratva*. Outside of Russia, maybe only a few know what it is although the name still has power. Inside, everyone fears it. The drug lords on the street, they answer to the *Bratva*. The men and women who peddle their flesh, the grifters, the thieves, the politicians, they all answer to the *Bratva*. No one takes a piss in the criminal underworld without the Petrovich *Bratva* knowing and granting approval.

You want something illegal, dangerous, illicit? The *Bratva* will deliver it to your door, but then they own you. It is the same for all these people who hire me. They want to own me, but I belong to no one now. Only myself. Alexsandr, the man who'd picked me up off the street and trained me to be a killer, decided that I had lost my love for the Petrovich family and kicked me out. To Alexsandr, loyalty to the Petrovich *Bratva* came first. It was a good trait for the general of the Petrovich army to have. Admirable even. For Sergei to decide Alexsandr should die was inconceivable. And as no one in the *Bratva* would avenge Alexsandr and cross Sergei, the task fell to me.

And since everyone on the outside seems to be aware that I'm seeking redress for Alexsandr's death, then so does everyone inside, including Sergei, the new head of the Petrovich family. The new king of the *Bratva*. His silence on this issue is telling. Sergei is as much a threat to me as I am to him. But for now, I pretend I am undisturbed that Sergei has killed my mentor.

The information provided to me by the Watchmakers about the new mark seems innocuous. One man, a doctor, living in Seattle. His name, social security number, and date of birth are given, along with the type of death requested. No need for discretion. The means of delivery are simple, then, and on my terms. It's just the way I prefer it, but something about this makes me anxious.

A quick Internet search reveals that the doctor in Seattle is a transplant surgeon. I wonder if he deals with black market organs, selling them or facilitating the purchase for rich patrons. The Internet only reveals that he has a toothsome smile, a full head of hair, and a plastic-looking wife. Perfect, pretty, but empty. The idea of running up to Seattle to research the mark displeases me. I don't want to be away from the girl in 224.

I return to the bathroom and look at the video tape of Mr. John Brown, my current mark. Sergei contracted me three months ago to find Mr. Brown and return him to Moscow. Mr. Brown's real name is George Franklin; he is an accountant from Chicago. He was caught skimming money from the *Bratva* transactions, and instead of running to Mexico or Singapore or somewhere else, he's trying to hide in plain sight. It is a rather inspired idea, but he's only tried to hide once.

I've hunted people all my life. Everyone leaves a trail. Mr. Brown's mistake was his dog, a tiny yippy thing. Rather than leaving it behind, Mr. Brown has carted that dog with him everywhere, zigzagging from Chicago up to small towns in Wisconsin. Now he's back in Minneapolis, Minnesota, not a few hundred kilometers from his home city. He's been buying the dog specialty food wherever he went.

I can fairly predict where he'd go next based on the availability of the food. I'm not to kill Mr. Brown. Simply find him and return him. But plans change. I haven't killed Mr. Brown yet because he has information. The video feed shows Mr. Brown spreading peanut butter on himself for his dog to lap up. Disgusting. I'll be doing everyone a favor by getting rid of Mr. Brown.

Swinging my scope over to room 224, I flip on my night-vision goggles. I can only see the outline of her body. She is leaving the apartment, and she appears to have a basket with her. I track her down to the basement laundry. When I first walked the building, I noted the basement laundry facility. It was dank and musty, with only a few lights and disgusting floor.

The girl from 224 should not have to clean her clothes down there. Someone should clean her clothes for her, but I know she could not afford that. Her refrigerator holds few items, and when she does eat, which seems far too seldom for my own peace of mind, she eats noodles and other cheap food. Her roommate does not make any more money, either. The two of them are poor and so obviously prey that it is a miracle they've survived on their own to make it to adulthood. The one male in their lives is worthless.

I watch again as her outlined form leans over the washing machine. She places her clothes inside and then leaves. She returns to her apartment and heads to her bedroom. It is too dark for me to tell what she is doing in there. Is she touching herself again? Can she bring herself off? I think she may be reading a book. I watch her, and the time that passes is meaningless. Nothing is more interesting to me that watching her, even if it is just the outline of her form. I should be doing so many other things. Researching my potential mark in Seattle. Pinpointing Daniel's position. Searching for the weaknesses in Sergei's coterie of advisors. Instead, I am mesmerized by her.

As I watch, I notice that her breathing has evened out and her head has flopped to the side. It appears that she has fallen asleep. Her laundry is sitting wet in that dank basement. Before I can give it another thought, I head out of my apartment, down the one flight of stairs and across the street to the back door of her apartment building. This door has no outside handle, but the lock is so simple that all it takes is a plastic wedge and few jerks of a keycard to get the lock to give way. I jog down to the basement and open the door.

Inside, a man is leaning over a pile of laundry. He jerks around at my entrance and fists something pink and lacy in his hand. Looking around, I take in a quick inventory. The washing machine he is leaning over is the one that my girl used. My nostrils flare and blood zings into my eyes. The *mudak* is fondling her panties.

With a roar, I charge. He shrinks back and raises his hands to defend himself. I grab the wrist of his fisted hand and crush the bones. His cries of pain are music to me, and my rage lessens. The pale pink cotton falls to the ground and, as he tries to wrest away, his sneakered foot nearly crushes it. I hold on to his wrist with one hand and reach down and pluck the panties off the ground and stuff them into my jeans pocket.

"What the fuck do you think you are doing?" I ask him through gritted teeth.

His teeth chatter and he responds with barely legible words. "Laundry. Doing laundry."

He is a lecher and a liar. I squeeze his broken wrist tighter and he cries out again. Using my other hand on the collar of his T-shirt, I twist and pull him close. "These are not your clothes, you filthy motherfucker." I am tired of my girl being surrounded by the dregs of humanity. Mr. Brown living next door with his perversions. This little man trying to steal her panties. How many other women has he done this to? I should kill him right now. My hand releases his T-shirt to grasp his throat. I could squeeze the life out of him.

But before I can say another word, I hear footsteps. It's her. Somehow I know it is her. The thief and I exchange glances. I push the *dolboeb*, the fuckhead, away and shove her clothing back into the washing machine. I see a dark corner and a bulb. I bat the hot bulb with my hand and break it, feeling the burn immediately.

This side of the laundry room is plunged into darkness. It is the perfect place to stash this man. I push him into the corner. "You make noise, you so much as breathe too loudly, and it will be the last sound you make."

He nods his comprehension, cradling his broken wrist. Grabbing the one chair in the laundry room, I pull it in front of him and situate it so that I am partially lit but that he would have to push past me to get out.

I do not have a book or magazine, so I pull out my phone and pretend to be checking the Internet. I'm holding my own breath because this will be the closest I have ever been to her. My hands shake with anticipation. I clench my phone harder to keep her from seeing how she affects me. I do not want to frighten her, so I say, "Allo," as soon as she turns the corner.

This is still unexpected and she jumps, placing her delicate hand to her chest. She has no idea that the action draws emphasis to her beautiful breasts. I want to see those breasts exposed to my gaze. I want to touch them with my hands. I want to rub my face between their valley, thumb her nipples, and lick every round inch of those swells. My cock hardens at the thought. I'm grateful that I am leaning over so she can't see the evidence of my arousal. Perhaps it is better that I've never been this close. I'd come at the first touch of her hand on my bare flesh.

"I-I didn't see you there," she stammers sweetly. Her voice is clear and melodic. I'm completely entranced.

"*Nyet*, it is my fault. I apologize for startling you." Is it uncouth to remain seated? With fuckhead behind me, I feel like I cannot stand up. Him and my aching cock.

"That's okay." She smiles at me, and I bite the inside of my cheek to keep from groaning. "I've just moved in, so I don't know everyone in the building. I'm Daisy Miller."

Daisy. I roll her name over my tongue. It fits her, like her smooth soft hands and her clear complexion. The women in Ukraine, some of them would wash their faces in goats' milk to keep a perfect countenance. I wonder if this is what she does. Her skin is creamy but golden as if she lives outdoors instead of within the stained brick walls of this dirty run-down apartment complex. Her eyelashes are thick and rest like lace curtains against the curve of her cheek.

"Daisy Miller," I repeat. "Like Henry James?" I've read a few American classics to better understand the world. It has not helped. The Daisy Miller of Henry James's story is light and intangible, all beauty and no substance. It does not match this woman.

She frowns at me, clearly not following my conversation attempt. "Beg pardon?"

"Is nothing."

She holds out her hand and offers it to me. I want to get up and touch it but I cannot. Instead, I slide the chair slightly forward and lean toward her, offering my own hand in greeting. She looks at me uncertainly like I'm some *dolboeb* who won't cross the distance to her. I should've beaten that man unconscious so I wouldn't have to be worried about him. I rise up slowly to see if there is any reaction, and I hear a slight movement. Gripping the chair as I stand up, I swiftly lift and then bring down the leg of the chair on some body part of the thief. It might be his calf. I hear a choked sound.

"Do you hear something?" Daisy looks around, and I take the opportunity to shove the chair back. The sound is cut off. The thief has received my message.

"I do not. Nick Anders," I say, walking toward her. My given name is Nikolai Andrushko, but I tell that to no one. I pull her tiny hand in mine and lift it to my mouth. It smells of lemon and detergent. I brush my mouth lightly over it, amazed I do not fall onto her and ravage her like an animal. Rather than tempt myself further, I let her hand drop to her side. She is blushing now, and her other hand is covering her mouth. I rub a thumb across one flushed cheek. "Daisy. It is a lovely name."

"Thank you."

I hear more sounds in the corner. "This place sounds like there are animals in the walls. I think unsafe, perhaps, for someone like you?"

"Like me?" She frowns. She does not like this. I grapple for a better response.

"For anyone. For women, especially alone. Come." I draw her toward her washing machine. "Let's finish this."

"Um, you don't have to wait for me. I'm just going to drop this all in the dryer and then come back when it is done."

"*Da*, I will watch," I offer. I want to wait with her, but I have a loose end I must take care of.

She looks uncertainly at me again, and I offer her a benign smile. It is enough, because she quickly transfers her items from one machine to another, although it is apparent she is separating out her tender under-things to take somewhere else. She pauses and then looks back at me, still flushed. Is she embarrassed? She shouldn't be. She should know that her delicate items only make her more desirable. I frown, wondering if the jackal behind me can see. I spread my legs and cross my arms, hoping to make a bigger barrier so he cannot see. I do not want anyone to see her private things. I wonder if she should wash them again.

Her unease is evident, and I know I should leave her. Not just because of the wary glances that she flicks toward me but because everything about her is in direct conflict to my entire existence. I can scarcely breathe standing this close to her, watching her in the flesh.

Her thin but capable arms are moving swiftly to lift and carry her clothing. Her hands are delicate with elegant fingers, perfectly shaped for her body. I imagine those fingers stretched around my shaft. There are freckles on her cheeks and forehead. Standing so close, there are details here that I could not have captured from my scope, my night-vision goggles, my paltry imagination. Daisy is a riot of colors with her chestnut-colored hair and her blue eyes. Her pale skin is lovely even in this dimly lit basement. It is a good thing, I decide, that I've yet to see Daisy fully exposed in the sun. I may die.

Ah, but that would be a happy death.

CHAPTER **THREE**

DAISY

He's not leaving.

My stomach is all nervous flutters. I should be concentrating on the machines, but all I can think about is the tall, gorgeous man standing down here in the laundry room with me.

He kissed my hand. He touched my cheek. It's like something out of a romance novel. I want to giggle like a schoolgirl, but I suspect he would think I'm silly. So I bite my lip and haul my basket of clothing to the dryer. My fingers tremble as I push quarters into the slot. Regan complains that the landlords charge us for the washer and dryer, but I like clean clothing, so I view it as a necessary evil.

I notice things about him. I notice that he's wearing nice clothes, or at least, nicer than mine. I notice that he's got tattoos on his fingers, and that when they touched mine, they were callused. The tattoos are a bit unnerving, but I have seen a lot of tattoos on people on the streets. Perhaps he simply appreciates the artistry of them.

I pick up a pair of wet jeans and shame hits me. They're old and baggy, and there's a bleach stain on one cuff. There's nothing in my basket that could impress a man like him. I sneak a glance over at him, just in case he's not watching me.

He is, though.

I flush and glance away again, hastily shoving my old, worn secondhand clothing into the dryer. Now I'm just being an idiot. *Be bold, Daisy!* I tell myself. *He kissed your hand!*

"So your name is Nick?" *Duh, Daisy. He just told you that. Could you come up with a stupider question?*

"*Da.*"

"It's a lovely name. Is it Russian? You sound . . . foreign." Oh dear. Now I sound really foolish. Regan would laugh at my Pollyanna ways.

"I am from Ukraine."

I glance over at him again, and he's watching me still, his flicking gaze cataloging my movements. It's not an unfriendly gaze, even though he's not smiling. It's intense, though. All gray eyes and piercing stare. Like he wants to know all my secrets. I smile at him again. "I like your accent," I say shyly. "It's not one I've heard often." Ever. Maybe on the Internet in a video once. It sounds like he is caressing his syllables with his tongue, but I don't say this. I'm not quite that bold yet.

"You are too kind. I know other languages but I am never able to shed my roots," he says, and that accent makes my pulse flutter all over again.

I wish he would talk more. He seems on edge. Is it because I'm trying to flirt with him, and I'm pathetic at it? "Which floor are you on?"

He swiftly answers. "Second."

I light up. "Me too. We're neighbors." I finish tossing my laundry into the dryer, and then there's nothing else to do. Should I continue talking to him? I'm suddenly out of answers. I clutch my laundry basket, feeling helpless. He hasn't moved from his wide-legged stance over in the shadowy corner of the laundry room. "I . . . guess if we're on the same floor, I'll see you around?"

He inclines his head at me. "*Da*, I will see you." He looks down as if he's embarrassed by something, and then he adds, "I should like that."

"Me too. It was nice to meet you, Nick." I feel my cheeks heat. "I'm in 224, if you ever need to borrow detergent or anything. Just let me know."

Again, he inclines his head.

I feel a little silly for offering up so much information, but I can't help myself. "Well, bye now." I turn to the door, feeling as if I've just flubbed my first chance at flirting with a man.

His gaze moves to the flip phone I have shoved in my pocket. "Give me your phone," he says and puts a hand out. "I will give you my number. You call me if you need anything."

My cheeks pinken, and I pull out my small flip phone. It is a disposable, the cheapest model. Regan's made laughing comments about me getting a smartphone so I can use the GPS and not get lost in the "big city," but that's more money each month than I want to spend on something so frivolous. Not when I don't have a job yet. But I hand it to him and try not to feel ashamed of how pathetic it is.

He says nothing, simply examines it, and then flips it open and begins to type with one thumb. I watch his tattooed fingers fly and wonder at the markings on each knuckle. It seems impolite to ask what they mean. After a moment, he snaps my phone shut and hands it back. "You call me, *da*? If you need things. I will call you if I need . . . detergent."

I nod mutely, give him what I hope is a friendly smile (and not a terrified one), and escape.

It seems I have two friends now. Regan and my Ukrainian neighbor who is so incredibly handsome that I could stare at him all day. I clutch my laundry basket to my hip and leave, feeling his eyes on my back. Once I am safely back in my apartment, I pull my phone out, flipping it open and paging through my tiny list of numbers to see what he has put there. A personal message? Something flirty?

Nick.

Just Nick.

I won't have the courage to call him, of course, but I'll think about it day and night. And when I touch myself tonight? It will be Nick's face I'll imagine. Tomorrow, I will borrow Regan's laptop and research all I can about the Ukraine. I want to learn about him.

There's something about Nick that draws me to him, that makes me stare at his phone number in wonder. I have met a few other men this week, some for longer than the short conversation I just had. But no one has tried to kiss my hand or given me their phone number.

It's a personal connection, and I don't have many of those. A personal connection with a tall, mysterious, handsome man? It is the stuff of my wildest dreams.

It's more than that, though. There's something about Nick, and I lay down on my bed, considering. After a moment, I realize what it is. He has intensity. There is something so vibrant, so aware, so *alive* about him that it sings to me. I am drawn to it like a moth to a flame. Is it because my father has always been a shadow of himself and because he did his best to break me? Nick, I think, would never be broken.

I like that about him.

NIKOLAI

Daisy, she reminds me of the paintings by an American painter from a city not so far away. The pictures are full of rolling hills and symmetrically planted wheat. Those images look pure, wholesome, and peaceful. Even her name evokes the same images. Whereas I am like the dark tormenter envisioned by Dante and made grotesque by Hieronymus Bosch.

At fifteen, I was ordered to terminate an art curator who had a predilection for American art and American boys. It was a satisfying job, as I learned much about art from watching the curator. The order to put him down had nothing to do with his pedophilia and everything to do with money. Always about the money.

It was the last hit I made under Alexsandr's watch. I still didn't know why he had released me, if it was the way I carried out the hit that made him decide I was too much of a liability or just that I was getting too old to control. It *was* rather messy. But after watching the curator for two weeks, I couldn't merely put a bullet in his head. I rub the inscription on my chest again. *Death is mercy.* And those boys he'd kept had deserved their own revenge. Still the memory of it reminds me of how similar I am to this broken, run-down building with its bricks falling out and its interior filled with trash.

"Can I—can I stand now?"

I turn toward the thief. "Get up," I command.

He struggles to his feet; he is maimed. His fortitude is impressive. He hasn't pissed himself, and he was quiet for the most part. I decide to let him go with just a warning.

"What is your apartment number?" I ask.

"122," he says. He looks small despite his size. Now that I've had a moment to collect myself and look at him, I am surprised to see that he is about my height, but he has no strength.

"I suggest you look for a new place to live. I do not care what you do with other women's clothing, but you are not to be near her. You are not to touch her or breathe the same air." I'm still looking at the dryer. My lip curls at the thought of the animal's hands on her clothes. I cannot allow them to touch her body. I spy a bottle of bleach, old and probably forgotten. It will ruin her clothes, but I can buy her new ones. Ones that haven't been worn before; ones made of material as pure and precious as she.

"B-b-but you didn't even know her before you came down here!" the thief whines at me.

I whirl around and pin him back against the machines with one hand to his throat. My earlier feelings of leniency have fled. I squeeze tightly. "I've ended lives over a lesser slight. Move and live. Don't move. Die. Simple." I am puzzled by this man's lack of comprehension. The deprivation of oxygen is perhaps affecting his thinking, and I ease my grip. "This is not such a hard choice, right? There are so many other dumps you can live in."

"But my security deposit," he coughs out.

Money, always money. Still holding him around the throat, I dip into my pocket and pull out two one-hundred-dollar bills from my wallet.

"Enough?" I wave them at him. His eyes widen, and he nods vigorously. He reaches for the money, but I hold it away from him. "Uh-uh. Tell me what you will do."

"I'll move out."

"When?"

"Today."

"*When?*"

"Now," he gasps.

I nod and let him go. He grabs the money and runs. I will check later to see if 122 is empty. If not, I will make it so.

Now I need to fix Daisy's clothing problem. One that she isn't aware she has.

I have no change, so I bypass the coin slots with two thin sticks of plastic from my lock kit. Angling them into the slots, I make the machine believe it is being fed two coins. I'm not stealing, really. I have no clothes to wash. But if Daisy returns to find me here, waiting, I will need a cover story.

I set the machine to a long wash and sit down to wait for her return. Daisy's dryer dings to signal its completion. My body tenses at the thought of her return. I have had little interaction with a girl like Daisy. Most of the women I've known, I've paid for. For the money I give to them, they treat me however I want, which is mostly to service me and then go away. I do not care what the whores think of me—but with Daisy . . . with Daisy, I care.

She stops short when she sees me. Obvious surprise is evident on her fine features. I offer her a small smile, my facial muscles protesting at the unfamiliar use.

"Hi again," she says tentatively.

"Your dryer, it is done," I reply. Her expression is no longer surprise but wariness. Neither emotion is one I want to invoke, although what I want from her is not fully known, even to me. Desire, yes. Want, yes. Tender emotions, yes . . . or no. I am beset with uncertainty and in unfamiliar territory, so I respond with stoicism, which in turn makes her even more cautious. I can see it.

It is devolving so quickly. *Nikolai, do something*, I command myself.

I swiftly walk over to her. Taking her hand, I gently guide Daisy to her machine. "I'm sorry, have I frightened you? I just wait for my own things." I gesture toward the machine I manipulated earlier.

"No, I was just surprised to see anyone here." She stands in front of the machine and makes no effort to withdraw her clothes. A light pink stain upon her cheeks gives me a clue. She is embarrassed. I have no idea why, but I turn away and then to go sit in my chair. Her unease is distressing me, and I do not know what to do to make it go away other than to leave her. My throat feels tight. Maybe if I visit a whore again I will pay her to teach me to flirt.

My own cheeks feel hot, and I pretend to read my emails while Daisy empties the contents of her machine into a plastic basket with broken webbing. A cry of dismay has me ricocheting out of my chair, but there is no threat to her. Daisy is staring at her belongings, one item in each hand and the stains from bleach I placed in her dryer are obvious. Guilt strikes me hard, harder than I'd imagined.

"What is it?" I ask, pretending I don't know that I have likely ruined her only clothes. She bows her head, and I wonder if she will cry. Please, *kotehok,* please do not cry.

In the end no tears fall, but her fatalism, her resigned acceptance of this loss, makes me feel even worse, as if I have physically squeezed a little of her happiness from her.

Abruptly I stand again, and the chair rattles backward into the machine.

"*Kotehok,* what is wrong?" My hand hovers over her bowed shoulders. I want to touch her but feel too guilty.

She sighs and then turns to me with a slight shake of her head. "Just my luck, I guess. I must have put the clothes in a machine that had bleach in it." She holds up a pair of jeans that look too big for her, with ragged cuffs. There is a large discoloration on the back. The shirt she holds in the other hand has the same problem. "The jeans I might get away with, but this shirt?"

"It was me," I declare. I fist the shirt in my hands and tug it from her. "You must allow me to fix this for you."

"No. What?" She tries to pull the shirt back, and the frayed fabric rips in our hands.

Now she *does* look like she is about to cry, and she bites her lips to keep back her tears. I cannot withhold myself from her any longer. My hand drops to her shoulder, and I pull her into me. "It is my fault. I do not know how to run these machines. You must allow me to make it up to you."

She leans into me and I rub her back—just her upper back—in small circles, as I did for a sex worker in Amsterdam who offered to teach me to cuddle. Then, I did not like it. I rubbed her back for a few seconds and then made her leave. But this is . . . amazing. Daisy's little body is resting lightly against mine. I can feel muscles in her back, which suggests that Daisy is strong. The blades of her shoulders are sharp against my hand, which suggests Daisy is not eating enough. I want to scoop her into my lap and feed her with one hand and stroke her pussy with the other.

She does not borrow my strength for more than a second before she is pushing away from me and brushing the hair out of her face. "It's not your fault." She shakes her head at me. "I'm sure it was something I did."

"*Nyet.*" I take her hand. "You come with me. I will not be able to sleep tonight knowing I have ruined your things with my ineptness."

She tries to scramble for her things, but I pull her away. "Wait," she says.

"Daisy," I plead with her. "You must allow me to do this, or I will not be able to live with myself."

She stares in my eyes. While I am tempted to shut them for fear of what she may glimpse if she delves too deeply, the truth rests at the forefront. My steady gaze must have convinced her.

"Seventy dollars," she finally says.

I smile at her and nod. I have no idea what she means, but I take this as acquiescence. I pull her out of the basement and head for the back door.

"Where are we going?"

"To my bike," I say. My hand is still grasping hers. I'm afraid if I let go she will disappear.

My rented Ducati sits untouched in the parking lot between our buildings. I have only one helmet, which I hand to her. "Put it on," I say, and then because I sound like a *mudak*, an asshole, I add, "please."

"I can't take your only helmet." She looks mutinous. I have no car, only this bike, and only one helmet.

"Will you wear it to the motorcycle shop? It is only a few kilometers away. I will take side roads and go slow." I offer her a compromise.

She gives me a slow nod in agreement and pulls on the helmet. All the tension built up from fighting the *huesos*, the cocksucker from earlier, and convincing sweet Daisy to come with me melts away. I swing my leg over the bike and motion for Daisy to climb aboard. Turning, I flip her visor up.

"Hold tight, even though we go slow, okay?"

"Okay," she replies. Her eyes are glittering with excitement, and I smile back. It's feeling less foreign.

I ride slowly through the streets as Daisy clings to me. Her breasts are pressing against the thin cloth of my T-shirt, and I can feel that she is enjoying the thrill. I want to believe that her arousal is because of me, but it is likely the simple vibration of the machine between her legs. At high enough speeds, the vibration might be enough to bring her off. I'd love to try that. I wonder if she is wet between her legs, whether the cloth of her panties is damp, or whether she is so turned on that the denim is soaked. I rock slightly on the seat, and I feel her press against me instinctively. I groan and don't even try to hide it, confident the wind will carry the sound away. My cock feels enormous at the thought of her wet, the thought of her coming while riding behind me.

When we arrive at the motorcycle shop that rents and sells these bikes, I scoot forward and try to think of something to reduce my erection. Her neighbor pops into my head, and I'm able to stand upright. Not wanting Daisy to be exposed to the men here, I tell her to remain on the bike and to leave the helmet down. "Else someone might try to steal it."

This is a lie, of course, but Daisy simply nods.

Inside, I buy Daisy a helmet and ask, "I need clothes. Where can I buy them?"

The gum-chewing clerk gives me a hungry look. "Honey, I can fit you out. What do you need?" Her gaze drops to my crotch, and I resist the urge to cover my groin with the newly purchased helmet.

"For my girlfriend," I say. She wrinkles her nose as if the idea smells.

"There's the mall just up the highway, 'round the bend. Take the Lindau Lane. Can't miss it." She emphasizes *mall* as if it has some special significance.

I nod my thanks.

Outside, I stand in front of Daisy, blocking the shop's view of her, and I offer her the new helmet.

"I'm sorry for making such a big deal out of this. What are

you going to do with another helmet?" She shook her head in dismay. "I wasn't thinking."

I shrug. "I needed one." For her only, but I did not say this out loud.

She looks at me doubtfully, but I give her my best impassive look. It is a good one; she feels discomfited and can no longer look me in the eye. Suddenly I feel like a fuckhead over this, but how to fix it eludes me.

I reach under her chin with my fist and tilt her eyes up to meet mine. "It is for you. Only for you. You can keep it to ride with me or you can throw it away."

An odd light flickers through her eyes, and I can't catch it. I don't know how to read her yet. I'll learn, though. The light is fading fast, and I don't want to be out with Daisy on my bike when it is too late—when the dangerous drivers are out. Alone, I can avoid these people, but with my precious cargo, I would be worried.

I pull her helmet over her head, carefully brush aside her hair, and affix the strap beneath her chin. I repeat the gesture for myself and climb on. This time, Daisy needs no instruction on how to hold me; her arms wrap around me immediately, and she presses her cheek against the middle of my back. Her thin, strong arms are wrapped around my waist. In this position, I would like to drive for hours just to feel her body against mine.

DAISY

Everything I've been taught says that I'm being a reckless fool.

I met Nick two hours ago in the laundry room. I let him dazzle me. I let him kiss my hand and hug me, and now I'm on the back of his motorcycle. The after-school specials that my father let me watch would say I'm being stupid. That nice young women don't run off with strange men on motorcycles.

But . . . I don't care.

I am tired of being cautious and being sheltered. I want to be wild and reckless, and I want to spend a bit more time with this man. If that leads me down a bad path, I'm going there with eyes wide open.

I don't know how one holds properly to a man on a motorcycle; this is my first motorcycle ride. I cling to him, pressing my body against his. My breasts rub against his back and bounce when we hit a bump, and I gasp at the sensation. Am I holding him too close? Do I care? I will just feign ignorance if he asks. I like the feel of his big body pressing against my thighs and my stomach far too much to stop.

It feels wicked. I've never, ever been wicked before, and I never realized until now that I wanted to be.

And I never realized how big malls were.

He drives the motorcycle into a large parking lot that has more levels than my apartment complex, and I see a massive building ahead of us. It looks like the mall. My goodness. I had no idea it would be so . . . enormous. I feel a flutter of excitement in spite of myself. I have never been to a mall, much less been to this one, but I've seen it advertised on television. My father wouldn't let me go, no matter how much I begged. Too open and unsafe, he would tell me.

I feel a flare of anger at my father. How much of my life has he robbed from me? For a moment, I'm viciously glad that I have abandoned him . . . and then guilt sweeps in and carries any anger away.

Nick parks his bike in one of the front parking spaces and pulls his helmet off, shaking out his hair. He's gorgeous. I watch him under my helmet. I could drink in his profile forever. He is handsome, his features fine-boned but still masculine, his eyes pale and intense. He puts the helmet down and indicates that I should get off the bike.

I comply, swinging my leg over the bike and feeling clumsy as I do. The jeans I'm wearing are baggy and old, and they slide a little when I stand up. I hitch them surreptitiously as he puts up a kickstand and gets off the bike himself.

Before I can lift my hands, he's removing the helmet he bought just for me. For some reason, it doesn't feel like control as much as it feels like . . . tenderness. He's achingly sweet, this Nick, despite his hard, intense exterior. I think that is why I trust him.

When he pulls it off, he smiles at me, as if pleased to see my face. "We are at mall."

"So we are," I say breathlessly. "Thank you for driving me."

He tilts his head, as if trying to determine what I mean. "I will shop with you. Is only fair."

His accent seems to get thicker from time to time, as if he forgets to control it. I feel a little flustered at the thought of him shopping with me. The clothes that were ruined were panties and bras, two shirts, and a pair of jeans. "You don't have to. It's not necessary."

"*Da*. Is necessary." And he crooks his arm for me, like a gentleman, to escort me into the mall.

All my protests fade at the sight of that elegant, polite elbow. I slide my hand in and move a bit closer to him, letting him lead me inside.

Once we pass through the glass doors into the mall, I gasp. This place is a wonderland.

"Is that a roller coaster?" I squeak. The mall is at least four stories tall, and it is so big that the sounds echo. Even if I squint, I can't see to the far end of the building. It's like it goes on forever. Big, potted plants line the median of the enormous walk-way, and there are colorful banners hanging high overhead that broadcast sales and specialty stores. There are lit signs and ele-gant window displays and people everywhere.

It's overwhelming and incredible all at once. "Oh, wow." I look over at Nick to see if he's impressed, too, but he's watching me. Color hits my cheeks, and I glance away, looking around again. I don't even know where to start, and all the stores look so expensive. "Do you know which store is cheapest?"

He's silent, and when I look over, he's frowning at me. "Why cheapest, Daisy?"

I blush at the way he says my name, like his tongue has to caress the syllables before they leave his mouth. "Well, we are only spending seventy dollars. I want to get as much as I can for my money."

And then I flush even brighter, because it's not my money, it's his. And all he owes me are some panties and a pair of pants. It feels wrong to try to fleece him out of extra clothing simply because I need it.

"Daisy," he says quietly. "Do not worry about money. Buy clothes you need. I will pay, *da*? Do not look at prices."

This makes me frown. I don't want to argue with Nick. I want to kiss him. But I'm not bold enough for that, so I figure that I will simply pick out inexpensive clothes and that this will com-plete our shopping trip. "All right."

I see a large store that advertises shirts for five dollars and head in that direction, but Nick takes my hand and tugs me down the wide-tiled hallways. I'm sure I'm going to have a sore neck from whipping my head back and forth as I stare in amaze-ment at all the stores. There is a store for everything from mag-nets to hats. Finally, Nick stops at a store with big, gold letters at the top and black marble trim. Inside, there are several tall, severe people dressed all in black who seem too beautiful to be Minnesotans. No one who lives on a farm looks like these folks. The windows are full of posing mannequins in silks and leathers and skimpy bras and underwear. I suck in a breath as Nick heads in, his hand clasped over mine to keep me at his side.

I don't know where to start looking. Then, I spy a sale sign at the back of the store and untangle my hands from Nick, heading there.

The items on sale are all way too large or out of season. Or ugly. I pick through them anyhow, flipping tags on anything that might seem like it could fit with a little bit of hand-sewing.

Nick waits patiently nearby, and when I glance over, he's scanning the room, eyes ever-watchful. I wonder for a moment what he's looking for.

I can't find anything I like. The items are so expensive, even on clearance. Fifty dollars for a bra? It's insane. But I know Nick won't let me leave here without at least buying something. So I grab one plain bra that is twenty dollars and clutch it under my arm to hide it. For some reason, it feels weird for Nick to see my undergarments. "Let's just get this one."

He looks at me for a long moment, glancing at the bra I'm trying to hide with my crossed arms. He reaches toward me and grasps the tag. Examines it. Then he looks at me.

"Do you pick out the lowest price item, Daisy?"

His English needs work, but I know what he means. I shrug, feeling silly.

Nick holds his hand out for it. *Oh.* My face flushes bright red, and I hand it to him, trying not to be too embarrassed—or titillated—at the thought of Nick's hands touching my bra.

He heads to the counter, and I linger a few steps behind. His voice is low and smooth as he speaks to one of the black-clad sales clerks, and he hands her the bra. A moment later, she comes from behind the counter, a measuring tape in her hands.

"Sweetie," she says as she approaches me. "I was talking to your boyfriend, and he is concerned that the bra you picked out won't fit. Let's get you measured, okay?"

I cast a startled look at Nick, but he watches me with a cool gaze, as if daring me to protest. The woman puts a hand to the small of my back and leads me to the dressing rooms, and she measures my breasts while my cheeks flame red with embarrassment. She gives me a size—34C—and we leave the dressing room.

"You were right," the saleswoman sings out to Nick. "That one is much too big. We'll find her something more suitable."

He merely nods, ignoring my protesting glances as the woman heads to one particular part of the store.

"Now," she says. "These are similar to what you had, but I think we can find something in your size." She pulls out a plain, smooth bra in a nude color. It is boring. It *is* like what I picked out, but I flip over the tag. It is no cheaper than the fancier items.

And for some reason, I put my foot down. I have worn boring, plain clothing all my life. My father insisted on approving everything I wore, and as a result, I have never had anything pretty or bold in my life. So I think for a moment and shake my head at the nude bra the woman holds out to me. I head instead to a nearby rack and look at the bras there.

They are lacy, frilly things. One is a silky pink and white gingham with a lacy design along the cups. It's incredibly beautiful, and I touch it longingly.

And then I look to Nick, as if seeking approval.

He nods, and I could swear he looks pleased.

"I think I want this one."

"That's a great choice," the saleswoman enthuses. "But you'll need the matching panties."

"*Da*," Nick says from afar before I can comment. "She needs several sets. Bras and panties. Shirts. Shoes. Dresses."

I shoot him a glance, but he has his phone out and is scrolling through something. He's not watching.

"Don't worry about him, honey." The saleswoman pats my arm. "He told me you are to get everything you want."

Everything? I want all the pretty things in the store. I finger a pair of lacy, pink garter belts that match the bra and panties I've selected. "I'm not sure it's appropriate for him to be buying me this stuff."

"Are you kidding?" the saleswoman asks with a laugh. "Guys come in here and do this for their girlfriends all the time."

I'm not Nick's girlfriend, and I'm still not entirely sure it's right, but I'm weakening at the sight of all the pretty things around me. As if sensing my hesitation, the woman puts the garter belts in the pile.

And I don't tell her no.

I move to the next rack. It has a yellow, floral pattern. It's sweet and pretty, and it makes me happy to see it. When I pause over it, the woman adds the bra and matching panties to my stack. I wonder if Nick told her to be aggressive.

By the time I say "enough," her arms are full of colorful, beautiful undergarments in a rainbow of colors and soft, pleasing fabrics. There is nothing plain or ordinary—or even serviceable-looking—in the stack. They are all soft, sultry things.

And even though I shouldn't let a man buy them for me, I'm giddy at the thought of owning them.

The saleswoman is having fun dressing me. She takes me to some of the racks at the front of the store after we've picked out piles of lingerie, and she adds sweaters and skirts and a few blouses to my overflowing arms. When I protest, she looks over at Nick, who nods approval, and she then takes me to the jeans counter, where we go through the same routine. Protest, look to Nick, pile onto my arms.

When we head to the counter, I hesitate. "It's too much."

"*Nyet*, it is not," Nick says. "You deserve beautiful things." And his hand touches my back and rubs my shoulder blades.

I like that touch. I want more, but I don't ask for more. I glance around as the saleswoman rings us up. There is a couple nearby, and they're holding hands as the woman browses through a rack. I look at their clasped hands with a bit of envy. Would Nick hold my hand like that if I asked him to?

The total the woman calls out startles me. It is more money than I brought with me during my escape. "No," I protest, but Nick simply pulls out his wallet, and I watch as those tattooed fingers unfold several hundred-dollar bills. I spy more of them tucked into the billfold.

I'm shocked. He's not poor.

I don't know why I feel so momentarily betrayed by this information, but I am. I feel like Nick has lied to me. Our building is old, run-down. Why is he living there if he casually carries around so much money? I want to ask him, but it seems rude.

Instead of feeling scandalous that I let this exciting, strange man buy me panties, I feel . . . like a charity case. It's no longer fun and a daring whim. Now I'm just sad.

Does he do this for everyone? Find women in need and purchase them things? He might. He has a hard exterior, but I sense a kind, lonely heart underneath. I thought he and I had our poverty in common.

Seeing all that money makes me realize he is nothing like me, and I feel smaller.

The woman stuffs the receipt in the bag, and I take the handles before Nick can. I'll keep that receipt and return all the pretty things, and then I'll give the money back to Nick. Based on Nick's behavior in the store, it's either throw a big argument now or simply allow him to think that he's getting his way and come back another time. I've decided.

It's silly because now that I know he's not poor like me, I feel alone all over again.

I bend my head as we leave the store, staring at the shiny marble flooring of the mall. Nick's hand is on my shoulders, guiding me. A friendly hand.

Nothing more.

I'm so stupid. Here I am, caught up in fantasies and daydreams, thinking this man might like me, when he is simply a rich man who is being polite.

We walk a few steps outside of the store, and Nick halts. I barely notice until his hands are on my shoulders, and he's suddenly standing in front of me.

"Daisy," he murmurs, and his fingers touch my chin to make me look up at him. Those intense eyes are devouring me. "What is wrong?"

For some reason, my lip trembles. "I . . . you shouldn't have bought me these things."

His eyes narrow. "Why?" His accent is so thick it sounds more like *vyyy*.

"That woman . . . she thought you were my boyfriend."

He stills and when he speaks, his voice is hard. "You have a boyfriend already? He will be jealous?"

"What? No." I shake my head. "No boyfriend. I just—she doesn't realize you were just being kind."

A harsh laugh escapes him. "Daisy, there are many things you can call me, but 'kind' is not one of them."

It is an odd thing to say. He has been nothing but kind to me. "It's too much money."

He considers this for a moment, and then he puts his hand out for the bag. I hand it to him, feeling crushing disappointment. Why am I so hung up on lovely, silky panties? Perhaps it's not the items themselves, but what they represent.

Old, timid Daisy would never wear such flimsy, sweet, colorful things. And new Daisy wants them more than anything. I want to see that gleam of approval in Nick's eyes as he sees them on me.

I want to feel special to him. I wonder if he realizes how messed up I am. I'm already clinging to him. I'm a strange, needy little package.

Nick reaches into the bag. He pulls out the receipt, and to my surprise, he crumples it in his hand and tosses it into a nearby trash bin. Then he holds the bag out to me. "Now you have no choice but to accept my gift, *da*?"

I look at him with wide eyes. "But, Nick. The money . . ."

He leans in. His pale eyes seem to caress my face, his stare almost too direct. "Which part bothers you," he asks after a moment. "The money or the fact that she thinks you belong to me?"

I feel trapped under Nick's gaze. He's staring down at me as if the world hinges on my answer. I feel the same way. I need to find a way to admit how I feel without embarrassing myself. Regan would have something smooth and funny to say in this moment, but all I feel is stupid. Like I'm reading way too much into things and making both of us incredibly uncomfortable.

"Just the money," I whisper. The thought of belonging to him makes me feel hot and breathless. For some reason, I think belonging to Nick would be nothing like my father's oppressive control. Nick would let me run free, I think. Give me just enough to let me do what I want, but he would always be there to protect me if I needed him.

His hand reaches up and touches my face. Ever so softly, his thumb grazes across my skin. Prickles of awareness shoot through me, and I feel goose bumps rise. I should push his hand away. I should.

I don't.

Instead, I meet his gaze, incredibly drawn to him. That small, simple touch is mesmerizing me. He leans in, as if he wants to tell me a secret—or kiss me—if I lean in to meet him. The thought makes my pulse flutter all over again.

As he does, I notice his open collar has shifted, and I can see a hint of black on his neck. I'm fascinated. "Is that a tattoo?"

It is the wrong thing to ask. He stiffens, his eyes going cold. He pulls back and shrugs his shoulders, and the enticing glimpse of tattooed skin is gone. He drops his hand, and I'm left cold and alone all over again.

"So," he says. "The clothing is a gift."

I've offended him. How awful. I should apologize. But he's not looking at me anymore, and I can't find the way to form the words. Instead, I clutch the bag closer. "Thank you."

We walk toward the next store in silence, and I see another couple holding hands. Suddenly, I want that, too. If I brush my hand against his, will he take it? Or will he ignore me?

This, I think, will tell me how he feels about me. If he's as messed up over me as I already am over him. A normal girl would not be so attached so quickly . . . but I'm not normal.

I switch the bag to my other hand, leaving one free. Very carefully, I brush it against his as we walk.

He glances over, and I think he realizes what I'm doing. I'm more obvious than I think. I should be embarrassed.

Nick's fingers lace with mine, and we walk, hand in hand, to the next store. My heart thrums in my chest like it is dancing.

Today is the best day of my life.

Three stores and three large bags of clothing later, I glance at the clock on the wall. "I should get going. I don't want to be out too late." That, and if I spend any more time with him, he will continue to throw money my way.

This makes him unhappy. He frowns fiercely, and his hand clutches mine tighter. He glances at his watch. "It is barely night."

"Yes it is," I tell him. "Regan told me it's not safe to hang out outside of the building after dark, though, so I should head in before it gets too late." Regan knows the apartment and knows more about the world outside than I possibly can, so when she warns me, I listen.

"I will go with you to your door."

"I—you don't have to."

"I do." And he frowns in my direction. "I will keep you safe."

"Of course." I swallow hard, reluctant to leave. I like being here with him. Like talking to him softly about things. While we've shopped, I have told him about Regan and my life. Well, as much as I tell anyone. I tell him I'm from a farm, just like I told Regan. I tell him I'm an orphan. I tell him I'm here to find a job and go to college, which is the truth.

Tomorrow I planned on going to the nearby stores and looking for a job that would support me. I need a job desperately. But . . . I want to see Nick again. And I clutch his hand a little harder. After today, am I going to see him again? I can't wash my clothes every day in the hopes he will show up. "Do . . . do you want to go out for coffee tomorrow?"

His cold demeanor melts a little. "Is this—?" He gropes for a word. "A date?" The word sounds foreign on his tongue, like he's never been on a date, let alone used the word before.

"My treat this time," I tell him. "A thank-you for the clothing." Even with my meager savings, I can afford a couple of coffees and some sandwiches. And I want to see him again. "I'm not sure what time because my day is pretty busy . . . but I'd like to get together."

Nick nods. "We will meet. You text me." We walk out to his bike and arrange my bags to ensure they don't fly away, anchoring them with straps. Then he is putting the helmet back on me, and we're ready to go home.

I never want to go home ever again. I want to stay here with him, feel the flutter in my stomach when his fingers brush mine. I want that forever.

We drive home in the twilight, down the streets of the nearby neighborhoods. When he pulls up to the crowded apartment building, he coasts up into the parking garage and then stops in front of the elevator.

He's silent as we head into our building. I'm silent, too. We go up the elevator to the second floor, and I head immediately toward Regan's apartment. If he asks me to go into his, I don't know that I have the sense to tell him no.

Not with the memory of his hand on mine, driving me wild and turning my thoughts toward sexual things. We get to the second floor, and I glance around. "Which door is yours?" How close has he been all this time? I can't believe I've lived here for almost two weeks and haven't seen him before now.

He's silent for so long that I worry I've offended him . . . or worse, that he doesn't want to tell me. "It's okay," I say in a soft voice and turn away. "It's not a big deal. I was just curious."

His hand grasps mine before I can retreat. "*Nyet*, Daisy. I . . . I apologize. I do not live in your building."

"You don't?" I think back to him downstairs and frown.

"My washing machines were broken. Some *mudak* puts bleach in the dryers, so I come borrow yours."

I laugh, relieved. So he doesn't live in this building and didn't want to confess? I feel better. "I'm just down the hall," I say shyly, and I gesture toward the doorstep of my apartment. I put my hands out for the bags that he has insisted on carrying for me. "That's me."

"*Da*." He holds the bags for a moment longer, and then he hands them to me. His fingers caress mine as we switch the handles from his fingers to my smaller ones, and I can't help but gasp at the sensation that moves through me at the gentle caress. My nipples won't stop hardening while I think about it.

He's my first flirtation with arousal. I'm twenty-one, and I've never been touched so intimately. I think of how scandalized my father would be at the thought of me riding on some man's motorcycle, of me asking him for a coffee date tomorrow. I can't help it. He's forbidden fruit, and I'm Eve standing in front of the apple.

Nick gives me a stiff bow and waits. I realize he won't leave until I'm safely in, so I give him a trembling, distracted smile and race inside, breathless.

Regan and Mike are making out on the futon sofa. His hands are in her shirt, and I'm pretty sure her jeans are unbuttoned, judging by the way they sag against her bottom. She's sprawled over Mike, her hips are nestled between his legs, and her tongue snakes across his lips. She glances up at me, gives me a dopey, passion-glazed smile, wiggles her fingers, and then returns her attention back to Mike.

"I'm just going to my room," I breathe, and I leave them behind. Normally I'd be scandalized by Regan's behavior, but right now I couldn't care less. I want to go to my room so I can think privately about my Ukrainian.

My Ukrainian. Just the thought makes me ache and throb between my legs, which is delicious and terrible all at once.

I head to my room and sling my bags onto the floor. I shut the door and flop down on my bed. I lay there for a long time, thinking. My window is wide open—but I don't even glance at it. Tonight I'm not missing the stars. Tonight I'm thinking about my Ukrainian.

My Ukrainian. As if he belongs to me. As if he is harboring the same silly crush I have. He held my hand. Bought me panties because he ruined mine. This doesn't make attraction. I tell myself this even as I pull open my phone and text him.

With my cheap, terrible phone, it's difficult to text complete sentences, but I manage to type, Let's meet @ coffee shop dwn street nite aftr tmrw. If I agree to meet him tomorrow, he will think me too eager. I'll add a day in there, just so it seems like I'm busier than I really am. I think for a moment more and then send, 6pm k? Then I lay back on the bed and wait, unable to do anything but lose track of the world and daydream.

My phone buzzes sooner than I anticipate. I snatch it up, flip it open, and read the message.

This is not good neighborhood. My apartment is safer. You come to me?

The thrill of excitement fades away under a pang of alarm. Go to his apartment? Now that I have been able to catch my

breath away from him, I realize that it would be too forward of
me to go to meet him mere feet from his bed. Have I made a bad
move, then? Was asking him for coffee akin to me saying "I want
to sleep with you"?

I'm naïve, but I'm not stupid. For some reason, this invitation
makes me angry. I snap back a text. Nvrmnd.

Never mind?

I'm not meeting u, however nice, at yr apt.

So you think I am nice, Daisy? I am pleased.

I am flustered at his flirty response. Im afraid I hav 2 dcline. It's
hard to text on my stupid phone. I have to constantly click the
number key until it scrolls to the right letter, but I do it anyhow,
because texting is safer than talking.

He answers immediately. Apologies. Coffee is fine?

He knows he's offended me. For some reason, that deflates all
of my anger, and I'm left feeling a bit foolish. Maybe in the
Ukraine it's not a big deal for guys to invite girls to their apartments. Maybe it's not a big deal if you're dating. But we're not,
and I know I'm a ninny. A Pollyanna, as Regan likes to call me.
But this Pollyanna is cautious.

So I reply after thinking it over carefully. K, I send back. The
coffeehouse is a nice, well-lit, central location for us to meet. And
I will tell Regan where I am and have her pick me up. If anything
weird should arise, I'll have her come and get me. The coffeehouse is safe enough.

I will see you in two days, he sends back.

I have a date. *No, not a date*, I tell my fevered mind. It's simply a thank-you. He bought me clothes and gave me a ride on his motorcycle. It's nothing more than that.

The next day is frustrating. I've worn a modest sweater over a white, high-collared blouse. My hair is pulled back into a sleek ponytail, and I am wearing makeup and pressed slacks. I look ready to go to church as I pass out my resume to every business I can find near our building and fill out applications. Most are not hiring. The economy is bad, it's the wrong time of year for jobs, and I have no work experience at all. The only thing I have going for me is a willingness to work any hours for bad pay.

In the end, the only leads I have are a nearby gas station that needs someone for the overnight shift and another restaurant that also needs someone for a late shift. They promise they will call me.

Job hunting complete, I return home and mope for the entire evening. I wish I'd told Nick that we'd meet tonight, but I had to pretend to be a strong, independent woman. I hate that.

The next day follows much the same—I job hunt until the afternoon winds down, and when I can stand it no longer, I head to the coffeehouse a bit early and get a booth. I bought lip gloss at the corner store and put it on in the bathroom so I can look my best when my Ukrainian arrives. Then, I return to the private booth in the back of the coffeehouse and open the newspaper I've bought, scanning for jobs as I wait.

And wait.

And wait.

It isn't until six thirty that I realize I have been stood up.

CHAPTER **FOUR**

NIKOLAI

I'm glad that she has declined my invitation to come to the apartment. As I glance around, I realize that I will need to work quickly to furnish this place so that it looks presentable. I wonder if I could ask Daisy to help me. This particular apartment was ideally situated because it was a corner unit on the second floor. It is high enough that someone cannot crawl through the window but not so high I can't jump down without injury. The corner affords me a larger view, it is close to the stairs, and I could possibly rappel to the opposite apartment building. I have not tested it, concerned that someone might spot me, but I have crossed wider spaces with nothing more than my belt and a steel wire.

I peer into the apartment across from me, one flight up from Daisy's. Inside two male students live together. Their residence is sloppy and filled with beer cans and pizza boxes. When they are not in classes, they play video games. I study their interior. Tonight

I will order things and have them delivered. A sofa. A table. I will want to see the bed in person. Only the best bed for Daisy. I shake my head. I've spent so much time alone in the past years that I have become delusional. As if Daisy will ever be in my bed.

A text sounds from my business phone. Not Daisy. The number I have given her is for my personal line. I have only three numbers in it. Alexsandr, Daniel, and now Daisy.

Call me.

The text is from Jules Laurence, a paper forger and computer hacker I've used in the past. Contact from him is disturbing. I call as directed.

"Allo," I say when the connection is made.

"Nikolai," he pants in my ear. "I'm so sorry."

He is blubbering now. The apology is all the explanation I need. He has sold me out.

"They threatened my Sarah. I had to tell them. I had to."

I say nothing. My silence will draw him out. I know this about him, but I thought that he had more honor. My lip curls in disgust. There is no honor, only self-reliance.

"It's the *Bratva*. They are scared of you and want to eliminate you before you get to them. They know that you're just waiting to hunt them down after Alexsandr."

"Alexsandr was months ago," I say mildly. "If I was to do anything to them, wouldn't it have been done by now?"

"The waiting was killing them. Plus, they know you. They know you wouldn't accept Alexsandr's death without retribution. That you've done nothing so far only incites greater fear."

Good, I think. Those *mudak*s should be shaking with fear.

"I have no allegiance," I tell Jules. "I accomplish the tasks set before me and move on."

Jules gasps his disbelief in my ear and apologizes again. "I'm sorry. I had to tell."

"Why are you calling?" I sigh. There is nothing to be done. I must eliminate the threat and return.

"I just thought that maybe if I told you, then . . ." His voice trails off.

"You thought I would not hurt you? That you need not fear me?" I can almost see him nod through the phone. "Then fear not. As you say, death is restful. It is living that is fraught with terror."

A quick inhalation is the only response to my words. Then, more sobs. "Please. Sarah is pregnant. I had to do this."

"I will show you my mercy, Jules." I hear him catch his breath. Enough of this ridiculous posturing. I command, "Tell me."

"They will be coming via the West Coast in hopes to confuse you. I'll send you the boarding gate numbers. I'm tracking it." A swallowed sob follows and then Jules continues. "Anything you need?"

"I think you have been overly helpful."

"Then you'll take care of it, and we'll be even?" His voice is hopeful, but I can offer him no assurances.

"I don't know," I reply honestly and hang up.

I glance at my watch. If the *Bratva* assassins are coming from Russia to the West Coast, I have less than forty-eight hours to apprehend them. I will have to fly directly to Los Angeles. Quickly I pull up the commercial flight schedule. I do not want to mess with private planes and their need to file flight plans and traveler manifests with the authorities. Using one of my identities, it is safer for me to fly coach, just one more anonymous businessman. My evening with Daisy will have to be put off. Fuming, I reach for my secure line to tell Sergei exactly what I think of his interference. I will do this task asked of me in my own way and time. But I force myself to draw back. Sergei will know soon enough what I think of his actions.

Instead I must contact Daisy and ask her for a different date. She will either take my delay as disinterest or worse, inconstancy. A dull ache behind my eyes begins to throb. Pressing a finger on either side of the bridge of my nose, I press down until the pain recedes. I will put this disturbance of my plans with Daisy in Sergei's payment column. So much he has to pay for. If only he knew.

I wonder whether I should text or call. What would Daniel do? He would text, I decide.

> Daisy, I find that an emergency in my business requires my absence for two days. I apologize for this but I cannot delay. Would you consider coffee on another date? Three days I will be back.

A considerable amount of time passes without a response. Impatient, I try to focus on the details in front of me. I cannot allow the *Bratva* to come here.

Pulling a bag from the closet, I quickly pack a change of clothing along with my laptop. The suit I will wear is nondescript, as are the shoes. I pull a latex face mask over my own. It is suffocating, but the padded cheekbones and the rounded forehead change my appearance dramatically. The high collar of the businessman's shirt easily covers the bottom of the mask as well as the dagger at my neck, the one that Daisy noticed earlier. I am Mr. John Anderson now.

I loop a specially designed belt through my slightly baggy pants. The metal trim at the top and bottom can be removed to form a garroting wire. I cannot bring anything more dangerous on the plane besides myself. I have killed with my bare hands and will do so again if necessary, but tools make survival easier. But then I am going to Los Angeles. I have a storage locker there with a few necessities.

Thirty minutes later, I am walking purposefully through the airport. I am going to a very important business meeting, I say to myself. People mill about me but take no notice. I am simply one of many travelers. At the security checkpoint, I remove my shoes and my belt without being asked. Never bring attention to yourself.

My carry-on and laptop are scanned and then released. I hold my breath as the belt reverses and the agents look more closely at my belongings. But the wire looks like nothing more than gold trim. It's a gaudy piece for a sedate businessman like me, but they approve it anyway. The agent nods at me and wishes me a good flight.

"Thank you," I reply.

"Traveling for business or pleasure," he asks as I pass through the body scanner with my hands raised.

"Business."

"What'd'ya do?"

I cannot tell if this is part of the security check or casual curiosity. "Sales of plastics."

He nods but I can tell he's lost interest. The security line two over is examining a bosomy woman. A female agent is rubbing her hands along the passenger's breasts and then her waist. The agent in front of me licks his lips and adjusts himself. I walk by him, and he doesn't even acknowledge me. Weak. I grab my belt, shoes, and bag, and I am out of the security checkpoint before the agent has finished his leering.

The plane is in the process of boarding when I arrive at the gate. I pull out my phone and pretend to check my messages like all the other passengers. Daisy has still not responded. I rub my finger across the screen imagining it is her hand. Perhaps her cheek or her lovely breast, the one that she pressed against me as she leaned against me as we rode the motorcycle together.

I clutch the phone as I think of Jules's sobs over Sarah. Would I not do everything to protect someone I cared about? Retribution is what I have planned for Sergei because of Alexsandr's death. If they threatened Daisy, wouldn't I sell out everyone I knew to save her?

I would. Even though I'd known Daisy but a minute, she was too good not to live. I'd betray everyone in my vile life to ensure that she would live. The people in my world had short life spans. Each moment we breathed was a gift, and it was one that we did not deserve.

When I killed, I targeted those who were the dregs and vermin of the world. Someday someone would take me out, and no one would mourn. But if Daisy was killed? Some light in the world would have been snuffed out. I want a piece of that light for myself, even if just for a short time. I know I do not deserve it—nor will I be able to keep it.

Every interaction with her is a lie, but for once in my godforsaken life, I want something fresh, clean, beautiful. Yes, I'd give up a lot of things to taste that, just once, and if it takes a battalion of lies, deceit, and manipulation to achieve that, I'll do it. I will hate myself, but the truth would disgust her. Someone like Daisy would never, ever spend time with someone like me. Even standing next to her is a gift to be treasured. To be allowed to touch her hand is a miracle.

Even if she does not agree to see me again, I will go to her and beg for another chance. On my knees, if necessary. The business phone vibrates in my breast pocket. Knowing I would look strange if I took out another phone, I ignore it. There would be time enough when I boarded to slip it out and read Jules's information.

The line of passengers moves quickly. Because I have only my bag, I go directly to my seat. I have booked tickets in two other names. Those people will not appear. I do not like to sit next to strangers.

"Would you like me to place that in an overhead for you, sir?" A flight attendant holds out her hand.

"No, thank you. I'll place it under the seat in front of me." I push the bag under and stretch my legs around it.

She smiles vacantly at me, having mentally moved on to the next passenger. As soon as she leaves, I pull out my phone and look at the message. LAX Singapore Air SQ21.

The weather is good on Jeju Island, I respond. It is my peace offering. Get somewhere safe and far away from me.

Sarah has always wanted to visit. The relief in the text message was palpable.

You should go for at least three months. I will not text him again.

Thank you.

I force myself to sleep on the flight. It might be the only rest I get in the next forty-eight hours.

Arrival comes swiftly, but it is early morning, and the rental car lines are minimal. I am in my Taurus and on the freeway to my storage locker in Brentwood within fifteen minutes. The outskirts of the flashy suburb are filled with cracker-box houses that look like little cartons set in a row. The people inside are probably more content than those in the larger houses. People with bigger houses and more money are never satisfied.

At the storage unit, I open a case that holds a few of my implements. The .40-caliber Glock 23 handgun I purchased from a drug dealer a year ago lies nestled inside. I like this gun because it belonged to a police officer, who traded it to the dealer for something. Maybe blow. Maybe girls. After I am done with the two men from the *Bratva*, I may leave the gun. The police officer can then be confronted. It will be my good deed, a balancing of the scales—although removing the two is not a bad deed. No one would say that, not even the man who employed them.

Sitting on a trunk, I carefully dismantle the Glock. The shaft is clean, and despite the lack of use, it still looks good. I dry fire it as if I am cleaning out the thirteen-round magazine. As I count out the bullets, I smile. A buyer who was not in law enforcement would be limited to a ten-round magazine.

Everything is in perfect working order. The suppressor is stuck down my sock, and the gun is tucked into a shoulder holster concealed by my jacket. The rest of the tactical weapons are left in the case, which I slide onto the passenger seat of the Taurus. Twenty minutes later, I am on my way back to the airport.

The Taurus is traded for a Lincoln Town Car, and my suit is now a hundred-dollar warehouse purchase, ill-fitting and wrinkled. I hold up a sign waiting for Ben Nelson. To the rest of the people here, I am merely one poor driver waiting to pick up his passenger.

The heat is stifling, and the press of bodies near the baggage and transportation claim makes me edgy and tense. I suppress the urge to pull out my gun and shoot until I have space around me.

I spot Bogdan, a high-ranking member of the security force in the *Bratva*, and an unknown man sauntering down to the baggage claim check. Bogdan is an unimaginative killer but very loyal. You must give him specific instructions because he does not know how to improvise. I wonder what Sergei told Bogdan. *Go find Nikolai in Minneapolis. Kill him and find the mark. Return.*

As they stop at the baggage claim, I contemplate what they have brought on their commercial flight. What would they be so dumb to have packed? I'll search it later. I glance at my watch and then take a phone call. I pretend that I am at the wrong terminal and move out quickly. In the town car, I follow the two. They are headed to Portofino, just as I suspected. They will want to be on the beach, not because they like the ocean, but because they want to ogle the women in bikinis. I wonder why Sergei has not sent Vasily. Do I not warrant Alexsandr's successor? At least Vasily would be a true challenge. Bogdan and his friend would be a task for an apprentice, not someone who has been hunting since he could hold a stick in his hand.

I leave the town car in a parking garage and pick up my case. Inside the basement of the hotel, I pull off my suit and stuff it down the incinerator. A row of uniforms are hanging in the laundry facility. I choose a bellman's uniform with its convenient white gloves and pull it over my thin pants and a tank. The laundry room contains carts and master keys. I tuck the Glock in the back of my pants and place the case of other weapons at the bottom of a luggage cart and head upstairs.

I keep my head lowered and am soon called on to deliver a guest's luggage to their room. I complete the task and then continue up to Bogdan's room. Once there, I don't bother knocking. They will not open the door. I pull out my gun, attach the suppressor, and use a master key I've pilfered from the maids downstairs. Bogdan looks up as the door swings open. I pull the trigger. He falls. I swivel, locking the Glock on my new target, and I hit.

They both fall to the floor in agony. Quickly, I enter, shut the door, and have them both trussed with duct tape. My favorite. The whole process has taken less than thirty seconds. The second man, one I do not know, spits at me, and I hear a grinding of his teeth. Bogdan must have heard it, too, because he shouts no. I step back from the second man, who is now foaming at the mouth.

"Cyanide?" I ask Bogdan. He closes his eyes and nods.

"In his tooth." Bogdan says, hanging his head.

"A new recruit then."

"*Da*, they are so earnest." Bogdan and I both watch the man. The poison he has swallowed is fast-acting. That's positive. In the past, Sergei would give his foot soldiers dimethylmercury. It took a long time for them to die. And it was painful. It was as if Sergei wanted to punish them one last time for failing him. But the downside was that the man, angry about the painful death, could be coerced to give up secrets. This unknown foot soldier is unconscious, and he will soon be dead. I turn away. There is nothing to be done.

"Bogdan, why are you so careless?"

He shrugs. He doesn't know. I believe this. Sergei does not surround himself with anyone who is smarter than him. It is too dangerous. That person will eventually want to throw you over. I go into the bedroom and rip the pillow cases into strips and hand the cloth to Bogdan. He ineptly tries to bind his hand, so I do it for him. "It will heal, you know."

"We were just coming over to warn you, not harm you," Bogdan whines.

I glance at the dead body of his companion in obvious disbelief.

Bogdan tries to smile, but it is a grimace. Smiling is something that comes hard to all of us. Not to Daisy, though. She seems to smile constantly. I shake my head to get her out of there. Time for business now; pleasure later.

"Why kill Alexsandr?" I ask bluntly. I want to hear Bogdan's story. His will be the one told throughout the *Bratva*.

"He fell in love with wrong woman." Bogdan tongues his tooth, the one with the poison, as if taunting me. I want to beat Bogdan for lying, but I wait. Patience. We both know that if he intended to use the poison, then he would've done it earlier, perhaps as soon as I had shot him. The stink of nicotine from Bogdan's clothes almost overwhelms the sulfur, blood, and now piss from the dead man. I rifle through Bogdan's clothes until I find his cigarettes. I place one in his mouth and offer him a flame. He nods in gratitude, takes a few puffs, and begins.

"She comes home two weeks ago. Angry. She says to her papa, 'Alexsandr is a *mudak*.' Sergei answers, 'What's new?' "

I nod. Alexsandr is an asshole. We all know this.

"She yells at her papa that she wanted to marry Alexsandr, but he refuses to marry her. He won't marry her, but he'll fuck her anytime he gets the chance."

Heaviness sets in. Alexsandr killed because of a woman. This makes more sense to me than the claims that Alexsandr was disloyal, yet I cannot shake the feeling that I do not know all of the story. I think of Daisy again, of fucking her, of her being angry that I cannot marry her. I see her face crumple and cry. I shake my head again. Daisy. I must not think of her now.

"Because she gives voice to the truth, Sergei thinks Alexsandr must die?" I ask.

Bogdan gives a negligent shake of his shoulder. "Sergei says to his daughter, 'I'll take care of this. No man fucks with the *Bratva*.' Then he is gone."

"He does the deed himself."

Bogdan shakes his head. "Don't know. He takes Daniel with him. Maybe Vasily, maybe Grigory."

I'm shocked to hear Daniel's name. He plays a deeper game than I suspected, but I will pursue that threat later. I need to understand the extent of my vengeance. "Is she happy then?"

"No, she finds out two days later. I guess she wanted a fucking." Bogdan curves his lips around his cigarette. I swallow down the urge to make him eat it. "She comes storming back, screaming and crying. She fights with her papa. Nonstop. She screams that he has ruined her life. He tells her that it is his right to protect and avenge what is his. She does not come out of her room for days. He says he is sorry."

"And now you are here to tell me this story."

"Sergei knew you would not be happy."

"Yet he acted anyway."

Bogdan looks away, draws hard on his cigarette. It is almost ash. I make no move to take it from his mouth. With Bogdan's hands behind his back, he cannot move, either. He drops it to the carpet and then spits on the cigarette. When I watch it burn, he shuffles over on his knees and rubs it out, grimacing at the burn through the wool of his trousers.

"So, you let me go?" Bogdan asks, hopeful.

"I cannot do that."

Bogdan tries to lean forward; perhaps he thinks to attack me on his knees. Some men could take me from this position, but not Bogdan. I move back with ease, and he falls forward, his nose now crushed in the carpet.

"You should take poison, Bogdan. It seems fast-acting." I stand to leave.

"Stop, Nikolai. Don't do this."

"What?" I turn and put my arms out. In the plate window beyond, I can see myself, thick cheeked in my red bellman's uniform. I look like a clown. A clown with a Glock 23 and suppressor. I lower my arms. "You come to me, Bogdan. I have job to do. Then I'm done. Don't interfere."

"You'll never get out," Bogdan snarls. "None of us ever do."

"That is what they said when I was six and taken in by Alexsandr's crew. That I'd never get out. But I did."

Bogdan looks torn between wanting to hit me and cry. He does neither. Instead, he begs me. "Don't leave me here."

"I cannot take you with me, Bogdan. I am in the middle of a job, one that you interrupted." I turn to leave.

"Take me into your network. Make me disappear. Please."

I hate it when they beg. It is an attempt to manipulate me through unsavory means. Through feelings, when they know I have none.

"I know you have a network you work with. I can be part of that network. You just need to give me a little hand." Bogdan offers this.

"Bullshit, Bogdan," I chastise, "always trying to sell out. At the first sign of danger to yourself, you are bargaining. What else will you bargain with? What information can you provide?"

"Anything." Bogdan is beginning to cry. Soon, no doubt, he will piss himself. The room already smells like a urinal.

"I cannot trust you, Bogdan. You have no allegiance."

"Neither do you. We are no different!" he cries.

Whatever sympathy I have for Bogdan disappears. I curl my lip at him. "You and I are nothing alike. I would not sell out a trusted friend or partner for my life."

"You would for a girl."

For a moment my heart stops. How does Bogdan know of Daisy? It takes every ounce of control I have not to attack him, to act nonchalant. To pretend like terror isn't taking over my body, because if I let it, I will start fileting off his skin until he gives me answers. I force myself to relax.

"A girl, Bogdan? Don't make me laugh. Is there some Pravdian whore I'm in love with?"

Bogdan sniffs with one side of his nose. "Someday there will be."

Ahh, Bogdan knows nothing. I walk toward the hotel room door, relief washing through me like a balm.

"Someday," Bogdan screams behind me. "Someday, like Alexsandr, some girl will be your downfall."

I stop with my white-gloved hand on the door and my back to Bogdan. "Then I will have lived for something important in my life."

"Bring me your mercy then," Bogdan pleads. "You know I cannot take the poison. You know this."

Bogdan is Catholic. He crosses himself before each kill, rape, assault. He believes that if he takes the poison, he'll go to hell. Not because of any of the deeds he committed, but because he believes taking his own life means that his last deed will be a sin. I rub the inscription on my chest. I can hear the whimpering pleas behind me. Mercy, then.

I turn and shoot.

When I arrive at the airport, I am met with the news that my return flight is delayed. I bargain with the ticket counter, offering more money and nearly losing my temper in an effort to get a quicker flight back. My phone has remained annoyingly silent. I do not know if Daisy has gone to the café without me. Whether she has decided she will not talk to me again.

Daisy is not a girl to wait on. If she has gone to the café, there will be dozens of wolves circling her, scenting her distress, and wanting to pounce on her. My nostrils flare, and the ticket agent's hand moves to hover over a distress button.

"Sorry," I say to alleviate her concern. *Durak*, idiot. I give her my best crestfallen look, the one I saw on Daisy's face when she thought I spent too much money on her at the mall. She does not realize yet I will keep buying her things to give her the life she deserves. Already, I have ordered her a leather jacket she admired and passed by at the store. I had it delivered to my apartment for when I get home. I will give it to her after I ruin the one tissue-thin coat she owns.

This is the right gesture because the agent smiles at me and removes her hand from the panic button.

"There's a flight that leaves in forty minutes, but you may not be able to make the gate."

I will make the gate. "Sounds great." I hand her my ticket, and she keys in the change.

I make the gate and arrive in Minneapolis without further delay, but I've still missed our date and had no response from Daisy. While I know she is not at the café, I run there anyway. *Perhaps she likes the place so much she returns,* I hope stupidly. But of course she is not there.

"Fuck. Fuck. Fuck." I kick the brick wall of the restaurant, but it does not alleviate my frustration. Two girls walk by and stare at me in horror. I want to bare my teeth at them and give them something real to be afraid of. Closing my eyes, I lean my forehead against the brick wall. The crisp night air should be refreshing, but all I can think about is how my sweet Daisy would have been here alone, waiting for me. She could've been cold and needed my arms. Had she felt unwanted? I release a low moan of despair. I wonder if I've already allowed her to slip away.

I decide to text her again.

> Daisy, I am here at the café. I know it is two days late but my business trip was unavoidable. Forgive me. Please.

I lean against the brick wall and will the phone to respond. I wonder at her cell phone. It's cheap and must be hard to send messages. This is good in that it prevents her from texting other males, but bad in that it makes it challenging for her to communicate easily with me.

The next time I see her, I will break her phone, accidentally of course, and then she will allow me to buy her a new one. Cheered by my new plan, I decide to go to the cellular phone carrier located three blocks away and buy the phone right now. That there will be a GPS locator in the phone is only so that I can keep track of her safety—or so I tell myself.

My phone dings, and I raise the screen immediately. It is her. My breath quickens.

> Why didn't u txt or call?

Good question. "I was busy shooting two Russian criminals," was not the right answer.

> I did text three days ago before I left. Did you not get it?

I do not get an immediate response. Was it possible that she did not receive my message? I take a screenshot of the message I sent as proof. I think it must be her phone. Perhaps I do not have to break it. I will explain to her that her phone is already not working right and that I should replace it. Perhaps the gift will make her forgive me more quickly. Instantly, I feel much better. *Good job, Nikolai,* I think. *This is smart.*

As you can see I send message. One thousand apologies for
being so disrespectful of your time. Please allow me to make it
up to you.

Inside the store, I pick out the latest smartphone.
"With a new contract, sir?"
"No, without." I will have it activated after I gift her the phone.
The purchase is completed before I receive another response
from her.

Oh. I didnt get ur msg. Felt stupid. Didn't know how long 2
wait.

Ah gods, I made her feel alone and uncertain. I should knife
myself in punishment.

I beg of you to flush this incident from your memory. Give me
one more chance. I promise I will not fail you this time,
lapochka.

lapo-what?

I tell you when I see you.

I wait for her response but none comes.
I go back to my apartment and wait. The night grows long,
and there is no response. Perhaps Daisy is right to have rejected
my attempts at reparation. Why should she want to be with filth
like me? The past forty-eight hours weigh upon me. I have killed
two men while she struggles to feed herself. I kill men for money,
and if she knew the truth, she would spit in my face. I knew from

the moment she caught my eye as I was watching Mr. Brown that she was an angel. But thoughts of Daisy make me ache. My cock is stiff and my balls are drawn up tight against my body.

Suddenly, I remember that I have something of Daisy's. The jeans I wore during the laundry confrontation lie folded in the corner. In the back pocket, I pull out the pale pink cotton that once touched Daisy's ass, her pussy lips, and the soft thatch of hair between her legs. I lift the cotton to my nose, but it smells only of detergent; the soap had washed away what I knew must be a delicious scent.

Still . . . I unzip my jeans and pull out my cock. It is hard to imagine Daisy in this place, this desolate space I call my living quarters. Closing my eyes, I fantasize that my hands are Daisy's hands and that I've just removed these panties from her body. In my imagination the crotch of the panties are still soaking wet from her arousal and I use the moisture to wet my cock.

I picture her falling to her knees and tonguing my length. My cock would stretch her lips wide. I'd tunnel my hands in her hair and tug her head back so I could slide in and out with ease. She's innocent, so she'd not be able to take my whole length. Instead, she would have to use her hands, twisting and turning and pumping me. I wrap the pink cotton around my engorged member until the cloth and lace are binding me tightly, imagining the pressure is from her lips. The bite of the elastic is really her tight fist enclosing my engorged flesh. In my fevered imagination, it is her skin next to mine, her body under me and wrapped around me.

The image shifts and Daisy is now sitting on my mattress, watching me tug at my cock. "Touch yourself," I tell her, and she tentatively reaches down between her legs. "Spread your thighs wider. I want to see you."

She obeys. In my imagination, her arousal visibly glistens her center, and I can hear the juicy sounds of her cunt as she fingers herself. I want to draw it out, but I can't, and I spurt long, white threads of come onto my stomach. I stumble over to the mattress and fall backward, my hand clutched around my still-aching member. It is not enough. The phone has remained silent. The entire apartment seems like a tomb.

I'll never be good enough for Daisy but I ache and I am . . . lonely. I reach over to the phone with my free hand and call a number.

"Massage Heights," a perky voice answers.

"I need a house call," I say.

"Do you have a preference?"

I begin to tell her I don't, but then I say, "Medium height, light brown hair, not too thin."

"Gl—" she starts to say a name, but I stop her.

"Tell her she'll be Violet for the night."

"Sure. Violet."

"Violet" knocks on my door thirty minutes later. I let her in. She looks nothing like Daisy. Her dirty hair is bleached too light. Her eyes are hazel and not blue. She is too thin. I can see her ribs when she opens her coat to show me her thigh-high stockings and garters. She smiles at the sight of me. I shake my head at her naïveté. Because I look young and have a firm body, she automatically thinks that I will be a better lay, but I'm strong and I could hurt her. She has no instinct of self-preservation. She will likely be dead before she hits her quarter-century mark.

Her outfit would be sexy to anyone else, but I am unmoved. I glance over my shoulder toward Daisy's apartment. Afraid she might be able to see in, I walk over and close the blinds. It is a stupid act. My Daisy is too trusting to peer in windows, looking for me.

The girl I've named Violet pulls off her jacket and looks for somewhere to place it. I take it and throw it on the kitchen counter.

"Um, you just move in?" She takes in my empty space.

"Yeah." I do not want her to remember me as "the Russian guy," so I make a conscious effort to speak with American slang. "Haven't got any furniture yet."

She shrugs. "Where do you want to do this?"

I sit down on a chair and pull out a condom.

"Just a BJ?" She looks surprised at my nod. "And a condom. Aren't you the responsible boy."

Not responsible, just smart. I open my jeans and pull out my cock. It is flaccid, but its quiescent length still makes Violet's eyes widen.

"That's quite a package you've got there."

"I want you to suck me," I say.

I do not want to have conversation with her. I want a fuck. I want relief. I jack myself and think of Daisy and the crumpled panties that rest on my washstand. I am erect instantly.

The prostitute comes forward and kneels between my legs. The floor is hard, and I consider getting her a pillow, but I do not want her to touch my things. I barely want her to touch me.

Her hands run up my jean-clad leg, and her mouth descends. I grab her hair and pull her face back. One glance at her too-knowing face and my erection subsides. I want for no one but Daisy. This fake flower I have purchased will do nothing for me. I stand up, and she falls aside. Walking swiftly across the room, I gather up her coat and pull out a hundred-dollar bill from my pocket. I would offer her more, but she would remember me more, talk of me.

"Sorry. I have appointment I have forgotten."

She looks at me uncertainly, but she quickly grabs the bill and shrugs on her coat. "If you change your mind, just say you want Violet again."

I nod. I won't be calling. But then, neither is Daisy.

CHAPTER **FIVE**

DAISY

"You sure you want this job, honey?" The elderly man looks at me with more than a little skepticism. "You seem too nice to be working the overnight shift at a gas station, if you don't mind me saying so. Not the safest job for a young girl."

I swallow hard, my hand smoothing the dark blue collar of the company polo I have been given to wear. It's my first day, and Craig—the elderly owner of the gas station—is showing me how to run the register for a few hours before he leaves for the evening and I am all alone until two a.m., which is when the next shift arrives.

It's not that I truly want this job. I don't. It pays minimum wage. The counters are dirty and everything in the store has a fine layer of dust on it. I feel very young as Craig gives me another skeptical look, but I don't have a choice. I have no money. I have less than two hundred dollars in my savings, and my cupboard is getting barer by the day.

"I want the job," I tell Craig with a smile. "Don't worry about me." This is the only place that has called me. Of course I want the job. I *need* the job.

"All right," he says reluctantly, and we go behind the counter of the gas station convenience store. There are things I have to learn—how to swipe the lottery tickets in the machine, how to turn off the gas pumps, how to change out the flavor bags in the soda machine. There are a million things to remember, and I make notes on a notepad so I won't forget. Last, he shows me the cameras in the convenience store. He shows me the panic switch if I should be robbed, and the baseball bat that is kept under the counter, and then the Taser that is kept, dismantled, in a compartment behind the time clock in the storage room. They are there "just in case," Craig tells me.

"Has this place ever been robbed?" I ask when he shows me the Taser. I am getting a little uncomfortable with all the safety precautions. It reminds me of being home with my father. Of sitting up nights with weapons in hand, waiting for a strike that never comes.

How bad can a gas station be?

"Twice," he tells me, and my heart stutters. "But only on holidays. We won't make you work those days." He pats my arm. "I live just down the street. You get any troublemakers in here, you call me, okay?"

I nod. Craig's number is at the top of my notepad in big, bold numbers. I won't forget.

It's eventually time for Craig to leave, and I give him an impulsive hug when he does. I like him. He's a sweet old man. He reminds me of my grandfather, who is long dead. Craig seems pleased by my hug and pats my back; then he pushes a knuckle at the notepad still clutched in my hand. "Remember. You call me."

"I'll remember," I say warmly. "I've got this."

He leaves, and I am alone, manning the store. I take a deep breath. I can do this. It's what the new Daisy would do. Old Daisy would be terrified, so I won't be her. It's a case of mind over matter, and if my hands shake when a customer comes in to buy a soda, I ignore it. I ring him up, hand him a receipt, and when he leaves, I exhale. Father would never expect me to be so strong, so independent, but here I am, working my first job like a normal girl. I'm terrified—Father's endless fear of everything and anything out of the normal day-to-day has left its shadow on me, but I'm stronger than my fear.

I *can* do this.

It's not so bad after that first customer. Because it's late at night and most people pay at the pump, the gas station isn't all that busy. Regan has let me borrow one of her textbooks, and I read it and go through the homework from time to time so I can be prepared when I can afford classes. I read her textbook in between customers and manage to chat a little with the people that buy cigarettes and lottery tickets and beer. My feet ache from standing on them for so long, but this job isn't so bad. And by the end of an evening shift, I will have sixty-two dollars before taxes. Craig told me we get paid weekly, so I like this job more and more.

It's some time after ten at night when the door chimes, letting me know there is a customer. I look up from the textbook and straighten so I can greet the person at the door.

I recognize the high cheekbones, the slashing brows, the piercing gray eyes and the deep scowl on his face.

Nick.

I freeze. I don't know what to do. I'm hurt that he never bothered to show up the other day, and I'm embarrassed, too. His texts seemed sincere, but it's easy to lie when you're not speaking face-to-face. But acting like a jealous wife when it was just a coffee date would make me look stupid. Should I play it cool and casual? Do I even know how to do that?

I try to form a "hello," but my throat closes up. Instead of being the confident, carefree woman I should be, I stare at him mutely from across the counter and give a tepid wave, like some sort of idiot mime.

Real smooth, Daisy.

That frowning gaze remains focused on me, and I watch his gray eyes flick back and forth, studying everything. He pauses at the gas station logo on my shirt. Glances around at the empty convenience store. Then back at me. "Why are you here, Daisy?"

My mouth opens for a greeting . . . and then snaps shut again. Why am I here? That wasn't what I expected him to ask. I make a feeble gesture at my shirt.

"This is not safe," he states. "You should leave."

"I . . ." I swallow, my words choking in front of his disapproval. I am being such a ninny. Why does it matter if Nick approves of my job or not? "I work here. The next shift doesn't get here until two."

Nick looks upset at this. His mouth flattens into a grim line, and he shifts on his feet, scanning the empty parking lot. "This is not job for woman like you, Daisy. You must quit."

Those bossy words drain all of my awkwardness away. A woman like *me*? Someone who should be sheltered and locked away from the world? Now he sounds like my father. My mouth works into an angry scowl. "Are you buying something? Because if not, I think you should leave."

For a moment, he looks astonished that I am talking back to

him. Like, completely, flat-out astonished, as if I've just cussed him a blue streak instead of disagreed with him. And instead of getting upset, a smile curves his hard mouth.

That smile makes me all flustered again, but I'm still mad. I remember why I'm mad, too. He stood me up. Didn't even have the decency to show up in person and tell me why he couldn't be there. No, he let me sit at the café for hours and make a fool of myself. Everyone there thought I'd been stood up for a date. And then he tries to make it better by sending a few texts.

And I feel even stupider, because I'm clearly making more out of our friendship than it is. If I meant something to Nick, he wouldn't have humiliated me like that.

Like I was nothing. Like I didn't matter.

He puts a hand on the counter, and I stare at the letters, which I now know are Cyrillic, tattooed on his knuckles. "Daisy," he murmurs, his voice that achingly delicious thrum that I hate myself for liking. "You are not answering my texts, and I must explain myself."

"There's nothing to explain," I say. "We had a coffee date." *Oh no, I used the word* date! "And you didn't show up." Now I feel my face flushing at my choice of words. I shift on my feet and step backward since he's moved closer, and I scan the parking lot. Someone has pulled up in a beat-up PT Cruiser. A boy my age, wearing a knit cap, long hair sticking out underneath and in skinny jeans. He's walking in, which means Nick needs to get away from the counter.

But Nick isn't moving. His fingers drum on the counter once, and still he studies me. "I must apologize," he says. "Something came up and I had to leave town. I tried to send you message."

I look at him in surprise, my expression softening. "You left town? Family emergency?" A family emergency will make every-thing okay. It's awful, but I hope for distressing health for an aunt or uncle, and then hate myself for thinking it.

"*Nyet.*"

I know that is "no" from hearing him speak previously. I wait for him to explain more, but he says nothing. After a moment, he types something into his phone. Mine dings, and he's sent me a photo. The attachment has a little broken picture and asks me to download.

"I . . . can't get your picture. I'm maxed out on my data." I'd have to buy a new phone or add more money to this one, and I can't until I get paid.

"Then it is likely you are not receiving many of my messages."

I stare down at my phone, chagrined. I'm still mad at him, but now I'm feeling slightly stupid about it. Like I'm the one being unreasonable. I don't know what to do. I look at Nick, but he's simply giving me an enigmatic smile, as if that will explain every-thing.

For some reason, that smile makes me angry all over again. It's like he's saying, *You see? It's not my fault your things are cheap.*

The customer enters the station and comes immediately to the counter, giving Nick a wary look. He halts in his tracks, his gaze flicking from me to Nick and back to me again, as if he isn't sure whether to flee or remain.

"Are you purchasing something?" I ask Nick again. "If not, I'm going to have to ask you to leave."

The customer's eyes widen. He takes a step backward.

Nick simply grins at my sassy tone. He taps the glass counter and points at a scratch-off ticket. "I will take lottery ticket."

I calmly pull one off the roll and ring him up. After he pays, he steps away.

And my heart sinks with disappointment, just a little.

But he doesn't leave the store. Instead, he loiters by an endcap of motor oil, holding that lottery ticket. He's not scratching it. He's still watching me.

The other guy steps up to the counter. "Clove cigarettes, please." He looks exceedingly nervous, as if Nick's presence bothers him. When I hand him the cigarettes, he practically snatches them off the counter and throws his money at me, eager to leave.

Then I'm alone with Nick again.

I'm not nervous like the other guy was. Nick doesn't scare me. He fills me with hurt and embarrassment, but he doesn't scare me. I think of the other day, when I sat in the coffee house for too long, everyone staring at me with pity in their eyes. I'd worn my new favorite bra and panties, just so I could feel pretty for him.

Not that it mattered.

He approaches the counter once more, still holding that lottery ticket in his hand.

"Do . . . do you need to cash that?" I can't think of another logical reason why he would still be here.

"Is for you. Present." He slides it across to me.

I shake my head. "I can't take it. I actually need to give you some money back. The other day, you spent too much—"

He raises a hand, silencing me. "You must let me apologize to you, Daisy." His voice is a silky caress, his gray gaze intense. "If I had any other way, I would have been there to meet with you. I promise you this."

The intensity of his words makes me feel heated, my pulse throbbing low. Strangely enough, I believe him. "You should have come and talked to me. You know where I live. A text is so . . . meaningless. Like I don't matter to you."

"You matter." His gaze is suddenly so piercing that I feel

pinned to the wall with the intensity of it. "Never doubt that you matter to me."

I feel warm, flushed. Uncertain. "You should have come and told me in person, though. I wouldn't have missed that, and you know my phone is junk." I'm whining. I know it. I wanted to see his face when he apologized. It's mostly just an excuse to see him again. But he's here now, and I'm being a baby about my feelings being hurt.

"*Da*," he agrees. "I should have. I did not. It was rude." He inclines his head, acknowledging this. "Will you meet me again?"

"For coffee?"

"For coffee, *da*."

"I don't know." I'm not used to having friends, much less guy friends. I don't know how I feel about my theoretical abandonment and the missed messages. It still hurts, and I don't want to be set up only to get hurt once more. "I don't want to go to the same place."

I'm still embarrassed by the sympathetic looks the baristas kept sending my way.

"I will do better, then." Nick pulls out a piece of newspaper from his coat pocket and lays it on the counter.

I give him a quizzical look, but he only gestures that I should open it. After a moment of indecision, I do. It is a movie theater schedule. I consider it, touched. Did he notice how hard I'd stared at the posters of the new movies at the mall? How I'd wondered what it would be like to go to one?

I hadn't mentioned it, but Nick had watched me so intensely. He must have noticed and remembered. He'd remembered and was asking me to go to something that he knew I'd love.

"You want to go to a movie?" I ask.

"With you, I will go anywhere." His mouth is still that flat, too-serious line, as if this is a grave matter we're discussing. "But we will start with movie. Tomorrow night?"

"I'm off tomorrow night," I agree eagerly. "I have every other night off. Craig doesn't want me to work every night in a row. Says it'll mess up my sleep schedule too much." And here I am, spouting information like a ninny. I can feel my cheeks pink with embarrassment.

"Then we go?"

My fingers tremble as I run them along the edges of the schedule. Once again, I am speechless. Is it simply an apology? Perhaps he just wants to see a movie and not go by himself? Perhaps he needs a friend. But the words that blurt out of my mouth are none of these sensible thoughts. "Is this a date?"

His mouth cocks up on one side in a smile, a real smile, and I get a flash of brilliant white teeth. He's so beautiful that I feel hammered by the sight of him. "*Da*. Yes. A date. If not tomorrow, then day after."

I should say no. But Nick is smiling at me and the movie theater is calling my name, so I pick up the paper and say, "It has to be tomorrow night, or else I'm working. I can't ask for time off yet."

He scowls, his big shoulders getting stiff. "This is not job for you, Daisy. You should quit. It is dangerous."

"Don't you start that again, Nick." I tuck the paper into my slacks pocket. "I'm my own person, thank you."

He considers this, and me. "Say my name again," he demands.

That feels . . . intimate. I look around, but we are the only ones in the store. No one will hear me repeating his name just to please him, and I want to please him. So I take a small, shuffling step forward and tuck my hair behind my ear in a nervous gesture. "Nick," I say, and my voice is shy, and I can't look him in the eye.

He exhales slowly. "*Ty tak krasiva,*" he mutters.

"What does that mean?"

"It means . . . I am sorry I hurt your feelings." He leans closer to me, and we are only a foot apart, the counter between us. "My friend Daisy."

Somehow, I don't think that's what it means at all.

But I don't ask. I'm wrapped up in him. He's leaning close enough that I can smell aftershave and see the faint stubble of a shadow on his neck. He's gorgeous, all masculine power, and I wish he wasn't standing so far away from me. I want to touch him. I want him to lean closer.

I want him to lean across this counter and kiss me. He seems to want it, too.

We stare at each other for a charged, electric moment, neither of us moving. Then, he gently brushes my hand with his fingertips. "I will text you tomorrow. *Before* the date. This I promise."

And then he is gone.

I'M STILL ASLEEP THE NEXT morning when my phone buzzes on the bedside dresser. I fumble for it and drag it close and then flip the clamshell open. On the tiny, outdated screen, there is a message.

1800—your doorstep.

Good morning to you, too, I think. I rub my eyes and then begin the laborious process of texting back on my old phone. I want to send something flirty back, something bold. Something to make him think of me all day long. But I type and delete a half-dozen messages before finally sending back: Shld I bring n xtra swtr?

Then I want to punch myself in the face for being so silly.

Should I wear a sweater? Why not ask him if I should wear granny panties? God. I am such an idiot.

Nyet. He responds quickly. I will keep you warm if you need it.

And just like that, I am all flustered and giddy again.

I bound up from bed, no longer tired. I had a late night of work, but I know I won't be able to concentrate. I have a date. I have a date!

It's my very first one. I am twenty-one years old and have never dated anyone. I want this so badly. I think of Nick, and I am afraid. Will he kiss me? My fingers touch my mouth, and I imagine his lips pressed to mine.

He's beautiful, confident, and everything I am not. I worry he will stand me up again and I will be a fool twice over. I could understand him wanting just a friend. But dating? Dating is something entirely different.

I need Regan's help. She'll know what to do.

I toss my phone on my bed, and then pause. It's almost noon. I have a few hours yet. This means I have plenty of time to get ready. I head into the living room and Regan is there on the couch, chatting with Becca. I wave to the two of them and pad into the kitchen for breakfast while they chat.

Becca is Regan's friend, and she's intimidating. She's got perfect red hair with subtle blond highlights in it, and she dresses in expensive clothing. Whereas Regan seems to radiate a cheery warmth, Becca is her opposite. She's icy and aloof, and I can feel her judging my ratty pajamas when I walk in. She's a childhood friend of Regan's, and I get the feeling that she's not impressed with our apartment, that she only tolerates being here because of her friendship with Regan . . . and her disapproval extends to me as well.

Becca's hard on my newfound confidence. I try to like her since she's Regan's friend and since she drops by frequently, but I always feel as if she's judging me and finding me lacking, and it rattles me. I wish, briefly, that she wasn't here, because I want to ask Regan about what to wear on my date.

I make toast and munch on it while standing in the kitchen. Becca and Regan are having an animated conversation about classes and boyfriends. Becca has just dumped her latest fling and wants to go "on the prowl" at a local club. Regan's not sure Mike will be happy if she goes, and I can tell she wants to tell Becca no, but doesn't have the courage to.

Becca's almost got Regan talked into going to the club when Regan glances my way. Her gaze brightens. "Hey, sleepyhead. Glad to see you're finally up."

I smile sheepishly and move to sit across from them in the living room. "I had a late night at work."

Becca's eyes gleam, and she shifts her attention to me, suddenly interested. "Are you working somewhere fun, Pollyanna?"

I wince at the nickname. Regan called me Pollyanna in front of Becca once, and now it's all that Becca calls me. I don't think she means it with the same affection that Regan does, however. "No, I'm working at a gas station."

She recoils slightly, her interest evaporating. "That sounds awful."

I shrug. "It's not so bad." I need it—and the money. If I can work a full forty hours a week for the next two weeks, I can make rent. If not, I don't know what I'll do. I haven't factored in groceries or bus fare, but I will worry about one thing at a time.

"We're going to a club tonight," Becca says in that sly voice of hers, tossing her shiny red hair. "Gonna pick up some men. You want to come?"

I look at Regan, and she crosses her fingers at me, giving me a helpless, pleading look behind Becca's shoulder. She wants me to go. I am guessing it's because if I am there, it will help rein in Becca. I wouldn't mind going because I've never been to a club before, but I have plans. "I can't go. I have a date."

Both women perk. "You have a date, Pollyanna?" Becca asks, as if I've just declared I have three heads.

"That's awesome," Regan says, getting up from the futon to move to my side. "With who?"

"Just someone I met in the laundry room." I don't tell them about the ride on his motorcycle or the shopping afterward, or that I'm wearing panties he bought me.

But now Regan is frowning. "Wait. Is this the same guy that stood you up the other day? That wasn't nice." She remembers how hurt I was.

"I'm giving him a second chance," I say stubbornly. "And I won't be talked out of it."

"Oh, Pollyanna," Becca says in a chiding voice. "You know you don't have to date a guy just because he asks you out. There are plenty of nice men in town. You need to go out with Regan and me more. We'll introduce you to some nice guys." She brightens. "Like, say, at the club."

Regan snorts. "You just want us to go to the club with you so you don't get drunk and hook up with a loser again."

Becca sticks her tongue out at Regan.

But my roommate's attention is back on me. "So where's he taking you?" Regan practically flutters around me with excitement. "Someplace swanky?"

"We're going to the movie theater," I say, voice shy. "I'm excited. I've never been. I don't know what to wear."

"Oooh," Regan says, and looks over at Becca. "First-date clothing time! I know someone fabulous with outfits."

Becca stands and grins like a queen accepting patronage. "Lead me to your closet. We'll help you dress for your date. And *tomorrow* night, we'll all three go pick up men."

Regan groans good-naturedly, but she doesn't disagree.

"I'll go out with you," I agree. "But I'm not picking up men. I have Nick."

"And I've got Mike," Regan says, but she sounds less determined than me, more resigned.

Becca only gives us a smug grin, as if she's gotten exactly what she wants. She leads the way to my closet and begins to dig in.

"Boy, this is nice shit you've got." Becca whistles, lifting up a pale pink blouse Nick bought me. "You're able to buy this stuff on a gas station salary?" She fingers the tag still on the sleeve.

"Um, no," I can't explain it to them. I can hardly explain it to myself that my small selection of clothing was bought by some guy I barely know. It sounds . . . stupid. "The guy I have the date with? Nick? He poured bleach on my clothes accidentally and then felt super guilty, so he took me to the mall and bought me some replacements."

Becca's eyebrows are nearly at her hairline. "This shirt cost three hundred dollars." She shoves the tag into Regan's face.

"I know. I couldn't stop him." I squeeze my fingers together in anxiety. What do they think of me for letting a stranger buy me these things? I should have protested more.

"Why stop him?" Regan asks, laughing. "If some guy wanted to buy me expensive clothes, I'd sure let him! This is beautiful stuff, Pollyanna, but not really date wear. In fact," Regan pushes my hangers aside, "all of this looks very conservative."

"I know!" Becca leans over to peer at the clothes. "I didn't even know this brand made conservative clothing."

They're right. Except for the gorgeous and naughty underthings, all the clothes Nick has bought for me are modest. The jeans are tight, but the blouses are intentionally oversized. The saleslady said it was a very hip look, and I liked it. But none of it was something you'd wear to wow a guy on a first date.

And I want Nick to remember me. "What do I do?"

Becca turns and gives Regan a smug look. "We go through *her* closet. If you want slutty, she's got it."

Regan mock gasps. "Whore," she says to Becca affectionately, and then grins and turns back to me. "Come on. Let's see what I've got that will fit you."

By the time six rolls around, I am ready for my date. My long brown hair has been pulled into a ponytail, the ends curled; my fringe of bangs is trimmed and perfect. I am wearing a light dusting of makeup with gray eyeliner that makes my eyes seem bigger and bluer than ever. My lashes are curled and darkened with mascara. My lip gloss is just a faint sheen of color.

Even though it's just a movie theater, it's a first date, and both girls insist I should "wow" Nick. I have no dresses, and they think I should wear one, so I've borrowed from Regan. It's black, and it has lacy sleeves that caress my arms all the way down to my wrists. The neckline is high and the bustline modest. It almost looks schoolgirlish, until I turn around and the entire back is made of the same sheer black lace as the sleeves are.

Becca declares it perfect—not too trampy, not too sedate.

Regan has let me borrow a pair of hoop earrings and a small sparkly necklace that caresses my throat. I have also borrowed a pair of black, low-heeled Mary Janes that Regan insists she never wears.

I feel pretty. I'm me, but just a little better than usual, with a little more pizazz.

I glance at the door repeatedly as it gets closer to our meeting time, worried that my date won't show. Will Nick stand me up again and make me feel stupider than ever for trusting him?

But at six on the nose, the doorbell rings.

"That's me," I say breathlessly, throwing my purse over my shoulder and scooping up my phone.

"Have fun," Regan tells me. "Call me if you need a ride home." She's smiling, though I know she's a little worried for me. Becca's gone and Regan's home alone, staying in just in case I need her. She's a good friend.

I pause before opening the door, smooth my ponytail and bangs with nervous fingers, adjust my collar, and then put my hand on the knob.

When I open it, I can't help but smile at him.

He's so beautiful, my Ukrainian. I know I have the silliest crush on him, but I don't care. From his high cheekbones to his arching brows to that cleft in his chin, he's all elegance. He's wearing a nice trench coat, his clothes entirely covered up by the length of it. He looks the same as he does every day—incredible. For a moment, I feel silly that I've gone to such lengths for a movie date.

But his eyes warm as he sees me, and I'm glad I did. His gaze travels over me, pauses on the jacket in my hands. "Allo."

"Hi, Nick." I smile broadly at him.

He puts a hand out for my jacket. "You must allow me to help you with that."

I hand it to him and turn my back obligingly, an excited shiver going down my spine. A man is putting my coat on me!

To my horror, I hear a rip, and then a muffled curse in Russian. I turn around to see that Nick's large foot is standing on one of the sleeves of my threadbare jacket, and it has ripped it entirely away.

"Oh no." I take the jacket from his hands and clutch it to my chest. I should be horrified that I've had another piece of clothing destroyed, but all I can think is that this might make us late for our date, and right now, the date is so much more important than my stupid jacket.

"I am *mudak*," Nick says in a flat voice. "Leave your coat. I will buy you a new one."

"That's not necessary," I say quickly. "It's not that cold out."

He grunts agreement, and then he crooks his elbow at me. "Shall we go, Daisy?"

I slide my hand against his arm and let him lead the way. We step down to the curb and toward what must be his car—no motorcycle today. It's a dark gray. Nondescript, with tinted windows. A sedan.

"Wait here," he tells me as I stand on the curb.

I shiver as I do. My dress isn't warm at all, and my back is almost entirely exposed. I will need to buy a jacket with my first paycheck, I decide. Maybe they will have something in my size at the thrift store . . .

My thoughts trail off as Nick pops open the trunk of the sedan and pulls out a large box. He hefts a leather jacket—a women's leather jacket—into his hands and then holds it open for me. "Here. Come put this on."

I approach him, eyeing the jacket. It's one I admired in the store the other day. He had this one already waiting for me? "Nick! Did you tear my other jacket on purpose?"

"Of course not," he says in a tone that indicates he is a terrible liar. There is a hint of a smile playing on his lips. "I am *mudak*, yes?"

"You are sneaky," I tell him, but I let him put the coat on me. It's cold thanks to the wind, but it's heavy. As soon as it warms against my skin, it will be perfect. "And thoughtful. Thank you, Nick. You must let me pay you back."

"*Nyet.*"

"Nick," I say, protesting. "You can't keep ruining my stuff and then replacing it."

He cocks his head to the side. "I do not admit to this, but if it would happen that I accidentally mar something of yours, should I not replace it?"

"It's just . . . too extravagant and *wrong.*" I struggle to explain my feelings of indebtedness to him.

"The wrong is from me, Daisy. You must allow me to right my wrongs, or I do not deserve to be with you."

I know that there is something odd about this statement, but I can't figure it out right now.

He opens the front passenger door for me.

I sigh and get into the car. We will argue about this later. I slide in to the passenger seat and then look around as he heads to the other side of the car. The interior is stark, no signs of the car being used at all. It could be a rental for all I know. I want to open the glove box and see if there is anything in there, but that feels nosy.

He gets behind the wheel and I buckle in, and then we are off to the theater.

We're quiet on the drive there. I feel like I should say charming, pleasant things to break the ice, but I can think of nothing. My mind is a giddy blank. So I twist my fingers in my lap and hope he's not disappointed in my lack of chattiness.

He glances over at me. "Are you tired?"

"Tired?" I touch my cheek. Do I look tired to him? Washed out? How embarrassing.

"You work late."

I tilt my head at him, curious. "How did you know?"

"You told me you worked until two in the morning."

"Oh."

He stares out the windshield, not looking over at me. A moment later, he admits, "Also, I was worried about you. I drove past after we spoke to check on you."

"I was fine," I tell him. "The owner lives down the street, and he said I could call him if anything happened. Plus, they have a Taser and cameras and a baseball bat behind the counter. Lots of things to keep me safe."

Nick's mouth tightens. "This does not make me feel better."

Chagrined, I go silent and burrow a little deeper into my coat. The newness of it is delicious, as is the heavy, decadent scent of leather that permeates it. "It's a job. I'm fine." I won't quit, either. It's not stubbornness that makes me keep the job. I need the money. I need to be able to support myself if I'm going to stay here in this new life, and I will continue to pass out resumes in the hopes of a better job. But if I can't find something else, at least this way I will have some money.

"I do not like this," he tells me.

"I didn't ask you if you liked it," I retort.

He goes silent.

I say nothing else. He's frowning fiercely as we pull into the parking lot. I feel as if I've messed things up already, and we haven't even gotten to the date destination yet.

It is worse than silent when he stops the car. He pauses for a moment, as if contemplating something, and I wonder if he's changed his mind about dating me. I'm almost in tears at this point. The only talking we've done is to argue.

I feel so stupid. I've ruined our date already. Poor, stupid little sheltered Daisy goes on a date with a man and immediately argues with him about money. Maybe we should call this off. Maybe he doesn't know how messed up I am inside. That underneath my calm exterior, I'm a terrified mess who's tasting her first days of freedom and doesn't know how to be a normal girl. He probably wants a normal girl.

I can't be her. I wish I could, but I don't know how.

He gets out of the car and I suck in a deep breath, shoring up my courage. Time to be Bold Daisy and take charge of the situation. Nick opens the door for me, and I get out.

And then I pause there and wait by the car.

He offers me his elbow, but I shake my head at him. His gray eyes grow cold and bleak, his expression shuttered as if I have rejected him.

It's now or never. "Can I ask you something?" My words are all breathless, my voice small.

"What is it?" His accent is thicker. It almost sounds like *vat*. I wonder if his accent gets thicker when he's upset. He looks upset, as if I've betrayed him.

"Are you sure you want to date me?"

His brows furrow. "Why do you ask me this?"

I wring my hands, unable to help myself. "You don't approve of me. Of what I do. You keep buying me things because it's clear what I'm wearing is not good enough for you. You seem like you're angry, and . . . I don't know how to deal with that." I try to smile to fix my words, but I'm ready to cry. I wanted this date—and him—so badly. "I'm not the most normal girl, Nick."

For some reason, this makes his mouth quirk in a half smile. "Why do you tell me this, Daisy?"

"I just don't want you to be disappointed." My gaze drops to his mouth and I stare at it. "In me."

His hand clasps mine and he lifts it to his mouth again, brushing my knuckles over his lips. No kiss, just touching my skin to his mouth. "Why would you think I am disappointed in you?"

"You want me to quit my job, and I'm not going to quit it. You keep buying me new clothes."

He sighs, but he doesn't let go of my hand. Just keeps rubbing my knuckles against his mouth. "I buy you clothes because it pleases me to see you wear things that suit you. You deserve the finest things, Daisy. It is only proper that I wish to give them to you."

It's not proper at all, I want to say, but I am entranced by his sweet words and the brush of his lips on my skin.

"I do want you to quit," he continues. "Because I worry for you. But if it is important to you, you stay there, *da*? I will just watch out for you." His expression cools. "Or do you not wish to date me now?"

"I want to more than anything," I blurt, and then wince at my own voice, at how eager I sound. "It's just that . . . I'm nervous."

I've never kissed anyone, and I'm scared I'll do it wrong and then you won't want to see me anymore. I think for a moment, and then decide that I should reach out and kiss him. If we wait until the end of the date, he might not want to kiss me, and I want that first kiss more than anything I can think of.

"Why are you nervous?" His lips move against my skin, and I feel the soft whisper of them all the way down into my panties. It's like he's touching me everywhere. My nipples are hard through the filmy fabric of the dress, and I am not wearing a bra.

"Are you going to kiss me on this date?" I ask.

He looks surprised at my words. "Do you wish for me to kiss you?"

"Yes," I say firmly.

"Then, *da*, I will kiss you." His face relaxes.

"Let's kiss now," I tell him.

He moves forward toward me, and I am pinned between him and the car. He leans in, and his gloved hand touches my cheek. It's all I can do to keep from trembling at the caress, but I am held by those gray eyes—and the hint of possessiveness I see there. He's concentrating on me so hard, as if he's determined to get this right.

I part my lips and tilt my face toward him. I've stopped breathing. I want Nick's kiss so badly.

He moves closer. His mouth grazes over mine in just the barest brushing of lips. It sends a ticklish flutter through me, and I make a small noise in my throat. My lips part a bit more. Is that all I'm going to get? Just a tease of a kiss?

I decide that's not enough. So I lean forward a bit more and as he pulls back, I try to kiss him more. I end up pressing my mouth to his lower lip, and I'm not sure who is more startled—Nick that I've tried to kiss him, or me that I've messed it up like an idiot.

His eyes widen.

I fumble backward, humiliated. "I'm sorry. I—"

His hands move to cup my face and then he's tilting my mouth toward his all over again. This time, the kiss is not a soft, gentle graze. This time, his mouth presses against mine firmly, and his lips part over mine. Mine part as well, following his lead, and his tongue slicks into my mouth, tasting me.

It is divine.

I whimper, and he makes a soft noise in his throat that might be a groan. His tongue strokes into my mouth again, flooding my body with heat, and I want to do more than just receive. I want to reciprocate. Is that wrong? So I hesitantly touch my tongue to his and wait for a reaction.

Nick tears away from my mouth, breathing hard. He presses

his forehead to mine and mumbles something in Russian. But he doesn't seem displeased. Instead, it seems as if he's trying to control himself.

I feel oddly . . . proud. I'm flushed with desire and my skin feels sensitive, but I want more. Does he? "Thank you," I murmur. And I wait. The kiss is over. Does he seem pleased?

He presses a kiss to my forehead and looks at me, and his gloved fingers curve my jaw as if tracing it. "I will kiss you, Daisy. I will kiss you all night. I will do more than kiss you if you wish. Simply say the word."

I suck in a breath. My pulse has centered between my legs and throbs there. I'm not brave enough to say the word. Not just yet.

But oh God, I want to.

CHAPTER **SIX**

NIKOLAI

Daisy looks like a schoolgirl with her high-necked dress and the shoes with the straps across the top of her foot. But the heels on the shoes and the sheer lacy back that makes me swallow back a gasp are anything but childish. A whisper of something naughty and darker lurks here. Perhaps it is my own wishful thinking, but I can't help but wonder what Daisy has experienced before me. Yes, she is innocent in some things but her eyes hold knowledge of something more. I want to know all of it.

Part of me wants to cover her body entirely, to protect her, but another part can barely control the urge to rip off her clothes knowing she must not be wearing anything underneath. These are not items that I have bought for her, but perhaps she is wearing my panties. I think of them as mine even though I know I shouldn't.

Everything with Daisy is doing something I know I should not. Every detail out of my mouth is a lie, and not even a good one, because a hit man needs no cover. We are in and out, seen only when we make the kill and sometimes not even then.

I do not know for how long Daisy will tolerate me; how long until she starts piecing together all the false threads of the story I've given her. I must speak less, for that is the only way to eliminate errors.

"What movie?" I ask sharply. I immediately regret the tone of my voice when she looks wounded. I try again and give her a small twitch of my lips, which I hope she understands to be a smile. "I mean, what movie would you like to see? You pick. I always pick wrong."

She peers up at the digital display that lists the movies currently playing. Her neck is lovely, and she has pink, glossy lips. The lights of the theater are reflecting off of the gloss, and the temptation to slide my tongue across their plumpness weakens my knees. I lick my lower lip to see if I can taste her, but the fleetness of our connection leaves almost no trace. "I guess it's between the superhero movie and the horror. I guess superheroes?"

"*Da*, good choice." I'm not really listening to her. I just enjoy watching her lips part and her cheek muscles round when she smiles. She smiles often. My fingers itch to caress her, but she's not said I can kiss her again.

I almost suffer untold indignities due to my inattention when Daisy begins to pay for the tickets. My hand slams down beside hers on the counter. Both the ticket boy and Daisy jump.

"I am sorry, but you cannot pay, Daisy." I pull the money out of the ticket counter's hand. It is slack with shock. I fold the worn bills and press them back into Daisy's hands.

"But I haven't paid for anything yet. I can buy a ticket," Daisy protests.

What kind of man does she think I am? Or perhaps she does

not even think I am a man. "*Nyet.*" I pull out my wallet and shove money at the counter clerk. "Two," I bark. When the ticket boy does not move, I lean forward and bare my teeth. "Two. Now."

He quickly obeys, and I grab the tickets and drag Daisy behind me.

"I could've paid," she is saying. "I have money. You can't pay for everything."

I do not even answer that. It is full of ridiculousness.

"What do you want to eat?" I wave my hand over the candy, ice cream, popcorn, and soda. There is a virtual restaurant inside this theater.

Daisy folds her arms across her chest and looks mutinous. "Nothing," she says, "since you probably won't let me pay for that, either."

"Then I will buy one of everything," I threaten. I do not even know why we are arguing about this. Whores never argue with me. No one argues with me. They do things because I pay them to do things, or they do things because they are afraid. I have no experience with girls like Daisy: honest, sweet, delicious Daisy.

Her face has closed down, and there is a distance between us now. She has gone somewhere else and that, more than her anger and more than her frustration, worries me. With her I am always fucking things up.

"I am sorry," I say. "I've offended you again. Please tell me what I should do."

My plea softens her, and she lays a small hand on my arm. "Nick, you can't pay for everything. I don't want—" She pauses, as if struggling to say the words, and then she continues. "I can't be dependent on someone. Not again. It's not fair to you. We barely know each other."

I try to understand her, but her words make no sense to me,

and worse, they make me afraid. I cannot let her get to know me. I can only put up a façade that she might like until it crumples.

The image of a British flesh peddler springs to mind. I eliminated him two years ago for ruining merchandise he was supposed to be preparing for high-end buyers. He'd developed a taste for his own stable but had never revealed to anyone that he carried syphilis. Buyers do not like receiving diseased product. But Harry Winslow III had a certain light that drew people, particularly women, to him. It was part of what made him such a good pimp. Even though I did not like Harry, I realize that I could use some of his charm now. I swallow my bile at pretending to be a disease-carrying pimp and try out a bit of Harry on her.

"Duckie." Harry was always calling someone *duckie*. "It's quite all right. I've got plenty of blunt to cover this." Harry's women always seem pleased at his big roll of cash. It made up for his very small penis. I'm fairly proud of my effort and smile at Daisy, but instead of softening, she looks confused.

"What's a duckie? Is that a Ukrainian word for something?" Daisy asks. "And blunt? What's a blunt?"

I tilt my head back and close my eyes. This is all a disaster. "How about popcorn?"

I order it before she can protest.

"Want butter?" the clerk asks me. I shake my head no. Butter is bad.

"No butter. No salt." I nod at the clerk. Daisy starts to say something, but when I turn to her with a raised eyebrow, she just sighs and turns away. Perhaps she does not like popcorn.

Inside the theater, we sit and say nothing as first the previews run and then the movie. As the characters are separated into clear divisions of good and evil, I look at Daisy. She is rapt. She is so engrossed by the action that she has forgotten I am next to her.

The movie is pissing me off. I hate it. The crowd inside is almost hissing at the bad guys who want nothing more than the power to live free. Perhaps their methods are not as pretty as the "good guys," but life is not so clearly black-and-white. This time it is my arms that are crossed and my attitude that is bad. I do not point out that the velocity of the bullets does not work that way or that the guns used are all wrong. A semiautomatic rifle would never be used by a real professional. Only bolt action. Something tells me that Daisy would not care.

When the movie is over and the lights come on, Daisy turns to me with wide-eyed amazement and a smile on her face, and I feign appreciation for the movie.

"Wasn't that great?" she asks.

"Yes. Great." I stand up and shove my way down the crowd and out into the night air.

"You seem like you didn't like it." Daisy tilts her head and examines me, like how I will respond to her question will determine whether I get to see her again.

I debate lying to her again, but she is already suspicious. I've told so many half-truths and mistruths to her, so just this once I think that maybe truth is not damaging. "I did not like the ending."

"Really?" Daisy looks surprised. Obviously, I should've lied. "It's the only way it could have ended. Good prevailing over evil, you know?"

"The villains had a hard life. They did not know any other way forward," I mutter.

Daisy gives me a look like I am a bug she has never seen before. "Well," she begins and then stops, as if uncertain what to say, "I guess so. I wasn't really looking at it from the villain's point of view. But they're the bad guys. You're supposed to want them to lose."

"Real life is not that easy," I say involuntarily. I do not know why I have said this. What does she know of me other than I live somewhere and have money? If she would know the truth, it would be the end of it. Her delight would turn to dismay. I try to keep back the words but they spill out of me, as if I can make her understand somehow. "Sometimes people do bad deeds to relieve the pain of others."

Her response is not what I expect. Instead of being angered by my words or arguing with the sentiment, a bleak look passes over Daisy's face. "I know."

Strangely, that response gives me hope.

We drive back to Daisy's apartment in silence. I think we are both wondering about the other's past. Daisy is not all perfect lightness and airy innocence. There is darkness in her, and it makes her all the more appealing. If there is darkness inside her, perhaps she will understand the darkness inside me. "I'm sorry for tonight," I say when I park in front of her building.

"Sorry?" She chokes on the word. "That's a horrible thing to tell a girl on a date. Are you sorry you invited me out? Sorry that you allowed me to pick the movie?" Her response is sharp and unhappy.

In my misery, I accept each phrase as a lash against my skin. Her words confuse me. I have done something wrong, perhaps been too aggressive. She looks heartbroken, and I do not know what I can do to fix this. My hands ball into fists, and I wish I could beat myself for my stupidity. What can I say to save this night? I have never done this relationship thing before. Never dated. I have only experience with women who take money from me, but each gift I buy for Daisy is one that I must force on her. Is she tolerating my company? Does she desire to be free of me?

At my lack of response, she gets out of the vehicle and shuts the door carefully. Her intentions are louder than if she had slammed the door and more painful than if my fingers were caught in the pinch. I see now that when she is truly upset, she retreats—and that all the delight in her is snuffed out. I hate that more than anything.

I follow her up, brooding and uncertain. I know not what to do. In the end, I do and say nothing. Not even when she pauses at her door and says, "Good night, Nick," in a kind voice. It sounds like good-bye, and my objection dies in my throat as I think of what soft words to say to her to convince her of my worthiness. When the door shuts behind her, I lean against it.

So many things I do well. I track. I synthesize information into discernible patterns. I follow through. I kill. Those things I am competent at. Courting, I am not.

In my own apartment, I do not allow myself to look at Daisy. Now that I have met her, kissed her, and held her, the invasion of her privacy would be too extreme. There is enough about me that would not be palatable to her, and somehow I know that *this* would be too much.

I won't watch her again.

I begin to do my search on the Seattle mark, scouring the deep web for information about the black market sale of organs. I find offers, sales, but no reference to the surgeons. I note the three deals that originate from the Pacific Northwest in the last month. Only three. That seems low. Perhaps the Seattle mark is too dumb to know about the deep web and instead uses some message board closer to the surface.

Once I found a child trading site on the most popular social networking site, as if no one would find them in their private group. I exterminated the administrator of that network for free. A penance, of sorts, for other lives I have taken. *Death is a mercy.* I wear my motto on my chest. I live it.

As I click, click, click around the net, I think of my evening with Daisy and how terrible I was with her. I wonder if I can make amends. I wonder how I even begin. For a long time, I sit in my rented chair with my laptop and think of the sadness I brought to her and the darkness that dims her bright smiles. I do not even allow myself to fantasize about her. Until she is happy again, I will not use her in such a low fashion.

There is perhaps one I could ask for help, but to do so could endanger Daisy, bring her to another's notice. Yet he has hinted that he would welcome something akin to friendship from me. I pick up my phone. Then set it down. I return to it seconds later and type out a message before I can think.

What is best place to take date? I text to Daniel.

I don't wait long before there is a response. This is the most important piece of information you've ever given me, Nik.

Mudak. I respond.

I know I'm an asshole. Only assholes are in this business. I'm going to take this as a sign you want to be friends with me. I knew I'd wear you down eventually.

You are old lady Daniel? I thought you were young disaffected American soldier.

This time the response is not so quick. I'd be more open to sharing if you didn't think I was your enemy.

I contemplate the potential repercussions. It is not friendship I seek. Only to share information.

Nik, you asked for dating advice, not the best wire to garrote someone or whether I prefer cyanide or dimethylene.

Daniel's desire for this friendship seems odd. I do not know what to make of it.

You have other friends like me. Bogdan mentioned a network, but I work alone and have since I left Alexsandr. In a network? I add.

He's getting it! Yes, there is a small network of us that share information. We've never brought you in, because, well, the others think you aren't very good at playing nice.

I do not play nice. This network intrigues me, though. When I worked with Alexsandr, there were often new recruits brought in. Early on, at nine or so, I tried to make friends, but Alexsandr made short business of that. No friends. Rely on no one, he commanded. Not even him.

To enforce this concept, he'd make us fight each other for a reward. Sometimes the reward would be chocolate or some sweet. Sometimes the reward would be a better weapon. But winning always meant having extra. And when you had nothing, extra meant everything.

He responds. You have rules. You live by them. It's enough for us.

I'm perturbed. Daniel has been watching me for longer than I have suspected. How long? I ask.

Only a couple of years.

Still, that is too long. He could know about Daisy. A chill washes over me. I open my folder marked *D-ArmS*. Daniel, Army Soldier. Based on his weapons, his precision, his American accent, and the source of his gunpowder, I've marked Daniel as a former army sniper.

I have left him alone because his work has never interfered with mine. I know that there are others out there like me, specialized killers, but as long as they do not interfere with my business, I have ignored their existence, much as I had hoped they ignored mine.

Do you threaten me?

No, you suspicious bastard. I'm inviting you to be a part of the network. Information share. Get out. Be safe. Make good decisions. Give you advice on first dates. If the woman has kids, go to the zoo. If she's single, movies are good.

Children? I've never dated a woman with children, but clearly Daniel has. I open my file and next to companions, I type, "dated woman with child/ren."
Movie was not good, I share with Daniel.

So you're already on a second date. Good call. Some girls don't put out until the third date. Just FYI.

I type, "dates girls who do not 'put out' until third date."

Advice observed. Zoo or what other options?

Does she have kids?

Perhaps Daniel has not dated a woman with children and is trying to extract information from me. I place my cursor next to "child/ren" and begin to press the delete button. I pause and then add "may or may not" to the companions line.

I take a deep breath, and my fingers hover over the touch screen. If I tell him she has kids and he is watching me, he may consider that a threat. If I tell him she is single, I risk revealing something more. But I have started this conversation by texting him in the first place. Perhaps I am ready for the risk.

You know the answer to that question.

Yes, I do, but you know things about me, too. That's called information sharing! You're already doing it and didn't even know it.

I do not like not knowing things.

I know, which is why I'm telling you that if you give me something, we can move on from here.

I understand now. Daniel wants an overt show of good faith. Even if I tell him something that I am sure he knows, he will accept this as an olive branch.

She has no children.

Take her on a picnic. It shows you've thought of her, planned for her. Take her somewhere private. You'll have to talk to her, though, and from our conversations, you're a pretty terrible conversationalist. You may want to practice that.

Da, spasibo. Yes, thanks.

I have a plan, and now I can sleep. Tomorrow I will renew my campaign, apologize for my misdeeds, and pray that she will accept me.

CHAPTER SEVEN

DAISY

Regan and I are playing flip cups and drinking. It's a silly game, but since she's introduced me to something called cinnamon schnapps, everything seems silly. It's harmless drinking, to get intoxicated in our apartment with the door locked and the evening done. I mentioned to her that I'd never drank alcohol before, and she wanted me to get my first experience in before we went to the club. We've put Becca off for another night, claiming I have to work. Regan says that Becca's pouting, but she'll get over it.

So we drink.

Drinking, of course, leads to a game. Flip cups. She pours shots into disposable cups and lines them up on the table. We drink a shot and are supposed to put the cup on the edge of the table and then flip it over with a tap. I'm terrible at this game, and by the end of one round, we're getting sticky alcohol all over the carpet, so Regan suggests a different game.

"It's called Never Have I Ever."

I giggle drunkenly and take another sip from my cup. The alcohol burns my stomach, but it's a good, interesting burn. "How does this game work?"

"I say 'Never have I ever something.' If you've done it, you drink. If you haven't done it, I have to drink."

I furrow my brows, trying to keep this clear in my mind. Maybe the alcohol is already getting to me. I probably have no tolerance for liquor. "What have I never done ever?"

"No, no," she says, laughing. "I say 'never have I ever drank alcohol' and you would not drink, because you haven't before tonight, see?"

This is confusing. "But I'm drinking now." Perhaps Regan isn't so good with alcohol, either. Her rules make no sense. My head is fuzzy, but I'm having so much fun. I can't stop giggling into my hand.

"That was just an example!" She sighs and grabs the bottle, refilling both of our red plastic cups. "So, I'll start since you clearly need more examples. Never have I ever eaten . . . frogs."

I snort with laughter. "I haven't eaten a frog. So do I drink?"

"No, no. Since you haven't done it, you don't drink. I do because you haven't. Understand?"

"Um." I still don't quite get it, but I'm willing to play along.

She nudges me with her cup. "Your turn."

I think for a moment. "Never have I ever gone to college. Is that right?"

Regan tips her cup back, drinking. After a moment, she swallows and nods. "That was a good one."

"So how do we win this game?"

She shrugs. "If you're still conscious by the end of it, you win."

Oh. I stare down at my cup. She's refilled it, and it looks entirely too full. Already my nose feels full of cinnamon and my throat and belly burn. I don't want more, but I'm enjoying myself too much to protest.

"My turn. Never have I ever had anal sex."

"What?" I am shocked. We've gone from frogs to . . . *that*?

Regan shrugs and drinks, but there's a laughing grin on her mouth. "Just curious if all the Pollyanna-ness was hiding a dark, dirty side."

I do have a dark, dirty side, but it's not quite that dirty. "I haven't even had sex, Regan!"

She waves a hand at me. "You're supposed to wait for my next question."

"Oh." I think for a minute, trying to formulate a question.

"So you haven't had sex? Really?"

I shake my head.

She looks impressed. "Kudos to you for holding out for marriage."

"I'm not," I blurt, and then I giggle because I sound so eager. "I just haven't been asked yet."

"Mmm. Think Nick will ask you?"

I feel all flushed and warm at the thought of Nick. Nick, who kissed me before the movie and then treated me like I'd offended him afterward. I don't know how to read him. He was beautiful, though, and sensual. And so very alive. I shiver, thinking of his icy eyes. "I don't know if he'll ask me," I admit. I'm a little sad at the thought.

"Would you say yes if he did?"

"Yes," I say, and this time I'm unflinching.

She looks surprised at my answer. "Really?"

"Really," I agree. I am fascinated with Nick, but I also want to know what sex is like.

Now that I am free from my father's prison, I want to do everything I can to live my life. And if that means having irresponsible sex with an impossible-to-understand man? I will do so. I touch my mouth, thinking of Nick's lips on my own. I wanted that kiss to go on forever. Is it because of Nick or because I want to be kissed more?

I think it's because of Nick, but I can't be sure. I don't have any other experience to back it up with.

"He's that sexy, huh?" Regan gets all dreamy eyed. "Man, I want to get a good look at him. The next time he asks you out, invite him in."

I don't know if he'll ask me out again, though. I stare into my cup awkwardly and try to think of a question that will for sure distract Regan from thoughts of Nick. "Never have I ever . . . owned a car."

Regan snorts and doesn't drink. She simply shakes her cup at me, and I drink that time. "You're not even trying," she protests. "Never have I ever had a man give me oral."

My eyes widen again. Regan and Mike have sex all the time. "I thought everyone did that." Not that I am an expert, but in the books I've been reading, the men always give oral to their women and love it. "So . . . Mike . . . ?"

"Not drinking on that one? Man, you are innocent." She tips her cup back and sighs after she drinks. "And not everyone does that. Mike for *sure* doesn't."

I feel like I'm learning all kinds of things about Regan right now, and her happy, carefree life seems to have a little tarnish on it. "Never have I ever . . . kissed a man I don't love?"

"You can't ask that unless you have done the same," she points out even as she drinks.

I think. I've only kissed two men: my father, who I do love even though I also hate him, and Nick. I don't know how I feel about Nick. I've only known him for days. It's too early for me to be in love with him, but what I feel for him is as intense as it is bewildering and maddening. I don't want to confess this all to Regan, though, so I shrug and take a drink anyhow.

"Never have I ever . . ." Regan slurs her words and then thinks. "Given a blow job in public."

I give her an exasperated look. "Is that all you think about is sex?"

"Sometimes," she says. "But those are the fun questions to ask."

"Well, I can't answer any of them," I tell her. "I haven't done anything."

"Anything at all, Pollyanna?" Regan looks skeptical.

I stare down at my cup. The liquor is starting to feel too strong, and my stomach is upset. I feel anxious. It's not just the alcohol, it's the feeling that I'm not fitting in with my new friend. "I . . . my father was very controlling. He didn't let me do much. That's why I left."

It's a start, but it's not enough. I want to confess that my father is terrified of being outside of the house. That he's not left it for the last thirteen years. That even when I was little, I had to go to the grocery store by myself and get things because he couldn't leave. That he controlled what I wore, what I ate, what I read, what I watched.

That I felt smothered and trapped with him.

And that I miss him and feel guilty when I think about him.

But I can't say all this to cheery, sex-obsessed Regan. So I simply shrug and stare down at my still-too-full cup.

"Wanna prank call him?" Regan asks. "Kinda childish, but who cares?"

"Prank call?"

"Yeah, you know. Pretend to be a pizza place and call him just to mess with him. Total passive-aggressive revenge on the parental units for messing you up as a kid."

I'm drunk and so this sounds like a good idea to me. I grin and nod. Regan pulls out her smartphone and hits the speaker button and then places it in front of me. I dial as we chortle and drink.

The phone rings once, and I realize I don't want to call my father. I don't want to pretend to call him, because if I hear his voice, I'm going to be sad. I've abandoned him. I've given up on him, and I feel like the worst daughter possible.

I hit the button to hang up.

"Aw, man," Regan says, and she tips her cup back to drink.

But I am frozen in place. I've just hung up on my father. That's our phone code. One ring, hang up, and then call back immediately. That's how he knows it's me and not a stranger. That's how he knows it's safe to answer.

He'll be waiting for a call.

Guilt twists my gut. I have to call back. It seems cruel not to. I hit the big redial button on her phone screen and wait.

My father answers immediately. "Daisy?"

His voice is hoarse. I can hear the unhappiness, the strain in it. My own voice freezes in my throat. I can't say anything.

"It's okay, Daisy," my father says, and he sounds so, so sad. "I just . . . I want you to know I'm sorry." He takes a ragged breath. "I didn't realize how unfair I was being to you. I know you had to run away. And I'm sorry. If you want to come home, you can. I'm not mad."

And he quiets.

My eyes are wide and I stare at the phone with a mixture of

terror and longing. Longing, because going back home to my father means a return to the familiar. It will make him happy to have me back under his thumb again. All will be right in his world.

All of this terrifies me because it is the last thing I want. "I'm sorry, Father," I say and hang up the phone.

I stare down at it, panting. I am so anxious and unhappy at hearing my father's misery that I feel as if I've taken it all into myself. How selfish of me to run away. My father isn't well. I know this, but I can't help myself. I have to get away. I have to.

"Well, that was . . . depressing," Regan says, and she tips her cup back to finish her drink.

I put mine down. "I think I need to throw up." It's more than the too-strong schnapps. It's my father's unhappiness and my own sense of failing at being my own person. I'm too boring to play fun games with Regan. My job sucks. I've been sheltered from everything, and I don't know how to fit in. And the worst of it all? A gorgeous, sexy man asked me on a date, and I somehow ruined it.

I make it to the toilet before I puke my guts up. At least the world is kind to me in that aspect.

I'm moping at work the next day.

It's not a hangover. I didn't drink enough to make myself ill, not like Regan, who hung out in a dark room all day and complained about her head.

I am sick at heart. I'm an awful person. I've abandoned my father, knowing his fears, to selfishly chase after my own life. And where has it gotten me? I am not making enough money to go to college. I am sitting alone in a gas station at ten o'clock at night, handing out cigarettes to customers.

This doesn't seem like the life I'd dreamed of when I lay in bed every night, praying that I could escape my father. I wanted a life and freedom, and now I feel more trapped by my guilt than ever. I have spent all night crying, and my eyes are red and puffy and aching.

My choices weigh me down as the night drags on. I can't concentrate on Regan's borrowed textbook, my normal reading. I'm too focused on the what-ifs.

What if I am doing the wrong thing?

What if my father is alone and something happens to him?

What if Nick never calls me again? He's been silent since our date two nights ago.

I am an awful person, because it is the last item that obsesses me most. I check my silly disposable cellphone at least once an hour, hoping for a missed text, but there is nothing.

It's foolish of me to obsess over one date and one kiss, but I can't help it. I want more. Maybe I'm the only one. Maybe Nick didn't like the way I kissed, and picked a fight simply to end the date.

The door to the gas station opens, the chime alerting me. I look up from another fruitless check of my phone to see Nick walk in, dressed in dark clothing, a somber expression on his face. It's as if my thoughts have conjured him.

I don't know what to say. I stare at him mutely as he comes to the counter as if he wants to purchase something, but I know he doesn't. Nick doesn't seem to ever need anything, even me. He's always prepared, always independent. I wish for a moment that he was as shaken at the sight of me as I am of him.

I wish I'd worn makeup. I wish I wasn't wearing this stupid work polo, and that I'd done something special with my hair. It lays flat on my shoulders, unattractive. I tuck a strand of hair behind my ear. "Can I . . . can I help you?"

"You know I come to see you, Daisy." His accent is thick today, his voice soft. His hands flatten on the counter, those tattoos catching my eye. They're inches away from where mine rest, but he makes no move to touch me.

I wish he would. If he touches me, then I know everything is okay. That he wants me.

"It's nice to see you," I say after a moment. I try to smile brightly at him. I'm not sure how to act after a failed date. I can't be mad at him. I want him to want me too badly. "How are you?"

He studies my face for a long moment. "Something is wrong. You are sad."

I try to shake my head to deny it, but I feel my face crumple even as I do. A loud sniff escapes me. "It's nothing."

The chill in his icy eyes intensifies, and his hand brushes mine on the counter. "Who has hurt you? Say their name. I will handle it. They will never bother you again."

For some reason, I find this declaration incredibly sweet. It only makes my eyes stream tears even harder. I swipe them away. "It's n-nothing." My voice has such a childish warble in it. I can't believe I'm crying in front of him. I'm a wreck, though. It's my father, and my guilt, and the fact that I know he's here to dump me.

"It is not nothing," he says thickly. Through the stream of my tears, I notice his hand lifts from mine. A second later, he is coming behind the counter, and he envelops me in a warm, delicious hug, pulling my body against him, my face brushing against his coat.

I am lost.

I burrow against him, letting the tears go. For the first time in years, I am being held and comforted by someone. It feels amazing. I didn't know what I was missing until Nick put his arms around me.

I've been so lonely. I'm trying to be so strong, and it's so hard. I feel completely out of my depth.

And I desperately, desperately want him to like me despite the fact that I am an awful woman who has abandoned her mentally ill father.

His hand strokes my back. "Shhh," he comforts me. "I will make it better for you. Tell me what I can do. Tell me who has upset you."

I huddle closer, not speaking. I want to stay in his arms forever. He's strong, and warm, and so comforting. After a few moments of weeping, I realize how uncomfortable this must be for him. He probably came here to let me down easy, and found himself comforting me instead. I reluctantly pull away, wiping my eyes and then smoothing a hand down the front of his expensive jacket. "I'm sorry. I shouldn't be doing this."

He bares his teeth as if he would snarl. "Let them fire you."

I blink up at him in surprise. "I . . . no. I mean, I shouldn't be crying on you. I'm sure you came here to break up with me—"

Nick's fingers brush my cheek in a tender caress. "No, *kotehok*. Break up with you? Is this why you cry?"

I can't meet his eyes. It's one reason, of course—I want him to like me as much as I like him. But it's more than that, too. I can't talk about my father, or else he'll learn what an awful person I am. So I simply shrug my shoulders and look away. I am so ashamed to break down in front of him.

His fingers continue to stroke my cheek gently, and when I try to pull away, he holds me against him. I am pinned between his big body and the counter, but I'm not afraid. I know instinctively that Nick would never hurt me. "Hush, Daisy. Do not cry. I came to apologize to you. I acted badly when we parted."

I pull back in surprise. "You're apologizing? I don't understand.

I thought I did something wrong. I haven't been on many dates, so I didn't know—"

His eyes are no longer ice; they warm as they gaze upon me. His fingers continue to stroke my cheek, as if he can't help but touch me. "I always speak wrong when I am around you. My words never come out right." His fingers brush over my mouth, oh so gently. "I want to get things right, but I just make worse. You deserve better."

If only he knew what a small, mean person I was on the inside. I shake my head, and my fingers continue to smooth down the front of his coat, and I wish it was bare skin I was touching. "No, that's not true—"

"*Da*," he says, and there is a flash of self-hatred in his eyes that startles me. "You are too good—"

I lean forward to kiss him, silencing him before he can disagree with me. It's impulsive, but I can't resist. His mouth is so close to mine, his touch maddening, and I want to put my mouth on him. I'm clumsy, though, and my mouth brushes his chin and lower lip, and I cringe inwardly. I am a terrible kisser.

But the effect is the desired one—he stiffens against me with surprise, and he goes silent. A mere moment later, his fingers brush my chin. He parts my mouth, and then presses his lips to mine in a proper kiss. A hot, wet, slick, tongue-filled kiss.

I'm stunned by his visceral response. Heat pulses through my body, and I open my mouth for his possessive invasion. I may have started the kiss, but it's clear Nick has taken charge now. His mouth slants over mine, his lips caressing my own. His tongue slides against mine, and my breath hitches at the intensity of sensation it brings. My nipples harden as I press against him, and I'm shocked—and intoxicated—by my own response. I thought the kiss we'd shared in the parking lot was wonderful, but it pales in comparison to the need surging in this one. I am weak in the knees . . . and I want to experience more.

His fervor should frighten me, but I hunger for it. This is what I have wanted all my life. In Nick's arms, I feel truly alive. My hand slides to his neck, and I brush my fingers over the hot skin of his nape. I wish he wore no shirt so I could touch all of him. I need much more than a simple kiss. "Touch me," I breathe against his mouth when he breaks the kiss.

He gives a soft groan—he hears my words.

I cling to him, lifting my mouth for another kiss even as his hand slides around my waist and he drags me closer to him. I want—

The door chimes, jarring me back to reality. Nick releases me immediately, and I stumble away from him, turning to the counter in a daze. A lone man walks in wearing a camo baseball cap, jeans, and a dirty T-shirt. He barely glances at me and heads to the back of the store for the beer.

The moment is gone.

I press the back of a hand to my flushed cheeks, trying to cool them down. My nipples ache, and I hope they aren't visible through my shirt. I've never felt quite so aroused, and this is all from just a kiss.

Well, not a *simple* kiss. Kissing Nick is anything but ordinary-feeling.

I glance over at him, but he's not looking in my direction. His gaze is riveted on the man in the store, and his eyes have gone cold again, calculating. He moves down a nearby aisle and watches the man, though he feigns interest in a long-expired box of Pop-Tarts.

The man comes to the counter with a soda a minute later and points at a pack of cigarettes. I ring him up, and he leaves without saying a word about the fact that he found me kissing a man a short moment ago. When he's gone, I turn back to Nick.

He comes to the counter again, but he stays on the other side of it, like a customer. I'm disappointed, because I know he won't kiss me again. To my surprise, he puts a smartphone down in front of me. "I purchased this for you."

I stare at it. For a moment, I think it's his phone and that he's going to show me something on the screen. Then I realize he has purchased a *phone* for me. "I have a phone, Nick."

"Is better phone." He nudges it toward me. "I think your other phone does not work so well. Sometimes I don't get your texts very quickly." His eyelids shade his expression, like he's embarrassed that he wishes I responded faster to his texts.

He's spending too much money on me. It makes me uncomfortable. I know smartphones aren't cheap. I priced them out when looking for a disposable, and the data plan alone is more than I can spend a month on something so frivolous. Not when I am eating ramen noodles every night of the week. "But why did you get me a phone when I already have one?"

"Take it. Is so you can text complete sentences."

I give him a hurt look. "I text the best I can."

Nick sighs and reaches across the counter to grab my hand before I can pull away. He rubs a thumb over it and shakes his head. "Again, I misspeak. Around you, my tongue is foolish."

The smile he gives me is wry, self-deprecating. "I am greedy man, Daisy. I want more from you than just a few words. I want all of your attention. When you think of me, you text me. I don't want you to hunt for short words because is easier to type. I want everything you have to say. This makes it easier." He gestures at the phone. "Take it for me?"

I eye the phone. I hate the thought of more charity, but the ability to text Nick with ease fills me with anticipation. "Once I get my own, you will take it back?"

"*Da*." His eyes gleam; he knows he has won the battle with flattery.

I give him a shrewd look. "If I say no, are you going to find a way to break my existing phone?"

"I am wounded you think such things of me, Daisy," he says, but there is a boyish grin on his face.

"You're terrible," I tell him with a laugh. "None of my things are safe around you."

"Not if I think you deserve better," he says, and he has gone all serious again.

I sigh and take the phone, since I know I have about as much choice in this as I did with the jacket. "Thank you, Nick."

He looks as if he wishes to say more to me, but after a moment's hesitation, he simply nods and leaves, and I am left alone in the store all over again.

I clutch it to my chest, watching him disappear into a sedan parked outside. I kissed him. He didn't kiss me until I'd made the first move. Was that stupid of me? He didn't ask me out again.

But then I think of his words. *I came here to apologize.*

And he brought me a gift. I feel giddy with excitement despite my initial misgivings, and I run my fingers across the screen. It is the latest model of a popular, expensive brand of smartphones, and I know Regan will envy it. Nick has already programmed my name into the phone as D8Z, and the background is a picture of white daisies. How sweet. I flip through the apps and on impulse, click on the photo album to see if he has left me anything there.

It is blank. I'm disappointed to see that, but it doesn't mean I can't return the favor. I experiment with the camera for a long minute and manage to eventually take a selfie blowing a kiss at the camera. His number is the only one programmed into my phone—under nothing more than "N" for his name—and I text him the picture, along with a quick message: Thank you for being so thoughtful.

His reply comes while I'm with the next customer, and it takes everything I have not to grab at my phone when it vibrates. He doesn't send me a picture back, but the text makes me smile. If I am rewarded with such beauty by a simple gift, I shall buy you a car next.

Don't you dare.

CHAPTER EIGHT

DAISY

"Come on, Pollyanna," Becca groans. "Why are you walking so freaking slow?"

"I'm coming," I yell at her from several paces behind on the sidewalk. I'm trying to text and walk at the same time, and I'm not good at it, but I'm not willing to give up on my message. Since Nick gave me the phone yesterday, I've been obsessed with it . . . and with Nick. Even though I was initially skeptical about the gift, I admit to myself that I adore the phone. Texting is so much easier.

And since he's given it to me? We have texted nonstop.

He texted to me all night last night as I worked. His text, Good night, milaya moya, was the last thing I saw when I went to bed. When I awoke, I texted him a Good morning, and we'd been texting off and on all day.

He won't send me pictures, which makes me sad. Says I don't

need to see his ugly face constantly. He's crazy—I think he is beautiful, his profile noble, his eyes slightly sad. If he sent me a picture, I would stare at it all day long. It would look much better as the background of my phone than the sweet, girly daisies he has set up for me.

I missed out on this by being homeschooled, this playful tease of flirtation. I'm also glad that I'm learning to flirt with Nick instead of someone else, because he seems just as bad at it as I am. Like we're learning together. Maybe he was homeschooled, too. The idea of Nick as a high school student makes me smile. He seems like he was born world-weary. I can't envision him as a carefree child. Of course, I can't imagine myself as one, either. Perhaps that is why we've bonded so quickly. Our old souls recognize each other.

Nick keeps asking me to send him more photos, though. I refuse to do so until he sends me one of himself, so we are at an impasse. It has become a teasing game to us, one that continues even now.

> Why do you not send me a picture of you, Daisy? I did not
> realize you had such cruelty in you.

I giggle to myself as I read it again. I am composing the perfect response, but I type slowly. You should see my skirt. I am feeling very bold. It's very pretty. Becca says I look like a nun, but I like it. I

Becca's hand, with its long pink fingernails, close over my screen, sending the message before I can finish it. "Dude. Seriously. Walk faster. I'd like to get to the club before it closes?" She casts me an annoyed stare.

"Sorry." I lower my phone and give her a guilty look, but I don't feel all that guilty at the moment. Not really. I'd rather be at home texting Nick and chatting instead of out with Becca and Regan, but Regan insisted. Becca wants to go to a club to pick up a new man, and it's clear that what Becca wants, Becca gets. Regan reasons that because both she and I have men we are seeing, we can keep each other company and drink at a table while Becca tries to meet a guy.

My phone buzzes in my hand, but Becca is shooting me dirty looks and Regan is patiently waiting down the street, so I force myself to ignore it and jog a little to catch up to them. I'm wearing the Mary Janes that Regan gave me—my only dress shoes—and a knee-length swingy skirt with a sparkly tank top. The clothes are new, and I love them. They're full of color and flash, and I am tempted to send Nick a picture anyhow . . . but I don't. I won't give in on this.

I catch up to Regan and Becca and rub my bare arms briskly. I wanted to wear a sweater, but Becca declared it "frumpy" and shamed me into leaving it at home. I wish I had it now; the walk from the bus stop to the club is longer than I would like. I haven't been to this part of downtown, and despite the late hour, the streets are noisy and crowded with people. I can hear a thrumming bass beat somewhere nearby, and it vibrates in my ears.

Then we are at the door of the club. It's a downstairs club, below street level. We wait our turn to get in as Becca chatters excitedly to Regan, and my phone vibrates with another message. I will check it in a minute, I decide, as soon as Becca turns away. The anticipation of what Nick has sent me burns warm in my belly.

The doorman checks our IDs. He stares at mine for a long moment, as if not quite believing I am twenty-one, and then ushers us inside. We are swallowed up by the club, and the pounding beat blasts in my head. The interior of the club is dark and feels a little misty; there are lights flashing everywhere and bodies pressed to each other on the dance floor.

It's like I've entered another world.

Regan says something, and I can barely hear her, even though her mouth is moving. I shake my head, and she yells it louder. "Let's find a table and get some drinks."

I nod and she grabs my hand to lead me through the crowd. With my other, I shove my phone in my purse.

A few minutes later, we are situated at the back of the club at a cramped table sandwiched between several other cramped tables. Becca is eyeing the dance floor, her arms raised above her head and moving to the beat. She clearly can't wait to dance. Her breasts bounce with her movements. Men are watching her as she gyrates, and I suspect that this is exactly what Becca wants. She thrives on attention.

I am starting to shrink into myself. The club is noisy, and I don't want to be here. There are people everywhere, and I'm getting a headache from the noise. This is about as far from my sheltered old life as I could get, and I'm not sure I like it. Like my father, I like my day neat, ordered, and controlled. This chaos in front of me is as far from control as I can imagine.

As soon as I sit down, Becca tosses her purse on the table and disappears into the crowd, swaying to the music. Regan just looks at me and rolls her eyes as if to say, *What do you expect, that's Becca.* I simply smile and look around, trying to have a good time for Regan's sake.

She pats my hand to get my attention as I stare, wide-eyed, at our surroundings. "I'll go to the bar and get us drinks," she shouts in my ear over the blasting music. "You stay here and hold the table."

I nod, and a moment later, she vanishes into the crowd as

well. Now I am all alone. I glance around at the nearby tables, but they are empty, littered with belongings that have been tossed into chairs. A balding man is seated alone at a nearby table, and when I look over, he waves.

I freeze in place, terrified that he'll come and hit on me. Isn't that what happens in clubs? I avert my eyes and pull out my phone so I can look busy. I was probably just rude to the man, but I don't know what else to do. So I try to make myself as small as possible, concentrating on my phone.

I have three texts from Nick.

Nick: You what?

Nick: Are you all right, Daisy?

Nick: Text me back. Now, or I am coming down there.

The last one was sent five minutes ago. Oh dear. My cutoff message had him worried, and now he's making empty promises. He doesn't know where we are, but the protective sentiment is sweet. I type a message back quickly. I'm here. Sorry.

Nick: Good. Very good. He responds immediately.

D8Z: Sorry. Becca grabbed my phone.

Nick: I should cut off Becca's hands.

D8Z: It's fine. I was just walking slow. Distracted by sending you messages. We are at the club now so I should be fine. I'll probably be slow to respond for the next few hours. Becca and Regan are determined for us to have a good time tonight.

Nick: I would rather you were with me tonight.

I smile at my phone's screen, the chaos of the club momentarily forgotten. I would rather I was with him, too.

D8Z: It's just a different sort of thing than I am used to. I will just try to have fun. Don't worry about me.

Nick: If you need me, say the word. I will be there to rescue you.

D8Z: I'll be fine.

I cap my message with a smiley face so it seems friendly. Regan returns a moment later with three drinks, chatting with a guy. I lock my phone screen and put it back into my purse, returning my attention to my friend. After a few more minutes of talking that I can't make out, he waves and leaves, and Regan shoots me a relieved look. She gestures for me to lean in.

"He was trying to pick us up for his buddies," she yells in my ear, the club equivalent of a whisper. "Wanted to know if we were meeting someone."

My eyes widen and I shoot a look back at the retreating guy. I want to shrink under the table. I don't want to be picked up. I want Nick. "But you're seeing someone, and so am I," I yell back at her. The words feel good to say. Nick is my boyfriend, isn't he? Maybe? I'm not sure what to call it.

"I know," she says back. "That's why I sent him packing." She pushes a drink toward me and gestures for me to try it. It's reddish and there's a stick in the cup with some fruit speared on it. I taste it, and it's fruity and sweet, but the alcohol flavor overwhelms everything. I put the back of my hand to my mouth and cough at the taste. Next to me, Regan chugs her drink like it's nothing. Maybe I'm being a sissy. I take another game swig, and it burns my throat. It doesn't taste better on the second try.

We nurse our drinks for a bit, but it's hard to talk in the club with the pounding music searing into your eardrums. Becca hasn't returned to the table, and I see her surface occasionally in the pit of dancing bodies. She's clearly having a great time. I'm content to sit in the shadows and watch her dance, but Regan looks restless. She's finished her drink, and she is watching the dancers, tapping her foot. She gets a refill on her drink and downs it almost as quickly. I'm still working on my drink, which is not even halfway empty.

When a young guy comes up, speaks to her, and then gestures

at the dance floor, she glances at me. It's clear she wants to be out there and having a good time. I wave her off. I will just sit here by myself, then. I pull my phone out again, but Nick hasn't texted me back. I put it away, not wanting to bother him.

A few minutes later, the music shifts to something slower, and a DJ rambles something into a microphone. His mouth is so close to the mic I can't make out what he says, but the dance floor clears momentarily, and someone takes the center of the floor, moving in an intricate dance as everyone else circles around to watch. I'm eager to see the dancer, but Becca and Regan return to the table a minute later, both sweaty and having a great time. Becca is flushed and laughing, and Regan's cheeks are pink with delight, her blond hair sticking to the sides of her face.

Becca slides into the chair next to me and leans in. "You going to go out there and have fun, Pollyanna?" she yells at me. "We brought you here to loosen up."

"I'm fine," I tell her. "Really."

"You can't hide in a corner all night."

That is exactly what I want to do. But I just smile at her words.

The music changes and the crowd screams enthusiasm. "All you ladies get on the dance floor," the DJ yells into the microphone. "It's time for 'Ladies' Night!'"

The crowd cheers, and both Becca and Regan surge to their feet. When I don't get up, Becca grabs my hand and tugs on it. "Come on," she says. "You have to go out and dance to 'Ladies' Night'!"

I don't want to dance—at least, not the way the couples on the floor have been dancing. They grind their hips together and put their hands all over each other, and I want no part of that. But right now, the floor is filling with women, and they have their hands in the air as they dance along to the rollicking beat of a song that seems familiar to everyone but me.

After a moment's hesitation, I give in and abandon my purse and the safety of the table. I don't want to be seen as the friend that won't have fun. Becca and Regan are my first friends. I want them to like me.

So I go out on the dance floor with them and I dance. I'm awkward and reluctant at first, but soon I am laughing and dancing along with the others to the pounding music. It's all women and we jump around and dance like fools, but it's all fun. For a few minutes, I am having a great time, and I feel alive all over again.

The music changes far too soon, and the crowd on the dance floor shifts. Another hard, thumping song starts, and the people change, press closer. I'm not ready to give up on the dancing just yet, so I continue to move to the beat, lost in my own world. I'm feeling sweaty and warm, and my skirt is twirling, and I wonder what Nick would think if he saw me now, with my hair flying around my shoulders as I am having a great time. The song playing is something dirty, the lyrics something about grinding, and I notice there are couples starting to dance nearby, hips pushed together. I remain on the dance floor, looking for Becca and Regan, but I don't see them anywhere.

Someone grabs my hips and begins to rub up against me from behind. I'm startled to feel him against me. He didn't ask permission; he just came right up and grabbed me.

I try to jerk away, but the dance floor is an oppressive crush of bodies, and it's hard to move without running into someone else. The man pushing up against me mistakes my actions and drags me harder against him, assuming I want his touch.

I want to slam away from him. I want to fling him from me, jab a knee between his legs for daring to touch me. It's my body. I should be the one in control, and I want to punish him for making me think otherwise.

But there are so many people nearby that I can't do anything. Whenever I raise my arms, I'm jostled, like a minnow caught in a riptide.

I panic.

I have no control over any of these people.

I can't breathe. Hands are rubbing up and down on my arms, and I freeze in place. The man continues to roll against my hips, and I can feel his erection prodding against the thin material of my skirt. This man that is trying to dance with me has an *erection*, and he's pushing it against me.

It's too much. I blindly shove away, trying to get out of the crowd. The music is splitting my head now, and my friends are nowhere to be seen. I squirm away from the man only to run into someone else, and new hands grab at me. There are people everywhere.

I hate it. I hate people. I want to go home where it's safe.

A muffled whimper escapes my throat, but the club is so noisy I can't even hear it. I can't breathe; air won't get into my lungs. It's too hot in the club and there's just no air. The bass has pounded it all away. I stumble, pushing my way off the dance floor, heedless of the fact that I'm pissing off people as I shove past them. Finally, I emerge from the crowd and arrive at the tables. I spot the man who waved at me earlier. I'm on the verge of tears now. I ignore his attempt to get my attention again and snatch my purse off of the table I share with Regan and Becca, who are still missing.

And then I run out of the club. I don't stop running until I'm out in the street. It's dark outside, and the music is still pounding in my head. I run away from the door and stop about halfway down the block, and then I curl up against the brick wall.

I feel as if I've been assaulted.

I've never been touched like that. Never. So casually, so ruthlessly. I just wanted to dance, and I was manhandled by a man with an erection. It's too much for my senses to handle, and I sob quietly to myself.

"You okay, honey?"

I look up at the face of the big bouncer. He's fat, middle-aged and balding, and he looks irritated that he had to come to check on me.

"I'm fine," I tell him. *Go away. Go away.*

"Anyone bothering you?"

Just you, I want to say, but I realize he's trying to help me. So I shake my head and say nothing until he goes away. I can't stop trembling. It's cold outside, but I like the crisp air. It feels so different from the steamy atmosphere of the club and the pressing bodies. I want a shower. I feel dirty. Someone touched me without my permission, and it was awful.

The man calls down the street at me, one more time. "You need me to call you a cab, girlie?"

"I have a ride," I call back hoarsely, and when he turns away, I wipe at my cheeks, trying to stop crying.

I'm not good at that. I can't seem to stop. I'm glad Regan and Becca can't see me like this. They won't understand. Only one person seems to understand me.

I get my phone out and stare at the texts I sent him earlier.

Nick: If you need me, say the word. I will be there to rescue you.

D8Z: I'll be fine.

Then I send him three little words. I'm not fine.

NIKOLAI

My phone is on vibrate because it is too loud in this club. This basement club is a death trap. I can see only three exits, and the space is over capacity. Drunk people are stumbling everywhere. I could kill at least half of them by starting a stampede.

It is clear to me that Daisy can never be left alone. She is too trusting and too willing to try out new things without the leavening effect of fear. She's not experienced enough fear in her life, I think. The mere fact that she wants me in her life is evidence enough of her precious naïveté. But it is the one thing about her that draws me to her, and I do not want to stamp it out. So I've followed her here. It is easy with the GPS. There are men who smile at her, who pass their hands over her back. I want to howl that she belongs to me; she is mine.

My jaw is sore from grinding my teeth together. I hate that she is here surrounded by sweaty palms and unclean thoughts. I see the lust in the eyes of the men around her. She exudes freshness in this stale air, and they want a taste of it. I fold one hand over the fist I've made and squeeze; the cracking of joints relieves a tiny bit of tension. I repeat the gesture with the other hand. I try to shake my shoulders and roll my head to ease the pressure, but none of it really works. The only way I will feel good is when I've removed myself from this box, and I won't do that until Daisy is ready to leave.

I do not need advice from Daniel to know that I cannot drag Daisy out of this place. I've already made multiple missteps with her. The only thing I can do now is to wait, collect information by watching my mark, and then use that information to acquire the mark. It is different work than I've done in the past. The ending steps must conclude with her liking me instead of her dead on the floor.

I sit in the corner of the club, unseen. Occasionally, a drunk girl will stumble back here and try out her wiles on me, but a cold stare seems to penetrate even the densest of heads. Their hindbrain knows the truth their muddled consciousness does not. I'm a danger, and these girls in here don't want dangerous.

I've encountered some that do; some that are turned on by it and some that are attracted to it. But not tonight. Tonight is filled with little dolls, tottering on their tiny heels, clothed in their tiny dresses. A man and a woman stumble back beside me. The dark corner provides them with a false sense of privacy. He lifts her skirt and they begin to copulate. In the cocoon of space beyond the dance floor, I can hear the sounds of their sloppy sex mix with the beats spun out by the DJ. I wonder what the man would do if I reached over and stroked a hand down the back of the girl. Would he even know, lost in his own pleasure? She is glassy-eyed from either the drink or the heat or both. It's not passion I see in her eyes when they meet mine. It's triumph. We stare at each other for a minute. She is suffused with excitement at being watched, so I turn away and seek out the object of my own desire.

Daisy is now on the dance floor, no longer texting me. Her purse is abandoned on the table. Vultures circle around it. If left there much longer, no doubt someone will come along and pilfer the contents. Daisy works so hard for what little money she earns, and since I cannot stand guard over her body here inside this club, I will protect her belongings. As I rise to walk to the bar top that Daisy has left, I feel a hand on my shirt.

I look down and it is the red-tipped fingernails of the girl, still being tupped by the drunk male, who has no idea that his partner's attention has so completely detached from his experience. "Stay," she mouths at me, her matching red lips forming words that I cannot hear. "Stay, and I'll do you next."

I shake off her hand like it is a snake. I hear a mewling cry behind me as I walk away. The man takes it to be encouragement and not disappointment. "Yes, baby," he groans, and I roll my eyes. He is like that man of Daisy's roommate. So much about his own pleasure and about not seeing to the one he is with.

But perhaps it is because he does not have a Daisy, someone whose pleasure in everything brings its own delight. The crowd parts for me as I walk forward, mostly because I do not hesitate. Or because they understand instinctively that I am not moving for them. There is a light-fingered hand that rests on Daisy's purse. It is not her hand, and it is just as I feared. I glance quickly at Daisy, who is dancing, her skirt twirling around her and her body being watched by so many in this club. My blood heats and instinct makes me want to shut this place down, but first, before I go to her, I rescue her purse.

My hand slams down on the table beside the thief's hand, making its owner jump. The girl is not her roommate or her friend who has come with them tonight. Some other woman with painted nails and a painted face. She grimaces and then smiles at me, smoothing down her brown hair with one hand, not moving her other from Daisy's purse. She intends to either pretend this purse is her own or to try to make a move on me. Neither will work, and I glare at her, trying to impart the message. She is too dumb to get it, for she moves closer to me, her fingers running down the front of my chest. I glance again at the dance floor, but Daisy has been swallowed up.

Impatiently, I grip the offensive hand in mine. "If you do not want me to break your wrist with one squeeze of my hand, you will do two things immediately. First, you will remove your hand from my woman's purse. Second, you will remove your hand from this shirt. It is attached to the body that belongs to the owner of the purse."

Her hands slip away after an infinitesimal pause. Daisy has reappeared from the crowd, looking upset and distraught. I wonder if she's seen the whore's hand on my shirt. I turn in anger to face the intruder, but she's melted into the crowd. I hesitate, wondering if Daisy would be upset if I were here. I think she would be. This is not the zoo or a picnic, as Daniel had suggested. And I've given Daisy multiple opportunities to invite me with her . . . none of which she has accepted. I allow the crowd to hide me as I watch Daisy snatch up her purse and head for one of the exits. She does not wait for either of her companions but instead pushes her way out. I follow behind. Before I can reach her, another man intercepts me.

"Bro," he says. "There's no exit here."

"I disagree," I say, pointing to the illuminated sign above the door, which spells out the word in red letters.

"It's an emergency exit only." He points to a red sign attached to the door. It says emergency, but it means nothing to me. Daisy has exited that door alone.

"I do not care what the sign says." I begin to move past him but he pushes me back.

"Look, dude, my man is making his move out there, so just use a different exit." At first, I cannot comprehend what he is saying. Daisy is a woman. She has not gone to make any moves other than to get fresh air. But then it comes to me. These are not places you visit alone, only in packs. There is a predator outside, and his teammate is inside deterring any interruptions, making a clear path for the predator.

My right arm comes up and knocks the hand off my chest. The left hand comes up to hold the neck of the offender off the ground. "He touches her in any way, and I will come back and rip your head off your body like it is the stem of an apple. One twist and you will be done." I drop him to the floor and make no notice of the way he slides down the wall, gasping and spitting. I run out the door, unconcerned now what Daisy will think of me following her to this club.

I will create another lie, a hundred of them if I have to. Outside I see nothing at first. I take a second sweep of the alleyway and hear a grunt and sound toward the end. I sprint there, and I see Daisy struggling in the arms of a man.

He has my Daisy. Rage blinds me for a second, the blood sweeps over my eyes so that I cannot see, but I can hear—and my well-trained body can feel. I pull the man off her with two hands, and I send him spinning backward. But I do not let him go, for he is a coward and cowards run.

As I pull him away from Daisy, I notice that she tries to swing at him—tries, and fails. And when she fails, she seems to crumple inside of herself. As if she has tried to be brave and it is too much for her.

The man in my hands fights me. I twist the back of his collar until he is choking from the pressure of the cloth. I run my other hand lightly over Daisy's shoulders. She is shaking, and there are wet tracks running down the front of her face.

"Are you all right?" I ask her hoarsely. While I was tending to her silly purse; while I was listening to that *mudak* inside, this vile creature was making my Daisy cry. I hear his weak gurgles and feel his struggle against the grip. If he were smart, he would loosen his shirt and run away, so I quickly let go of the collar of his shirt and grab the back of his neck and pull him close to my side so I can wrap an arm around his neck. I'm holding him like he is a bag tucked under my armpit. It is too close to Daisy, so I back off slightly.

"Are you all right?" I repeat.

She nods and wipes her face so that the tear tracks go to her temples instead of down her cheeks. "Nick, what are you doing here?"

I think for a minute, trying to invent a good lie, and come up with nothing. Hit men are bad liars. At least I am a bad liar. I tell her the truth. "I worry about you, Daisy, and come to this club."

"How did you find me?"

Now I do need a real lie. "I was driving past and saw you on the street."

She considers this for a minute, and I think she might buy it, but the man in my arm says, "He's fucking lying. Saw you on the street? What a crock of shit."

I squeeze my arm tighter. I could easily twist his neck and put an end to his misery, but not while Daisy is looking on. Her face displays uncertainty caused by the *mudak*'s words.

"I drive around a lot at night." I lie again. "I can't sleep." Not a lie. I hardly ever sleep. It's not a welcome place for me.

"Did you—did you follow me?" Daisy stutters out.

"Oh this is rich," the soon-to-be-dead man snorts out. "You're a stalker, and I'm the bad guy?"

"One moment, Daisy," I say. I must take care of this trash before I can explain myself to Daisy.

I drag the predator down the alleyway. There is no real place to hide from Daisy's gaze. I push the male up against the brick exterior wall. "I will tell you what I told your friend inside. I do not like anyone touching Daisy. She is not for you. But you touch her and make her cry, so you must be punished."

"No way, man," he protests. His legs kick futilely at me. I lower him to the ground and turn his foot to the side with mine. Three swift kicks to his Achilles tendon has rendered him unable to stand.

He cries out sharply.

I muffle it with my hand and lean him against a wall. "See what I can do to you with just my boot out here in front of God and everyone? Think of what it would be like alone. Maybe I will come after you one night as you are walking home. What could I do to you then?"

He cries then. "Okay, enough, enough. I didn't even want the fucking bitch."

I kick him again for disrespecting Daisy, and then I let him crumple to the ground. Daisy is watching me, because what else is she going to look at? Her hands are covering her mouth. I tell myself she is horrified at how close she came to being hurt instead of about how I maimed this stranger. Lie.

"He'll be fine," I say brusquely as I take one of her hands and lead her out of the alley.

"How'd you get here so fast?" she asks. "I just texted you."

I felt it, but I hadn't looked at my phone, too intent on following Daisy outside. I'm tired of lying to Daisy, so I don't answer. I've parked down the street in another rental, something else I will have to explain to Daisy. So many lies piling up. I hear the click, click, click of her heels against the pavement and realize I am walking too fast. I slow down immediately.

"Nick, talk to me." Daisy pauses. "Did I offend you again?" She sounds as if she's ready to start crying again.

This makes me stop. I turn to her, seeing her upset, unhappy little face staring up at me with hurt clearly evident in her eyes. "No, Daisy, I am the offense." I search her eyes. This is the truth. Can she see me?

Her hand brushes lightly against my cheek, a tentative offering.

I close my eyes and turn my face into her hand so she is cupping my jaw, and my lips are touching her fingers.

"I thought maybe I interrupted something when I texted you."

She's so kind to me, so trusting. I feel like I've been given a charge to protect her because she cannot protect herself.

"I am *durak*," I say against her hand. "Stupid. Come, let's go to car, and I will tell you everything." Not everything, but perhaps enough.

I hold the car door open for her, and then I drive. I do not return to our neighborhood, but instead I take her out to one of the many lakes that are scattered through the city. The moonlight is reflecting off the lake's surface, and I know that this peaceful spot is the right place to make my confessions.

"Daisy," I say and ask for her to look at me. "I must tell you that I have not been honest with you, always."

She looks back at me with sad eyes, so old in her innocent face. "I know, Nick."

"You do?"

"Yeah, I do. I mean, you're not a terribly good liar, and a lot of times you're contradicting yourself. Are you . . ." She swallows, then asks, "Married?"

"Married?" She asks this like it is the worst thing ever. It is one truth I am grateful to give to her. "No, never." I hold up my hand like I am swearing an oath to her.

She sighs with relief. "Then what is it?" I weigh how much to tell her, and she can see it. "No, Nick, tell it all to me. Don't pick and choose."

Inwardly I grimace. I cannot tell her all, but I tell her some. "I am from Russia, born in Ukraine, but I grow up in the streets of Russia. In a *Bratva*. Do you know what that is?"

She shakes her head no, so I explain. "It is a family of sorts, but not a good one. We don't like each other."

"Sounds like a real family to me." She gives me a shy smile.

"Maybe. But this family is bad, so I leave the family, and I do odd jobs around the world, and then I come here for another job."

"Doing what?"

"Computer work." This is not a lie. Much of my work is done on the computer today. She accepts this because she can see it is the truth, even though it is only parts of the truth.

"I do not live in your apartment, Daisy. I live across the street."

"I remember you told me. Why did you lie about that?"

I had forgotten. What lies have I told her and lost track of? I am *mudak*. "I had no excuse for being in your building."

She does not push me further, but simply seems to be meditating on this. "Do you lie to me because you think I'm naïve?"

"No!" I am startled. She thinks the worst of herself, as if there is anything about her freshness that could be bad. "I think you are a wonder, Daisy. A wonder."

My words make her blush, and the moonlit pink in her cheeks heats my own blood. But, I am not an animal, and I remain on my side of the car. "I have no real roots. I rent cars and an apartment. I am glad that you did not come over. I have nothing there."

"It's not like I have much," Daisy admits. "I just feel out of my element with you. It's like, because I'm a virgin, I just don't get what is going on."

We both startle at this admission. Daisy claps her hand over her mouth, and even in the dim light, I can see she is bright red. Her confession changes everything and nothing for me. I knew, from the moment I saw her touching herself, that she was innocent. Or maybe I had hoped. But to hear the truth from her made me dizzy with pleasure.

I cannot bite back a groan.

"It's bad, isn't it?" She sounds ashamed. "You don't want a virgin. No one does. I'm such a loser."

"How can you say that?" I pull at the hands she has pressed to her face. "If the entire club knew the truth, I would have had to fight every one of them to take you out of there untouched." I pull her to me, not willing to have any distance between us, and her lax body allows it. "Your innocence is precious."

"Is that what you like then? That I'm innocent? And when I'm not, you're done? Poof? Out of there?"

"*Nyet*," I bite out. How can I fix this? "You could be with a hundred men and still be innocent to me. I've done so many bad things in my life." I pause, feeling winded. How to explain? I want to hit myself. What would Daniel do? He'd have counseled me to have practiced more, but how could I have anticipated this? "I feel like I am not worthy of you."

"Me?" She lets out a small huff. "I feel like I'm not experienced enough for you." She smiles like we are a pair of fools.

And we are. I curve my own lips upward. "You are just right for me." I look down at her hands and then into her eyes. "Am I right for you?" I hold my breath.

"Would you teach me?" Daisy asks.

"Teach you what?" I am hearing her say things, yet they make no sense to me. Perhaps I am dazed from the loss of blood that drains from my head to pool in my lap when Daisy takes my hand and places it in her own and then rests them both high on her thigh.

"You know . . . touch me?" I can hear the blush in her voice as she speaks. She's eager, but still embarrassed. "I don't want to be a virgin. I want you to teach me about sex. And orgasms. All those things. Will you show me how?"

"How?"

"How to get off?"

I've died. The Madonna in heaven is staring me in the face. I was sure I would go to hell, but there is an angel sitting in my car asking me to stick my hand in her warm cunt and bring her to orgasm. Surely that is heaven.

But the corporeal flesh beneath my hand clenches at my over-long silence. She's tense, anticipating rejection.

"I am sorry," I admit. "I felt like I had died and gone to heaven. You ask me if I would like to give you pleasure? There is no answer but yes."

"Right here?" she whispers, her eyes gleaming with antici-pation.

"Yes, here." I would never be able to drive home in this state. I run my hand up her arm and cup the back of her neck. Tugging gently on her hair, I tilt it backward so we can look at each oth-er's eyes and each judge the sincerity of the other's statements. "I will do as much or as little as you want, sweet Daisy."

She struggles with something and then admits, "I'm not exactly sure of what I want. I've read some books, but I don't know how much is reality."

"Then I decide for you, *da*? You trust me?" I thrill at the idea of her trust as much as the idea of her want. She nods, but I need to hear the words. "You trust me?"

A small smile peeks out. "*Da*," she repeats, her mouth form-ing the Russian word for yes. "I trust you."

"So I will kiss you first, my kitten, and then we will do other things." I stroke the back of her hair, and she nods her assent.

I drop my hand to the back of her neck and pull her close. I soak in her scent and open my mouth so that I can match the rhythm of her breathing. As she exhales, I inhale until our breaths are one symbiotic loop. The air in the vehicle no longer exists. Only the puffs of oxygen that are exchanged between us exist. There is noth-ing but her and me.

I pull her mouth against mine, gently at first, and when her lips part, I stroke them with my tongue. Little lapping strokes until she's comfortable with the feel of my mouth against hers. My patience pays off when she opens and her little tongue darts out. The first stroke of her tongue against mine is so shockingly erotic that I nearly come in my pants. The simultaneous urge to devour her and push her away so I don't embarrass myself grips me.

My one hand on the back of her neck tightens, and the other reaches up to caress her jaw. I want to touch other places. I want to cup her breasts, thrum my thumbs across her nipples. I want to reach between her legs and circle her clit. I want to push one, two of my fingers inside the wet heat between her legs.

I want all of these things, but settle for just stroking her cheek, jaw, and neck. Her skin is soft, and I feel the roughness of my fingers catch against the tender flesh. All of these things swirl in my mind as we kiss. So little of our bodies are touching, but I am enflamed. My fingers rub over the wildly beating pulse in her neck. This reveals her own passion to me, but she is so innocent that I cannot bear to take her here in the car, even if she would let me. I break the kiss and lean my forehead against hers. Our breaths are short pants now.

"You want more?" I ask.

Her hands, once resting on my shoulders, stroke down the front of my chest, feeling the hardness of my pectorals. I've never cared about my appearance before. My body is merely a weapon. But as her fingers wander and explore, I'm proud of the fitness of my body and that she finds pleasure in the muscles she discovers.

"You're very strong, aren't you?" she asks in a wondering fashion. I nod. Inside I feel like I could lift a car if she would repeat her words to me in that same breathy tone.

"So that I can protect you," I reply. I lean back and give her greater access to my chest. Her hand moves lower, over the ridges of my abdomen and along the v-lines of my torso that arrow into my jeans. My cock is pressing insistently against my zipper. And my breath catches as her hand hovers over the bulge.

I swear I feel the heat of her palm through the layers of fabric, and that my penis is reaching toward her touch. This time I cannot prevent a moan from escaping, and she hasn't even touched me. Just the idea of her touching me is enough, and I come.

Wetness dampens the denim, but I'm not ashamed, because her look of pleased wonder is intoxicating.

"Did you just—?" She can't bring herself to say it.

"Yes, from just the thought of you touching me. It is enough." I admit.

"I've never—" She cuts off and begins again. "I've never seen a man in real life."

"Do you want to see it?"

She nods quickly.

I reach between us and unzip. My release was only a small one, only in anticipation, and my cock is still hungry and hard. It springs up between us, and the wetness shines in the dim moonlight.

"Can I touch it?"

I grit my teeth and nod. I'll come again, I fear. I try to think of unsightly things. Things that will reduce my excitement. I cannot think of anything but her, cannot see anything but her soft hand lowering and then encircling my girth. I am not a small man. The whores have told me this—some in delight and some in fear. Her hand barely wraps around it. I reach around her hand and pinch the base of my cock hard—so hard that another man might cry—to lessen my arousal so that she may touch me.

Her index finger lightly touches the tip, and my cock bobs its head in response. Two more fingers stroke down the heavy vein. My eyes roll back in their sockets. This light petting is so incredibly erotic that it will fuel my fantasies for weeks.

"It's really soft," she murmurs, almost to herself. "I thought it wouldn't be . . . well, I don't know what I thought it would feel like, but not like this."

I pinch myself harder and warn her, "It's a little sticky from my come."

She then does something that I never would have imagined in a million years. She lifts her fingers to her mouth and licks them, tasting my release.

I nearly shoot all over her. Instead, I fist my penis and squeeze it so hard some come releases from the top, and my balls try to climb inside my body for fear that they are next in line for abuse. But the pain dulls my arousal to an ache, and I'm calmed once more.

"Kitten," I say, releasing my cock and zipping my pants quickly. "I cannot have you touching me again tonight. I am too weak. And you have not even begun to understand the pleasures of your own body. Please, allow me to show you what a release is like."

She looks disappointed and embarrassed. "I-I-I don't know if I'm ready."

I nod. "You tell me when you've had enough." I want this experience to be perfect for her. Releasing the catch for the seat, I position it as far back as it can go and recline on it, propping myself on one side. I pat the seat. "Lie down here."

She does so, but I can tell by the way she plucks at her outfit that she is nervous. I begin to stroke her, long languid strokes down the front of her body from her shoulder to the knees. Her breasts quiver underneath her shirt, but I ignore them. I want her to relax at first, be comfortable next to my body and languid under my touch.

Each pass of my hand settles her. I match her breathing once again. It is a trick I've learned to calm others, and it works here. Soon her arms are no longer tense and her thighs are falling open. Now when I stroke down her front, I linger over her breasts and rub a bit harder over her thighs. Her breath and pulse pick up.

If there were light in this car, more than just the silver moonlight, I would see the blood coloring her cheeks, the tips of her breasts, and her neck. The flush might be all over, and I cannot wait to see the sight. For now, I content myself with the visible signs of her arousal.

With the next pass of my hand, I allow myself to cup her breast and feel the turgid nipple beneath the fabric.

"Your body seeks a release," I tell her.

"How do you know?" Her voice catches as I rub my thumb across the hardened point.

"Because your body is tightening up. Here, your little nipples are taut and ready to be suckled. The skin is stretched tight across your cheeks, and your pulse thrums madly in your neck." I whisper kisses across the apple of her check and lick the throbbing pulse point. "Between your legs, the blood pounds hard, and your pussy is catching and releasing. I can tell by the way your hips shift and lift to press against my palm." I allow my hand to drop down between her legs and lie lightly above her pubis.

She pushes involuntarily against me.

"I revel in these signs," I tell her, whispering the words against the delicate swirl of her ear. She shivers as I trace the outline of the lobe and lick the tender skin behind it. "These signs tell me that my woman's body sings for me."

"Your . . . woman?" She struggles to get even these words out.

"Yes, mine," I say and this time, I press my hand harder between her legs and curl my fingers to cover her sweet cunt. And like I predicted, I can feel the fierce pulse of her heart at the very core of her. Even better, I can feel dampness between the fabric of her panties and her skirt. "Are you wearing panties I have bought you, Daisy?" I ask. "Did you think of me when you pulled them up your legs and squeezed your thighs together? Did you wonder what it would be like if it were my hands there instead of the silk and lace that I purchased for you?"

She gives me what I want. A panting, breathless "yes."

"May I see?" I ask. She nods her head, and it is enough. I pull up the hem of her skirt, and beneath it I see light-colored panties, the color of which is unknown to me. I guess. "Blue?"

"Blue," she agrees, and she gives me a tense smile.

I soothe her brow with one hand across it. All these things, the pauses, the light touches, the talk, it is all designed to make her come hard. I will own this first orgasm of Daisy's. No matter what happens to us, I will ensure that she will never forget this moment in her life. That she will think of this day, the evening, this moment, and that the mere thought of how hard she comes will arouse her once again.

For this, though, I need more than one hand. I curse myself for starting this in a car, of all places. But I will improvise. A good assassin is the king of improvisation. There is just enough space between the steering wheel and the front of the seat for me to kneel. I am bowed over, but the awkward position is meaningless to me. I could sit in this position for hours if it meant that I could bring Daisy to orgasm. This is not a punishment position; it is one of immense reward.

Her face looks down upon me with some trepidation; fear and uncertainty have crept in while I have been busy repositioning myself. I place my hands on her lower thighs and give her yet another truth. "I am so hungry for you, Daisy, my teeth ache. My mouth waters at the idea of tasting your nectar. My hands itch to stroke every inch of your body."

My words relieve her, and she smiles tenderly at me. I place kisses on the sides of her knees. I rub my hands up and down her legs, stroking a finger behind each knee and the tender skin at her ankles. I lick the inside of her thighs and raise her skirt up even higher so that I may kiss her rounded belly. Over and over, my hands sweep her legs, thumbs almost touching her silk-covered pussy but never quite making contact. Her hips push up against me, and I feel the wetness from her desire rub against my chest as I lean over and learn the contours of her ribs and belly.

Her hands have crept into my hair, tugging at me, urging me downward. She is an innocent, but her body knows where she burns hottest and who can provide relief.

Only me, I vow. It shall be only me from now on who brings her to release. I want all of her orgasms from now until I am dust. I move downward and breathe hotly over her mound. Her hands tug on my head, and she makes me pause as I am about to mouth her through the delicate panties I've purchased.

"Are you sure you want to do this?" she asks. Her lower lip is between her teeth.

"Why wouldn't I?" The question seems so ridiculous. Every man would want to be here if they knew the treasure that they would receive.

DAISY

I'm an awful person

I should be a wreck right now. This thought goes through my mind even as Nick's head moves under my skirt, the stubble of his shaved chin grazing my naked thigh. There are so many things that I should be thinking about right now. I should be questioning him about why he was following me. I should be sobbing with fear over the man that nearly attacked me.

Instead, I'm panting and eager for Nick's touch. His mouth is hovering over the silk of my panties, so close that I can feel his breath on my skin through the fabric. His breathing is ragged, but so is mine. And I've seen his penis, and I've touched him.

If he's stalking me, I shouldn't *want* to touch him. It's not smart. But . . . there's a part of me that is desperately wicked. That's thrilled that he's fascinated enough by someone as boring and plain as me to want to focus all of his attention on me, to be the center of his world. And I am entranced by what he offers—the chance to pleasure him with my exploring touch, and the chance to be pleasured in return.

It's that promise of pleasure that overrides all caution—it drags me under.

He wants me. No one can fake how quickly he came. And now he wants to go down on me, something that Regan says Mike won't do for her. I'm terrified, even as I'm shaking with anticipation. It's supposed to be the most erotic thing a man can do to a woman, and I feel like I've been thrust from complete ignorance to a sexual buffet of experiences. He's giving me so much that I simply can't process all of it right now.

"I can smell you," he says, and his voice is thick. "You are very wet, *da*?"

His words are crude, startling . . . arousing. I gasp. It feels like all the air in the car has disappeared, along with my sanity. He's right, though. I'm wet, so wet. Even now, I try to clench my thighs together to feel my slick flesh rub against itself.

"Tell me how it feels, Daisy, and I will touch you."

Nick wants me to speak the same dirty words he uses? I don't know if I can. It feels so personal, and I can't imagine telling another person in the world my secret fantasies. What if I ask for the wrong thing? What if he laughs at me? Or worse . . . what if I bore him?

I am paralyzed by indecision and my own pitiful lack of knowledge. I've read novels, but many of them did not go into great detail. They just wax rhapsodic about explosions and fireworks and being pierced. I want to make sure I have things exactly right before I ask for them.

I don't want him to think me foolish.

When I don't answer him, Nick's hands move and they frame my panties, the triangle of his fingers outlining my most sensitive areas.

"Do I frighten you, *kotehok*?"

I shake my head. I want this more than anything, and my own cowardice is going to cost me the chance to explore if I'm not careful. "I don't know what to ask for. I'm sorry if I'm disappointing you."

"Not disappointment," he says, accent thick. "Never. And you wish for me to guide you to pleasure this time, Daisy? *Da*, I do so, on the condition that you show me what you learn next time we touch."

Oh, that sounds so much better. I nod eagerly, my enthusiasm returning. "Show me." I want to come just like he did, just as quickly, and just as fiercely. I still have the taste of him on my tongue, and it's driving me crazy. Even now, I lick my lips, wanting to taste more of him. "Do you think you'll come again?"

Nick laughs, but it sounds almost pained. "Of this, I do not doubt, lovely Daisy."

He makes it sound like I am the most exciting woman in the

world, and it makes my pulse flutter all over again. I shift in the seat of the car; the ache between my legs full of need.

"But first," he says in that delicious, low voice that I love, "I will please my woman until she screams."

I have never screamed with intense emotion in my life. But I don't correct him. Maybe tonight I will.

"A woman's cunt is soft, delicious thing," he tells me. "Like flower with delicate petals." His thumb strokes down the center of my panties, and I feel him outline the seam of my sex. I am so damp that the panties stick to my skin, and it makes the visual obscene. I am horrified and fascinated by it all at once.

"Should I be this wet?" I ask him.

"Only if I am lucky man." His mouth brushes over my panties, and I suck in my stomach involuntarily. It's like I don't want to get in the way of his touch. "You will give these to me tonight, Daisy," Nick tells me as he tugs at my panties, at one of the small, white bows that are set at each hipbone. "So I will dream of this moment tonight when I sleep."

His words make me feel so erotic. Like the damp seeping in my panties is the sexiest thing he's ever had happen to him. I make a wordless little whimper, and am embarrassed at how loud it is in the car.

"Slide these off your hips, kitten," he tells me, and his voice is a persuasive purr. His fingers tug at the hem of the panties, and he glances up at me with those gorgeous eyes. "So I may look at all of you. You show me, *da*?"

"Yes," I tell him, and the excited quiver in my voice is matched by the one in my fingers. I'm fumbling as I pull at the fabric, and then it moves down my hips and onto my thighs. The thatch of my hair is displayed to him, and I feel naked. He has not even seen my breasts, and yet I am showing him my most feminine parts.

Nick groans as if in pain, gazing at the sight of me. His hands take control and he has my panties in his grasp. He tucks them into the pocket of his jacket, and then I am naked from the waist down, my skirt bunched up at my hips.

"Part your legs," he commands. His gaze is riveted on my flesh. "Show me your desire."

I suck in a breath again, but I do as he commands. I like that he's in charge and is telling me what to do. I feel better with him in control, guiding me.

But he simply stares and stares, and then his gaze flicks to my nervous one. "You are most beautiful thing I have seen."

And then it doesn't matter that we're in his car and that he's hunched over awkwardly and that I'm sitting with my clothes all rucked up. I am beautiful and sexy in his eyes. I spread my legs wider for him in an invitation, hardly daring to breathe at my own boldness.

Nick mutters something in Russian, and his mouth grazes along the inside of my thigh. I tremble at the feel of him there again. It feels more severe with my sex bare to him. I've got nothing left to shield myself.

He looks up at me, and his eyes are dark, his pupils dilated. "I'm going to touch you with mouth, Daisy."

I nod, unable to look away from him. I'm twitching with need. I want him to do this. I *need* it.

Almost in slow motion, his firm, hard mouth descends on the curls of my sex. I watch as they press to my mound, and I feel him there. It sends an excited thrill through me, but it's not blowing me away.

I must be wearing my emotions on my face. "Patience, *kotebok*," he says. "I have not yet begun pleasuring you."

"I know," I say. "I just—"

And then he licks me.

My words die in my throat. I'm stunned by that private, utterly personal lick. It's right up the seam of my wet flesh.

He groans. "Perfection."

I'm stiff, my senses on overload. It's almost too much for me to absorb. I push at him, not sure I like how personal this is. I'm not good with personal. I don't know how to handle it.

"No, Daisy," he tells me, and his voice is ragged. "Let me have more. I will make this good for you."

Then he burrows, and I feel his mouth part my flesh. His tongue glides along my slit, going deeper and stroking along hot, needy skin. My body jumps in response. His hands trap me in place, pushing down on my thighs so I will keep them apart for him. And he slides his tongue along my sex again.

I whimper. The sensations are overwhelming: tickling, wild, and erotic. I'm really not sure I can handle it. My hands go to his hair again, but I'm not sure if I'm pushing him away or encouraging him for more. "Nick—"

He lifts his head to gaze up at me, his mouth slick with my own wetness. "The way you say my name with my mouth on your cunt—it is a dream." He lowers his head again, but not before adding, "I want to hear it when you come."

I love his words. They're so naughty and direct, even when I can't be. And they take the fear out of me. I relax a little, and encourage him with petting motions as his mouth moves back to my sex—my cunt, he calls it—and begins to explore with the tip of his tongue. He makes light, tracing motions, outlining each fold, and I watch, breathless, as he bends over me.

I like his mouth there, but I'm still waiting for the fireworks. He's avoiding my clitoris, and I wonder if he knows it's the most sensitive part. If not, I don't want to correct him. I'm more interested in watching him, the way his lashes look like dark fans as he bends his head and licks me.

It's nice—pleasant, even—and tickly now and then. But it's not the explosion he had. I guess it's not the same for women.

His tongue glides to the top of the slit of my sex, and then he flicks it over my clitoris.

I stiffen as fire rushes through me. "Um—"

"Feel good?"

"Uhhh." I can't think of a coherent thing to say. I push at his head because I want it back there again. That's where the fire is.

"Sweet Daisy," he murmurs. "Now I make you come." When he bends his head low again, I am filled with anticipation so sharp that it aches.

But instead of flicking his tongue across my clit this time, he puts his lips against it and sucks firmly.

I cry out, shocked at how good it feels. My hands flutter over his hair; I need to hold on to something to anchor myself, and I'm afraid I'll tug every lock of hair out of his head if I keep touching him. So even as I spread my legs wider, I brace myself against the car door. The intensity is almost too much, but he doesn't lift his head. He just keeps sucking, and occasionally he flicks his tongue against my clitoris.

I don't notice that his hands are moving until I feel one finger press at the base of my cunt, to the center of my core. It's big and thick, and I gasp when he pushes forward. It feels as if he's searing his way inside my body.

"Be calm," he tells me just before he presses his tongue to my clit again. "Let me pleasure you." And his finger presses deeper until it's seated deep inside me.

Now I am moaning and writhing at the onslaught of sensation. In all the times I have touched myself, I have focused on my clitoris, never like this. Even as his tongue presses against my clit in a teasing, circular pattern that makes me mad, his finger presses deeper. There's an aching burn and a tightness, but it feels so good that I don't even think about asking him to stop. I bear down on his hand, unable to stop my hips from moving or stifle the soft cries that fill my throat. It's building now. The intense pleasure I was wondering about? It's arrived, and it's every bit as wonderful as I imagined.

"So tight," he tells me. "*Bozhe moi.*" His murmurs of Russian platitudes are stifled when he flicks at my clit again with his tongue. I feel another finger join the first, and I feel impossibly stretched, to the point that it's painful.

But I don't want him to stop.

I throw my head back as I mindlessly say his name over and over again. My eyes are closed—I can't watch him anymore, because it makes things too intense, and my senses can't handle his beautiful face cradled between my legs, those long lashes fanning over intense eyes focused entirely on pleasuring me.

His tongue's not stopping now, pressing faster and faster against my clit in a steady pattern that is as maddening as it is wonderful. My hips rise to meet his mouth, and I'm pushing up against him, even as my hand is braced against the car door for support. It's the only thing keeping me from collapsing. My entire body is stiffening, and I feel it building, that warm, delicious curling sensation that I need more of but don't know how to get. All I know is that I'm getting closer.

His fingers pull out from my warmth, and I feel an aching, momentary loss. Before I can protest, he sinks them deep again. There is a stabbing ache followed by a blissful shot of pleasure that moves right through me, and the curling need increases.

Nick thrusts again with his fingers, and I am there.

Fireworks.

I am shuddering and gasping, on fire from the pulsing intensity of my orgasm. I cry out his name, and I am lost. Heaven. Pure heaven, and Nick has given it to me.

I will never be the same again.

CHAPTER **NINE**

DAISY

Now that I have opened a Pandora's box, I can't go back to the sleep of an innocent. My dreams that night were filled with Nick's face, Nick's hands, Nick's mouth. When I wake up, I am restless and panting.

And when I move through my day, he is ever-present in my mind, an intriguing puzzle I intend to figure out. I sleepwalk through a late breakfast and clean our apartment and buy groceries—all the while Regan lays on the couch, nursing a hangover. She texted me late last night, asking if I was okay. I told her I met Nick and got a ride home, and that seemed to satisfy her.

If only she knew what had gone on in the car.

I am scandalized and titillated by what happened. Prior to last night, I only dreamed of what occurs with a man, but now I have so much more knowledge, so many wicked things to consider.

I touched his penis. I made him come. And then he pleasured

me with his mouth—only his mouth, because I wasn't ready for more.

I'm still not ready for more, not yet. I like teasing around the edges, playing with the concept of sex without going all in. Of course, I say this in the light of day; last night after our steamy session in the car, Nick walked me to my door and gave me a chaste kiss. I'd been the one to cling to him and beg him to come inside with me so we could explore more.

He'd turned me down. I'd said I wasn't ready, and he would honor that.

I think of him when my phone buzzes, and I toss the sponge down on the now-clean kitchen counter and run to my room to answer it in private.

To my disappointment, it is work. Craig has texted me. Had a no-show. Can you come in early?

I can't afford to say no, though I am secretly hoping that Nick will ask me on another date of some kind. I sigh and text back. Of course. What time?

Six. Will pay overtime.

Thank you.

I have two hours before I have to go in to work. It's not enough time to do anything, except perhaps more cleaning. And there is no text from Nick, which makes me feel odd and anxious at the same time. Did I go too far with him? Does he no longer respect me because I am slutty when he touches me? Should I play coy? I don't know how relationships work; my father only let me watch children's television shows, and all the romance novels I read were stories from a different century. In those, the women are all impoverished heiresses and the men are all rakish dukes.

I feel too sheltered. Regan and Mike are casually sexual, but there is an undercurrent of unhappiness in their relationship. I don't want to copy it.

But I can't understand why Nick isn't texting me. It must be something I did.

I move to my window and open it wider, leaning out and enjoying the breeze on my face. The sunlight is pure and crisp, the weather gorgeous. I love the sun. I turn my face toward it and sigh with pleasure, and then I scan the street below with interest. There are cars moving along the street in busy lines, and people walk down the sidewalk, bags in hand. It is a normal day.

My gaze slides to the apartment building across the street, and I think about what Nick told me last night. He doesn't live in this building. I haven't given it much thought until now. I stare at the windows on the other side thoughtfully, trying to see a face behind the glass, but there is nothing.

I was driving past and saw you on the street, he said last night.

I know it's a lie. He can't always be driving and conveniently running in to me. I consider this for a moment, and then head to my bed. I sit on the edge and regard my phone. The phone he purchased for me. I pick it up, hesitate, and then make up my mind.

I text him. You're watching me, aren't you? That's how you knew where I was last night.

His answer is swift, which means he has his phone close by and is watching it. Does this bother you?

It bothers me more that he has not texted me until now.

Are you mad at me?, I send. It's needy and ridiculous, but I can't help myself. The only man I know how to deal with is my father, and he made his frustration known by angry words. I can't handle silence.

Never, Nick sends back.

D8Z: Then why the silence?

Nick: I wanted to give you space in case you had regrets or you feel I push you too hard.

The only thing I regret was that I was too scared to do more. But I don't tell him this. I'm just relieved he's not unhappy with me.

D8Z: I want to know if you're watching me, Nick.

Nick: And again, I must ask. Does this bother you?

I consider this. I should be furious, but I'm not. Perhaps because his intervention last night was so timely? I can't be mad if he has protected me with his watching. Still, I want to know the why of it.

D8Z: I suppose it depends on what the purpose is.

Nick: Purpose? Must there be one?

D8Z: Why else would you watch a total stranger? I assume you've been watching me for a while? Since before we met?

Nick: You are clever, my Daisy. And I am a poor liar. Da, I watch you. I saw you and thought you were the most beautiful creature I have ever seen. I cannot stop myself from watching and wondering about you. Never did I think to actually speak with you, though. Have I frightened you?

D8Z: Should I be frightened of you?

Nick: I would never hurt you. Never. I only wish to protect.

This seems to align with what I know of Nick. I think back, realizing that if his intentions were bad, he could have hurt me that day in the laundry room. Instead, he took me shopping and bought me expensive things. I'm wearing a pair of the panties he bought me right now, and my hand flutters to the waist of my jeans in thought.

Nick: I have scared you, haven't I?

I consider this. I know it's not normal for a man to watch someone from afar, but Nick has been my closest and truest friend since I arrived. I am fascinated and besotted with him. I'm not mad. I'm not entirely comfortable, but I'm not mad.

D8Z: Which window is yours? In the other building?

Nick: I will show you. Look for blue.

He's there even now? Is he watching me? I lick my lips, ashamed to feel my nipples harden and the flesh between my legs grow wet with arousal. I peer out the window, looking. Then, I see it. It is a window with the shades tightly drawn, directly across from mine. The blue is the merest hint . . .

And I blush to realize the blue is my panties that he had taken from me last night.

D8Z: How often do you watch me? What do you see?

Nick: I see treasure beyond value. I see beauty without compare. I see your every gesture exudes pleasure and joy in even smallest things. I see delight in simply existing. I see you, Daisy.

Heat curls through me at his words. Oh, my. I know he's trying to redirect me with flattery, and it's working. I'm breathless at his romantic text.

D8Z: Are you watching me now?

Nick: Da. Do you want me to stop? For you, I will. I do not wish to make you uncomfortable. I treasure your opinion above all things.

It's on the tip of my tongue to tell him "yes, stop," when I realize I am breathing shallowly with excitement. The fact that he watches me feels naughty and wicked, and I love the feeling. It's scandalous to consider, and I think that is why I enjoy it so much. I do want him to keep watching me . . . but I want it to be on my terms.

D8Z: We need a signal, I think. If you're going to watch me, let me know first.

Nick: Anything you desire, kitten. I am yours to command.

D8Z: My father and I had a signal when we knocked on the front door or called, so we knew who it was. I want a signal to know you're there. So I know.

I am in control, I realize. If I don't want Nick to watch, I can shut my window. I can tell him to stop. I think he would. For the first time in my life, I am running the show, and I feel heady with the power of it. I control Nick's happiness with a mere thought.

It is all at my discretion entirely. Knowing he watches me changes nothing . . . except perhaps it makes me aroused to think he's watching me, even now. My hand touches the waistband of my jeans again, and I think of stripping them off in front of my window, all so he can see from afar.

Will he come in his pants again at the sight?

My breath catches; I am panting, and my nipples ache. I want to tell him to come over so we can explore sex some more, but it's not a good idea. I have to work tonight, and if he comes over, I won't want him to leave.

Across the street, at Nick's window, the blinds open a bit, and there is a bright flash, like that of a mirror reflecting light. It flicks once, twice.

Nick: That is my signal to you. Anytime you are curious if I watch, look out your window. If I am, I will give you a signal.

D8Z: I see it.

I see it, and I wonder how much of me he sees. I smile at the window and touch my fingers to the glass as if to say hello.

Nick: I wish your hand was on me and not the window, dasha. Meet me tonight.

D8Z: I can't. I'm working.

Nick: Tell them you quit. It is not good job for you.

I shake my head at the window, as if to silently say, "I'm not quitting." Always, he suggests I quit, and I ignore it. He doesn't know what it's like to see two twenties in your wallet and realize there is no more coming in. I text him again, not wanting to change the subject.

D8Z: So if I ask you to stop watching me, you would?

Nick: Always. You mean more to me than anything.

His words make me warm, and they fill me with pleasure.

D8Z: I'll let you know if I want you to stop. I'm only allowing this because I like the thought of you watching me.

Nick: Oh? You like it?

I grow bold and smile at the window. I'm incredibly aroused at the moment. I keep thinking of last night, the hot feel of his flesh under my hand. I can't wait to experience that again. I decide I want to play with Nick, leave him wanting me and distracted.

I face the window, and my hand slides to my breast. I cup it, picturing his hand there, and gasp at how good it feels to tease my own nipple.

And then I look at my phone, waiting for a response from him.

It comes an eternal moment later.

Nick: Daisy . . . do you tease me?

I feel a sense of glee mixed with my desire. He's realized what I'm up to. Want me to give you something to watch, I text back, feeling so bold and pleased with myself. I want to do this. I'm nervous but excited at the same time.

It takes an agonizing year for his text to come back, but it returns.

Nick: Nothing would give me more pleasure than to see you touch yourself for me. Words cannot describe what I am feeling right now.

My breathing comes shallow and thin, and it's rasping with

excitement. I think of Nick touching himself as he watches me. Does he have binoculars? Is he holding them in one hand and grasping his penis with the other? I shudder at the thought of that and pull my T-shirt off before I can second-guess myself and let shyness take over. I'm wearing one of my new bras, and it's lacy and white and so pretty that I feel sexy just wearing it. I'm glad I chose it today, and I bite my lip as I ease one strap down my shoulder, my other hand still clutching my phone.

Nick: Bare your breasts for me, dasha, please. I want to see you touch them.

D8Z: Only if you promise to touch yourself, too.

Nick: Yes.

That one single word fuels my imagination, and I slide my bra down my shoulder all the way. My face is burning with shyness even as my body hums with excitement. For some reason, this is easier than the thought of undressing in front of Nick if he were here in person. It allows me to be bolder. The air caresses my now-bared breast, and my nipple is erect, the peak tight and aching. I still cling to my phone in the one hand, but the other is free, and I graze my fingertips over my breast, thinking of last night.

I want to show him more than just my breast. I face the window and tease my nipple a moment longer, and then I slide my hand to my jeans, asking a silent question.

My phone vibrates with another text immediately.

Nick: Show me.

A shuddering breath escapes me, and I set the phone down on my bed so I can have both hands free to unclasp my jeans. I wiggle out of them and kick them aside. I am standing in my room, in front of my window, in nothing but my panties and my bra, one breast exposed. I bite my lip, considering. I am on the second floor. Can anyone see me but Nick? Do I care? I'll never know if they do. Nick's responses are gratifying, though. With shaking fingers, I slide my panties down my legs, strip my bra off, and then wait to see Nick's response.

My phone vibrates on the bed, and I turn to it.

Nick: Touch yourself, kitten. Show me where you liked my mouth.

I suck in a breath at his words. It's one thing to tease him with the thought of touching myself, and it's another to see it written down, realizing he is, in fact, riveted to my every move. I leave the phone on the bed, and my hands pluck at my nipples, wishing they were his mouth, his hands. I'm not content with just touching my breasts, though it's sending little jolts of pleasure through my body. I know he will want to see more.

So I let one hand slide to my belly, and then lower.

My fingers brush the curls of my sex. I'm already incredibly slick, the moisture dampening the hair there. I gasp to feel the fluid there, and a racking shudder rips through me when I brush over my clit. His mouth lingered here last night, sucking and licking, and I remember it. I remember how his mouth gleamed when he looked up at me. I wonder if he liked my taste.

My wet fingers go to my mouth, and I paint my lips with the juices of my sex, knowing that he watches. Will he find that erotic? I taste my own musk and think of him, even as my fingers dip to my sex again. I can't slide a finger inside myself while standing, not like he did to me last night, so I pet and soothe my clit, rubbing the wetness back and forth even as my other hand plays with my nipple.

I'm so aroused that when my phone vibrates on the bed, I come instantly, knowing that he just texted me again. It's like the message is the catalyst, and I'm shivering with my quick, hard release. It leaves me aching for only more, though, and I feel momentarily sad that he's not here and is instead watching me across the way.

I wish Nick were here.

I wipe my sex-wet hands on an old T-shirt and toss it into the laundry, and then I pick up my phone to see Nick's text.

Nick: Again, you make me come in my pants.

D8Z: I'm glad. I like the thought of being so irresistible.

I curl up on my bed and slide under the covers with my phone, feeling languid and peaceful. If Nick can't be here, the phone is my connection to him. If I can't be under the covers with him, I'll be under the covers with the phone.

Nick: Ah, Daisy. You are too good for one such as me. Why you even speak to me, I do not know. I do not deserve such a gift.

D8Z: Silly man. I like this relationship, Nick. I like you, and I like that you let me control things. You let me steer. It makes me feel strong. Unafraid. That is the best feeling in the world.

Nick: You wish to be driving us, kotehok? I will let you drive the Ducati the next time I see you. Would you like that?

D8Z: I . . . don't know how to drive.

I'm ashamed to admit it. It's one of the things my father never let me learn because he wouldn't leave the house to show me, and going to a driver's education class would have meant interacting with a class full of others, and the thought was anathema to my agoraphobic father. I think, also, it was part of his way of keeping me trapped at his side. I'm excited by just the prospect of exchanging my state-issued identification card for a real driver's license. It is a skill I lack, and one I haven't had the courage to admit to Regan yet because I'm afraid she might laugh at me for being so backward.

Nick: Then I will show you, little flower. And then you will drive me everywhere, da?

I smile at my phone.

D8Z: Da. :)

NIKOLAI

"So, *dasha*, you don't know how to drive. This is easy." I point out the pedals. "The big one is stop and the little long one is go. Press both softly at first, until it feels right to you."

"All my firsts are with you," she says, giving me a sly little grin.

I like that. My cock likes it, too, and I want to pull her hand over to touch my hardness, but I think it is too soon for that. She is not a whore to be ordered about. She likes to be in charge, and I am happy to wait for her direction, but eventually I will show her how much pleasure she brings to me. "No one else would treasure you like I."

"No one?" She arches her brow now.

It is not arrogance that drives me, but possessiveness. I am afraid she wouldn't like either, so I simply shrug.

"What if someone else would . . ." She pauses and thinks for a moment. My frame tenses up, but she says, "Teach me to drive?"

"*Nyet*, I would not like that."

"What would've happened if one of my customers had touched me? You seem upset when you come to the station."

"I would have killed him."

"Ha. Ha." She sounds out each syllable so that it is not a laugh but a mocking sound. "No, seriously."

I look at her steadily. No, I think, no joke. I would cut off the hand of a man who touches you. I'd start by sawing off each finger slowly, because death ends the suffering. He'd need to suffer.

When her eyes dim and her countenance takes on a worried look, I say, "Kidding."

Only I think we both know I am not.

She turns to start the car.

"Push in the brake, then press the button. Wait for the engine to engage."

She follows my instructions.

"Ease up on the brake."

The car jerks forward as she releases the brake—too swiftly—and then engages it in a rush. We both jerk forward.

"Sorry, sorry," she rushes to apologize.

"It is nothing. Just, gently."

The second time, it is smoother, and she begins to make big circles around the empty parking lot. We practice braking, turning, and accelerating slowly, and then more swiftly. In no time she is maneuvering the rental with ease. Perhaps another time we will try the bike. I wonder what else I can teach her—what other firsts I can show her.

My time with her might end swiftly, but I want her to remember me. The more firsts I experience with her, the longer I will be imprinted in her mind. Enough firsts and she will never forget me.

Time passes quickly, and we stop only because I hear her stomach grumble. She protests when I pay for her meal, but I ignore her protests.

"What else do you want to learn?" I ask as we gulp down sandwiches. Daisy wants to return to the vehicle, and I want to make Daisy happy.

She shrugs and beams a happy smile at me. "God, everything."

A thought strikes me. A woman alone in the city should be a woman armed. I will teach Daisy to shoot a gun. It is one area in which I have extensive expertise. "Let's go to the country," I say.

"You can drive out there on the long roads and practice at a faster speed."

Daisy beams at me. This is a good idea, I can tell. Better than a picnic. I will tell Daniel next time we talk that his skills with women are outdated.

I lead Daisy to the passenger side of the car. "When we get away from traffic, you can take over."

Inside the car and on our way west of the city, I broach the topic. "Perhaps another time, I could teach you to handle a firearm. I am worried about you alone at night at the gas station."

Daisy laughs at this suggestion. "I actually know how to shoot a gun already."

I shoot her a look of surprise. This is not the response I expected. It is not that I've never seen a woman handle a weapon. There are women who do the work I do, and there are women in the *Bratva*, mostly those who trade in sexual favors, but plenty can handle a knife with ease and guns are plentiful.

"My dad taught me." Daisy is subdued. Her eyes go distant, sad.

I sit straighter, as I know little about Daisy's past. I only know her present. That she is alone, poor, and with few resources and no family—or so I thought.

"What happened that he would do that?"

At first she shrugs, a French, enigmatic shrug that could mean many things. "I lived on a farm. In this direction actually." She waves her hand out the windshield down the long highway road we are taking.

"Fathers teach all their daughters to shoot on a farm?" I ask. I know only a few agrarian families and, now that I think about it, they probably all can shoot a rifle.

"Varmints," she says quietly. Sensing she has something more to say, I wait and soon my patience is rewarded. "My mother was killed by a stranger. Or, at least we think it was a stranger. He's out now. Served two years in juvie."

Out of all the stories I imagine Daisy sharing with me, none was this one. "Your mother was shot?"

My imagination gallops away from me. Was she involved in some criminal activity? Did she steal something?

"I know. It sounds unbelievable, right?" Her voice is choked up, and I want to pull over and comfort her. Instead, I can only reach out and squeeze one of her hands.

She returns my grip and holds my hand between both of hers. "My dad and I don't know why it was her. When he got out of juvie, the murderer sought my father out and said he was next. It changed my life. My dad is afraid to leave the house. He took me out of school, and we became hermits. One day he brought me downstairs to the basement. He'd set up a seven-yard shooting range down there with a barrier made of hundreds of phone books, which I guess were destined for the recycling station. For months, I went down every night and shot a gun into the wall of phone books."

"What gun?"

"Baby Glock."

"That's a good gun. A .38?"

She nods. "You know a lot about guns."

"I did a job once," I say vaguely. Still truthful. "I'm sorry about your mother and your father. And he only served two years?"

"He was a minor, and he pled it down to involuntary because he was high on meth." Daisy looks down, and I feel wet, hot tears splash onto our joined hands. "They were lenient, even though he took my mom away from us."

My heart aches for her. When I am done with this job for Sergei, when I bring retribution to Sergei's house, I will return and find this man and kill him for Daisy. We may never be together again, but I will do this. I vow it silently. For now, all I can do is comfort Daisy in her time of need. I pull over onto a side road. Unbuckling my seat belt, I reach over and pull Daisy onto my lap. She hugs me, but only for a moment before she pushes back.

"Thanks. I don't know why I got so emotional." She swipes away the tears with the back of her hands.

"There is no need for apologies. Your response is normal," I assure her, rubbing her back in steady, firm strokes.

She tilts her head and smiles at me. "Is there no emotional response that will make you uneasy?"

"None from you." I lean forward and kiss the base of her throat. Her pulse flutters in response. "I want all of your emotions." All of them. I treasure even her anger. Indifference is what I fear.

Daisy melts against my chest, and it is not sexual desire she arouses in me this time, but fierce protectiveness. I hug her and then say, "Do you want to drive now?"

She nods her head and takes the wheel.

We drive for a long time, and I tell her about my time watching the curator. Not that he had a predilection for young boys, but the art that he managed and how it spoke to me in ways that surprised me.

"I'd love to see art like that," Daisy says. "I've only seen pictures of it. My father regulated everything in my life, even my connection to the Internet."

I begin to understand why she is so innocent, and I fear for her.

"Do you still have a gun?"

"No, I left it at the farm."

"I will buy you one then." Tomorrow we will go and get one.

Or I would get one. There were always guns on the street for purchase. The weapons I have are too big for her delicate hands.

"You can't keep buying stuff for me," Daisy says with exasperation.

"Why not?" Harold's girls vied for his gifts more than they wanted his attention. Even the whores were more interested in my pocketbook than the actual fucking we did. This I did not understand about Daisy. "I have money. It is of no consequence the purchase of a gun."

Daisy shakes her head. "If you have so much money, then why are you living in a dump across the street from me?"

I tell her a little truth. "I am, what you say, investigating someone."

"Oh my God, are you spying on someone? Like a guy who is cheating on his wife?" Recognition gleams in her eyes. "That's how you started watching me, right?"

"I am observing someone. He has taken money from someone I work for. That someone would like it back."

Silence fills the car, and I wonder what it is that Daisy is processing. Does she understand the ominous tone of my words? But no, she surprises me again. "He must be an awful man, to steal money from someone."

"*Da.*"

She flushes, but then shrugs. "I guess watching me is pretty boring compared to that."

"Never."

"Never?" She laughs. "All I do is sleep and then go to work at the gas station."

"I do not like that place," I announce. "Bad things will happen there."

She rolls her eyes at me, as this is an argument we have had before. "I told you Craig, the owner, lives right down the street."

I shift in my seat but she is not looking at me. "There are bars on the windows. That tells you it is dangerous. Safe places do not have bars."

"I need the money," she says, her chin firmly set.

I heave a sigh and rub the side of my neck. Patience, I tell myself. "I cannot watch you all the time."

"I've never asked you to!" she exclaims in a frustrated voice.

I am equally frustrated. "One day I will not be there, and the man down the street will not be home, and someone will come and try to hurt you."

"What's my alternative, Nick? To not work? Sit at home and let a man take care of me?"

Yes, I would like that, but even a man as dumb as I knows better than to give voice to that sentiment. "Perhaps we can find you another job. At a library or a museum."

Daisy's face falls, and she looks dismayed. "My resume is a big blank, Nick. I don't have schooling, and I don't have work history. No one at a museum would hire me. I don't have the skills for anything like that."

"I didn't realize that there were skills you needed for that," I admit.

"There are." She is abrupt in her response. "It's not like I want to work at the gas station. It's that at the age of twenty-one, the only job I can get is working at a gas station."

She sounds frustrated and resigned, and I am helpless in this situation. I can give her money, but she will not accept it. I cannot give her a job. I have few marketable skills myself outside of a military organization.

I am restless after my drive with Daisy. There are loose ends that need to be taken care of. The accountant. Sergei. Daisy is making me think of the future when before I'd only considered life on a day-to-day basis, moving from one job to another. In between tasks, I spent time perfecting my craft. Firing my weapons and honing my body. I read some, visited museums, slept with whores. That life has made me ill equipped to do anything useful.

I am not even certain of the full extent of my accumulated wealth. I do not live expensively, but neither do I own anything, preferring to live out of hotels and rentals. My bank balance is very healthy, but I've never done anything with it.

Not only do I have no real skills outside of killing people, I'm not educated, even though I try to brush on a patina of learning through my reading of books—mostly strategic military tomes and the few classics like Henry James—and my visits to art houses.

I have so little of worth to offer Daisy. That I could buy her a phone or a few pieces of clothing or even pay her rent is the only thing I can provide, and she rejects even that. I want something more with Daisy. I want, perhaps, to not kill anymore. To live with her in a tiny apartment and eat food made by her hands and make love to her every evening. And maybe some mornings. Also afternoons.

But I cannot make love to Daisy until this matter with Sergei is resolved. It is time to settle these issues so that I can lie down with Daisy without fear of danger to her and me.

I WATCH MY MARK. MR. Brown is moving around his apartment getting ready for bed. Either I've missed his daily perversion, or he is too tired for that nonsense tonight. He heads for the bed, and the dog trots obediently behind. I wonder if the dog would attack Mr. Brown if it were allowed to, like the pack of boys had attacked the Milan curator.

The uncomfortable silence in my apartment is interrupted by a chime from the second bedroom. I consider ignoring it, but then think it may be Daniel.

"Allo," I answer.

"Nikolai." Not Daniel. Sergei. The head of the *Bratva*. His voice is nearly unaccented. He told me once that accents are as dangerous as fingerprints and that an accent will always give away your history and ultimately lead your enemies to your family. I had no family, I told Sergei. He clapped me on the shoulder and replied that he knew, and that's why I was the perfect weapon.

Perhaps it is why he felt he could kill Alexsandr without a second thought. Sergei believed that I was a machine, a gun that Alexsandr pointed and fired. And now that Alexsandr was dead, he believes that I am a weapon that Sergei now controls.

I have done nothing to disabuse Sergei of this notion. In truth, I am doing Sergei's bidding right now. Tracking this errant accountant and then disposing of him.

"Sergei. What is it that you need?" I wonder if he has cleaned up the bodies left at the Palisades. That must have been a mess.

"I was wondering whether you have heard about the passing of our friend Bogdan. He was in Los Angeles taking care of a problem for me and wasn't able to follow through due to some digestive problems."

"Bogdan always drank too much. His liver give out?" I ask.

"Liver and heart. Actually, an all-organ failure," Sergei replies.

I click my tongue against the roof of my mouth. "That's too bad."

"Bogdan's young wife is full of distress. You know she is pregnant."

"I did not." This I did not want to hear. "Bogdan lived a dangerous life. She was unaware?"

"No, she was aware. I think she didn't know the extent of his debts, however." Sergei's voice was light and smooth. He was probably imagining with glee all the things he would require of this young widow.

My nostrils flare in disgust. Sergei should be eliminated for the mere offense of being a cliché. As a soldier in the *Bratva*, Sergei once held himself to strict standards. Once he was the leader, he fell victim to the power and what he viewed as the spoils due a victor. Forcing himself on a grieving widow would be exciting for Sergei. That she would resist him would be like an extra serving of dessert.

He once raped two sisters, forcing the father who owed him no more than a few thousand American dollars to watch. Sergei had laughed like a movie villain. I wanted to kill him then, but instead, I squeezed the carotid of the father until he passed out and then discharged my gun into the ground. Sergei was bigger than me at the time and eighteen to my fourteen, but I was more feral. He stopped, but hate had burned in his eyes.

"You do not like this?" Sergei asks, prompting a response.

"It is not my place to render a judgment." My non-answer is all the reply we both need. "But I do not think you call about Bogdan."

"Nikolai, you were never one for small talk, which is why you are still a soldier in the *Bratva* and not a leader."

"I'm not part of the *Bratva*," I correct him. "I have not been part of it since I was fifteen." That was how old I was when Alexsandr kicked me out. At the time I was hurt, but in the past weeks I've wondered if this was Alexsandr's biggest sacrifice and the most generous action he could have ever taken. Bogdan wanted out and could not leave. Sergei would've eventually wanted to punish me for putting a stop to his activities. Alexsandr made me leave, and in doing so gave me freedom.

"Once a part of *Bratva*, always part of *Bratva*," Sergei sneers.

I smile into the phone at the sound of his temper. Another sign of Sergei's weakness. He does not deserve the power that he's been given, but Alexsandr did not want to lead, and Sergei was Petrovich's nephew and the oldest male progeny of the Petrovich family. The responsibility fell on his shoulders, but he did not wear the mantle well. The *Bratva* would be in pieces within ten years.

While some may believe that criminal organizations should never exist, the Petrovich family serves an important role. There are many families that relied on the income the *Bratva* generates, and if it is not Sergei controlling the flow of guns, illegal substances, and secrets, it will be someone else. Crime does not go away. It can only be contained.

I remain silent, however, because Sergei does have power and the resources of the *Bratva* at his disposal. There were some who believed in the structure of the family with religious fervor; they were good people and they would do Sergei's bidding without question because he was the head of the family now.

It does not pay to unduly antagonize Sergei, particularly when I suspect that he is calling me because I am taking far too long with the accountant, Mr. Brown. His next words confirm this.

"This job is taking up months of your time. It is extraordinary. Is our accountant really that clever of a man?" Sergei asks. *Clever enough to steal millions from you*, I think, but know better than to say this.

"It's a delicate job. I do not want to draw the wrong attention."

"Just drug him and bring him back," Sergei commands.

"Do you want someone else to do this job?" I ask.

I hear Sergei breathing heavily and then a sharp sound as if he is striking his wooden desk with something. "*Khuilo.*" Fucker, he calls me, but he tries to make it sound like a laugh. We both know he is not joking.

I wait.

"Give me a timeline then. When will you be done? I have other tasks for you."

I shrug, but he cannot see it. "You are not the only contract I take. I have a job I will be doing after. Then, I will see."

"You little pissant, you listen to me." Sergei has lost control now. He is yelling. All pretense is over. "You were born in the gutter to *pizda,* and the *Bratva* took you in and made you what you are today. We own you."

"Calling my dead mother a cunt is not going to make this job go faster," I respond mildly, but I am gripping the table so tightly that the edging is cutting me and blood is beginning to loosen my hold.

Sergei curses again. "*Pizdets na khui blyad!* I know where you are, and if you don't get this job done within the next week, you'll be the mark."

Fucking load of bullshit? That's all he had in the barrel for me? I felt insulted by his lack of creative invectives, but the thought that he knows where I am concerns me. I'd need to finish up with Mr. Brown just to ensure Daisy's safety. I didn't need a better version of Bogdan coming to town.

I needed to see Daisy shoot a gun. I needed to make sure she had one.

Later, I followed Daisy to work that night to ensure that she was safely ensconced inside. Outside, I find the exterior satellite feed cables and attach a tap so that I can monitor the security feeds remotely. I should've done this weeks ago. Feeling a little better about Daisy's safety, I head to her apartment complex. Mr. Brown is waiting for me.

I don't bother knocking. The door opens easily for me, and I know from a previous search that Mr. Brown has only one weapon, which he keeps in his bedside table. Why allow intruders to get so far into the residence before being able to mount a defense? It makes no sense to me. I have trip wires on the door, so easy to set up with a few cans or bells and very hard to disable unless you are already inside. They are low-tech safety measures that Mr. Brown couldn't be moved to employ. His loss.

Even his small dog could not be moved to provide any defense, because Mr. Brown insists on the dog being locked inside the bedroom with him. The front rooms of the apartment are dark, which allows me to slip inside and move around undetected. I pull the rickety shades and carry an uncomfortable metal chair into the living room. Mr. Brown will sit here, and I will stand.

There is no surface I feel comfortable touching, even with my gloves on. "Mr. Brown," I call, "You have a visitor."

The sound of my voice awakens the dog, and soon the dog wakes Mr. Brown. I stand in the corner—in case Mr. Brown decides to shoot first and ask questions later—but it is just an outsized precaution. Mr. Brown likely has never pulled any trigger, unlike Daisy.

"Who is it, Peanut?"

Peanut? I shudder at the grotesqueness of the dog's name, given Mr. Brown's perversions. The dog trots out obediently and comes up and yips at me. I kneel down and give the dog one of his special treats. Over my head, I hear the whistle of a bullet followed by a sharp retort.

My eyebrows climb my forehead. Mr. Brown has actually

shot at me, and because I bent over to feed the dog, I've avoided having to dodge a bullet. I remain crouched. My eyes are adjusted to the night, so it is easy for me to see him waving the gun around. I will have to disarm him.

I give Peanut a final pat and move stealthily to creep around Mr. Brown. He does not sense me, and I'm able to easily rise up behind him and remove his gun from his hand. The gun is small and lightweight. Perhaps I will give Daisy Mr. Brown's gun. But no, Daisy shouldn't be touching filth belonging to Mr. Brown.

I wave the gun toward the chair. "Please, Mr. Brown, sit down."

"I'm not Mr. Brown. You have the wrong person," he says, but he obeys nonetheless.

"George Franklin, formerly an employee of the Petrovich *Bratva*? Currently on the run and in hiding?"

Mr. Brown gasps and then begins to plead with me. "What do you want? I have money. Lots of money. I'll give you anything."

These encounters are so similar that I wonder if there is some script that is handed out to criminals. In case of capture, use these bargaining tools. Alas, I must surmise that these work on occasion or the bribes wouldn't be offered.

"You do have some information I would like, Mr. Brown," I reply. "You managed the money for the *Bratva* and got stupidly greedy, but I don't care about that. What I care about is why Sergei had Alexsandr Krinkov terminated." I put up a hand to forestall any fakery. "I know it is not about Sergei's daughter."

Mr. Brown closes his mouth and then opens it again. "I'm not certain what it was about."

"Well, then." I lift Mr. Brown's gun up and chamber a bullet. "There is nothing with which to bargain."

"Wait, wait." He lifts his hands. "I heard them arguing about the cattle. Alexsandr didn't think the *Bratva* should be in that business. Guns and drugs, yes, humans, no."

I lower the gun and gesture for him to continue.

"Alexsandr said that the children were too much. He didn't want to be part of it and said that Sergei's uncle would never have participated."

"It is just the age, not the act itself that bothered Alexsandr?" Oh Alexsandr, our priorities are all so perverted.

Mr. Brown shakes his head. "I don't know. I didn't care. I was leaving. Now you have your information, you can leave, too." Mr. Brown is brazen in his requests, but why not?

"A little information share and you expect me to let you go? Who do you think sent me?"

"Sergei," Mr. Brown replies sullenly. He looks down at his feet, and then to his dog, who has not moved from my side.

"Do you think I can return to him and say that the job is not done without suffering consequences?" I shake my head at him. "Do not treat me like I am a foolish child."

"What do you want from me?" Mr. Brown holds his hands up in plea. "I'll give you anything."

"You are a man out of ideas, yes?"

"Yes!" He is willing to agree to anything right now.

"You have no contingency plan? You just thought you would take your money and run around the Midwest and that no one would find you?"

"Yes." Mr. Brown begins to cry and rock in his chair. "I've been on the run for so long. I stopped here because I was just so tired."

"So you give me the information that Sergei wants from you . . . because he did not ask for me to kill you, but to return you home to him."

This terrifies Mr. Brown. He hugs himself and sobs openly now. "Don't send me back. Just kill me now. Promise me."

I rub the inscription on my chest. Death is a mercy. This man understands. The end is merely the beginning. Staying alive when you are maimed, when your family is being tortured, when you are being tortured—all are worse than death. I bring mercy.

"I promise," I say. "I will return to Sergei and tell him that I had to put you down, but first you reveal the information to me that imperils Sergei. Tell me this information that is so important that you must be returned healthy and hale."

Mr. Brown begins to talk, and it is forty-five minutes before he is done.

I shoot him once in the temple. I will take the dog with me. I'm not certain what I will do with this dog, but I do not want to leave him here to eat out Mr. Brown's brains as dogs are wont to do.

I pick up Mr. Brown's body and lay him in the tub. There I pour a mixture of sulfuric acid and hydrogen peroxide that will eat away at Mr. Brown's body until all that is left are his bones. The lack of obvious decay will ensure that Mr. Brown's body is not found for some time. I pay his rent for three months in advance.

It will buy me some time with Daisy. Three months to figure out what I should do with her.

In my own apartment, I burn my clothes—the gloves, pants, shirt and skull cap—in my own bathtub. The porcelain is remarkably hardy, and the smell of cotton and wool burning is not unpleasant. Afterward, I shower off the residue of gunpowder, smoke, and ashes.

I give the dog a pat on the head and go to check on the security feed of Daisy's gas station that I have hacked into. She is sitting on a stool, looking through a magazine. No one appears to have harmed her. Perhaps Daisy is right. She is fine.

Briefly, I wonder if she will miss her neighbor, but she has not mentioned him even once. I continue to watch her until her shift is nearing an end. I pour out some dog food for Mr. Brown's dog. He needs a new name. I cannot call him Peanut. The thought makes my stomach revolt in disgust. The dog is uncertain at first, but after pissing in two corners, he decides that my soulless apartment is just as good as Mr. Brown's. Cleaning up after the dog, I wonder what I will do with him. Perhaps Daisy would like a pet.

The rest of the night hours pass uneventfully.

As her shift nears its end, I trot down to the Ducati and speed off to pick her up.

"Hey, Nick." She seems pleased to see me, all bright smiles. "I didn't think I'd see you."

"Why not?" I am offended. Did I not tell her that I would watch out for her?

"I'm just surprised. Pleased, but surprised. I didn't get a text from you." She slings her leg over the back of the bike and tugs on her helmet. It is hard to talk to her while she is wearing it. I would need to buy those helmets with the mic capabilities.

I tug her close to me and pat her hands, which are folded over my abdomen. I am tired, and I suspect Daisy is tired. We both need to sleep, but I cannot sleep when I am worrying about her. When we arrive at her apartment, I broach the issue with her.

"Daisy, I am exhausted," I tell her honestly.

Her hand reaches out to brush against the skin under my eye. "You look it."

"You are tired, too, yes?"

She nods a little.

"Then let us sleep together. I cannot sleep without being next to you now. Not after." I pause meaningfully, and I am pleased when I see her blush. She understands then. "Just sleep, nothing more."

Daisy huffs a laugh and shakes her head. "I don't know if I should be offended that all you want to do is sleep."

"No offense is meant." I tell her. "I want you much, but we are both tired, and your first time should be when we are both fully rested. After, you will get no sleep for hours, maybe days."

This makes Daisy blush even harder, although it is nothing but the truth. Once I am inside her wet lushness, with her sweet cunt gripping my cock, I will not want to leave for days. We will need to arrange to have provisions brought to us every few hours, for I suspect that once I have Daisy, I will think of nothing else but having her again and again until our muscles are jelly and even the ability to think will have been suspended. But I cannot do this until the situation with Sergei is resolved. I cannot place Daisy in any danger, and thus I must remain vigilant at all times.

Daisy takes me by the hand, and I follow to her apartment. When she shuts the door, I pull out some string and ask her for a couple of cans or metal items.

"Why?"

"For safety," I respond honestly. She looks at me like my idea is full of craziness, so I tell her, "I will not be able to sleep if we cannot secure your residence."

"Nick, did you grow up in an unsafe neighborhood?"

"Yes." Truth. The streets were unsafe. In the *Bratva*, a non-Petrovich was a target until you could stand up for yourself. You needed to learn that skill quickly.

Daisy asks me no more questions. Instead, she digs around the trash and finds two metal cans. She rinses them out, and I dig a hole in the bottom of each with the little penknife on my keychain. The cans are strung together and rest at the top of the door.

"What about Regan?"

"If she leaves or returns, we will know. Just like with anyone." I want to keep track of everyone coming or going.

Daisy looks down the hall toward the bedrooms and then back up to the cans. It takes effort not to cover the area beneath my jacket where my gun resides.

"I think that there's a lot you should be telling me, Nick, or things I should be asking you about, but I'm too tired right now." She yawns even as she speaks this.

I nod, although at this point, I don't know what I am agreeing to. I spare a thought for the dog, but if he shits or pisses again, I will just clean it up. Tomorrow. All those things can be taken care of tomorrow.

"Come on," she says, and I follow her down to the bedroom.

I've seen it before, but being in Daisy's bedroom is completely different than staring at it through a scope. I run my fingers across the scarred wooden dresser that holds the clothes I've bought for her. I'm not sure who has slept on the bed before us, but I care not. All I know is that I will be cradling Daisy's body close to mine.

"Do you want clothes to sleep in? I don't have any, but maybe Regan's boyfriend has left something?"

I shake my head. "No, I can sleep in my T-shirt and jeans." I don't tell her that I'd rather be naked than touch his clothes.

Daisy picks out some clothes. I try to remember what we bought that would constitute nightwear. My blood heats when I think of the scraps of satin and lace that were in the lingerie department. I remove my jacket and hang it on the closet door. The gun is tucked between the mattress on the side of the bed closest to the door. I shuck off my boots but leave on my socks and belt. It will be easier to respond to threats the less clothing I have to don. I know Daisy is nervous, so I lie down in the bed, my hands tucked behind my head. And I wait.

CHAPTER **TEN**

DAISY

My mind is troubled as I head to the bathroom and change into a sleep shirt. It's soft and fuzzy, all warm and flannel. It's not cold in the house, but I feel obligated to Nick to wear thicker clothing to sleep in so I don't bother him. He looks exhausted and doesn't want to have sex, so I won't torment him by wearing one of the silky nighties I got when we went shopping together.

I exit the bathroom and give the cans strung above the door a quick look and then glance away as if they are no big deal. The sight of them bothers me. Not because they are there, but because they represent secrets. They make me think of my past with my father, and the many ways he had to ensure that we would never be surprised by intruders. I remember Bubble Wrap placed on windowsills.

I wonder if that is why I am so drawn to Nick—underneath it all, we are more alike than either of us realizes.

There are dark shadows under his eyes, but his gaze is watchful even as he relaxes in my bed. The frame is pushed against one wall, and Nick is lying on the outside. I will have to crawl over him to get into bed. I wonder if he does this on purpose because he wants to see me drag my body over his? The thought excites me, and I crawl into bed over him, blushing, my gaze averted. I lie stiffly, hoping, waiting for a furtive touch on my breasts, my sex.

But all he does is put an arm around my shoulders and draw me against him. My cheek rests on his shirt, and I lay a hand on his stomach.

"*Priyatnykh snov*," he says in Russian, and I guess he is wishing me pleasant dreams.

"Night," I murmur back to him, and he clicks off the light.

I listen to his breathing, my ear on his chest, but I'm wide awake. I can't possibly sleep with his big, firm body lying against mine. My hand is relaxed on his stomach, but I want to move it. I want to brush over his skin, feel the warmth of him, explore his body at my leisure.

But he's so tired. I don't want to bother him. I'm torn. I'm aching to explore him, but I'm frozen in place. It's like I've been offered the world and told not to touch.

His big hand strokes over my back. "What troubles you, *dasha*?"

"I'm fine."

Nick chuckles. "I can feel the stiffness in your body, little flower."

"Can I . . . should I get off you? I don't want to bother you." My hand smooths over his stomach, wishing I was feeling skin instead of fabric. "You need to sleep."

His arm tightens around me. "I enjoy the feel of your body against mine, Daisy. Your touch brings nothing but comfort. Now, relax."

I do, and my hand brushes over him in soft patterns as I wait for his breathing to even out. It does, and I am glad he has finally fallen asleep.

Ever so slowly, my hand creeps to the edge of his shirt. It is untucked. I am inches away from feeling bare skin, and it is a temptation I can't resist. My hand glides lower, and my fingertips graze warmth. His skin is scorching underneath my touch, but soft. So soft. I am riveted.

"Daisy," he murmurs, and his voice is thick.

I snatch my hand away, scalded by the sound of his voice. "I'm sorry. You're trying to sleep, and I'm bothering you."

He reaches over and grasps my hand again, replacing it on his lower stomach. "Do you want to touch me, Daisy? I will not object."

"I . . . you don't mind? I'm not going to keep you up?"

"I will not sleep, but *nyet*, I do not mind." His fingers caress my cheek. "How can I mind when my woman wishes to explore my body? It is not possible."

My hand lies on his stomach, unmoving for a long moment. I'm afraid to give in to my desires, feeling a bit put on the spot now that I know he is paying attention. In the end, though, my curiosity and my need win out, and I slide my hand fully under his shirt, pressing my palm to the warm flesh there.

Nick groans and shifts his hips, and I notice that the crotch of his jeans has risen. He's erect down there, all from my simple touch.

I'm fascinated by his erection and by the feel of his stomach under my hand. His skin is taut, and there are crisp hairs in a line down the center of his stomach. My hand has grown bolder, moving under his shirt, exploring. His belly button is a soft dip of skin surrounded by nothing but muscle. I trail my fingers along that line of hair, up and down, though I pause at the waistband of his jeans.

How much do I dare?

Nick takes that question out of my mind when, in the next moment, he reaches over my exploring hands and unbuttons his jeans. They have no zipper but five buttons, and I watch with amazement at the rapidity in which he dispatches them. Then his hand moves away again.

I see the stiff form of his cock pressing against the fabric of his underwear. As my fingers play with the hair below his belly button, I feel his breathing quicken. He's excited by my touch, and his excitement fuels mine, chasing away my shyness.

He likes my exploring, and that makes me bold.

I slide my hand to the bulge of his penis, and I stroke over the fabric-covered flesh. A low noise hisses from Nick's mouth, but he doesn't pull me away. He likes this. It makes me want to do more. I push at the fabric of his underwear, and the head of his cock is revealed.

It's thick and round, larger than I remembered it. The head glistens with a droplet beading the crown, and it makes me lick my lips. I remember the taste of him from last time, and I want more.

"Nick," I breathe, and my hand slides under the band of his underwear so I can grasp that heated rod of flesh. "Can I put my mouth on you?"

He mutters something in Russian, voice strained. His hand strokes my hair. "I am yours, little flower. Do anything you like."

"Will you like it?" I squeeze my fist around him, fascinated by how hard his length is, how hot and smooth and silky the delicate skin covering it is.

"*Da*," he says, and the word is thick. "I would love it."

I want it, then. I want to drive him crazy. I love the thought of my Nick losing control because of something that I've done to him. So I slide down his belly and move forward until I can brush my tongue against the head of his penis. I catch that droplet with my tongue, and I taste him. He is salty, the taste almost bitter, but strong. I am intrigued by it, and by the droplet that arrives to take its place immediately.

I tongue the head of his penis again, fascinated by the velvety texture of him against my tongue and by the way Nick goes all stiff with each motion of my tongue. I know that stiffness; it's a good one. It's a sign of him trying to keep control.

It's my goal to make him lose that control.

I press a kiss to the head of his sex, wanting to brush my lips over that impossibly soft skin. I like the feel of him against my lips. In the books I've read at the library, the heroine always takes the hero in her mouth and sucks on him. But it feels like there is too much of Nick to fit into my mouth. I ponder this even as I press small kisses to the head of his penis, letting my lips explore him gently. I don't want to do this wrong.

His hips shift again, and his penis brushes between my parted lips. If that's not an invitation, I don't know what is. I open my mouth wider, let my lips circle the head of it, and then I pull back, uncertain once more.

"Can I take your penis in my mouth, Nick?"

I look back at him for my answer, and his eyes are glittering in the darkness, his gaze intent on me. He gives me a small, jerking nod. "It is a cock, Daisy. A *khui*. Say that for me."

"*Khui*," I say. "I want to taste your *khui*."

I'm rewarded by his groan of pleasure, and his eyes close. I love that, the tension on his face, the way his body hums under mine. I'm the cause of this, and it's a delicious feeling. My hand tightens around the base of his penis—no, his cock, his *khui*— and I bend to take the head of it into my mouth again.

And I suck.

His breath hisses. "Teeth, Daisy—"

"Oh," I say. "I'm sorry. I didn't know—"

"It is okay, *dasha*." His hand soothes along my back, on the stupidly thick nightie I'm wearing. "A man's skin is sensitive there."

And he trusts me enough to let me put his cock into my mouth. I'm pleased. I open my mouth wider and take the head into my mouth again, this time letting it rest against my tongue. I turn my head and look to him for approval.

Nick only groans and brushes my long hair aside so he can see my mouth on him. "God have mercy, but you are beautiful."

He's so hard that I don't need to hold him to guide him into my mouth—the long, smooth curve of his cock seems to point right at it, and I gently suck on the head and move my mouth over it, exploring. I'm not sure how to do this, but I seem to be doing okay, if Nick's stiff body and softly muttered Russian epithets are any indication. But I'm not sure how to get him off. In the books, it's simply a process of putting a mouth to a penis and then the hero pulls the heroine away. Nick doesn't seem like he wants to pull me away.

And I'm having too much fun to leave.

So I change things up a little, and press small kisses to his cock in exploration. I move over the length of him, licking and nibbling with my lips. There is a vein on the underside of his cock, and I kiss it, too. The base of his cock is surrounded by springy, dark hair, and I find his balls oddly delicate. I'm not sure what to do with them, so I go back to his cock and begin at the head again.

I'm huddled over him in an awkward crouch, but I don't realize how close I am to pushing my bottom into the air until his hand slides over my backside, caressing and exploring. I suck in a breath when he pushes up my flannel nightie, exposing my panties, and his hand strokes over the seam of my buttocks and glides between my legs.

Oh, my legs are pressed too tightly together. I want his hand there. I shift on the bed and ease my knees apart so he can touch me again, if he wants to.

I hope he wants to.

I take the head of his cock into my mouth again and rub my tongue against it.

He groans once more, and his fingers glide along the silky line of my panties, heading back toward my sex. Unconsciously, I raise my hips, needing his touch. I'm distracted, my breath is coming as quick little pants as I tongue and lick at the head of his cock. I'm waiting for him to touch me, to rub me through my panties.

But he doesn't; instead, his fingers slide under the band of my panties, and I feel him glide one through the folds of my sex.

"*Bozhe moi*, Daisy. You're so fucking wet." I feel his finger searching for my opening, and then he thrusts it deep inside me.

I whimper, because it feels invasive . . . and yet good. I press back against his hand and my mouth flutters against his cock. The beads of arousal that drip down the head of his cock drag over my lips, wetting them, and I moan when his finger thrusts deep inside me again. What we're doing is so incredibly wicked . . . and delicious.

His finger thrusts inside me again, and I'm so wet that I hear the sound of his fingers moving in my panties. He mutters something else in Russian and then pulls his fingers out, and I make a noise of protest. It is replaced a moment later with another finger— no, his thumb, and I feel his index finger seeking out my clitoris.

And I'm suddenly having a hard time lining up his cock with my mouth. I'm trembling, weak with need. I was in control, but now he's driving me just as wild as I was driving him. I don't want him to stop, either. His finger finds my clit, and I cry out against his cock as he gives it a stroke with a fingertip.

"Take me in your mouth, Daisy," he tells me. "Like you will pull me into your throat."

Oh. Realization dawns, and I picture this and want to do it for him. I suck on the head of his cock again, even as he continues to work on my cunt with his fingers, and it takes everything I have to concentrate. I open my mouth wide, and his cock rubs along my tongue. With a little movement of his hips, he's pushing deeper into my mouth, and I open as wide as I can, taking him as far back as I can. My gag reflex works, and I release him, coughing, and then take him deep again.

"Ah, Daisy," he grits. His fingers move against my clit, his thumb grinding inside me. "You are perfection. Will you come for me? With your little bottom in my hands as I pleasure you? With your mouth on my cock?"

His words are exciting, and I can't help but push back against his invasive, wonderful fingers. I'm making small noises in my throat, even as I try to take him deeper into my mouth. I pull on his cock with my tongue and my mouth, and he hits the back of my throat, which startles both of us. I rear back, and Nick cusses. But he liked that, so I try it again.

It's getting harder for me to concentrate; his fingers are hammering into my panties, and I'm losing control. I can't keep his cock in my mouth. My lips are greedy for him, but my body is quivering and distracted, and my breath is coming in weird little pants. All the while, Nick is murmuring encouragement. I settle for rolling the thick, blunt head of his cock against my lips, letting the wetness move over them as I kiss it frantically and work my hips against his fingers.

Then, it's there; that odd, wonderful tightening deep inside me that tells me I'm coming. I cry out, my body shuddering, and then Nick's cock jerks in my hands. A warm spurt splashes across my lips, and then I realize he's coming, too. I pull back, but he continues to come, and it's on my hands and face, and now his belly and jeans.

He cusses something again, and I feel his fingers slide out of my body. There's an embarrassingly wet sound as they leave my sex, and then he's rolling off the bed, heading to the bathroom.

And I'm left there, crouching on the bed with his semen splattered on my face and hands, my sex throbbing and slick from my own release. And I'm not entirely sure what to do. We didn't cover this when we played around in the car.

To my relief, Nick returns a moment later, and comes to my side with a towel. Tenderly, he wipes at my face and hands. I can do it myself, but there's a possessive look in his eyes that dares me to contradict him, so I don't. He cleans me up, wipes down his belly, and then tosses the towel into the laundry hamper near the bathroom door. To my surprise, he returns back to the bathroom, and I hear water running. A moment later, he appears with a wet washcloth.

"Take your panties off."

I gasp. "Why?"

"So I can take care of you."

My face burns with embarrassment as I slide off my now-wet panties. Nick draws me close to him and moves the warm, wet washcloth between my legs, bathing me. His gaze is on my face the entire time, and to my horror, I begin to get aroused all over again.

"Are you sore, Daisy?"

His whispered words are embarrassing to me. "It hurt a little, but it wasn't a bad hurt."

He brushes my hair away from my face and tenderly kisses my

mouth. "I must remember to be more careful with you. You are treasure, and I don't want to hurt you. I just . . . lost control of myself. I had to touch you."

"I'm glad you did," I say shyly, and I wrap my arms around his neck.

He gives me another long kiss, and then he nods at the bed. "Come. Now we sleep, *da*?"

And this time, when he pulls me against his side, I'm able to relax and go to sleep. I curl up against him and think that Nick being in my bed—and in my life—is the best thing ever.

I'm so glad I ran away. My hand pets Nick, but it's not an exploratory petting, not like before. It's a comforting, soothing, just-checking-to-make-sure-you're-really-there sort of motion. I think of the circles under Nick's eyes, and I feel a momentary stab of guilt that I've kept him awake. He's exhausted, and whatever his job is, it must be taking a lot out of him.

I consider this for a moment. "Nick."

"Mmm?" His voice is sleepy, and he hugs me tighter.

"Do you still watch me?" It's occurred to me that I work late hours, and he seems to know intimate details of my job.

"*Da*."

"While I'm at work?"

He is silent for a long, long moment, which means he is trying to cobble together a bad lie. After a moment, he heaves a sigh. "*Da*. It is not a safe job. I worry."

I sit up in bed, regarding him. "You're exhausted. You can't be up all hours watching me."

His eyes regard me in the dark, now wide awake. "You said you did not mind."

"I said I don't mind if you watch me and I know about it. But there's a difference between watching and stalking. I'm fine at work. They have security cameras and everything." I give him my most stubborn look. "I don't want you watching me there, okay?"

"Is not up for discussion—"

"Nick," I say in a warning tone. "I'm serious. If you can't respect that about our relationship, I don't know that we can have one."

His eyes go cold. "Do you put an ultimatum on me, Daisy?"

"Yes, I do," I say. And my heart squeezes with pain, but this is important. "My father trapped me in our house for twenty-one years because he needed to control everything I did. The reason why we—why you and I—work so well is because you let me have as much control as I want." I reach a hand out and lay it flat on his chest, a silent entreaty. "But if you can't respect my boundaries, you're no better than him."

He is silent for so long that I know he's angry. I expect him to get out of bed and leave. But he doesn't. Instead, he looks at me with those sad, tortured eyes and brushes a finger along my jawline. "*Da*. I do this for you, Daisy. I will only watch you here in your apartment. This is all right?"

"Yes," I say, relieved. "*Spasibo*."

He laughs, surprised at my Russian. "Why do you thank me?"

"For caring enough to care about how I feel."

He pulls me close again, snuggling with me on the bed. "I do not think you realize, Daisy. You are everything to me."

CHAPTER ELEVEN

DAISY

"Man, this weather is awful." Regan peers out the window at the pouring rain and recoils when it thunders. "You sure you want to walk to work? I can drive you."

"It's only two blocks," I say, reaching for my coat. I shrug it on and then head to the window that Regan is peering out. It does look awful outside. I hesitate, watching the rain slant sideways. By the time I get to work, I will be soaked, and it will make for a miserable evening. There's no point in taking the bus, though, not for a walk of two blocks. I consider Regan's offer. "If you drive me, can you pick me up, too?"

She gives me a thumbs-up and then just as quickly frowns. "Oh. I'd have to borrow your phone. I dropped mine yesterday and now it won't work."

I glance out the window again, at the furious storm, and then I reluctantly pull my phone out of my pocket. I don't want to give

Regan my phone. It's my only connection to Nick while he's out of town. I'll miss his sweet, thoughtful texts that make the hours at work pass faster. But it's either that or sit in soaked clothing behind the counter all night. With only a little hesitation, I hand her my phone. "If Nick calls, just let it go to voice mail."

"Of course," Regan says, pocketing my phone and not even glancing at the screen. "There's no dirty selfies on here, are there?"

"What? No!"

"I'm kidding, I'm kidding, Pollyanna." She waves a hand at me. "I'm not going to look at your phone. Don't freak out. I won't even use it. Just call it when you're ready to be picked up, and I'll hop into the car. I promise."

I nod. "I trust you." She's my only friend besides Nick. Of course I trust her.

"So . . . you and Nick are pretty serious, huh?" She turns away from the window and heads to the counter to grab her car keys.

"I think so."

"He's your first serious relationship, isn't he?"

I nod, though I can feel the blush stinging my cheeks.

Regan puts a hand on my shoulder, the look on her face serious. "I know you're pretty innocent, Pollyanna. Do we need to have a birds-and-the-bees talk?"

"I know how sex works, Regan!" I can't believe we are having this conversation. Regan's not more than a year older than me. Sexually, though, I suppose she is vastly more experienced than I am, even after my few encounters with Nick.

"I'm just looking out for you, girlfriend." She pats my shoulder. "I'm glad to hear it, though. Don't let him pressure you into doing something you don't want to do."

"Nick's not like that," I protest. If anything, I am the one pressuring Nick into more sexual experimentation than he's asked for. I'm just so eager to experience all of what life has to offer that I can't hold back. I'm greedy with him. He offers me kisses, and I want more. "You don't have to worry."

"I can't help but worry," Regan says as we step out of the apartment and into the hallway. "You're just so sweet and innocent. I kinda thought you'd be with, I don't know. A different type than him."

"What do you mean, his type?" Now I'm curious what she thinks.

"I don't know. I just pictured you with some nice, equally innocent, sweater-wearing mama's boy. Not one that runs around on a crotch rocket."

I think of my Nick, with his tattooed hands and strong body and eyes that can be so cold . . . until they look at me. Then they have all the warmth in the world. "He owns a sweater," I mumble. At least, I am pretty sure he does.

"Like I said, I'm just looking out for you," she says, and there is concern in her eyes as we head down the hall and down the stairs. "I know it's none of my business, but I feel a bit like an older sister around you, and I'm just trying to make sure you don't get hurt."

"Nick would never hurt me," I say softly, and I know it's the truth. He keeps warning me away from him, as if certain I will wake up and realize he is bad for me. He doesn't realize that I love his differences. I don't mind that he's had a hard, ugly life before we met. I know what it's like to not want your past to define you. Only the present matters, and in the present, I am with Nick, and he is with me, and what I feel for him can't be contained by regular words or thoughts.

"Once you meet him, you'll see what a great guy he is." I think it's sweet that Regan is concerned. She is a good friend. She voices her concerns, but in the end, it is still my choice, and I have made it.

I feel naked without my phone in my hand. Surely I can go a few hours without Nick's texts, though I already feel their loss keenly.

"So are you expecting a call from Nick?" Regan asks. "Want me to call you up at the gas station if he calls?"

"I don't know that he'll call me," I tell her honestly. "He's out of town."

"Business?"

"I think so."

"What's he do?"

"Computer stuff," I tell her. Nick hasn't really said too much about what he does, and I haven't asked. It's clear that he doesn't want it to define him, and I understand that. I am no more just a gas station employee than he is . . . well, whatever he is.

From what Nick has told me and his sense of shame at his profession, I suspect it is something not entirely legal. Perhaps he pirates movies and sells them on the Internet. Maybe he is a hacker. Either of these is possible, and neither matters, though I do worry that one day his calls will be from jail.

But Nick is a grown man. I don't want to control him any more than I want him to control me. So I haven't broached the subject. When he wants me to know more, he'll tell me.

"Well, regardless," Regan says as we get to the bottom of the stairs. "If he calls, I won't answer."

"Thank you," I tell her. And a moment later, I add, "But you'll still call me and tell me, right?"

She laughs. "Will do."

With my phone and Nick to text, a night at work never seems to drag.

Without both, the hours tick by slowly. I stare at the security monitors for an eternity—the most boring television viewing ever, even compared to PBS—and think about Nick instead. Does he miss me? Is he thinking about me? Is he texting me and wondering where I am? I should have texted him to let him know Regan has my phone. I didn't think about it, and now he'll be wondering where I am. Poor Nick. His evening will be just as lifeless as mine.

When I can stand staring at the security cameras no longer, I decide to stock candy bars and lottery tickets. I don't like to leave the counter, even though Craig said sometimes you just have to. You pick a slow moment to go to the bathroom, preferably late at night. I have learned to pee fast and to not drink much prior to my shift. But boredom causes me to retreat to the back room for the occasional retrieval of a box so my hands can have something to do while I monitor my lonely counter.

The last person to purchase a slushie complained about the flavoring, so I decide to refill the machine by changing out the syrup bag. They're kept on a shelf in the back, so I pull out the step stool and climb up to get it, when I hear a familiar chime. It's the door, letting me know there is a customer in the store. That's hardly unusual in itself, but it's one in the morning, it's raining, and foot traffic has been slow. "Just a minute," I call out, tugging the box of diet soda syrup out from under a stack of root beer flavors. While I do, I glance at the security camera.

There are two men in suits that have entered. Both are wearing sunglasses. One has paused by the door and puts a hand inside his jacket and leaves it there. He scans the room as the other stalks around inside.

This . . . makes me anxious. I'm not entirely sure why. It strikes me as unnatural, even more so when they begin to speak in a language I recognize but don't understand: Russian.

My skin prickles with alarm. Do these people know Nick? There are surely not that many Russians in the city, are there? And why would they show up at a gas station at one in the morning in suits? I think about Nick's job, his likely computer hacking. Are these people looking for him? Maybe they are police, but that doesn't explain why they speak Russian.

I'm scared. I'm so terrified I immediately begin to shake, but I somehow manage to go to the stock room door and shut it—and lock it—before anyone can come back here.

Two seconds later, a hand jiggles the knob. I hear swearing, and then a man calls out to the other in Russian. They're clearly angry, and one slams against the door. I turn to the cameras but both have moved out of sight. They are probably at the door.

I am trapped.

My brain shuts down. I stop shaking. I've been trapped before. I spent twenty-one years trapped and cornered. I know how to function like this. The best thing I can do is to stop thinking, stop processing, and just exist. Do what needs to be done.

I calmly drag a shelf in front of the door, though it's heavy and I can't push it more than a few feet. Once they figure out how to open the door, it will fall over and block the way out, but I'm stuck anyhow.

I'm not helpless, though. I go to the time clock and the lockbox that is kept underneath it. I open it and pull out the C2 Taser gun. The bat is under the counter up front at the cash register, so I can't get to it. Calmly, I pick up the body of the Taser and then the battery pack that goes into the back. I slide it in and consider the air cartridge. These men look like they could carry guns. If I aim mine at them, I need to be faster. Better to have the element of surprise. I skip the air cartridge and will use the C2 as a stun gun instead. If they come close enough to grab me, I only have one chance anyhow.

I'm so calm as I slide the safety cover on the switch back and ready the gun. Then, I crouch in the farthest corner of the room, my hands tucked between my legs so I can hide the gun, and wait.

On the camera, I see one man return to the front of the store. He's watching so no one else comes in. The other continues to fuss with the knob on the stock room door, and I'm waiting for the click that will tell me he's worked his way in.

It comes a moment later, and I stiffen, though I am calm.

The door opens. Just a crack, and then it meets the shelf I have dragged forward. With another muttered curse, he shoves at the door, and the shelf careens forward in slow motion.

It makes an enormous crashing sound, boxes of candy bars sliding forward and smashing to the floor.

One man barks a command in Russian, and the one at the door answers, clearly annoyed. Then, he pushes forward, stepping over the fallen shelf, and I get a good look at him.

He could be my age, but there's something hard and familiar in his eyes that makes him seem older. His suit is rumpled, and he looks irritated at the shelf. He scans the room, and his gaze finally falls on me, huddled in the corner and crouching low.

"Come," he says to me, and he flicks his hand in my direction.

I don't move. I refuse to. I watch him with wary eyes instead.

He calls something over his shoulder at the other man, and he steps over the fallen shelf, moving toward me.

I tuck myself back further into my corner, doing my best to look frightened. I'm not; my brain is still numb.

The man steps forward, approaching me. His hand is out, but

I don't take it. I know he's trying to look not-scary but is failing. His eyes are too cold, too gleeful.

Then, he's standing right in front of me, bending over.

"Please don't hurt me," I whisper, since I know he wants to hear something like that.

"You come and no one gets hurt," he tells me, and his hands go to my arms as if to grab me.

I jam the Taser forward, shove it between his legs, and hold down on the button. Without the air cartridge in, it acts like a stun gun. It crackles with electricity, and I hear the *flick, flick, flick, flick* it makes as it contacts his flesh and sends shockwaves through his groin.

He jerks, shudders, and collapses.

I calmly stand up, though my knees ache from my crouch. It's clear he didn't expect me to fight back, but my father's anxiety has trained me well for this sort of situation. I step over the fallen man and climb over the shelf and out of the room.

The other man is clearly surprised to see me. He's bigger than the other man, his face hard. His eyes narrow when I am not followed immediately out of the room. I see the realization on his face; I have disabled his companion somehow. I clutch my stun gun closer, my hands sweating, and circle the shelves as he begins to walk forward, keeping distance between us. It's still raining, but I can run into the night, run all the way home.

"So," the man says, and his accent is thick, and sickeningly like Nick's delicious one. "You are his little flower, *da*?"

I say nothing. My hand is tight on the button of my stun gun. He's moved away from the door, but he's still too close for me to make a break for it. His words make my belly cold; this isn't a robbery. I knew it wasn't.

They've come for *me*, and it's something to do with Nick.

The man's hand goes into his jacket again, and it remains there. He has a gun, but he is not going to draw it. Not yet. I keep my hand low on the off chance he has not seen my Taser. I am stupid; I should have grabbed the air cartridge. If I got within fifteen feet of this man, I could shoot him with it and disable him and run straight to the police. But I left it in the other room and now I can't go back. I don't know how long the other man will be unable to move.

I need to do something other than hide behind shelves. But what?

The man's hard gaze remains on my face. "Yury," he calls out. Then he says something in Russian. There is no response, and the eyes narrow, the focus tightening on my face. He pulls the gun out of his jacket and shows it to me. "If you come to me, I will not have to use this."

I know that if I go with him, I am dead. I circle back behind another shelf as he takes a step forward. "If you kill me, Nick won't like it," I tell him.

He barks a laugh. "There are many ways to use a gun, little one. I do not have to kill, only disable. But, very well. We do it your way." He puts the gun back into his jacket, and pulls something else out. It's oblong, flat, and black. After a moment, I realize it is a phone.

When he runs his thumb across the screen and unlocks it, displaying the pretty floral wallpaper and the D8Z under the time, I realize it is *my* phone.

This rattles my unnatural calm. "How did you . . ."

"The blond *blyad*, she gets scared, and she sings like a canary, *da*? A little rope on the wrists, a little gun to the face, and she is very scared." His eyes are so cold. "And you will never see her whole if you do not come with me. I will mail her to Nick in pieces. Would you like that?"

I stare at my phone in his hand, trembling. This man has Regan. Happy, carefree Regan, who has been nothing but good to me. Who thinks of herself as my older sister and just looks out for my happiness. This is my fault. "Where is she?"

"She is in the back of my car." He gestures out the glass doors. "You may join her if you do not fight, little one. But if you do, it will be very bad for her."

My father has trained me for a hostage situation. I know the stupidest thing I can do is give in to what they are demanding.

But Regan is the one who will pay the price, and it doesn't seem fair. I don't know what to do.

I stare at the man, at my phone in his hand. "How do I know you didn't just take that from Regan and kill her?" My voice is so calm, like it belongs to someone else.

"So suspicious," he says, and chuckles even as he glances back at the storeroom, waiting for the other man to appear again, and his eyes are narrowed with anger even though he is laughing. He flicks his thumb on my phone—the phone Nick bought for me—and then turns it back to me. "Is proof, *da*?"

There's something on the screen, but I'm too far away to see it. "That could be anything."

"Suspicious. I like that in you. Suspicious but innocent. I see why Nikolai is so obsessed. Your cunt must be tight indeed." He lowers the phone to the floor and then kicks it down an aisle nearby.

I tremble. Nick is Nikolai to this man and not to me? I step closer to the phone. I'll have to sprint for it; it's only halfway down the aisle. I should leave it.

But I have to know. I have to.

Clutching the Taser tightly, I run for the phone. If he comes after me, I will stun him like I did the other man.

He heads for me as I scoop up the phone. I knew he would. I've made a stupid mistake, and now I will pay. I raise the stun gun as he rushes me, but he's too fast. His arm slams mine into a nearby shelf. Cans fly as my hand makes contact; the Taser tumbles out of my hand.

I don't even reach my phone.

He mutters something in Russian I don't catch, and his hand tightens on my wrist. I struggle against him; I'm dead now that he's got me. I know this, so I fight. I kick and scratch and claw at him with my free hand, ignoring that it feels as if he's breaking the wrist of my other with his tight grip.

The man reaches back, and that's the only warning I get before his hand slams into my face. The world tilts as black stars explode behind my eyes, followed by pain. I reel and stagger, trying to remain upright, remain conscious.

A hard hand grasps me under my chin, forcing me to stare into icy eyes. "Now we do things my way."

The man drags me out to his car, parked at the far end of the gas station, where the cameras' view doesn't quite go. It's almost as if he knows exactly how far their range is and has avoided it.

My head is reeling from his blow, and it's hard for me to focus. Now that he has me in his grasp, my struggles are futile. He's so much stronger than me, this man, and I don't know what to do. I jerk at his grip a few times as he drags me outside into the rain, but when he opens the car door and shoves me in, I go.

I go because I see long blond hair splayed over the backseat, and it terrifies me.

I nearly trip over Regan's sprawled body as I crawl into the car, and he shuts the door behind me. Immediately I try the handle on the other side, but the child locks are in place and it won't open. So I focus on Regan instead, my fingers brushing over her cheek. There's a massive bruise there, obvious even in the darkness, and her eyes are open wide and terrified. There's duct tape over her mouth, and her hands and feet are zip-tied together. Tears stream out of her eyes.

My poor friend. "I'm sorry," I whisper to her. This is somehow my fault. This is happening because these men want to hurt my Nick, and they came after me.

I sit her up as much as I can, and I put my arms around her, stroking her hair with my hands to soothe the sobs that come, muffled, from behind her gag. I should take it off of her, but I don't know what these men will do to her—or me—if I do. For once, our roles are reversed; I am the calm, knowing one. She is the small, terrified one. I have lived my life waiting for it to end in violence, and now that it is here, I'm so, so calm.

Will Nick find out what happens to me? I wonder this even as I make soothing noises in my throat to ease Regan's terror.

The man stalks away from the car and returns to the gas station, no doubt to check on his friend. He is so confident we can't escape from the backseat of the car that he abandons us. I study the backseat; there is a window partition that will not allow me to get to the front seat. I can kick out the backseat—maybe—but that will only lead to the trunk. What will I do in there? I try the doors again, but they don't respond.

The men return a moment later; the younger one is limping. He looks furious, and when they slide into the front seat, he pulls out his gun and waves it at me, cussing wildly in Russian.

The other man slaps it out of his hand and barks something

harsh. He looks as if he barely tolerates the other man. The younger glares and puts his gun down, but he gives me another ugly look.

He's mad at me, more than the other. He's going to make me regret using my stun gun on him, I just know it.

But until that moment comes, I smooth my hand on Regan's hair and hold her against me. "It's going to be all right," I lie to her.

The windows in the backseat of the car are so heavily tinted—and the darkness so black outside—that I can't tell where we're headed. We seem to drive for hours, but when the car stops, my stomach clenches in fear. It looks like we are in the middle of nowhere. Have they driven us out here to dispose of us? I think about the thriller movie Regan made me watch a few weekends ago in which the hero was driven out to the desert and shot. I shudder.

The back door opens. "Get out of the car," the bigger, meaner one says to me.

I do; there's no point in antagonizing him. As I do, I see a massive building in the distance that I can't make out. There are small lights on the ground.

On the other side of the car, the younger man slices the cuffs on Regan's legs so she can walk, but does not remove her gag. We're dragged across the grounds just as massive doors open and a small plane comes out.

We are flying somewhere?

Sure enough, they force us onto the plane and we are seated in what should be the lap of luxury. Regan's eyes are wide with fear and her breathing is ragged behind the gag. "We're going to be okay," I try to reassure her.

The larger one swings around. "Talk again and we'll shoot you in the leg. Maybe you heal from that. Maybe you don't." Tears leak out of Regan's eyes, and I can feel my face wet as well but I shut up.

Leather seats and plush couches line the interior of the plane, and there are televisions set into the wall. I've never flown, but even to my naïve eye, this looks expensive. There's a door in the back, and it looks as if it leads to another room. I can see a bed in the back, and I'm suddenly terrified of what that means.

The bigger man tosses me down into the first chair available. "Buckle in."

I fumble to do so. If I'm sitting here, I'm not in the back room with that ominous bed. I quickly belt myself in, and because Regan's hands are still cuffed as she sits next to me, I reach across and do hers, too. The men situate themselves nearby and relax, talking and laughing in Russian as the plane begins to accelerate and take off.

I look at Regan's silently begging eyes, at the bruise coloring her cheek, and I have no answers.

I don't know where we're going.

I don't know why we've been taken.

I only know two Russians with guns have come after me because of my relationship with Nick. And I'm terrified, but I'm frightened for him, too. What if they hurt him? He's so careful to keep me safe; this will devastate him.

I suspect that is the point.

"Where are we going?" I ask once the plane has leveled off and the roar of the engines dulls a bit. My voice sounds braver than I feel. Next to me, Regan tenses.

The younger man—Yury—laughs and says something to the older one. He gets up and heads over to us, my phone in his hand. "I think we will take some photos to send to Nikolai," Yury says, and he looks at me. His fingers curve over my cheek, caress my chin.

I remain still. I want to jerk away, but acknowledging that he's bothering me will only make it worse. So I stare blankly ahead and hold tight to Regan's arm.

Yury's thumb moves over my lips. "I bet you suck a good cock, eh?"

I recoil, staring up at him in horror.

He presses his thumb to my mouth again, and I shudder backward, even as he asks once more. "Do you suck a good cock? Is that why Nikolai risks everything for you?"

If I open my mouth to answer, his thumb's going to be inside it. I want to push his hand away, but there's a dangerous glint in his eyes that scares me.

"*Nyet*, Yury," the other man says in a weary voice. He says something else in Russian that I wish I understood.

Yury pushes his thumb against my lips again and then gestures at Regan and says something.

The other man shrugs.

"So. We take picture for Nikolai, so he knows we mean business." Yury gives me a cold smile. The thumb goes back to my mouth, and he pushes it hard against my lips. "I want him to see you suck on this."

I keep my lips firmly shut and glare up at him.

"Suck on this, or it will be my cock next," he says, and he glances at the other man for approval. When he's not told to leave me alone, his smile grows triumphant, and he gives me a smug look. "So, little *pizda*, which one do you want to suck?"

That is no choice. I part my lips and let him push his thumb into my mouth, feeling violated already. Hot, angry tears brim in my eyes, and I hate when they spill over my cheeks, even as Yury pumps his thumb in and out of my mouth in a gross mockery of what I'd been so eager to share with Nick only a few days ago.

"Beautiful. Nikolai will not be able to take his eyes off the sight." The camera flashes in my face, and he grins and tosses it back to the other man. "Is done. Now can I have the blonde?"

"Do what you like," the other says. "Just drug her so she doesn't fight and bruise herself more."

Yury laughs. "Long live Sergei Petrovich."

The other gives a disgusted sigh and waves a hand as if he is mentally done with his companion.

Yury grabs Regan, and I hear her muffled scream of fear behind her gag.

"No!" I fumble with my seat belt, even as Yury unhooks Regan's and drags her to her feet. She casts me a helpless look as Yury pulls her across the plane toward the bedroom. "Leave her alone!"

"Sit down," the other man commands me. He grabs my wrist when I pass by. "Sit down and shut the fuck up, or I will have to drug you, too. If I drug you, I cannot control what Yury does to you. Understand?"

Terror shoots through me. I want to save Regan, but I don't know what to do. The hand on my wrist tightens, becomes bruising, and I collapse back in my seat, watching my best friend disappear into the back bedroom with awful, horrible Yury. The door shuts.

It is silent. Awful, awful and silent.

"Has he mentioned us to you?"

I drag my gaze from the bedroom door to the big, scary blond man seated across from me. "Huh?"

"Nikolai. Has he mentioned us to you?"

"I don't know who you are," I whisper.

He makes a *hmph*ing sound that might be impressed. "I am Vasily. That is Yury. We are *Bratva*." He watches my face to see if it rings a bell. When it doesn't, his eyebrows flick up in surprise. "So. He has not. This is very interesting to me. I never thought he would truly get out, but perhaps it is so."

"Where are we going?"

"Moscow, of course. But do not worry. Nikolai will come after you. Of that, I have no doubt. And if you behave, you might even be alive to see him." The smile Vasily levels at me is weary. "If not, I am sure we will keep parts of you to make him think you are alive until he figures out otherwise. It is how things are done."

"Why?"

"Why what?"

"Why is this how things are done?"

He shrugs, and for a moment, that weariness threatens his features again. It's quickly masked once more. "I do not give orders, little one. I simply take them."

"Why take me? Why take Regan?"

"Your friend was in way. Is wrong place, wrong time." He shrugs his enormous shoulders. "Such is the way of things. Yury likes her, so she comes with us. When he gets tired of her, she will fetch a nice price on the black market." He points at me, wagging a finger. "You, however. You, Sergei will use to flush the snake out of grass."

"If he won't come to you, he must have a reason," I say desperately. I'm trying not to stare at the bedroom door. Oh, Regan. My poor friend. I want to weep. I want to go in there and rescue her, but that cold, tired look in Vasily's eyes dares me to do something.

And I am frozen in place. None of my father's training has prepared me for what to do if the bad guys don't leave.

He gestures with his hand, and I notice it is tattooed, much like Nick's.

I stare at that hand, riveted.

Vasily looks interested in my response. "Aha. Now do you see?" He shows me his neck, the dagger on his throat there, as if it should mean something to me. Nick has tattoos, too. But so do a lot of people. But it's the ones on his hand that look familiar.

That, and the cold, dead look that comes over Vasily's expression from time to time.

"You're in his . . . family, aren't you?" I struggle to think of what Nick told me of his younger years. That he'd grown up with a group of men that he worked with.

He taps his nose as if I've said something clever. "Now you see. But Nikolai grows tired of his jobs, so he must be taken care of. I like Nikolai, but Nikolai does not follow rules. Is not personal. Just business. You understand these things."

But I don't. Not really.

It must be obvious on my face, because Vasily sighs and mutters something in Russian. "What is it you think Nikolai does, little one?"

I thought Nick would tell me in time. That he would come to trust me. But it's not making sense. Why would someone that works in computers be in so much trouble? "A computer hacker?"

Vasily laughs. His big shoulders shake with mirth. "Computers? Computers, she says." He laughs and laughs. "You are very sweet, little Daisy Miller. Perhaps it is this he is drawn to." His gaze sharpens and he stares at me. "Tell me, if I threw you down on the floor and fucked you, would I be the first one?"

I gasp and jerk backward, shocked.

But he only nods. "*Da*. I suspected as much. It is written on your face. A virgin. No wonder Nikolai is beside himself with lust.

Rarer than unicorns in this age." Again, that tattooed finger wags in my face. "You are worth far more than your friend. Is why Yury will not touch you, though I know he would love to fuck with Nikolai by hurting you." He shrugs.

"What are you?" I whisper. "What is Nick?"

Vasily pats the breast of his jacket, where I know he keeps his gun. "Can you not guess, little innocent Daisy? Even after all these hints?"

I shake my head. I am blank. I am numb. I have nothing left to draw on.

"I am *ubitsya*. Assassin. Hit man." His smile is thin and bitter. "I kill for money. Just like your Nikolai." The fingers fan out, splaying the tattoo on the knuckles. So like Nick's. The expression in his eyes so similar. And I know it is the truth.

I am going to be sick.

CHAPTER **TWELVE**

NIKOLAI

I do not like leaving Daisy to fly to Seattle to study and plan for
the hit I will carry out for the Watchmakers, but it seems important that I obtain the details necessary to carry out this contract.
I am unsure what the resolution with Sergei will be but it is
unlikely that I will survive it. I want to make sure Daisy is taken
care of. This last hit will add to my bank account. I've never
thought of what I would do with the money when I am gone, and
I'd had no incentive to spend much while I was still alive. The
hollow feeling of hunger is never far away.

A local kennel agrees to watch the dog while I am in Seattle.
Not having a good story thought up about the dog, I've kept his
existence a secret from Daisy. So many secrets I keep from her. I
inform Sergei that Mr. Brown is taken care of and that I'll be
moving on to my next hit. If he needs me, I will be in Seattle and
away from Daisy.

On my way to Russia, I will need to stop in Switzerland, make a visit to the bank and ensure that Daisy can access the funds whenever she likes. I have to make a list of things to take care of. Take care of the surgeon for the Watchmakers. Eliminate Sergei. Provide for Daisy. I begin with the doctor. He has a regular routine.

While he is at work, his two kids are at school, and his wife is busy in the neighbor's bed, I go through his papers. Most of it he keeps on the computer in a locked folder. Password locked, not even encrypted. I shake my head at his poor attempts at security. The password-protected folder is opened with a few keystrokes, and I copy the spreadsheet and documents onto my flash drive and leave.

The spreadsheet shows income from the sale of harvested organs. There are notations by each. *A, D, Dx. Alcohol, drugs, disease.* He is selling tainted organs, which makes sense. He cannot sell the pure organs. Those would be noticed. But drug addicts, alcoholics, street people would provide a decent supply source. Likely the transplant doctor's organs have killed the wrong recipient, and now he is going to pay.

My fingers hesitate over the keyboard. In the past, this information would have been sufficient for me to carry out my task without question. It is not a child or a mother. But now, I wonder who my client is. Who is the injured party? I never entertain these morality questions, only maintained a few boundaries. To do otherwise would lead to madness. Do the hit. It's just a job.

I push away from the desk and lift my phone to text Daisy. It is the afternoon. She could be sleeping. Her night schedule is wreaking havoc with her body, she tells me. She felt like she was coming down with something. I need to take her away to somewhere warm, perhaps the Maldives. There are some private islands where she can recuperate and we could make love without worry of gas stations or Sergei. After, then. I allow myself just a glimmer of hope.

After.

Decision made, I return to the computer and type in a search for "failed organ transplant." There are many results, but one news article stands out. A twelve-year-old daughter of a Swiss banker has passed away due to some long-term illness. Ahh. That is it, then. The dangers of the black market where unregulated goods are traded with regularity.

Desperate people take desperate action. I understood this nameless man's grief and his pursuit of some kind of justice. But I despair at the ephemeral nature of it all. Taking out this one transplant surgeon only means that others will take his place. The market will still exist. The market for illegal goods, for depraved acts, for weapons and drugs will continue, no matter how many people I eliminate.

The inscription on my chest itches. Is death the mercy that I promise? I've not found peace in these years of killing.

No, peace is life with Daisy, on her farm, watching her grow round with my child. Peace is a future without killing, without the *Bratva*. Someone else could take my place, but I'd need to secure our future. First, by taking down this trauma surgeon and then by elim-inating Sergei in such a way that Daisy and I would be untouchable.

The information Mr. Brown imparted was helpful. He had heard Alexsandr's seditious whisperings that he was unhappy with Sergei's decisions for the *Bratva*. Mr. Brown thought to bring all the information he had been compiling on Sergei to Alexsandr in hopes that Alexsandr would pat him on the head and send him safely away. But Alexsandr wasn't the general of the Petrovich *Bratva* just because he was a brilliant military man. No, Alex-sandr loved the Petrovich family. He was a distant relative, and he may have loved a Petrovich daughter. In the end, Alexsandr's loy-alties were with the *Bratva*.

But the information Mr. Brown compiled was too valuable not to use, and so Alexsandr must have demanded a change. Change came. Sergei killed Alexsandr, and now Vasily is the general. But I have the information now, secrets like the ones Sergei has on so many others, and that information will be used to buy safety for Daisy and myself.

I drive along Interstate 5 to ascertain the best location for the kill shot. It takes me three passes to determine the best one. About three kilometers south of the hospital, the highway runs along a run-down neighborhood filled with graffiti, empty apartment buildings, and abandoned railroad tracks. A look through one of the buildings sitting some distance off the freeway shows evidence of it being a drug house. Perfect. Mr. Blue, as I have named him, visits a woman who is not his wife every Tuesday. The woman lives south of the hospital on Rainier Beach.

I take my binoculars and go from room to room to ascertain the best location for my hit. I make a tiny X on the floorboards, marking the optimal position of my SAKO rifle. I'd have to drive here. This would take at least forty-eight hours, but for now, I will return to home, report back to Neuchâtel, and hold Daisy.

They will give me the final details, and then the hit will be done. Now, though, Sergei.

Sergei will require a transatlantic flight, first to Switzerland and then on to Moscow. I could be gone for up to two weeks, but I couldn't leave Daisy for that long. Would she consider a trip abroad? That was a risky undertaking, but having her with me seems safer than her staying here to be robbed or raped at the gas station.

I bring up the security feed to the gas station. Another person is there. Not Daisy but it is early yet. She will not appear until later. I check my car's GPS. I wanted her to take that to work instead of public transportation. Daisy had argued, but I'd left her the keys. The car is still sitting in the parking spot between our two apartments.

I text her then.

Miss you. Will return tomorrow.

I receive no response.

She is sleeping then. I should sleep so that I am well rested when I see her tomorrow. I will be able to plan for Sergei better.

Thoughts of Daisy warm in her bed arouse me. In the shower, I take myself in hand, the warm wet of the water and the slick of the soap ease my strokes. I close my eyes and lean my forehead against the tiled wall. The remembrance of my fingers inside Daisy rocks me. She was slick and so tight. I had a hard time fitting both fingers in, and after she'd come, her walls were so swollen that even one finger seemed too immense for her. The thought of pushing in between that tight cunt of hers makes me shudder. I squeeze my cock tighter, imagining that it was her flesh that surrounded me.

She is eager, my Daisy. She would cling to my shoulders and the tiny heels of her feet would press into my low back as she urges me closer. I would pump inside of her, slow at first and then faster as I feel her clench her tight heat around me.

I'd need her mouth on mine. I'd need to fuck her mouth with my tongue as I fuck her cunt with my cock. I'd want to surround her with my arms, my body, and my scent. Instead of coming inside her, I would pull out and spray my semen on her stomach. Then I would rub it in until she had absorbed every ounce of me.

I come in my hand, spurting long jets of ropy semen into the shower. My hand is no replacement for Daisy, and I feel myself harden again, just at the thought of her name. With a flick of my wrist, I turn the water icy cold and stand there until my erection has subsided and I am nearly blue with the cold.

Sergei would need to be taken care of in less than a week. I cannot wait for Daisy much longer. If I don't end this now, I will not be able to think of anything but her and her warm welcoming body.

I check my phone once again, but there is no return text. The feed from the gas station shows the owner behind the counter. He looks unhappy. Perhaps Daisy is sick and stayed home. Maybe she would be fired. The thought fills me with more pleasure than it ought to.

The bed beckons to me, and with the phone in one hand and the other languidly jacking my cock, I think of Daisy until I drift off.

The buzz of my phone wakes me at once. I jackknife into a sitting position, my heart pounding. Daisy. I know it must be her.

"Allo," I answer immediately. She must be sick. I will be on the first flight home. Punching in the airline address, I start searching for the earliest flight from Seattle.

"Allo, Nikolai."

Dread wraps its fingers around my heart. I quickly look at the phone. It is from Daisy's number.

"You are a dead man, Sergei." I spit into the phone.

He laughs at me. "I can hardly believe that you've been late on your assignment because of a girl! A girl, Nikolai." He sounds joyous and amused. I'd cut out his tongue and make him eat it. "I actually thought you might be a boy lover given your purported monk-like existence. That last whore you hired in Amsterdam a few months back said that you looked like you were fucking a pillow you were so disinterested."

I hiss. Sergei had been tracking my activities for far longer than I'd expected. "Why?"

"Well, that's the right question to ask me. I thought for sure you'd parcel out more threats, but we both know that's a worthless endeavor." Sergei pauses, inviting me to say something, but I bite my tongue until I taste the tang of blood. "Why? Because I knew when I killed Alexsandr the lot of you hungry animals would come after me."

The animals? He must be referring to the other boys, the other hired killers that Alexsandr had trained. It did not occur to me that others would want to avenge him. What was it that Daniel had said? That I was not alone.

"You've misjudged then," I say, trying to sound calm and unaffected, but how can I? He must have Daisy. She is in their grasp. He could be trying to addict her to drugs. He could be—my thoughts splinter. I cannot think of Daisy like that.

"You know, we didn't know which one of these girls was yours, because this fancy phone with your number on it was in the blonde's possession, but we figured out with a little persuasion that it was the flower you were fucking." He pauses to take a breath and a swallow. Probably drinking vodka. "I've not taken her, your Daisy, because she's a virgin." Sergei sounds amazed.

I mute the phone and take the chair I was sitting on and bash it against the desk until it is in pieces.

Sergei is talking in the background. "I've never found the US to be much of a marketplace. Most of the girls there are dried up before they exit their teen years, but this one is what, twenty, and still a virgin? I'm delighted! I have just the businessman in mind for her. He sadly has syphilis from one of the products that was infected by Harry, but he'll be so happy to get this one. I think he believes that if he fucks enough virgins he'll be cured."

Sergei laughs, and I squeeze the broken wood so tightly in my hand that I begin to bleed in three places. It is enough to keep my voice level.

"I cannot imagine why you are calling me with this tale, Sergei. I took care of your accountant."

"You were supposed to bring him back, not kill him," Sergei thundered. He pounds his fist against the table so loud I hear it through the phone.

His show of anger has a calming effect on me. I open my laptop and pull up the GPS of Daisy's phone. The satellites take a moment, but she is pinpointed south of Moscow, at the location of the Petrovich country estate. It is a large, wooded compound complete with guards, fences, dogs, and trees. I copy those coordinates and send them to Daniel. If I am not alone, then this is his opportunity.

DAISY

When we land, my hands are zip-tied together behind my back. Yury places a pillowcase over my face, and I am led down stairs, across the tarmac, and into a car. I'm shivering with cold—and fear—but no one offers me a jacket. I'm tossed into the backseat of a car, the door shut behind me. All around me, there are people speaking in Russian, but no one seems even slightly concerned that they have a bound, hooded captive.

I wiggle around in the backseat of the car as it drives, but I am the only one back here. Regan is not with me. Fear strikes my heart, and I wonder where they have taken her. Why are we being sent to two different places?

Even though I am terrified, I am exhausted. I fall asleep in the car, so I don't know how long we travel. I wake up when the car jerks to a halt. I listen for doors to open and close, so I can count how many people are here.

I only hear one. That means there is just one person with me. I can take out one person, can't I? I flex my fingers behind my back and twist my wrists. The zip ties are cutting into my skin. It hurts, but the hurt is minor compared to the fact that I am helpless this way.

The back door opens, and someone grabs me by my legs. "Get out," I hear a voice say, and I'm disappointed to realize that it's Yury. I've been left alone with the person that scares me worse than Vasily. Vasily doesn't like me, but to him, I am a chess piece to be moved about.

Yury hates me because I tasered him in the balls. I'm terrified of what he will do to retaliate.

I wriggle my way out of the backseat and get to my feet. I'm unsteady, weaving. I haven't eaten since before heading to work, and I feel shaky and weak. My mouth is dry, and I have to pee, but I'm afraid to ask.

Rough hands grab my arm and drag me forward, leading me. I stagger as I walk, but Yury is moving at a brisk pace, and it's difficult for my shorter legs to keep up. He's not a very good guide, either. I stumble when my ankle hits something—maybe a curb? Then, a moment later, my face slams into something so hard I nearly black out.

Yury laughs, the sound cruel. "Stupid *pizda*. How can I be responsible for your well-being if you keep running into walls?"

Blood runs down my nose and into my mouth, and my entire face throbs and feels swollen. My teeth ache and I want to cry from the pain, but I bite my lip to keep from giving him the satisfaction. This is how he will hurt me. Vasily's boss wants me as a bargaining tool, but Yury will just make me miserable because he can. When he jerks at my arm, trying to pull me forward again, I hunch my shoulders, preparing for another wall, but there is nothing.

And then I am inside somewhere.

I can tell we're indoors; the air has changed, and our shoes make an echoing noise like we are in a big building. I still have the hood on, so I can't see anything. Yury's hand on my upper arm pinches terribly as he drags me forward, and then he slams me into metal that bangs against my shins. "Sit down."

I try to feel things out with my leg. It's a metal chair, I think. I gingerly sit on it and wait, my hands aching from the tie, my face and arms feeling like one giant bruise. It's too quiet. I want Regan back. Even knowing she is at my side would make things less miserable.

But I am alone with Yury.

The hood whips off my face a moment later, and I blink at my surroundings as my hair flies about my face in a cloud of static. We are in a warehouse of some kind. It's empty, though; rows of nearby metal shelves have nothing but dust on them. A single light bulb hangs from the ceiling, and everything is dark and ominous. There are folding metal chairs in front of a small card table, and this is where I am seated. Yury is hovering at my side.

He glares down at my face and cusses something in Russian. Then, he pinches the bridge of my nose. "Does this hurt?"

It hurts, but I won't give him the satisfaction of telling him so. I jerk away from his grip.

He grunts. "Good. Is not broken. Sergei would have my hide if I permanently defaced his little moneybag." He gives me a cold smile. "You had me scared for a moment there."

I glare at him, my face throbbing where he pinched it. "Are you going to sell me back to Nick? Is that the plan?"

Yury stares at me. Then he laughs as if I have said something hilarious. "You seem to think your boyfriend will be alive long enough to buy you back. You are funny woman."

I try not to be bothered by this, but . . . I'm scared.

I know Nick is one of the bad guys now. Vasily told me that he was an assassin. One of the *Bratva*. I'm guessing the definition Nick provided wasn't a complete one.

Nick kills people for money. He's as bad as the man that killed my mother and destroyed my father's life.

And it makes me a terrible, awful person because I want him to come through that door in the next minute and rescue me. I want him to show up and hold me close and tell me everything will be okay. That he has me. That I'm safe.

And I hate myself for it.

"No more jokes for Yury? Shame." My captor studies me for a moment longer and then inclines his chin. "Maybe you are ready for other things to go in your mouth, then."

I remember his threat from the airplane. "If you put anything in my mouth, I'm going to bite it off." He can punch me or slap me, but he can't hurt me, not really. He's too scared of his boss, this Sergei he mentioned.

His eyes narrow and he regards me for a long moment. "Go clean up in bathroom. You are disgusting with snot and blood running into your mouth."

I've won this round. "My hands are bound," I tell him, and I shrug my shoulders as if to demonstrate that I can't move them. "I can't stick my head under the faucet and clean off. And I have to pee. Can you untie me?"

"So you can fight me?"

Yes, I think, but I know that won't get me what I want. "Are you afraid I'll win?"

He snorts. I am triumphant when he comes to my side, but he

delivers a ringing slap to my face that stuns me. He grabs my chin in the next moment, when my head is still spinning. "Listen very closely. I am going to untie your hands, but if you try to run away, I will break your arm in my bare hands. I will tell Sergei it was accident, *da*? You can still spread your legs that way."

I shiver. I know he is serious. "I hate you," I tell him quietly. "I hope Nick murders you." And I'm a bit alarmed at myself when I realize that I mean it. My gut is full of terror and fury, and I would love nothing more than for Nick to come through this door and destroy Yury right in front of me. I hate him so much. I hate him because I know he raped Regan. I hate him because I know he would casually break my arm as easily as he slapped me.

I hate him because it's easier than hating myself for being responsible for all of this. All because I thought the man I was falling in love with was a computer hacker.

I am the worst kind of fool.

"You can hate me, *pizda*. But be smart and do not run away or it will be bad for you." And he pulls out a knife and slices through the restraints on my wrists.

I shake my arms and stand up. I want to rub my wrists, but I stare warily at Yury instead. Yury, who still has the knife out, regarding me. Waiting for me to spring, to do something stupid. He would love nothing more than if I tried to attack him, because then he would be justified in breaking my arm . . . or worse. So I simply say, "Where's the bathroom?"

He points at a door in the back corner of the near-empty warehouse. "Clean your face. You are disgusting."

I go to it. The doorknob has been removed and only a hole remains, but I shut it for privacy anyhow. The toilet is disgusting, the seat broken and ringed with years of grime, but I quickly relieve myself and then wash my hands in the sink with the equally dirty cake of soap there.

There's a mirror above the washstand. It's cracked, broken, and filthy, like the rest of the bathroom, but I can see my face. The bridge of my nose is puffy and turning purple, and I look like I've been punched in both eyes. Blood cakes my upper lip, and my mouth is swollen. I carefully wash my face with splashes of cold water, but it doesn't look much better once I get all the blood off. My wrists are masses of bruises from where the cuffs—and Yury—have held too tightly. I look terrible.

I am still better off than Regan, though. Tears flood my eyes as I think of her. It's my fault she's been taken, and I don't even know where she is anymore. *I'm so sorry, Regan.*

My face cleaned, I'm in no hurry to go back out and see Yury again. I slide down the tile wall and crouch on the floor, hugging my arms close to my body. He can just come and get me. It's quiet in here, and I feel a little safer with a door—even an unlocked one—between me and my captor.

My thoughts turn to Nick.

I don't know what to think about Vasily's words. He could be lying to me, but the tattoos on his hands and the way his eyes get cold when he's angry look so, so familiar to me that I know he's telling the truth. Vasily is an assassin, and so is my Nick.

I should have seen it earlier. The way he watches me. The way he has so much money. The frightening tattoos on his body.

The pain in his eyes, the loneliness.

I bite down on my knuckles to stifle the sob that threatens to choke from my throat. I am torn. Part of me wants to hate Nick for who—and what—he is. For lying to me. For letting me be so innocent and deluded even as he lies to my face. Has he been going out and killing people while I have known him? Does he murder someone and then come to me and kiss me? I am revolted by the thought. *I must leave town on business*, he told me, and I never thought to ask more. I'm so stupid.

Worst of all, I still have feelings for him. I think of the sadness in his eyes. The self-loathing. He thinks himself unworthy of me. And now that I know the truth, I understand why . . . but I can't stop caring for him.

I can't lie to myself—even with everything I know, I want Nick to come through that door and rescue me and hold me in his arms. I want Nick to make everything all right again. I want him to come and kiss me and make me forget.

But I'm scared of him now. Because I know the truth of what he is. He is like Yury. He is like Vasily. And I wonder if there are any other Daisies out there, huddled in warehouses, while Nick sits at a folding card table and waits for the captive to emerge from the bathroom.

This time, I can't muffle my sob.

Yury doesn't come into the bathroom after me. I remain there for hours, crouched on the floor, hiding in plain sight. I hear him talking on his phone, a one-sided conversation that might be about the weather or sports, for all the laughing he does.

Soon, though, I hear another voice. A woman's voice. She coughs and says something in Russian, and Yury responds. The woman's voice becomes whiny and pleading, and Yury's tone grows short.

Then I hear another man's voice. His Russian sounds different than the others, flatter.

And then, I smell food. It smells like french fries. My mouth waters.

Wary, I get to my feet and peer through the hole where the doorknob should be. I can see nothing. I will have to leave my sanctuary to see what is going on. My stomach growls, reminding me that I haven't eaten, and I'm terrified, but I'm even more terrified of not knowing what is going on.

I open the door and emerge from the bathroom.

Yury is still sitting at the card table. He's got a cigarette hanging from his lips and an ashtray parked on the table in front of him. Two other men are in the room. I recognize Vasily again, but the other man is a stranger. There is also a woman here. The woman is scrawny and bony, shivering in a heavy fur coat that looks like it was fished out of the garbage. Her face is caked with heavy makeup, her blond hair stringy.

The men are wearing long coats, their faces expressionless as they regard me. The new man holds a bag of McDonald's.

They all turn at the sight of me emerging. The dark-haired man regards me for a long moment and shakes his head. "Christ, Yury. I thought we weren't supposed to fucking hurt her. Sergei wants to sell her. She looks like shit, man."

I am startled—he's speaking English, and it's completely unaccented. This man—this newest assassin—is American?

Yury takes a drag on his cigarette and gives the newcomer a thin smile. "She is clumsy. Has accident." He shrugs. "Why do you care?"

"Because I get a cut when she gets sold," the man says bluntly. He tosses the bag on the table. "Some fine dining for you while you wait."

Yury grunts, and his gaze flicks to the skinny blond woman in the coat. "I see you brought me present."

"Galina has not paid her debts to Sergei, and now she messes herself up on krokodil," Vasily says. "Is only a matter of time. So Sergei says to bring her here. She wants to work off her debts." The man smiles thinly. "Problem is, no one wants her."

"So why bring the *pizda* to me?" Yury looks only mildly interested. His gaze flicks over the woman. The rest of them are ignoring her . . . and me.

"Because Sergei said so," the American says bluntly. "I don't give a shit what you do with her. I just don't want her to be my problem."

Yury nods. "I will think of something." He pats the folding chair next to him, and the woman thumps into it.

"Sergei sent us here to relieve you of guard duty. We'll take her off your hands for a bit." The American gestures at me.

My eyes widen, and I take a step back toward the bathroom. Yury is the devil I know. I'm scared of him, but I'm even more terrified of this new man because I haven't seen him before. He might be four times as sadistic as Yury. How can I trust any American that works with these horrible men?

"*Nyet*," Yury says. "We are having fun, aren't we?" And Yury looks over at me.

"Fuck you," I say, my voice trembling. And I flinch backward in anticipation of someone attacking me.

But the men only regard me with the same cold, shuttered expression I've seen far too often.

"See?" Yury says in a flat, mocking voice. "Fun. She likes me. And I am sure she will be friendlier once she has something to eat. She will be good to me, then."

I won't suck him off for food. I won't. I ignore the growling of my stomach.

"Whatever," says the American. "So you're going to stay?"

"*Da*. You may run off." Yury flicks his cigarette at the others. "I will call if I grow too bored. And until then, I will just play with my present."

The smile he gives the skinny woman makes me feel cold inside.

"All right, then," the American says. He looks at Vasily, nods, and begins to leave. The big blond man stays beside the front door, guarding it. Vasily isn't leaving.

A moment later, it is just me, Yury, and the woman—Galina. Vasily remains by the front door, but he could be a statue for all the attention he gives to the situation.

Galina and Yury remain seated at the table, and Yury looks over at me, where I hover near the bathroom door, trembling and uncertain. He points at one of the metal folding chairs. "Sit."

Should I fight him? Disobey? My face throbs, and I can see no advantage. There was nothing I could use as a weapon in the bathroom, and the warehouse is equally empty. After a moment's hesitation, I approach and sit across from Yury and the woman.

He nudges the bag of fast food toward me. "Eat."

I watch him to see if it's a trick, and when he doesn't move, I hesitantly reach for the bag with one bruised hand.

He gives me another thin smile and takes another puff from his cigarette.

There are a hamburger and fries in the bag and a napkin. I dig through the bag, hoping against hope that there is a plastic knife—something, anything—but there is not. After a moment's disappointment, I grab the burger and unwrap it, taking a huge bite before they can snatch it away from me.

Yury watches me with amusement. "Americans have such disgusting manners."

I ignore him, wolfing down the food. There's no drink, and

I'm incredibly thirsty, but I don't complain. After I eat the burger, I start on the fries.

Yury continues to watch me eat. The woman seated next to him seems to be rather out of it. Her expression is glazed and vacant, and she sniffs repeatedly as if she has a cold. As I eat, Yury cocks his head. "Give me your hand."

I still. This is the trap. I watch him, waiting.

He makes an impatient gesture. "Give me your hand."

Trembling, I extend my hand toward him. I expect anything out of this man except for what he does. He takes my hand in his and examines my fingernails. Then, he looks over at Galina and says something in Russian.

She obligingly sticks her hand out for him.

He pulls out his knife and grins at me.

My stomach churns.

Galina continues to sit there like a zombie.

"I think we will send Nikolai a little message. A little, how shall we say, 'Hurry up.' What do you think, *pizda*?"

I swallow hard. I want to know what he means, but I'm afraid. "What are you going to do?"

He examines Galina's fingers and makes a face, angling her hand toward me. It is covered in dark spots, and in several places, it looks scaly and gangrenous. "She has much love for *krokodil*. It is a cheap fix when you are too broke to afford the good stuff." He puts her hand down and gestures that she should give him her other hand.

Galina does, just as easily and blankly as before. It's like she doesn't realize he has a knife in one hand. I wonder if she realizes anything.

He examines Galina's new hand and then looks over at mine again. Then, he takes her ring finger and carefully pares the nail down with his knife. "The good thing is that Galina still has a decent finger or two, *da*? It makes our little message easier."

"What message?"

"Sergei says we cannot harm you. His buyer likes his packages whole. I understand this, but I think Nikolai needs a bit of incentive, yes? And what is more incentive than sending him his woman's finger?"

My hands clench into fists and I hide them between my legs, horrified. "No!"

At the door, Vasily calls out a lazy warning in Russian.

Yury rolls his eyes and waves a hand at me, ignoring the other assassin. "Stupid *pizda*. Did you not hear me say that I cannot touch you?" He points the knife at Galina's blank face. "But this one, she owes many, many dollars to the *Bratva*. And she has nothing left to pay with but her flesh." He sneers at the woman's hand. "Her rotten, rotten *krokodil* flesh."

As I watch, he carefully places Galina's hand on the table.

The woman could be a zombie for all the attention she pays. She stares blankly ahead, a hint of a smile curving her mouth.

When Yury lowers the knife toward her finger, I jerk to my feet. "No! Please don't."

"Do not worry," Yury says with an evil smile. "She is so strung out she will not feel a thing. And this will make your Nikolai work faster, *da*? So is beneficial to all."

He poises the knife just above her knuckle.

I run out of the room and back to the safety of the bathroom, but not before I hear Galina begin to scream.

I throw up in the sink until I have nothing left.

CHAPTER THIRTEEN

NIKOLAI

I sit coach the next flight out. It was the only seat I could get. I wouldn't arrive until tomorrow otherwise, and even that delay is too long. Despite the crowded conditions—the male next to me with the runny nose and the cough, and the girl to my right who thought I might want to show her around when we arrived in Moscow—I sleep. I force myself. I ruthlessly push aside Daisy's screams of pain and her ugly tears. I refuse to replay the words of Sergei as he talked so casually of raping Daisy and of selling her to a syphilis-ridden pervert in Dubai.

None of those things matter. What matters is that she is alive. Until she no longer breathes, my sole concern is rescuing her. After that . . .

Well, after that I would enact a vengeance upon the house of Petrovich and anyone else who had touched Daisy. It would be known throughout the world from Hong Kong to New York, in all the dark spaces, that if you touched something of Nikolai's, vengeance would come to you and to your family and that it would not be in the form of death. It would be in the form of financial ruin, permanent maiming. It would be people returned to you with their limbs cut off and their bodies riddled with drugs. It would be so you could look every day upon the slow, wasted bodies of your loved ones and remember that all of this could have been avoided if you had just left me alone.

That is the message I would deliver to Sergei, to the *Bratva*, to everyone.

But to do this I must sleep. And I do.

But I am unprepared for the horror that awaits me at the airport. At the gate, a curvy flight attendant from Atlant-Soyuz Airlines approaches me. She is pretty from a distance but up close you can see the signs of *krokodil* use, green scalelike spots are evident around her chin and near her ears. Soon she will not be able to hide the marks, even with makeup. Soon the body tissue will gray and die and her skin will peel away, leaving only bone.

"Mr. Andrushko?"

"*Da*." I nod in acknowledgment.

"This is for you." She holds out a box but her hands are shaking. The pupils of her eyes are tiny pinpoints and tears threaten to spill at any moment. I don't want to take the box. I want to shove past her and get on with my mission, but I reach out for it anyway.

A stone settles in my stomach, and each step toward the airport parking lot is like walking through cement. I choose a car from the back of the lot, pick the lock, and start the engine. I drive a little ways and then pull over. Inside, I see a small electronic device with an LCD screen and a bloody tissue. My hands shake when I lift the tissue-wrapped package out of the box. And when I see the severed finger inside, I wrench open the door and heave. What little I have ingested splatters the frozen ground on the side of the road. *My God, Daisy. What have I done to you?*

I lurch back to the car and pick up the video screen and watch as Yury forces his finger inside my Daisy's mouth; I watch as her tears and terror are captured by some laughing, cocksucking, miserable human being who will be flayed by my knife as soon as I reach them.

I don't want to watch the rest of the video but I force myself to. The scene shifts from the plane to a concrete room. The sound cuts out, and I can't hear her scream as a knife is produced, but I cry out when a close up of Daisy's finger being cut off flashes across the screen. But tears and puking will not save her. She has nine fingers, so what? At least she is alive.

I force myself to watch the video ten more times, looking for any clues that I can find. The finger looks desiccated already, not like any of the fingers on Daisy's hand. But the death of a limb can change the appearance. I push it out of my head. None of that will help me now.

Finally I head west. Alexsandr has a safe house there. There will be weapons and gear, and it will give me a moment to plan. Storming Sergei's quarters would be near impossible. There are a dozen mercenaries who guard the exterior and probably a dozen more loyalists inside. The GPS location of Daisy's phone is squarely inside the estate. It's possible that Sergei had the phone and that he has stashed Daisy somewhere else, but he has to know that I am coming, and so he has retreated inside his castle.

The hour-long trip takes me half the time. I am nearly out of gas when I arrive at the safe house. I take the precaution of circling the house to locate the underground cellar entrance at the back. Alexsandr and I dug this tunnel ourselves for five years. No one else knew of it. Creeping down inside, I walk lightly, stepping over three trip wires that are set. I wonder at the last time Alexsandr was here. The tunnel is musty, and insects are crawling through the boards we had lined along the soil walls. At the end of the tunnel is a small dirt cellar with a generator. The generator is humming, indicating that electricity in the upstairs is being used.

Someone is there.

I have no gun, but I have the garrote on my belt. I pull that off and hold it in one hand and climb the cellar stairs with the other in order to loosen the lock. Then I push the ladder hard, and the trapdoor on the floor pops open. Quickly, I move back to the tunnel to avoid ricochet gunshots, but I hear nothing. I duck and roll over to the generator and flick it off, kick the ladder out of the trap, and then run back to the tunnel opening.

An image of Daisy as she found her first orgasm with my tongue pressed against her fluttering clit teases at the fringes of my mind. No. Not now. I've been cold-blooded all my life. Daisy has brought me to life, though, and should she die, there are not enough ways that I can make a man suffer like I will make Sergei and anyone else who harmed her suffer.

I want to roar out my anger but now, more than ever, I need to swallow my emotions.

A curse sounds from above. "Goddammit, Nikolai. Why can't you come through the fucking front door like a normal person?"

It is Daniel. Despite the lack of voice modulator, I recognize him somehow. Maybe it is the cadence of his words, something a modulator cannot change. Or perhaps it is because he sounds exactly as I imagined. Still, I wait. The video that was sent to me has the voices of men in the background over the soundtrack of Daisy's tears and cries.

One of those men could be Daniel. That he is here in my safe house makes me suspicious. I clench the wire tighter in my hand. I can take Daniel, not because I know I am stronger or faster than him, but because through him is Daisy. Daniel does not have the same incentive.

The sounds from the upstairs are now penetrating over the pounding of my heart. My body tightens at the memory of the video, and I want to place my hands around Daniel's neck until he is blue in his face. I close my eyes and inhale to regain control. I cannot afford any mistakes. I breathe deep. Once. Twice.

There. I can hear. There are more than one set of footsteps above. No matter. I can take up to five by myself. The first victim down will equip me with weapons. I have a way out and an advantage. Anyone wanting to get me will have to drop down into the cellar space. Their body mechanics will require them to land with their knees bent. From here, I can swipe my leg under theirs and they will be on their back. In one more move, I can disarm them and shoot them, lifting the dead weight of the body as my shield. I practice the moves in my head. Swipe, attack, shoot, and spin. Swipe, attack, shoot, and spin.

"It's me, Daniel, but I expect you know that. Look, I'm going to drop a Glock down to you as a sign of good faith, okay? It's not your favorite handgun, but hey, no hammer right? Who doesn't like that?"

I consider this. A Glock has no external hammer like most handguns, but an elongated firing pin called a striker instead. It makes for quick and easy shooting, even when your hand is injured.

A light flashes at the top of the opening, and seconds later the Glock and the magazine drop into the dirt. I draw both toward me with my leg. No shots fired. I can barely see the Glock chamber in the dim light of the tunnel, but I dry fire it twice. It sounds and feels fine.

I load the magazine and shoot up into the opening where the trapdoor once sat.

"Jesus fucking Christ." I hear Daniel yelp.

I've got twelve bullets left. Murmurs are exchanged. The other voice belongs to a Russian. So two people, twelve bullets. No question. I consider heading out the tunnel and then circling around and picking the two off from the exterior.

"Listen, you hothead, what will make you come up here without shooting us?"

Nothing, no Daisy. If they had Daisy, I would come up, but I say nothing.

"Okay, listen. It is Vasily and me. Just the two of us. I'd say we were unarmed, but we both know that'd be a lie. I know where Daisy is. I promise you that as of an hour ago, she was fine. Unharmed, maybe a little mentally fucked up, but otherwise doing pretty good. Her blond roommate, not so much."

"Regan," I mutter.

"What's that?"

"The roommate you take? Her name is Regan," I say.

"Yeah, Regan. They hustled her off. I don't know where she is. I couldn't break my cover and leave Daisy. Nikolai, it was not Daisy's finger that got cut off. I promise you. It was another girl. She made a bad deal with Yury and had to pay up. Vasily was there."

"I want to hear from Vasily."

"Get over here, asshole," I hear Daniel mutter to his companion.

"What?" the voice is heavy and accented. It could be Vasily, or it could be a dozen others, but I'm going to play Daniel's game for a short while.

"Why?" I call out.

"Why am I here and not with my uncle Sergei, raping your

tender girlfriend? A virgin?" He clucks his tongue. "I don't know whether to praise you for finding such a gem or laugh at your lack of manhood in failing to take such a prize."

I cannot hold back and I shoot again in the hole. Eleven bullets. Two killers. Still enough.

"*Mudak*," Vasily curses.

Fuck you too, fucker, I think.

"Shut the fuck up, Vasily. We don't have time for this shit," Daniel growls. I hear a scuffle and then Vasily's voice returns, a bit chastised, a bit sullen. This is quite the play the two are putting on. If only my Daisy wasn't in the hands of a fucking madman, I would think this is funny, but I don't.

I am gripping the butt of the Glock so hard that the metal weave on the grip is imprinting itself on my hands. I want to unload the entire magazine until the two are bleeding on the floor.

"GET FUCKING ON WITH IT!" I roar. I have lost all my patience.

"Ah, Nikolai, I thought you were unmanned down there," Vasily says, ever cool. "But nonetheless, Alexsandr was right. Sergei is the wrong leader of the *Bratva*. The selling of our women, the pervasive use of *krokodil*, all of these things are killing us. It is not making us stronger, but weakening us. But even those things, maybe we forgive. But killing Alexsandr, kidnapping your woman, and turning you against us? *Nyet*. Sergei is just not fit to lead. In a generation or less, the *Bratva* will be broken, as Alexsandr said. So, we will help you recover your Daisy. You may kill Sergei. Then you must leave. Leave the *Bratva*, retire. No more kills. No more jobs. The name of Nikolai Andrushko will be wiped out of the books, and you and your

Daisy will cease to exist to us, just as we will cease to exist for you. Those are the terms."

I slide to my butt. All this because Alexsandr whispered in the ears of the *Bratva* that Sergei was unfit? My Daisy taken because Sergei feels his position at the top of the *Bratva* is imperiled? He was more stupid than I thought. But somehow I am still uncertain.

"What will make you feel safe enough to come out, Nick?" Daniel asks. "Because the more time you spend in the tunnel, the greater the risk to Daisy."

He is not wrong. Each minute that ticks by is a minute that Sergei could change his mind and decide to harm her more. But if this is a trap, then I have lost the chance to save her.

"You cannot take on the *Bratva* alone." Vasily reenters the game. "You know this. At best, you have a suicide mission on your hands—at worst, you die at the front gates and Daisy is passed around to the guards until she wants to kill herself."

The options in front of me are bad and worse, but I take bad because I have no choice. I exit out of the back of the tunnel. There is no point in sticking my head out of the hole and waiting for it to be shot off like a melon. At least from the front door, I'll have some cover. I walk to the front of the small cabin, and the door is thrown open.

I press against the side and both Daniel and Vasily walk out. Their hands are to their sides, empty but poised for action. I lower the Glock.

Daniel is six feet five inches. He has at least three inches on me. Vasily and I are more of the same height. Both are fit and hold themselves with a certain lightness that I associate with men who know how to use their bodies as weapons. I could take one, perhaps, but not both. Against my better judgment, I offer my left hand to Daniel in a gesture of agreement.

He takes my hand and squeezes it.

"I'm not doing this out of the goodness of my heart," he says. "I have my own agenda, and I'm going to need your help."

This, I understand. The transaction of favors has meaning to me. I nod and walk inside, showing my back to the two dangerous predators behind me. It is an overwhelming show of good faith.

Inside, I see a battery of weapons. Machine guns, submachine guns, knives, handguns, a stack of C-4 about two feet high. I would've never left this building alive.

Daniel sees me gaping at the C-4. "Right. I had to keep moving that crap so your shittily aimed bullets wouldn't hit it and blow us all to pieces."

I shrug. "You should have been more specific about your goals at the start. But, enough of this. What is the plan?"

DAISY

I hide in the bathroom until I am so exhausted that I curl up and fall asleep, not caring that I'm resting on dirty, broken tile. I will take germs over Yury any day. Hours pass, maybe a day. I've lost track of time. I sleep, but my dreams are full of Nick and guns. Nick, shooting my mother. Nick, holding Galina's hand down as he saws her finger off.

They're not restful dreams. When I am awake, though, I am cold, hungry, sore, and Yury is there. So I sleep the hours away, waiting for death or for Nick.

I am not sure which one I hope for.

I wake up, shivering, when a boot nudges me. I look up, squinting, and I see the big blond giant that had been guarding the door to the warehouse. "Come."

I get up, every bone in my body aching. I'm dizzy when I stand, and I weave a little. The giant's hand grabs me by the arm to steady me, and he drags me out of the bathroom. Yury is there by the card table. There is no sign of Galina, though there is a dark, rusty splash in the center of the table that I can't stop staring at.

I wonder if they sent the finger to Nick. I wonder at his reaction. Would Nick regard it with the same cold, emotionless expression I see on the face of the man holding me upright? Or would it be the sad-eyed, lonely Nick that I fell in love with? Will he be unhappy to receive what he thinks is my finger?

Or will he even care? Do I even know the real Nick at all?

That is the thing that scares me the most, I realize. It's not that Nick is a killer and has an awful past life that has caught up with him. It's that I don't know if the man I've fallen in love with is real or not. It's that I don't know if I know the real Nick at all.

Because I still love him and I still want him, but I don't know if I know him.

"Come," Yury says, interrupting my thoughts. He holds out a zip tie, and I realize my hands are going to be bound again. His grin is vile. "I will enjoy it if you fight."

I don't fight. I cross my wrists and hold them out, waiting. My numb movements remind me of Galina, and I flinch in realization.

Yury seems disappointed that the fight has gone out of me. He ties my wrists tightly in front of me and then gives me another shove, pushing me away from him. He barks something at the blond giant, and a moment later, the hood is tossed back over my head.

"Where are we going?" My voice sounds overloud in the stifling hood.

"You are lucky," Yury says. "The sale has gone through. We will take you to airport and fly you to meet your new owner." He laughs. "Maybe after he is tired of you, he lets me have a round, eh?"

I shudder and hunch my shoulders, as if I can somehow shrink away from these awful men.

Vasily says something, and Yury replies in a nasty tone. Then, the blond nudges my arm.

And I am led out to a car once more.

Vasily's giant hands are strong, but they are kinder than Yury's. He doesn't shove me into the car as much as he prods me into the right direction. I am led to the backseat, and the door is locked again. I hear the men get into the front seat, and then we drive.

And drive.

And drive.

I begin to doze off again. It's hard for me to stay awake. My breath under the hood is muffled and hot, and my head aches so badly that I wonder if something is wrong with me. All I want to do is sleep. Maybe because sleep is an escape. It's the only one I have right now.

"Stop here," a voice says, and I jerk awake.

I hear Yury say something in Russian.

Vasily responds. I catch the words "Coca-Cola" mixed in with his Russian, and I feel the car pull to a halt.

Yury sighs and bites out furious words, but the car remains running. One door opens and shuts, and I hear feet crunching on gravel.

I wait in the backseat, my body tense. Are we . . . on a snack run? That seems insane.

"*Bozhe moi,*" Yury says, and I perk up. I have heard that before. He honks the horn and screams something in Russian. I can't tell if he's mad that the other man is taking too long, or what's going on. The hood isn't tied down over my head, and I wiggle, moving my chin, trying to slide it off without being obvious. I'm desperate to see what's going on.

A moment later, the car door opens, and then it slams shut again. I hear Yury's feet crunching on the gravel as he spits Russian out at someone. He sounds furious. Now that I'm the only one in the car, it's safe for me to reach up and snatch the hood off of my head, and I do so, blinking my eyes and looking around.

I am alone in the car. We are parked outside of a gas station in what seems to be the middle of nowhere. Immediately, I try the door handle. It doesn't respond. Damn it. Frustrated, I turn around and tear at the backseat, trying to get to the trunk. Maybe if there's a car jack, I can put it through the window.

The sound of a fight catches my ears, and I pause, pressing my face to the heavily tinted glass in the backseat.

I can just barely make out what looks like a scuffle. Someone is fighting. . . . Yury? Who would be fighting Yury? Hope flares in my heart. Nick? But the man in the distance is dark haired and too tall to be my love. To my surprise, the other man grabs Yury in an efficient choke hold and presses something against his neck. Yury flails for a moment and then goes limp, and the man hugs his limp body. He drags him back behind the building.

I lose my breath. Oh God. Did . . . did someone just murder Yury?

What does that mean for me?

I drop to the backseat, hiding. My breathing becomes terrified panting. If the killer doesn't see me, maybe the car will be abandoned and I can run away. The big blond assassin is nowhere to be seen, nor does he return to the car. Both he and Yury are possibly dead.

What do I do now?

Fear crawls through me as I hear the car door open; the warning chimes ominously. Someone slides into the front seat. I remain as still as possible, hoping against hope that he is simply searching the car for money and will leave a moment later.

But the keys go into the ignition, and the car starts.

"You okay back there, Daisy?"

It's the American man's voice. The assassin from the warehouse. One of the men who brought Galina to Yury.

I sit up cautiously, sliding to the far end of the backseat despite the fact that there's a window partition separating us. I study the back of his head. "Who are you?"

He snorts. "You can call me Daniel. Nikolai sent me."

My heart slams in my throat. "Nick?" I breathe, relief rushing through me. "But . . ." I pinch off the words, frightened. How do I know to trust this man? He could be lying to me to try and get more information out of me. Even though it kills me, I say nothing else. I simply watch him.

"Did Yury hurt you?" Daniel asks me. "I can't do anything about it now, but just let me know so I can anticipate Nick losing his shit and stay out of the striking zone."

"Where's Regan?"

"Who's Regan?" He sounds as if he couldn't care less. As I watch, he flips on the turn signal and begins to drive away from the gas station.

"My friend. The blond girl that was with me when . . . when they took us."

He shrugs. "Right. Her. She was sold onto the black market a few days ago, if I don't miss my guess. Sorry about that, but she's a problem for later. My problem right now is Nick, and Nick wants you, so here I am." He gives me a thin, mirthless smile in the rearview mirror. "Betraying the *Bratva* and bringing down the house with a crazy sonofabitch. Ain't life fuckin' grand."

I digest this. Does he think Nick is crazy, or is he referring to someone else? Another party I'm not aware of? There are so many things going on that I don't understand. It makes my head—and my heart—ache. I press my hands to my forehead, but that causes a sharp stab of pain radiating from my nose. "Where are we going?"

"To a hotel in Moscow." His gaze flicks to the rearview mirror again. "Gotta reunite Romeo and Juliet."

NIKOLAI

The best weapon in battle, particularly a battle in which you are outmanned, is surprise. Deception is one of the ways to engineer surprise. Sun Tzu declared that all war is deception and that a wise warrior misdirects the reaction. Sergei is a criminal who longs for the recognition of others who possess wealth: those born to oil, minerals, or perhaps who own a technology company that rules Europe. Those men are feted in magazines and are called oligarchs.

For Sergei, whose financial resources might rival the oil barons, he will never have the respect of those he deems his peers, because he is a leech. He orchestrates oil deals, but never owns any oil. The weapons he trades are stained with the blood of others. He transports dirt, the nutrient-rich soil from Ukraine, to Russia. In Ukraine, he leaves enormous holes that he fills with garbage. This is Sergei's legacy. It is one of destruction and waste.

I suddenly realize what drove Alexsandr. For those who love the *Bratva*, and Alexsandr did, Sergei's fall further into the abyss—whether it be from the sale of young girls to diseased foreigners or hooking our own on flesh-eating drugs—is ruining the

Bratva. Soon it will be nothing but a hole full of garbage. He will never be able to fuck the society women or drink vodka in their special clubs. He will always be other.

I have no allegiance to the *Bratva*, but for Vasily, it is his life. Daniel, his allegiance is more occluded, but I am committed to trusting Daniel, no matter his loyalties and agendas. Relying on another sits uncomfortably upon my shoulders, but I have no other choice, at least not one which will see both Daisy and me alive at the end.

Because it is easier to capture one man out in public than one woman in a conclave, we bait a trap.

All of this is taking too much time, and I'm chafing at the wait. Vasily returns to the *Bratva* headquarters. There is no reason for him to go to the estate unless he is called there. No one I trust— and I barely trust Vasily or Daniel—is with Daisy, but they both assure me that Sergei is serious about maintaining her virginity for the purpose of the sale. The sale could take place that week.

The Magvenodov family is my bait. The Magvenodovs are what the Petrovichs aspire to be—or at least what Sergei aspires to be. The patriarch of the Magvenodov family is a billionaire with homes in London, Hong Kong, and New York City. They own a British football team. They dine with princes and kings. Their names are whispered with jealousy and reverence, and there is no door that is closed to them.

The eldest son has a sad taste for the lads which, in Russia, is seen as worse than eating *krokodil* at the dining room table. Better to be eaten by drugs than admit to being a sodomite. I am sorry for Lev that I will use him in this way, but I am desperate. I cannot decide whether Daisy would want me to use every resource at my disposal to free her. The methods I use might be unsavory, but they will be effective.

I resolutely crush any stirrings of a conscience. Sitting outside his lover's apartment, taking photographs like a low-grade *shpion,* demeans both of us, but if I had to eat the garbage in the holes in Ukraine to recover Daisy, I would do so.

I capture the entire evening. Lev's father may actually be more disturbed by the intimate romantic scenes—Lev's boyfriend cooking him dinner or Lev gifting the other man a coat—rather than the sexual scenes. Lev's father has his own perversions, but they are more socially acceptable. Still, it is effective blackmail.

"Lev Dmitrievna Magvenodov," I quietly call out as he exits the building. The look of postcoital relaxation is immediately replaced with wariness. This man is no idiot. A person lying in wait for him outside his lover's apartment has no good news.

I wait in the shadows in case Magvenodov should decide to shoot and run. But he does neither. Instead, he walks straight toward me, and my unease at what I am going to ask him grows in proportion to his bravado. "*Kak vas zovut?*" he calls out.

"I am Nikolai Andrushko." I answer his question about my name.

"*Vy poteryali?*"

"*Nyet,* I am not lost." I pause and make a split decision. I swing the camera behind me and tuck the SD card in my pocket. It is enough that I am here. If he has any intelligence, he will know my leverage. If he is too dumb to recognize the danger, he would be worthless. "I come to seek your assistance."

I step out so that some of the light from the building washes over me, and I hold my arms from my side. With my body, I signal that I am no immediate threat.

"And what will I get in return?" Magvenodov asks.

"What is it that you seek?"

Magvenodov looks at the window of his lover's apartment. "I should say the photographs you have taken, but I curiously do not care. Perhaps I am relieved at no longer having to hide."

This isn't quite the response I was hoping for, so I wait. Brave and smart, but not as patient as me.

Magvenodov heaves a sigh. "What is it that you want? Money? Access?"

"None of those. I want you to meet with Sergei Petrovich. In public. Tomorrow morning. Ten."

"A mobster? What are you trying to get me into?"

"I have a"—I curl my tongue around the word and release it because it feels right—"loved one in the grasp of the *Bratva*. After tomorrow, Sergei Petrovich will no longer exist, and the *Bratva* will owe you a favor. Anything."

"You are in a position to make these promises?" Magvenodov pulls out a cigarette pack and pops two smokes up. He offers me one. I gesture for him to hand me the lighter so that I can help him light the cigarette. As he hands it over, I think he's not so smart then. He hands me a weapon and bows his head in front of me. But then, not everyone was raised by Alexsandr.

"Yes." I take deep drags on the cigarette, inhaling the nicotine as if it were oxygen. Magvenodov smokes more slowly, almost leisurely, as if he were enjoying an after-dinner coffee. My patience is waning now. I want to be ready to move to the next step. The distraction.

Magvenodov nods slowly, as if thinking something agreeable to himself. "Yes, I will do this."

"Good. Tomorrow at Baltschug at ten," I instruct. "If you do not come, it will go poorly for you."

The warning is unnecessary, because Magvenodov simply rolls

his eyes. "Do not treat me like I am a child. You want something from me, and I am delivering." He thumps his chest lightly. "And Baltschug? So we can stare at the Kremlin while we eat? So passé."

"You need only occupy his time for ten, twenty minutes at the most. Offer him nothing. Just the whiff of opportunity will render Sergei Petrovich weak at the knees. A disturbance will happen at the restaurant. Act concerned, but ensure no one interferes."

Magvenodov nods, but I make him repeat the instructions. "Offer him nothing. Do not interfere."

I give a curt jerk of my chin in acknowledgment. Magvenodov begins to turn away, but I grasp his wrist and pull up his hand to shake my gloved one. "Tomorrow then. You should think about London or Switzerland. Maybe even America. Easier to breathe there."

And then I walk away, disappearing into the shadows. I'm on to the next play. Behind me, I've left the only bargaining chip I have, but my spirit feels lighter. The microcard with the incriminating photographs belongs to Magvenodov now.

CHAPTER **FOURTEEN**

NIKOLAI

The suite at Hotel Metropol is carefully outfitted. I roll up the Aubusson carpet that covers the nearly century-old parquet floors. The Bolshevik officials resided in these suites after the revolution. It makes sense for Sergei to meet his fate here.

I have a kit ready that includes plastic sheeting, a gun bought on the street after my meeting with Magvenodov, and cyanide pills. A black duffel, large enough for a body, is stuffed inside my case. A quick look around the room assures me everything is in order. We are just missing two pieces: Daisy and Sergei.

Because I would never be able to get into the Petrovich compound by myself, I am tasked with retrieving Sergei. I must leave Daisy to Daniel and Vasily. For over an hour I argued with the two of them, but Daniel was resolute that there was no chance of me getting into the compound. Sick at heart but resigned, I left to seek out Magvenodov.

Now I am alone in the palatial hotel suite, but I appreciate none of it. I do not want to sleep because I know Daisy is out there, in danger. Anything could happen tonight, and the unknowing is like thousands of knives piercing my flesh. I use every trick I've ever learned to get my body into a restful state. Tomorrow I must be sharp and ready. Eventually, I drift off.

A few hours later, I awaken. The night still lingers but the rest has been enough. It must be, because I know I will get no more. I drive toward the Petrovich compound and sit in the rented sedan watching the traffic move by. The scenes from the video replay in my head and the screams I imagined Daisy must have made when she feared they would take her finger make me want to bend the car in half. Instead I must wait.

I wait so long I fear Sergei is not going to meet Magvenodov, that he is pissed off by the short notice, which amounts to not much more than a royal summoning. When I see the three-car cavalcade leave in the morning, I sigh with relief. Sergei may be angry, but he is too eager to lick the boots of the oligarchy.

The drive into Moscow proper will take Sergei thirty minutes. I speed up and pass the three vehicles. About five miles ahead of them, I cause a collision between a semitrailer truck and a livestock hauler.

The semi tips over, and the two drivers are out of their vehicles screaming at each other. Debris from the interior of the trailer litters the highway. Cars swerve in and out; their drivers try to avoid witnessing this misfortune lest it follow them home. The confusion allows me to easily pull over to the side in my stolen vehicle, and I race back toward Sergei's motorcade.

My heart pounds fiercely as I run along the tree-lined highway, and I am grateful there is still some foliage to provide me cover. Even though the traffic is still moving, it has slowed. I know my window of opportunity will be small. The drivers will move their vehicles or others, like Sergei, will simply drive in the ditch or on the shoulder to move forward. He'll not want to be late for a meeting with Lev Magvenodov.

I'm grateful for my regular workout regimen as the burn of the run begins to spread from my lungs outward. The chill air makes it hard to breathe, but I force myself to run faster and faster until I see the motorcade in front of me. The sight spurs me forward. I run past the vehicles and slip into traffic, knowing that the dash cams will pick me up. I pull my skullcap lower and raise the collar of my overcoat to conceal my features as best I can.

I run to the vehicle just behind the last SUV in the motorcade, which has allowed itself to be separated by two cars from Sergei's Maybach. This inattentiveness will serve me well. I pull out a heavy metal disk and throw it toward the front of the SUV, striking the hood. The driver predictably slams on his brakes and looks forward. With a quick inhalation, I sprint forward and grasp the driver's side door and wrench it open. Quickly I aim for the passenger side but there is no one there. It is only the driver. I catalog that detail but give it no further thought. It is just one of many signs of the sickness in the Petrovich *Bratva*. Sergei's laziness and lack of attention to detail will be his downfall.

"You're going to climb into the passenger seat or get your brains blown off," I tell the random Petrovich soldier in Russian as I get in.

He raises his hands from the wheel and nods. I cannot push the dead man out of the vehicle. Everyone in Russia has a dash cam, and I don't need this posted on the Internet later.

The Petrovich soldier does what I tell him, and I climb into the driver's seat and pull the car forward. He looks awkward sitting hunched against the passenger seat, my gun in his face.

"How old are you?" I ask.

"Twenty-five," he answers. Older than I am, but he still has an air of naïveté about him as if he can't believe he has found himself in this situation.

"Do you know who I am?"

He shakes his head. The line of cars moves forward slowly, but we are undeterred by death here in Russia. No one is gawking at the accident, for these types of roadside injuries are all too common.

"I am Nikolai Andrushko." I hear his quick inhalation of breath. "So you've heard of me?"

"*Da*. Alexsandr talks, I mean, talked of you some." The young man squeaks. He is so young and untried that I feel exhausted by the idea of having to terminate him.

"The girl that Sergei brought to the compound. She belongs to me."

Silence then. I think the baby soldier is afraid to speak, and when he does, his fear is evident in the high-pitched tone of his voice. "Yours?"

"Did you touch her? Did you look at her? Did you laugh at her terror?" I spit out. This is unfair, but I have no one else to vent to.

"N-n-no," he stutters. "I didn't see her. I only know that there was someone brought in who was important and who no one was to talk to."

We are nearing the city proper, and I debate what I will do with this kid. I cannot have him interfering with my business, but I am loath to kill him. He is so green he doesn't even know to use his cyanide capsule.

At a stoplight, I reach over and thump him over the head with the Glock. He slumps down, unconscious. I reach over and pull off his coat and hat. Unless the driver in the front knows this kid closely, I will pass. The function of the Petrovich motorcade is to simply provide protection for the interior vehicle. The bodyguards in the interior car will enter the restaurant with Sergei while the motorcade drivers stay outside.

Thankfully Sergei does not deviate from this typical procedure, and he enters the restaurant without glancing toward the rear SUV. Leaving the vehicle idling, I hop out and walk to the lead SUV. Popping the lock, I slide into the rear seat, strike the driver unconscious, and then turn to the passenger. He is another unknown.

"Sergei is using recruits for cover?" I shake my head. The Petrovich *Bratva* is going to hell. Sergei's uncle would've never used unseasoned soldiers for this task. Every one of the individuals in the vehicles would have been known to him by their first name. They would've worked for him for at least ten years. It was an honor for a Petrovich foot soldier to guard the head of the *Bratva*. The lack of a known Petrovich in either of these vehicles is a telling sign of the insidious sickness inside the *Bratva*, and it makes Vasily's actions all the more understandable.

Like Alexsandr, Vasily's loyalty is to the *Bratva* itself, not to Sergei. That he is facilitating Sergei's demise is an action consistent with saving the organization—it is not then considered insurrection.

I breathe a little easier. Vasily is a man of his word. Daisy would be delivered safely to me, and in order to uphold my bargain, I must dispose of Sergei without this being tied to Vasily.

I knock the other baby soldier out, too. I don't care that they will report back to Vasily that it was a dark-haired Ukrainian who attacked them. After tomorrow, Nikolai Andrushko will cease to exist. I'm here to ensure the death of only one man. Sergei.

The rest of the morning goes off without a hitch, so smoothly that I begin to worry. The waiter I bribed replaces the sugar with baking soda. Sergei drinks his supposedly sugared coffee and spits it out immediately, but the reaction of the baking soda with the Perrier he always begins his breakfast with causes foaming to appear at the mouth.

"My God, he's got rabies!" cries one patron. Others stand up and move away immediately.

"What kind of disease have you brought in here?" Magvenodov demands and shoves back from the table. Sergei holds his hands out, pleading with the wealthy oligarchs.

"It's nothing!" he shouts but no one there believes him. Sergei is vermin to them, and that he is actually foaming at the mouth only proves how he does not belong. I would laugh at him if I didn't want to twist his head off his neck.

His bodyguards are trying to help him, but they are being blocked by the staff. It is easy enough to slip into the melee and administer a syringe of curare to both bodyguards and to Sergei. Curare is a paralytic drug harvested from vines of the South America rainforest that causes almost no harm but renders the victim immobile for a short time.

When Sergei goes limp, it's easy enough for me to shoulder him and push my way out of the restaurant. The staff and patrons think I am one of his foot soldiers, coming to his aid. If only they knew the truth.

I drag Sergei out, his heavy body made more unmanageable by his paralytic condition. I fold him into his Maybach and take off for the hotel.

The private hotel elevator for the top floor of the Hotel Metropol is convenient. I encounter no others on my trip up to our suite. Sergei is fully awake and shooting poisonous glances my way. I feel almost jubilant.

"You look unhappy, Sergei. Is it because you cannot move

your limbs or because the whole oligarchy of Russia now thinks you are a diseased dog?" I don't even try to stifle a laugh. My joke at his expense only enrages him further. I drag him down the hall and into the suite. Dropping him by the door, I go to the kit and get out the plastic wrap and duct tape, and I position one of the heavy mahogany chairs in the middle of the plastic.

"I know. You are thinking, 'Just wait, Nikolai, until I gain full function of my limbs again. You will be hunted like the dog you are.'" I click my tongue at him, watching as a little saliva dribbles from his tongue. The curare is wearing off. I debate giving him another dose but decide against it.

He flops in the chair, and I tape his arms to the sides so that he can sit upright. Then his legs. I text Daniel that my quarry is secured.

I receive an immediate OK in return.

I sit on the sofa and disassemble the Glock, clean it, and reassemble it. It's larger than I would like for Daisy, but I can help hold it when she shoots Sergei. I wonder how long this can take. The drive from the Petrovich compound is only half an hour, but I suppose Vasily must mobilize the transport for Daisy. Perhaps news has already reached the compound of Sergei's kidnapping. In order to be able to effectively lead the *Bratva* after Sergei's demise, Vasily must appear as if he had nothing to do with Sergei's death.

"Why do you not kill me?" Sergei chokes out. The curare is wearing off.

"Because that is for Daisy."

He gives a weak cough and leans his head back to spit out his extra saliva to the side. It makes a slight splatting noise when it hits the plastic. "She's too weak. She'll never do it." His head lolls to the side.

"I wonder why you do this, Sergei? Why you take these risks?" I muse. Leaning my head to one side, I pull and crack my neck muscles. I do the same on the other side to relieve tension.

"What risks? Killing Alexsandr?" Sergei spits again, only this time some of the liquid hangs on the side of his mouth. He looks unkempt, like a beggar pulled from the streets.

The mention of Alexsandr kills my humor at Sergei's situation. I begin to pace, knowing that I shouldn't show my agitation to Sergei but do so anyway. "You knew that Harry was diseased and that your transplant source was selling organs from alcoholics and drug addicts and HIV patients. You knew you were supplying bad *krokodil* to your own people and killing them. These are the acts of a stupid man, unfit to lead."

"Is that what they tell you? Alexsandr thinks the *Bratva* business too dirty for us. Perhaps, he says, we should not do some of these things anymore. Alexsandr shows me he is too weak to be the enforcer of the *Bratva*." Sergei tries to sneer, but the lax control over his muscles make him look as if he is seizing.

"You have no sense of brotherhood," I scoff. "Alexsandr would no more betray the *Bratva* than he would cut off his own cock, but you kill him because he talks reason that you do not want to hear. Then you endanger everyone by taking Daisy." I stoop in front of him and point the empty gun in his face. "Daisy needs to see you die so that in the night, when it is dark, she can know that she does not need to be afraid."

"Where will you be?"

"Beside her." *Holding her hand and helping her pull the trigger*, I think.

"And you are not enough man to take her virginity, let alone her fear."

Sergei has no taunts that can touch me, but I tape his mouth shut because I am tired of hearing his drivel. I pull up my tracking program and wait.

DAISY

I watch Daniel with wariness as he pulls into the parking lot of the hotel. It's quiet, and there's no one around, but I don't trust this man. How can I trust anyone ever again? Everyone has lied to me.

Even Nick. It's his lie that hurts the most, honestly. It feels like I never really knew him, after all this.

When the car stops, I don't move. I wait with bated breath to see what this new man will do. He tells me he's working with Nikolai to bring down the *Bratva* leader, but I don't know that I can trust him or what he tells me.

After all, Nick was Nick Anders to me. He is not Nikolai, *Bratva* hit man.

Daniel comes to the side door of the car and opens it to let me out. I leave the car, every muscle in my body screaming caution. He sees my tension and leans in. "I'm taking you to Nikolai, little girl. It's not in your best interest to run. You have nowhere to go."

He's right, but it doesn't stop the thought from crossing my mind and lingering there. I don't respond to this, only raise my tied wrists.

He pulls out a knife, and I wait . . .

But he only slices through my bonds. "Come on," he says. "Stay behind me and keep quiet. We're going in the back way."

Daniel takes me to a service elevator in the parking garage and

then into a back door. We cut through a kitchen, an empty hallway, and then through what looks like a laundry room as we make
our way inside. We pass people in staff uniforms, but they deliber-
ately avoid making eye contact with us. It's like they see my bruised
face and the dangerous man I am with, and they want to pretend
we do not exist. It's probably easier that way; I don't blame them.

Then, we are in another elevator, a staff one. Daniel pushes a
button and waits at my side, his stance wary. I cannot help but
look at the perfect hang of his jacket, wondering where the gun
is. I wonder if I can grab it before he breaks my wrist.

And then what?

Fight my way into the hotel? Tell the manager that I have been
kidnapped?

And . . . then what? Will they take me back to the States, or
will they call the authorities? What if the men I am running from
are the authorities?

I'm so confused, so cornered. I clench my hands and wait for
instinct to kick in. Instinct will tell me what to do.

The elevator dings, announcing that we've arrived at our
floor. "Come on," Daniel says, and he puts a hand to my shoulder.

I flinch away, skittering backward a step. "Don't touch me."

"Sorry," he says, and he raises his hands in the air to show me
he means no harm. "Let's go, before Nikolai decides we're taking
too long and kills Vasily."

My heart goes cold at his casually tossed off words. *Let's go
before Nikolai kills Vasily.* Like he would do it in a fit of spite.
My Nick.

Daniel walks two steps behind me—probably so he can watch
my movements in case I bolt—and he shepherds me down the
hall to a hotel room door. 786. It's the last one down the hall,
and it offers a modicum of privacy from the other rooms. Once

at the door, Daniel knocks once, then three times rapidly, then once again.

It's a pattern I'm familiar with. Didn't my father and I have our own system of knocks and acknowledgments to let the other know it was safe? The door opens immediately on the other side, and there is Nick, who gathers me into his arms. I catch a glimpse of him. He looks tired, stiff . . . furious. His arms are trembling around me as if he can barely hold on to his control, and an animalistic sound escapes his throat. I sag into him, feeling safe even though I know it's ridiculous to feel safe here in the arms of a man who kills people for a living.

Some semblance of sense creeps in, and I push out of Nick's arms.

He grabs me before I can retreat from his anger, and his hands capture my face. His eyes are wild as he surveys my swollen nose and my bruised eyes, but his fingers are careful as he traces over my injuries. After a long, tense moment, he lifts my hand and examines it carefully. He pauses at the bruises circling my wrists, but he seems satisfied that I have all my fingers.

Then, before I can say anything, he whips out a gun and points it at Daniel's forehead.

Everyone in the room freezes.

"Nikolai," Daniel says warningly. His expression hasn't changed. "You know we're in this together."

"You let them hurt her," Nick growls. "You let them touch my Daisy."

"What were we supposed to do? Cuddle her in front of Sergei and Yury?" Daniel's voice is flat, unafraid. It's almost like he's daring Nick to shoot him. "Use your brain, dipshit. She has all her fingers. She was not raped. She is fine."

Nick is breathing hard, and his face is flushed with rage. The hand holding the gun aloft trembles, and I realize he's struggling to keep control.

Daniel's gaze flicks to me, and I realize he wants me to speak up and say something.

"Nick, you're scaring me." I don't have to fake the tremble in my voice; I'm utterly terrified at this moment.

It's my voice that breaks through his mindless rage. The gun lowers and goes back into the holster in his jacket.

And then Nick turns to me and his hands cup my face again. "Daisy," he groans, and he leans in to kiss me. It's a gentle kiss, mindful of my split lip. "My sweet Daisy."

I can't relax in his grip this time, even when he pulls me closer and wraps his arms around me. All I can think is that this man is an assassin and that he nearly killed a man just now. All because he thought Daniel hurt me. He would kill over bruises and a split lip.

I wonder what else Nick has killed over.

He seems to sense that I am not returning his hug, that I am shrinking away from his touch. He takes a step backward, and those intense eyes study me, full of hope and longing and relief.

"You are not hurt?"

I shake my head. I'm not hurt, not really. I'm bruised, I'm terrified, and I'm feeling so betrayed, but I'm not hurt. "Where's Regan?"

"No one knows. We find her, but later. Other things are more important right now." His hand reaches out as if he wants to touch me again, but he drops it just as quickly.

"I hate to break up this sweet little reunion," Daniel says in that droll, utterly American voice. "But where's Sergei?"

"In other room."

"Still alive," Daniel says, and I can tell by the way he says it that he's not pleased.

"*Da*. Revenge is for Daisy alone. This, I give to her." Out comes Nick's gun again, and he offers it to me, handle first. "It is only for her."

Daniel mutters a very American curse.

Nick shoots him a furious look.

I stare at the gun being offered to me and then at Nick. Nick, who I thought I knew. "You . . . want me to go in there and kill someone?"

"Is not *someone*," Nick says, and his accent grows thicker, a sure sign he is agitated. He takes my hand and puts it on the gun, forcing it into my grasp. "It is the fucker who took you from me. Who has stolen Regan. I give you revenge so you can sleep at night."

"Nick," I cry, wanting to release the gun, but his fingers are wrapped around mine. "I'm not going to *murder* someone."

"Let her go, man," Daniel says in a low voice. "She's not like us. Look at her. She's terrified of you."

It's as if Nick is seeing me for the first time when Daniel says that. It's like it's just now occurred to him that I won't like the idea of killing Sergei. It's like he's just now realized there's more to my reluctance than fear from being kidnapped.

I watch the light in Nick's eyes die slowly as he sees the way I hold myself back, the way I regard him with fear. I watch the hope in them—the terrible, awful love in them—wither away. Now, there is nothing but sadness as he regards me. Sadness and yearning.

"So," he says, and his voice is so cold, so even, so calm. "Sergei has told you who I am, *da*? And now you are afraid of me."

"You're a hit man," I say. "You all murder for *money*." The words taste vile in my mouth. "Why didn't you tell me?"

"And what would I say to you, little Daisy?" There is so much pain in his voice. So much self-loathing. "That I want to kiss you and make love to you even though I am not worthy of your small-est attentions? Far better to say nothing. It is easier to beg for-giveness than to ask permission."

I shake my head. This is a nightmare. This is all a nightmare. I want to go home and wake up in my bed, curled up against Nick's side, Regan asleep in the other room. I want things to be like they were when my eyes weren't opened to the truth.

But I can't go back to that. And now that I know the reality of who—and what—Nick is, I want to laugh at myself for not see-ing it before. There's a predatory grace in every motion that he makes. His eyes are cold at times, calculating. He handles guns like he was born to them. He's covered in strange, dangerous-looking tattoos. He grew up in a family of coworkers who are "not good" by his own admission. He's wealthy and pays for things with cash. He rents cars and lives in apartments across the street so he can watch people.

And he watches me. He's always showing up at the right moment.

It's so obvious, so chokingly obvious, that I feel stupid.

Nick's hand drops away from mine so quickly that I have no choice but to clutch at the gun he's left in my grasp. It's like his eyes are begging me to see him on the inside, past the trappings, but my mind is too bruised and unhappy at the moment to see anything but the fact that Nick is not who I thought he was.

His hand reaches up to brush my cheek, and when I flinch away, he flinches in return. "I knew I could not keep you," he says. His voice is hoarse with emotion. "Such a beautiful, innocent soul. I just wanted you for as long as I could have you. I knew it was wrong, and I did not care. Someday, I hope you forgive me."

Tears cloud my eyes, but I'm still trembling, still holding on to that gun.

"Sergei is yours to do with as you please," he tells me. "Whatever you choose, I understand. But I know something about monsters." Nick clears his throat and swallows. The Adam's apple is prominent in his throat, and I can't look away from it—from him.

"If you do not dispatch the monster that harms you, he will rise again and again in your dreams and you can never feel safe. Every day of your life, you will look around the corner and wonder if it is him. When you come home at night, you will fear the dark spaces of your rooms. Small things like your closet will become a place of terror. I save Sergei for you so that you can hold the metal in your hands and feel the power of the bullet and see the evidence firsthand of his death. That way you sleep at night and go out into the day without fear." He tips my chin up so we can stare into each other's eyes. "See the truth in my eyes and know I do this for you."

The truth of his words ring in my ears. He speaks of my father's life and maybe his own. I do know he does this for me even if I don't understand all of it; I know that Nick's statements to me are the truth. If he is capable of love, he loves me, and he doesn't want me to be afraid.

His hand cups my cheek and holds it tenderly. "But whatever you decide, kitten, I will support you."

Daniel makes a sound of protest in his throat, but Nick shoots him a furious look, and he goes silent. Nick turns back to me, and there is silent pleading for understanding in his eyes, but he nods. "It is your choice, Daisy. You hold his life in your hands, and I will honor your wishes."

"Even if I let him go?"

"*Da*, even that."

I wouldn't, though. I'd turn him over to the police so they can enact justice. That is the smart thing to do. But it's good to know that even now, I am in control. I nod at Nick.

He just watches me, heart in his eyes.

I swallow hard. I want him to take the gun back, but I suspect that if I offer it to him, it will be the end of everything. Nick will take it back and disappear out of my life as silently as he entered it.

And I'm not sure I'm ready for that yet. So I clutch the gun in my hand.

NIKOLAI

I have fucked this up.

Daisy is looking at me like I am no better than Moscow sewer rats. Like I am not better than Sergei. Daisy needs food and to rest, not to be forced into killing a man. Her body is trembling, and while her hand is clutched around the gun I've given her, she looks like a leaf could fell her.

I retrieve the gun from her hand. She resists at first, making a small sound of protest. Thankfully, she allows me to rest an arm around her shoulders. Carefully I direct her toward the sofa, where she collapses.

"Rest for a moment, Daisy. We talk later."

A soft, low sob escapes her, and it rips through me. Biting my cheek to corral my anger toward Sergei, I lay a blanket over her body. The warmth of the blanket and perhaps the enveloping comfort of the sofa allows Daisy to relax. Kneeling beside her, I stroke her brow and am relieved that she does not flinch from my hand. Whatever she has been through, she still allows me to touch her and she still takes comfort from me. It is enough. If this is all I have from her but she lives safe and happy for a long time, then it is enough.

"Nick, man." I hear Daniel settle into one of the chairs. "You gotta learn to be a little more subtle."

I flick a finger at him but say nothing so as not to bother Daisy. "I'm going to order us some food," I tell her.

"I'll take a steak. Rare." Daniel tosses his dirty boots onto the gold-inlaid coffee table. "I like to hear the faint moos when the dome comes off the plate."

Daisy shudders at this statement. "Gross," she mumbles.

I take her participation as a positive sign. As long as she remains willingly with me, it is positive. Even if she no longer loves me, even if she hates me.

"You should leave, Daniel," I tell him, flipping through the room service menu.

"Can't. We've unfinished business." He nods his head toward the room with Sergei, but his wordless gesture is unnecessary. Daisy knows what we talk of.

"Sergei, you mean?" she asks.

"*Da*." I crouch next to her again. "But we need fuel. Blinis? Meat? Cabbage soup?"

DAISY

I stare at him in a daze. Nick is offering me food like we're on vacation. Like it's normal to order room service while we have a kidnapped man sitting in the next room, waiting for me to execute him.

I can't process this. My hands curl and go to my forehead. "Nick . . . I . . ."

I don't know what I want to say. There's so much bubbling in my head. Nick wants me to go in the next room and shoot a man. A man who is our enemy. But that's what the bad guys do. They murder and kill.

I've always thought of myself as one of the good guys. But I look over at Nick and realize that I've fallen for someone who can't be considered one of the "good guys" by any stretch of the imagination.

He's a killer.

And it's awful, because I still want him. I want to curl up in his arms and have him stroke my hair and mutter Russian endearments to me like everything is going to be okay. His touch has always made things better in the past.

Does it make me bad for wanting him?

He doesn't seem to realize my distress. He's still crouching in front of me, his hands brushing over my shoulders, face looking up into mine.

It's still the same Nick as before, the same possessive touch.

And I suddenly feel . . . bad for accepting it. I've lusted after a killer all this time.

No, I correct myself. I've lusted after Nick. I knew his job wasn't legal, not exactly. I was fine with him being a computer hacker, but now that I know he's some sort of Mafia hit man, I have an issue with it?

The problem is with me—and my brain.

Oddly enough, I think back to the movie we watched together, back at home. It was a movie about superheroes, and I'd gone on and on about how I wanted the bad guys to get their due.

Nick had been offended. Hurt, even. He'd tried to tell me that the bad guys were just doing what they could. That they were making the best out of a bad situation.

I'd thought he was picking a fight with me. But maybe . . . maybe he was talking about himself.

I'm too quick to judge, I realize. I don't know Nick as well as I thought, but I can't hate him. Not when he's here to rescue me. Not when he's putting his life on the line for mine. Not when he's looking up at me as if the world begins and ends with my smile.

I can't hate Nick. I'm still hopelessly in love with him.

With the bad guy.

I wonder what this makes me.

NIKOLAI

Daisy is silent for so long that I worry about her. I caress her arm and repeat my question. "Food? Blinis? Borscht?"

She thinks for a minute, and a tentative smile touches her mouth, as if she seeks to reassure me. "I don't know what those are."

"Blinis are small pancakes served with caviar. Borscht is a beet soup. Is very good," I say, encouraging that smile. I would do anything to have her look happy again.

She considers this for a moment. "Blinis, I think. No caviar, though. And thank you, Nick." Her small hand touches mine.

Nodding, I bend down thoughtlessly and press a kiss to her forehead. She sighs deeply and then wraps her arms around me. Without another thought to Daniel, I capture her mouth and hungrily kiss her, sucking in her breath and giving it back to her in the next moment. I feel exultant.

Her lips are tentative at first but then her fervent passion leaks through, and we kiss as if we have been separated months instead of days. I run a hand down her back, feeling the fine bones of her shoulders and the individual bumps on her spine. These all reassure me that she is still alive, still possibly loving me. The bottom of her shirt has pulled up and I can stroke a tiny patch of skin.

I feel her shiver in response. This time I know it is not from fear or the cold, and I press her more tightly against me, my fingers dipping below the waistband of her pants. She moans quietly, and I respond with my own guttural sound of need.

A cough behind me interrupts the fog of desire that has swept over me. Daisy breaks away and burrows, embarrassed, into my chest. Turning slightly so that Daniel can see me, I send him a heated glare. "Go away."

"Can't."

In that moment, I want to go and shoot Sergei myself so that Daniel will leave us alone. Instead, I press another kiss on Daisy's forehead and place a room service order for a bottle of vodka, borscht, two orders of blinis hold the caviar, and two steaks, one with the head still attached.

"Daniel, go check on our guest."

Daniel releases a huge sigh as if my request is extremely burdensome, but he gets up and slips into the adjoining room without another word. After the door closes behind him, I kneel down by Daisy's side again. Her head is resting on her small hands, and she looks uncertain.

"Do you need anything?" I brush the loose strands of her hair away from her eyes and tuck the fine silk behind her ear. "I can get you anything."

"No." She struggles to sit up, but I press her down. "I can't lie here with you kneeling beside me. It makes me feel weird. Or weirder, I guess." She pushes into a sitting position, and this time I do not protest. Patting the empty cushion beside her, she gestures me forward. Stiffly, I sit beside her until she curls her body into mine. Lifting her, I situate her in my lap, tucking her legs in and resting her head on my shoulder. Her nose burrows into my neck, and a rush of joy permeates my bones.

"I'm sorry I never told you before what I am." My throat is tight as I await her response. She exhales, and I feel her body relax as she does.

"It's not like there was ever a good time, right?"

"Right." I'm so grateful that she is accepting and so, in this moment, I try to make her understand.

"When I was fifteen, Alexsandr sends me to Milan to take care of a curator of a small private museum. He is old, maybe fifties, and is surrounded by young boys. At first, I balk at doing this job. He is taking in young boys off the street and giving them a warm place to sleep, food in their bellies, clothes on their backs. Ignoring Alexsandr's summons to finish the job and return, I begin to watch. I take a chance and meet one of the boys who is delivering a painting. Up close I can see that he is scared of everyone. He scuttles through the streets, looks no one in the eye. I try to approach but he flees."

A mew of pain emanates from Daisy, and I realize I've squeezed her too tightly. "Sorry," I mutter and loosen my grip.

"It's nothing. Go on," she urges.

"So I watch and then I see. This curator takes in the homeless boys and makes them do things to him. Makes them watch each other. Makes them do things to each other." I pause, not wanting to give voice to the things I saw. "Do you understand, Daisy?"

"I do," she chokes out. Daisy is tenderhearted, and for a moment I think that maybe I should not share this story with her, but it is important she understands.

"Finally, after two weeks, I get one boy to talk to me. I tell him that the curator will be taken care of, and he tells me that the monster will always live within him. I do not want that for these boys, so I tell this one child, perhaps the leader, that I will help him kill the monster. And I do. The results were . . . messy," I admit.

"And for this, Alexsandr says I must leave the *Bratva,* for my loyalty was impaired by my feelings for someone else. He was right to make me leave, but I would've done it again if I had the chance, Daisy. I think your father is locked in his own prison because the monster who took your mother still lives. I do not want that for you."

We both fall silent. Room service comes and goes. Daniel comes out of the adjoining room and we eat together, silently. I know not what Daisy thinks as she has been quiet since I've told her the story.

After eating, she goes to the bathroom, and I hear the shower run for a very long time.

"Leave her alone, man," Daniel advises when I stand up and look at the bathroom door for the fifth or fiftieth time.

When Daisy comes out of the bathroom in a white robe, I offer her some clothes I've brought for her. Soft jeans, an undershirt, and a cashmere sweater. She takes them to the bathroom and emerges again, hair wet but fully dressed.

I offer her a glass of vodka, but she is uninterested.

"I'm going to go sit out on the balcony for a little bit."

I pick up a blanket and follow her out, but before I can cross the threshold, she places a hand on my chest. "I need a moment to myself, okay?"

The worry must show on my face, because she reaches up to stroke one hand down my cheek. Turning, I press a kiss into her palm. "Yes," I say. "I will wait for you. Always."

She nods and closes the door, separating us. I lean my forehead against the glass until I feel Daniel drag me away.

DAISY

A number of minutes later, I return to the hotel room from the balcony.

"Can I . . . can I talk to Sergei? I want to find out where he's taken Regan."

"He is yours," Nick says, and his tone is more brusque. He gestures at the half-open bedroom door and steps aside.

I glance at the door and then back at Nick, but he won't look me in the eye. He's scanning the room again, a pretense of safety keeping him from looking at me. I know he wants to clench me to his side—I can tell by the way his hands keep making fists—but he's giving me space. He knows I need it.

He knows me so, so well.

I swallow hard and push the door open, stepping into the bedroom of the hotel. It is opulent, this room, with an enormous mirror across from the king-sized bed and the dainty, old-world furniture that decorates the room. Sergei sits in a cleared space, taped to a chair sitting on plastic. I close my eyes for a minute, not wanting to process what the plastic means.

When he sees me, though, his gaze flicks to the gun in my hands, and he laughs. "So," he calls out. "They have sent the little flower to do the deed?"

I step forward, trembling. Even though this man is bound on the chair and looks helpless, I am still frightened of him. He's malevolent, this Sergei, and I can feel his evilness seeping out of his pores and into the air I breathe.

I look behind me, and Daniel has come to the door. He closes it and then leans against it, standing guard. He is there to make sure Sergei won't hurt me, I know, but his presence isn't reassuring. For a moment I wish he were Nick, but I guess that he needs time to process my struggle with who he is.

I want Nick, but I'm still unsure about the fact that he's a trained killer. Can the two be separated? Will Nick be the same if they are?

I approach the bed slowly. There is a wooden chair at the table next to the side of the bed, and I carefully place the gun on the tabletop and angle the chair so I can sit facing Sergei, who is still taped to his chair. The plastic makes crinkling sounds as I move around.

"Where is Regan?" I ask. My voice is so, so calm. I've learned this from Nick—that I can sound fearless even if I'm shaking inside.

Sergei's lips pull into a thin, ugly grimace. I notice he has dried tracks of drool around his mouth and wonder at it. "The little blonde? You will never see her again."

"Where is she?" I am responsible for her. I must know where Regan is.

"Even if I knew, *pizda*, I would not tell you." Sergei's smile is condescending. "Likely, she has been sold to a black market whorehouse. Once they have used her until she is diseased, they will harvest her for organs. It will be a slow and ugly death for your Regan, and she will curse your name every hour, upon the hour. How does this make you feel?"

I know he's simply trying to rile me, but his words hurt. I flinch.

As if he can sense my pain, Sergei continues. He nods at the gun on the table. "So, he has sent you in here to dispatch me, has he?"

"I'm not going to kill you," I tell him quietly. "I don't play games with death. I just want to know where my friend is."

"You will not kill me, *da*." He laughs again, as if he finds this funny. "Poor Nikolai. Lonely, discarded *Bratva* boy brought low by an innocent virgin who is repulsed by who he is. He drags me to you and places the gun in your hand like mangy cat bringing a rodent to its master for approval. He does not understand your disgust, because to him, it is job well done."

His smirk is so ugly to see. "But you are not like him, eh, little flower? The thought of killing one such as me repulses you, even though your Nikolai would not hesitate."

I say nothing. He's right about everything so far. I'm curious what else he will talk about if I remain silent. Nick uses this technique a lot. I see that now. If he doesn't know what to say, he waits you out. So I sit there and stare back at Sergei.

"Your lover cannot cut it with the *Bratva*, though, can he? Daniel, there—" He nods at the door. "He would not hesitate to cut my throat and think nothing of it. But Nikolai, he is a romantic. He is desperate for your approval, *da*? Shall I tell you a story about Nikolai?"

I wait.

"When he is a young boy, Alexsandr despairs of what to do with him. He tells me, 'Sergei, I have a young man I am training to be *ubitsya*. He is good, but I worry he is soft.' And I say, 'Why soft, Alexsandr? What makes him so?' He tells me that he has boy followed. That when others are experimenting with whores at the tender age of twelve and thirteen, Nikolai, Alexsandr's prodigy, has been doing the same at the age of nine."

I blink. I will not let him see me react.

" 'But do you know what he has been paying these whores to do,' he tells me. He says to me that Nikolai has been purchasing the oldest whore there. She is fifty, with a *pizda* that is as worn as an old sack. He wonders what a nine-year-old wants with such a woman. So he has him watched. And do you know what Nikolai does with this old whore, little flower?"

"No. What?"

"He has her hold him while he sleeps," he says with a sneer in his voice. "She sings him to sleep and makes him dinner, and he pays the old slut as if she is the finest piece in the land. He has affection for her. So, I tell Alexsandr, there is one way to make it stop."

A sick feeling comes over me as I listen. I picture Nick as a lonely nine-year-old boy, so desperate and starved for attention that he has to pay an elderly hooker to pretend to be his mother.

"So we send the boy to the brothel with a project, *da*? Kill the whore or be cast out of the *Bratva*. He must choose his family. And do you know what he chooses?"

"He let her live?" I hope, but even as I say it, I doubt it is the truth.

"*Nyet*," Sergei says. "She is old and diseased, and she owes much money to the *Bratva*. Nikolai does the hit, because it is how we have trained him. He is the creature we have made him." His smile is thin again. "However flawed. And he did not cry once, this Nikolai. This is the man you love. He kills because it is his life."

I think Sergei is wrong. I think Nick kills because it means nothing to him. It is simply a means to an end, something he has been trained to do, something that he is good at. I think that if the killing meant something to him that it would be worse. But to him, it is the same as opening a spreadsheet and typing in numbers. It is simply a job.

"I see you do not like my story," Sergei says. He shifts in the chair, and I flinch instinctively backward, which only makes him laugh again.

"Why did you tell me that story?"

"Because it will give me great pleasure to see the truth in your eyes when you look upon Nikolai. When you realize he is a piece of shit crafted by the *Bratva*. He can never be a normal man, little flower. He knows only to be what we have made him."

This is the wrong thing to say to me.

Sergei doesn't know it, but his words are working against him. Nick is who he has been created to be, just like I am who my father shaped me into. A little mentally twisted, a little sick in the head, and a lot lonely and needing of love.

That hasn't changed. I still see the same longing and need in Nick's eyes when he looks at me.

He's the same man, really. I simply know the truth about him now. There is no gloss left, no mystery as to who and what he is. It's almost a blessing.

Nick is who they have made him.

I am who my father made me.

I look down at Sergei. "So tell me," I ask, and my voice is curiously calm. "If I don't shoot you, what happens?"

He laughs, that sneer back on his face. "Little flower. What do you think happens?"

I consider. "I think I could take you to the police." I think for a moment longer and then add, "And I think you have enough connections that you get out. Am I right?"

He shrugs his shoulders, but I see from the gleam in his eyes that I have guessed right. No police station will hold this oily man. He has too many connections.

"And if you get out, you'll come after Nick, won't you? You can't let him live. Not while you breathe. It's either you or him, right?"

Even as I say this, I realize it for the truth. This is the sadness in Nick's eyes. He's letting me choose because he doesn't believe he deserves to live. He believes like Sergei does, that he is nothing but a worthless tool who is only good at killing men. He doesn't believe he is worthy of love.

And if I let Sergei go, Nick will disappear. He will go into hiding and wait for the kill to come.

He will go into hiding . . . like my father.

It hits me then. I look at Sergei calmly, at the way he smirks at me despite the fact that he is bound and helpless in the chair.

If I let this man go, I am condemning Nick to the same life that my father has—a life of fear, of constantly looking over his shoulder. It would be a prison of my own making.

Nick would never be free.

I think for a long, long moment and stare at Sergei's hard, ugly face. His thick, bushy eyebrows. The smugness there.

Nick is who he is because he was raised that way. He was created by his family of killers to be one, just like them. He didn't ask to become who he was. He has survived the only way he knows how.

I understand this. I am a creature of my upbringing as well. And I was raised to know how to shoot a gun, in case I ever needed to.

I stare at the gun on the table.

Sergei follows my gaze. He laughs. "So brave," he mocks. "How Nikolai would be proud."

I ignore him. The gun is an American one, a Glock, and not a Russian one, so I know how to use it. I press the magazine release button to check for ammunition. The slide is full. I push it back into place with the base of my hand. It's as if I'm in the basement of my house all over again. I pull the slide back and chamber a bullet. I only need one.

"Ah, this is part where I am to quiver with fear and beg for my life, *da*?" Sergei's voice is mocking. He clearly doesn't think I can do this.

"You won't beg for your life," I say calmly. "You don't think it's in trouble. You don't think I can do this. You think I'm going to let you go and that I will take you to the police. Then you will make a few calls, and you will be out by nightfall."

I remember the legal system in America and how full of holes it is. How even a murderer can go free in no time at all, if they know the right strings to pull. I remember this all too well. And I remember how helpless it made me feel last time.

But I am helpless no longer.

Sergei says nothing. He simply watches me, that mocking, derisive look on his face.

I carefully raise the gun to Sergei's head, flick off the safety, oh-so-calm, and pull the trigger.

I won't let this man destroy our lives.

In killing him, I have chosen Nick. I see his darkness, and I accept it. I love Nick for *who* he is, not what he is.

The shot is loud in the room, and I squeeze my eyes shut at the sight of Sergei's face contorting, at his forehead splattering with red, at the gore on the plastic.

There is a shout from outside the door, and Daniel surges forward as if he has been shoved. A second later, Nick has pushed his way into the room, muscling aside Daniel. He stares at Sergei, dead in the chair, and then his gaze moves to me with the gun in my hand. There is not pride in his eyes, but a question.

He truly did not think I would do it.

Then again, neither did Sergei.

I burst into tears. Great, sweeping sobs rip from my throat, and I toss the gun down on the table and move toward Nick. His arms encircle me even as I press my cheek against his chest.

"Daisy," he murmurs. "My love. You didn't have to."

I know I didn't. But I am choosing a life without fear. I am choosing freedom for Nick—and for me. I think of Sergei's analogy. *He drags me to you and places the gun in your hand like mangy cat bringing a rodent to its master for approval.*

If Nick is a cat seeking approval, I am an abused dog that bites the hand before it can slap. But I won't live in fear again.

I won't. And I won't have created that future for Nick. I love him too much.

I realize he still thinks I hate him, even as he calmly soothes my back as I cry. I look up at him and put my hand to his chin, even as I weep. I force him to look me in the eye. "I love you, Nikolai," I tell him. Nikolai, not Nick.

My Nikolai.

He stiffens and there is a question in his lonely, sad eyes. "Daisy, you know the truth. I am hit man—"

"You are my Nikolai," I tell him softly. "And what you do doesn't define who you are. We are both rising from our past."

His eyes look suspiciously wet for a moment, and then he crushes me to his chest in a hug so tight that I can't breathe.

I never want to leave his arms again.

CHAPTER FIFTEEN

NIKOLAI

I do not see Vasily before I leave. He gives us one week for Daisy's bruises to heal. They are all superficial but very painful. Daniel and I carry the body of Sergei to his car. He will take care of it. "Pigs," he says. I care not.

My attention is focused on Daisy. She cries at night, every night, and I hold her as she clings to me. Before Daniel left, Daisy makes him vow to find Regan. Her nightmares are a mix of fear for herself and for Regan.

"Your name, Daisy Miller, it is the character in a famous story, yes?" I ask her one night when she cannot sleep. I do not know if the time in the hands of the Petrovichs bother her more than the killing of the head of the snake. I'm afraid to ask.

"No." I can feel the soft shake of her head against my chest. I feed her a little more vodka. It has helped these past nights for her to fall asleep. "I've never heard of that before."

"*Da*, Henry James writes about a flower in bloom who stands outside of society but is lovely nonetheless." I do not tell her that the Daisy Miller in the story is an incorrigible flirt looked down upon or made fun of by everyone around her. "She has tragic ending."

"Great," she mutters. "I'm named after a girl who dies?"

"*Da*, your parents know of this?" I stroke her back and tip the vodka against her lips again. She swallows and snuggles closer.

"I don't think my parents ever heard of Henry James. My mom said I was named after all the wild daisies that grew on the farm."

"It is perfect name." I wish I could show her how much I love her, but her body is bruised and hurts all over. Later there will be time for loving. We have many days together.

After our one-week reprieve, Daniel arrives and escorts us to the Moscow Vnukovo airport. There, Daisy and I will take a charter jet to Switzerland. Winter is on the cusp here. I've bundled Daisy into a borrowed fur. I wear only a long-sleeve shirt and jeans borrowed from Daniel. Everything that Daisy and I brought to Russia will remain here.

"I've got a lead on Regan," Daniel says to Daisy. The mention of Regan's name brings forth her tears.

"Thank you," she chokes out.

Daisy nearly runs up the stairs into the body of the jet, but I stop to take one last look. Russia is a vast, mysterious land. There are portions of the northern country that few men have ever explored. In the winter, it is harsh and unforgiving, but every spring, the foliage comes out. The people here are resilient like the land itself.

My heart aches a little as I realize that I may never step another foot on Russian soil again. Nor that of Ukraine. I take deep breaths, wanting to suck in and preserve some of this land that has made me.

"You'll miss this place, huh?" says Daniel, shivering a little in his thick coat. Yes, he is from a warmer climate. In my shirt, I feel nothing but the cleansing air. The colder the wind, the more pure.

"You see harsh landscapes and acres of snow, and I see the warm blanket of winter sheltering the earth until it is time for the seeds to flower and rise again. We are a people of resilience and survival."

I feel Daniel shrug beside me, the wool of his heavy jacket barely moving over the gesture. "So you make a sacrifice, and that way you know your treasure is worth it."

I nod. Leaving a small bit of me here in Russia is not that big of a sacrifice when I get Daisy in return. She is the embodiment of the spirit of my homeland—beautiful, resilient, and powerful. "I am in your debt. Call upon me before I pass so that I may go into my rest unfettered." I phrase my request in such a way that Daniel cannot deny me. He shakes his head in rueful agreement.

"Go on then. I'll call in the marker soon enough." Daniel pushes me up the stairs but this time I am the one running up into the plane.

Inside, I sit next to Daisy. The craft is small but luxurious. There is no one but Daisy and me and the pilot. No others to see us leave. I don't ask who the pilot is, nor do I care.

"Why can't you return?" Daisy asks, reaching for my hand.

"The Petrovich interests are well protected here in Eastern Europe. Its tentacles are far reaching. In exchange for killing Sergei, I am allowed to leave on the provision that I do not return.

Daisy makes a choked sound. I rush to reassure her. "*Nyet*, do not cry kitten. You are my home now."

The flight to Zurich passes quickly, but the whole time I can think of nothing else but Daisy naked in a big bed. I ache to hold her and remind each other that we are alive. Her scent fills my nose, and thoughts of her in various stages of undress and in various positions torment me.

It is hard for me to rise from my seat when we land. I close my eyes momentarily and think of Sergei getting eaten by pigs. Daniel has promised me that he will deliver the body to a hog farm where the animals will eat all of Sergei. That is enough to kill off my erection.

I barely notice the lush appointments of the Baur au Lac hotel. I notice Daisy looking in wonderment at the crystal chandeliers and the acres of marble floors. "You like?"

She nods and then sighs. "I'm not going to get used to this."

"I like that," I admit. "It means I can spoil you every day."

"If you spoil me every day, I *will* get used to it."

"Not you, my Daisy." I kiss her fiercely then, in the lobby of this staid hotel. She blushes when I pull away, and I have to position myself behind her so that the few people loitering aren't shocked by my erection. Once we are inside the hotel suite, I draw Daisy into my arms.

She draws in a deep breath. "Nick, I want you to love me."

"I do." I tighten my hold.

"No, I mean, physically."

At first, I do not understand, but as she stares at me, a flush begins to spread. Suddenly comprehension takes hold, and I am instantly hard once again. "Yes, yes, Daisy." I spread soft kisses on her temple and forehead and draw back to check again that she is serious.

She nibbles her lip and her flush deepens. "For some reason, after all this, I feel embarrassed."

"Don't." I lead her into the bedroom, and the lush surroundings of hotel are the perfect setting. We have a view of the park, the lake, and the Schanzengraben Canal, but none of the scenery interests either of us. "We have left it all behind us now."

I sit her on the edge of the bed and begin to disrobe. I want to confess all to her and for her to see my imperfect body. The buttons on my dress shirt have become too small, and I pop two off in my haste to tug off my shirt. My undershirt follows and then my slacks, socks, and briefs. My cock is jutting out, hungry for her. I squeeze it to get myself under control, and I hear a pleased gasp from her.

"Do you want this, kitten?"

Her eyes are bright and her skin is flushed as she watches my naked body.

I'm filled with such relief that I want to lie down before I fall down, but I lock my knees and place my hands behind my head. "In Russia, your body tells the tale of your sins or your triumphs, depending on who looks upon you." I'm tense because even though she knows what I am, she does not know all I've done. And I am about to tell her so that we can go forward without looking back.

And so, I tell her about the tattoos that cover my body. "The stars on my knees mean I bow before no government. The marks on my fingers tell you I have killed, and the dagger in my neck that I kill for money. The markings on my shoulder indicate how high in the *Bratva* I was. These marks all told people I was not a man to be fucked with." I pause and close my eyes and pray for strength. "I would come to you unblemished, if I could."

"And the inscription on your chest?" her soft voice says. She hasn't moved.

"Death is mercy." I am still afraid to open my eyes. I feel her gaze upon me, and my cockstand lengthens. I cannot help my reaction to her, and truly I do not want to. I need her to know that I desire her at all times.

As seconds tick by, I wonder if I've made a mistake and misread her. That now that she has seen the true me, she will turn me away. As Alexsandr did. As did my family, whoever they were. I have been alone for so many years, and I do not know how I can go on if Daisy rejects me.

I hear a swish against the heavy Egyptian cotton sheets as Daisy stands, and then I feel the heat of her body as it nears mine. Her hand brushes over my right pectoral and my nipple, and I cannot stop the shudders.

She trails her fingers under my arm to my back, where she traces the wolf's head. "And this?" she asks, her breath light upon my skin.

"I am *Vor*, a wolf, a predator," I respond hoarsely. These light touches of hers are more erotic than a naked woman dancing in front of me. Or two naked women performing a lewd act. Her fingers trail off, and I wonder if she is done with me. I can scarcely swallow. Then I feel the press of her lips in the middle of my back.

"Oh, Nick," she says, her mouth moving against me. "My Nikolai. I love you, and it wouldn't matter how many tattoos you have or how many bad things you've done in the past. Your life is one I can't begin to understand, but I want to spend the rest of my life learning you."

Her words are like a knife against the bonds that held me. I spin around and grab her in my arms. My mouth is upon hers before she can say another word, draw another breath. I eat at her mouth as if it is the finest delicacy in all the land. My tongue delves deep into the wet cavern of her mouth.

I swing her legs up around me and tip her back into the bed. The mattress envelops us. I trail my mouth over her jaw and down the column of her throat, where I find her pulse thrumming madly. I bite it, and her hips rise up to press against me.

I thrust my thigh between her legs, and she begins to ride me. Her wetness is evident. I grind down harder and drag my mouth and tongue over her collarbone.

Her hands grab my head as she works herself into a frenzy. A release now, however, would be a weak one, and I need to be inside her somehow, either my tongue or my cock. As I ease away from her, she gives a tiny, mewling, "No, Nick."

"Shhh, kitten. Let me help you."

Her grip on my head eases and she nods, panting a bit.

"I will take care of you. Little release now, and then, when your tissues are swollen with need, I give you big release." I grin cockily at her. "One you will never forget."

"Is that right?" She shakes her head, and her mouth twitches with amusement. "Are you going to talk about it all night or are you going to do something?"

My Daisy. So fearless and so direct with her hunger. I wonder what I have done so right to have the gods smile at me like this. "Do something," I assure her. "But first, we remove your clothes."

"I don't have any marks," she says, looking at me through the lace shield of her eyelashes. It is a look designed to bring a man to his knees. It is good that I am already prostrate or I would've fallen over.

"I will make them," I promise. The silk shirt that I bought her from the airport store provides little resistance when I rip it down the front.

She gasps, but then laughs a little at my eagerness. "Nick! That was my only shirt!" she says, grabbing at the sides of the torn silk. I slide my hands up to cup her breasts. Her nipples are erect and ready for my mouth. I ignore her comments about her clothes and bite her nipple through the fabric. My kitten likes the nip because her protests die off, and her hands have left her shirt to slide along my shoulders. The touch of her fingers against my bare skin is heaven.

I squeeze one breast and pinch the nipple as I mouth the other one through the lace of her bra. My free hand reaches under her and loosens the clasp. Soon her bra is gone and her beautiful breasts are bared to my gaze and my touch. I place wet kisses around the mounds and then suck the nipple of the right breast hard into my mouth.

Her cries of pleasure echo above me, and I can feel her legs move restlessly below me. "You have the most beautiful breasts, kitten. I could spend all day between these mounds." I cup them and kiss both fervently. "I would lick the valleys and nibble on the peaks until you were coming on my thigh."

"God, Nick, please," she moans.

"Please what?" I tease her.

"I ache," she says.

"Is it your heart?" I place a soft kiss over her left breast.

"No, you've filled that. I feel empty *much* lower."

Her words wash over me like sunshine. "Such a beautifully worded request," I tell her. "How can I not suck on your pussy when you ask so nicely?"

She bats me slightly with her hand. "Nick, that's not what I said."

I shake my head and smile. Never had I thought sex could be like this. Joyful and playful, but still erotic. "I'm, what you say, reading between the lines?"

She laughs as I intended, but her giggles are cut short as I move lower between her legs. I pull off the skirt we bought and find a tiny thong underneath. It barely covers her sexy mound. I pull it aside and see the wetness of her arousal glistening on her cunt lips and between her thighs.

"You look delicious, kitten. I cannot wait to eat you."

A twist of my fingers and the thong string breaks.

"We're going to be broke if you keep destroying all my clothes," Daisy tells me, but I can tell by the way that her thighs fall open that she cares little about the scraps of fabric I have laid waste to.

"Mmmmm" is all I say. And soon I cannot say anything else because I am licking up her nectar. I place the broad flat of my tongue along her seam and sweep her from front to back in long languorous strokes as if I am the cat and she is the milk.

Her clitoris protrudes from its hood and begs for me to suck on it. I place my mouth over her and suck it in. With my hands, I reach up and squeeze her breasts. Her thighs are gripping my head, and her hands are tugging my hair with urgency.

I don't stop.

I suck and lick and bite and suck more until her pants turns to cries and her cries turn to screams. She shudders her release all over my tongue.

Into her soft swollen tissues, I slide one finger, softly breaching her innocence. She is slick and tight.

Her first instinct is to slide away. "No," she cries. "Don't. Wait. It's too much at once, Nick."

"No, kitten, we have just begun." And I begin again. I slide in one more finger, shallowly fucking her with just the tips. As her soft channel gives way, I slide my fingers in farther. I measure her reaction to ensure that the pain is minimal.

Her body is slicked with sweat, making her shine all over. I want to lick every inch of her—and I will. Her face is a study of concentrated eroticism. Her lower lip is clenched between her teeth, and her fingers clutch the sheets as I build her to another orgasm. Her channel is tightening its grip on my two fingers. I slide a third one in. Three fingers is still less girth than my cock, and I want to make this as painless as possible for her.

With my thumb, I work her clit. My fingers pump in and out of her in a steady rhythm. Her breasts are bouncing, and I cannot resist their call. I bend my head and suckle on one and then the other, still working my three fingers inside of her.

Her body tenses and her thighs squeeze my hand tightly as her body bows off the bed and she screams my name again. It is the most glorious sound I've ever heard.

I keep stroking through her orgasm, and I feel the muscles in her pussy tighten again in yet another release. She is shaking now, and crying.

"Oh my God, oh my God," she chants, thrashing her head back and forth. I pull my fingers out slowly and cup her mound, pressing my longer fingers against her cunt lips. She continues to spasm and shake, and I kiss her face tenderly, licking away the tears that spill out the side of her eyes. When the tremors of her orgasm have passed, she rolls into me and I hug her body tight.

"What was that?" she asks in wonderment. I choke back a laugh.

"You had an orgasm." I tell her.

"But I've had them before, haven't I?" She sounds delightfully bewildered, and if my cock didn't ache so much from the need to be inside her, I might've spent five minutes laughing. As it was, the pain in my groin prevented all but a weak chuckle.

"Yes, but they can vary in intensity." I pull the covers over her and get up to wet a washcloth for her. "But I will always make them that good for you," I say smugly from the bathroom.

"Is that right?" She still sounds dazed, and my chest puffs up with pride at how well I have made my woman come. I wring out the washcloth and test it against my wrist. Not too hot.

"What are you doing?" She looks curiously at me.

"I'm taking care of my kitten," I tell her. Pulling down the sheets, I press the washcloth between her legs.

"That's normal, right?" Uncertainty fills her voice. "I feel like I don't know anything."

"It is," I assure her. I pull down the sheet so that her lovely body is exposed. Shyness overtakes her and she moves to cover her breasts and her pubis. Instead of brushing her hands away and telling her that she should not feel shy with me, I roll her over so that her back and lovely buttocks are exposed. I squeeze some of the hotel lotion into my hand and begin to rub her back. Her muscles here are tight, perhaps because she is unused to such casual nudity.

With long strokes, I soothe her muscles and her nerves, pressing and rubbing all the safe places. Her shoulder blades, the curves of her small biceps, the dip in her lower back. As she softens and relaxes, I begin to learn her erogenous zones. I trail my fingers along the sides of her breasts and over the curve of her buttocks. Rubbing along her inner thighs, I allow the tips of my fingers to lightly touch her cunt. She moves restlessly against the sheets, but her arousal is only a small flame, and I want it to be a roaring fire. I want to see the wetness paint her thighs and hear her breathless gasps. I want this first time of hers to be a memory of glorious pleasure rather than pain.

The focus of my massage moves downward, and I pay particular attention to the sensitive ankles and tender soles of feet. She is sensitive around the backs of her knees and the inside thigh area. All the parts I have rubbed with my fingers, I follow with my tongue and mouth, avoiding the obvious erotic zones. Daisy moans, either in delight or annoyance or both.

"You're killing me," she says, and then freezes up, all my seductions for naught. The word "kill" has brought back bad memories. I frown at her back but lie down next to her and gather her into my arms.

"There are bad men in this world, and sometimes they need to be removed so that their harm cannot spread to others."

She shudders, and I hold her tighter. "Will this ever go away?" she asks.

"Yes and no. The stark feelings of guilt will fade, but you will not forget this moment." I debate what to say next, for I have no experience in comforting someone I love. I have no experience with loving, either. "I think you will find some peace, but it is okay to not feel it now."

"I know I shouldn't feel guilty. I shouldn't, because he's sold Regan off to God-knows-where, and he wanted to hurt me, and he wanted to kill you. I shouldn't feel guilty, and yet . . . I do." A sob breaks. She turns her head and cries softly into my neck, and her tears are like pricks from a needle on my skin.

"Shhh, kitten," I whisper over and over as I rock her. The tears subside eventually, and Daisy pulls out of my arms to lie on her back.

"I'm sorry," she says, unable to look me in the eyes.

"Nothing to be sorry about." I roll to my side so I can look at her. The need to touch her is strong, so I pull her to my side and rest my head on top of her. We both lie there in silence for some time until sleep pulls us under.

I awaken to a soft hand between my legs and tender lips at my throat. For a moment I think I must be dreaming and I reach down and cup myself. There I find a fragile hand. Daisy.

Her fingers still and begin to move away, but I forestall her movements. Instead, I grip her hand tighter around my already-hard cock and show her how to touch me.

"You like it rougher than I thought," she whispers.

You have no idea, kotehok, I say silently, but to her I say, "Yes, tighter, a little hard." And we begin to stroke me together. I pull her mouth toward mine, and we kiss, openmouthed and ravenous. We kiss and kiss while we jerk me to an orgasm. My come jets out in long, translucent ropes, the semen lubricating our caresses. I groan low and loud as she pulls at me harder. "Yes, just like that," I gasp out, and then I can say nothing for a long minute.

I wipe off her hand and mine with the discarded washcloth.

"You're still hard," she notices. My cock jerks in anticipation.

"I am," I tell her. "And I will be until I come inside of you."

Her blue eyes are on fire with desire for me. "Then come inside me," she invites, and I nearly spill again at her invitation.

It's everything I've been waiting for. "My hands are shaking." I raise my hands to show her that they are trembling slightly. "I let you get me off so that I can control myself enough to show you pleasure."

She shakes her head at me, amazed. "Nick, you don't have to try so hard."

"Never." I cradle her head in my hands. "You should shoot me when I stop trying. No effort is too much for you. Pleasing you is the greatest privilege that exists."

I can tell from the look on her face that she doesn't believe me, but it is the truth.

I drop my mouth to hers and kiss her until she takes my breath away and then gives it back. I begin to map her body once again, this time noting that her right breast is more sensitive than her left. With my hands, I mold her breasts and pinch and squeeze the erect tips. Someday our child will suckle here.

Reaching between us, I smooth her lubrication over her cunt lips and then onto my cock. My fingers slip inside her easily this time, our previous play having made her ready for me. Inside, the tissues of her cunt grip me, and I bite my lip hard to keep from coming.

Her hands stroke my shoulders and tangle in my hair. The touch is loving and genuine. I will never get enough of her. I rise up on my elbows and kiss her again and again, all the while plunging my fingers inside her. I grind my palm into her pubic bone, and she cries out in pleasure.

"I must taste you again." I push down between her legs and raise her up to my mouth like she is a feast, and then I eat at her like I'm a starved man until she comes and I drink down her juice.

As she shudders from her orgasm, I reach over to the nightstand and rip open a condom. Sheathing myself, I rub just the tip over her already-sensitive flesh, and she trembles and clutches at the sheets, her eyes dazed. I push in slightly, and because I've fingered her several times today, she is so very tight.

"Someday soon I'll take you without a barrier, *da*?"

She nods. "I'll get on the pill right away."

"Or maybe we make baby?" I spread my fingers over her belly. "Someday."

Her eyes glisten and she chokes out, "Someday."

I cannot hold myself back any longer. The tight grip of her pussy on the tip of my cock is exquisite torment. I push in slowly and feel the tissues give way. My eyes scan her face so that I can pull back or cease if there is any sign of pain, but there is none. When I'm finally seated to the hilt, it is almost too much. I want to stay inside her forever.

"I do not want to leave you, kitten. Ever."

"Then don't," she pants, her hands fluttering over my body. "We'll just make love in this beautiful hotel room until we die."

"A perfect end," I agree. Instinct takes over, and I must move. The first drag of my cock out her channel elicits a groan from both of us. It's the most glorious feeling. I thrust back inside of her.

There is nothing else that exists in this world, only her and me. I lift her so that we are virtually upright and her little clit can rub against my pelvis. My hand tangles in her hair and angles her head so that I can ravage her mouth. My other hand clutches her buttocks as I lift her off me and then drive back inside. Again and again we press against each other until I can feel her convulse around me. I let the ripples of her cunt flutter against my cock and listen to her cries against my mouth. When they begin to subside, I pound against her until my own release comes and I spill into the barrier between us.

Tenderly I rest her against the pillows. Strands of hair are sticking to her face, and I push them aside. She is too tired to do more than smile weakly at me. I feel like I have conquered a mountain. I could run a thousand miles for that smile. Swiftly, I dispose of the condom and climb back into bed with her. Pulling the covers up, I tuck her lax body into my side.

She mumbles something and then drops off to sleep. I stare at the coffered ceiling and make a dozen promises to different deities thanking them for their gift and swearing to keep her safe and happy for as long as I have breath.

"What will we do today?"

"First, we go to the Paradeplatz district and get you onto the bank accounts." I place my fingers over her mouth. "Do not argue. It will be done."

"I'm not with you for your money."

Daisy's mouth turns down at the corner, and I cannot keep myself from kissing it. I stroke my tongue over her pressed lips until they part, and then neither of us argues for several minutes. "Then we shall go to Paradeplatz where you will tell me what I should be wearing every minute of the day down to my briefs, and then I will help you pick out delectable bits of lace and silk that will touch your secret parts when my lips and hands cannot."

Daisy blushes and shakes her head, but she's smiling. "I hope you have a lot of money, because you clearly like spending it."

I lean back against the soft pillows. "I don't know how much I have, but it is enough for us to buy a few things."

Later at the hotel, I sit out on the balcony overlooking the river, sipping some coffee. Daisy comes storming out, waving the bank book. "Didn't you ever look at this?"

I shrug. "Yes, but what does it matter? I had nothing. So long as I was not hungry or could buy a necessary weapon, the amount was of no concern."

Daisy closes her eyes as if reaching for patience. "This is millions. Like I don't think you and I could spend all of it even if we shopped at the Bahnhofstrasse every day."

"Then we will not worry about it."

My lack of concern over this is bothering Daisy, so I pull the bank book out of her hand and lay it on the table. "I don't care what I have so long as I can be with you, *kotehok*. I am happy living in a box as long as you are sharing the box with me." I pull her down on my lap.

She has changed into one of the sleek black outfits we bought in one of the gold-lettered shops that littered the shopping avenue. Some of those shops had no price tags, which made it easier for me to buy clothes for Daisy without argument. And since many of the shops had agreements with the banks in the financial district, I merely signed a discreet credit slip without Daisy noticing. So much easier that way.

I lay my mouth over my favorite part of her neck where her pulse beats. There is the evidence of her life and her passion. As I suck on it, I can feel the flutter of her heartbeat speed up, and suspect that if I slipped my hand beneath her skirt, her delicate pink silk panties would be wet.

"Still, I think I should get a job when we get back, and we both should learn how to manage money," Daisy says, but I can tell her heart isn't in her scold. She tips her head so I can get better access to her neck.

"Are you sore, *kotehok*?" I took her only once, although she came several times. My bold question makes her squirm in my lap, and my cock responds predictably.

"Not really." She sounds a bit breathless. I suspect that Daisy's body, newly awakened, is just as hungry as mine. My fingers slide up her thigh, and her legs fall open. Between them her arousal is evident. It coats my fingers, and the thin barrier between my touch and her clit is soaked. I push the material aside and rub her slightly. She moans, and I pull her chin around so that I can kiss her. My fingers push into her still-tight passage, and I fuck her with my tongue and digits until she is crying into my mouth.

"Let's see how a bath feels," I suggest, lifting her in my arms.

"A bath?" She sounds disappointed.

"Yes, I want to fuck you while you are sitting in front of a jet in the bathtub. And then maybe eat you out." I don't give her any time to protest, fastening my mouth on hers again and walking directly to the bathroom.

We don't come out until hours later, when our skin is wrinkled and we have used up half of the hotel's hot water capacity.

CHAPTER **SIXTEEN**

DAISY

When we return to the States, we go to my apartment. It's quiet and lonely, dust on the counters and the food spoiling in the fridge. It's not the same without Regan. I still don't know where she is or what's happened to her. I'm terrified that we can't find my friend, and nightmares about what is happening to her keep me awake at night.

We were gone for six weeks. We haven't heard more about Regan. Daniel was in the wind, Nick said. We could trust him to bring her home safe. We just had to be patient. A number of past-due notices were on our door, and an eviction notice was stuck over them. Great. It doesn't matter anymore, I suppose, but the sight of that notice on the door upsets me. It's like no matter what I do, I am still ruining Regan's life.

Nick goes down and talks to the landlord and asks for a key.

The landlord comes up with Nick, grumbling about flighty girls and derelict tenants. By the way Nick is clenching his jaw, I can see Nick's patience is thin. The landlord lets us in, and there is crap everywhere, like some drug-addled neighbor broke in looking for valuable stuff.

I find Regan's phone by her bed. It's still broken. I'll have to charge it and call people. Her boyfriend. Becca. Regan's parents. I want to weep over all the bad news I must share. But for now, I've got to be strong.

Nick is always at my side. He rubs my back and helps me pack everything up.

After it is all taken care of at the apartment and the landlord is paid two months' back rent and three months of "nuisance rent" as he calls it, we are headed for a kennel where Nick says he is housing a dog. This surprises me, but Nick is a man of many secrets. I feel he will share them all with me in time. Besides, I've never had a dog, but I figure that he's an orphan like Nick and so the two belong together.

Besides, maybe it will help my dad.

Nick has promised that Daniel will find Regan, but Daniel is only one man, and the network of the *Bratva* is vast. I might never see Regan again, never hear her call me Pollyanna in that cheerful, laughing way of hers.

Because I am going home.

I realize, after everything that happened in Moscow, that I am different. I still feel that same joy at unfettered sunlight, pleasure in walking down the street and holding Nick's hand, and enjoy things as small as going to dinner together.

But I'm not as innocent as I was. I embrace that small, broken part of who I am. If Nick is darkness with a kernel of light inside him, I am light with the matching kernel of darkness. It's what makes us so perfect for one another.

Nick takes the phone to the cellular store so that he can obtain a list of Regan's contacts. The conversation with her parents is excruciating. I have no answers for them. Regan's boyfriend seems almost uninterested. He never even stops by the apartment. So when I pack my things, I pack up hers as well. I will hold them for her until she returns to claim them. Nick assures me she will, because Daniel is an expert at what he does I will have faith, and wait. And so I pack everything. I work slowly, partly in the hopes that Regan will pop through the door one day and surprise all of us, and partly because I am enjoying this time with Nick.

My sweet, broken Nick.

Despite the fact that I know the truth about him, he's convinced, somehow, that I will reach a breaking point someday and turn from him. So at night, he pulls me close to him, and we talk. I tell him of my upbringing, my sad memories with my father, and he tells me stories of hits he has undertaken. They are always hits on awful people: organ harvesters, drug users, smut peddlers. Never innocents. He reminds me of the stories behind his tattoos, and what they mean, as if seeing these brands of who and what he was will somehow drive me away.

But I listen to his stories without comment, and I kiss each tattoo as we make love. It will take time before Nick realizes that he is worthy of my love, but I am patient. How can I not love this man who watches me with such adoration in his eyes? Who worships my body and soul? Who treats me like I am the most precious thing he has ever touched and scarce believes he is allowed to breathe my air?

Every day that passes, I love Nick more and more. I don't care about his past. We will build our own future, together.

He's agreed to return home with me. My time in Moscow taught me a lot about myself, but it also taught me a lot about my father.

I now know that I handled the situation between us all wrong. I shouldn't have run from my father's control; I should have asserted my own. My father's obsessive control came from fear, and I allowed it to rule me. Now that I refuse to live in fear any longer, I want to return to my father's side and support him . . . and help him return to the real world.

Nick has promised to be by my side every step of the way.

We rent a sedan and pack it full of my few possessions and Regan's things. Nick has only one bag, and it is clothing. I am sad to see that my poor *ubitsya* has no personal possessions, save those that he has stolen from me, and his weapons, which he carefully stashes in the rental.

Even though it has been weeks since Sergei's death, and Daniel has promised to wipe us from the network's database, Nick will not move freely about unless he is prepared for any and all attacks. He will not let me be taken from him again, he says.

I'm fine with his protectiveness; I don't want to be taken from him again, either.

When we drive up to my father's farmhouse, it looks as lonely and abandoned as ever. Paint is peeling off the boards, the grass in the yard is knee high, and sheets of wood still board up the windows.

Nick gives me an incredulous look as we pull up. "This is where you lived, Daisy?"

I nod. I've got a lump in my throat at the sight of it. To me, it doesn't look like a prison any longer. It just looks sad. Lonely. I want to fix it because I'm not lonely anymore. Not with Nick at my side and his love fueling my heart.

We park the car, and Nick goes to my side and opens my door for me. I pretend not to see the gun hidden in his jacket, because Nick is not comfortable unless he is vigilant, and this is something my father will understand. Nick helps me out of the car and then his fingers link with mine. We hold hands as we approach the door, and I give my father the special knock to let him know it's me.

Moments later, I hear the fumble of the locks—all ten of them—as they are undone. The door opens into darkness, and there's no one there to greet us. It's my father's way—he opens the door and then hides behind it, just in case of an intruder.

It makes Nick instantly wary, and I watch his hand go up to his jacket, but I calm him with a pat on the arm and step forward. "Father?"

"Daisy?"

It's my father's voice. He sounds so old and tired. We step inside, and Nick shuts the door. As soon as we are in, the lights come on.

"You've come home," my father says, stepping forward, and there are tears in his voice.

I hug him close, surprised at the contact. My father hadn't touched me for so long—at least not out of affection. His normally tidy appearance is disheveled, and the living room is a mess. While I have been gone, my father has been falling to pieces. I feel guilty, and give Nick an unhappy look over his shoulder.

"I'm here, but I'm not staying," I tell him. I won't live under this roof again. "This is Nick. We're moving in together. There's a house for rent down the road, and we're going to move in down there."

We're going to get married, too, and have children, but I know I'll be the one to propose. And I like that, too, because I like the control. I just haven't told Nick all my plans yet. He still thinks he's not worthy of them. I'll give it time—and give *him* time to realize I'm not going anywhere.

My father is crying, but I only pat his back and murmur

things to him. I understand him now, when I didn't before. I tell him I won't leave him again, and that we can start over.

Because I know enough about myself to take control of what I want, now. With Nick at my side, I can be strong and fearless enough for my father and myself. And once my father starts to get over his crippling terror, we'll move forward—all three of us—with our lives. I want to go to college. I want Nick to go, too, so he doesn't feel like he is worthless and skill-less. My Nick loves art, and he talks about the curator so often. I want him to take art classes, and I know it'd please him.

It's a fresh start for all of us.

I think of this, and then I think of Regan, who said the same thing to me so many weeks ago. *Oh, Regan*, I think. *I'm so sorry. I pray that Daniel finds you soon.*

NIKOLAI

"Do not talk to me of this man."

Daisy and I have rented a small property just down the road from her father. We are settling in, but I have an outstanding obligation. Daisy would like for me to just forget it, but I am a man of my word.

"Why not, Nick?"

"This is what I do, Daisy. I kill people for money. I'm a killer. See, you recoil. You said, 'Nick, I understand you. Nothing you've done will make me stop loving you.' This is a lie, correct?"

My greatest fear is that the terror of the nights in Russia will fade, and Daisy's understandable revulsion will rise up and drive her away from me. Perhaps this is a test for both of us.

"No! No, it's not, and *yes*, Nick, there are some people who need killing. Those people who took Regan and me. Maybe that accountant you were watching. I don't know, but do you know, either? It eats at you, Nikolai. I can see it. How long can you act as judge, jury, and executioner before you're completely lost to me?"

She knows that when she calls me *Nikolai*, it cuts to the bone. I turn away and continue packing my bag. No disguise is needed this time. The trauma surgeon will be shot in traffic on his way home from a surgical treatment. I have figured the optimum distance, wind, and location from my one visit and satellite imagery. Freeway shootings are ideal. Few people expect them, and you can be in your vehicle and gone before anyone ever knows a thing.

"I am already lost, then." I must be strong against her sadness. I have been paid for this job, and it is something I must complete.

"You are wrong, Nikolai." Her face is turned up to me, the look on it so earnest and trusting. "I love you unconditionally. You can go off to Seattle and kill this doctor. He probably needs killing. You can come back to me because I will *never* stop loving you. I just wonder when you'll start loving yourself."

I pick up my bag in silence and walk toward the door to the house. With the knob in my hand, I ask, "Will you—" The words stick and I clear my throat and try again. "Will you be here when I get back?"

I am afraid to look at her, afraid to see her good-bye. But before I can leave, she throws herself at my back and kisses my neck.

"I will be here, my love. You'd better return to me."

I'm undone. Completely. I drop my bag and turn to grasp her close to my heart. "I will return to you the same man, I promise."

She kisses me with a fervor that leaves both our mouths bruised. I welcome the pain, the ferocity of her passion. I want to carve out that desiccated thing in my chest called a heart and give it to her. *Take me, love me.*

"I do, Nikolai, I do," she responds. I do not even realize I have spoken out loud. My eyes are wet, but I force myself to pull away.

It takes me two days to drive, but I need my SAKO rifle for this, and so I cannot fly. Seattle is cold, rainy, and wet. I stay in a motel on the edge of town and pay cash. I force myself to sleep, and then in the morning, I prepare everything.

The gun is dismantled and cleaned. I dry fire twice. My bullets are checked. I load and unload the weapon and then carefully place it into my bag. I rub my chest. I'm bringing death and it is a mercy, I tell myself.

I slip on my long-sleeved shirt and jeans. Black socks into black boots. The plan runs through my head over and over. At three p.m., Mr. Blue will leave the hospital and head south toward Rainier Beach. Approximately twenty minutes later, he should reach the kill zone. From there, I will have thirty seconds, a lifetime, to pull the trigger.

The entire morning goes exactly as planned. The GPS marker I placed in his car two months ago, before Daisy was kidnapped, before my life changed irrevocably, lights up and moves. I track him on my phone as I reach the destination. I pull on a mask. It's a Hollywood set mask and it looks like I'm slightly balding. It's a precaution. No one is likely to see me—but just in case.

I position myself in the abandoned house and wait. The countdown begins in my head.

Ten.

Nine.

Eight.

Finger on the trigger.

Four.

Breathe.

Two.

The head of the surgeon jerks back, and blood and matter splatter the seat behind him. I slide my finger off the trigger and listen. Almost imperceptible noises, like tiny mouse feet, rustle above me. *Daniel.* I drop my rifle and run up the stairs, but by the time I reach the upper level, it is empty. No, there is a small piece of white paper lying by the window.

I've found her.

P.S. Consider this an early wedding gift, you suspicious bastard.

I tuck the note into my pocket and return downstairs. I lift up the rifle and kiss it. *Daisy.*
My Daisy.
I want to be better than this. For her.
I turn out of the building and head out of Seattle—and back toward Daisy.

She asks me nothing when I slip into bed with her. She kisses me passionately and moans her sweet sounds as I lick between her legs until she shatters. Her fingers dig hard into my back as I thrust between her legs for hours. She pants her desire as I roll her over and take her from behind, my balls slapping against her, my hand pulling her head back so that I fuck her mouth with my tongue at the same time.

The next morning, when we have breakfast, she looks heavy-lidded with desire and walks gingerly.

"We need to install a bathtub," she says. I agree instantly. Daisy's body slick with water, slick with desire. I harden as I think of our time in Zurich and the hours we spent in the bathroom of the hotel.

I pull up bathtubs on the computer. "This is nice," I say, pointing at a model that has multiple jets.

"Those aren't bathtubs." Daisy ruffles my hair like I'm an innocent, mischievous child. "Those are hot tubs."

"We get both," I declare.

"Fine." She giggles and there's no argument about the price. I'm thrilled but suspicious.

"Why do you not ask me about Seattle, little kitten?"

"Because I love you, Nick," she answers serenely. She is like the Madonna, sweet and mysterious. Her love for me is unconditional, and I cannot allow her to think the worst of me any longer. I must allow her to love me as she allows me to love her in return.

"I did not kill him," I confess. I pull out the note that Daniel left. "Daniel completed the job. He left this."

"Oh, Nick." She hugs the note to her chest. "She's safe then?"

"Yes," I tell her, even though I'm not certain. She melts into me. Her hands flutter over my chest, stroking and petting in an attempt to comfort, to touch.

"I'm done with the killing, Daisy. I want to be whole for you."

Her eyes are shiny, but her whole face is lit up. "What will you do, then?"

I shrug. "I do not know. Maybe we both attend college together? We learn new skills?"

I've said the right thing; I can tell from the excitement on her face. "I'd like that."

"But first, we get many tubs and then fuck in them."

She giggles again and says, "Hundreds of tubs." My groin tightens.

We make small improvements to the house, but I think we both know it is temporary. Daisy is anxious to return to the city and to go to college. Her father is holding her back, though. Not intentionally. She worries. Her father has not had the cathartic release that Daisy had with Sergei, and although I promise her no more killing, one last hit must be carried out in order for her family to be happy and free.

It takes no time to find the young man who killed Daisy's mother. I broach the subject with Daisy because I cannot lie to her ever again.

"Your father, Daisy." I take her hands in mine as we sit one winter night in front of the fireplace. The pleasant smell of burning wood fills the small family room and makes me long to have this conversation over so that I can peel away her clothes and make love to her in the firelight.

She grimaces at the mention of her father. She had hoped that his recovery would be swifter.

"What about Father?"

"His mind is tormented by the loss of your mother, his inability to protect her, and his fear of her killer. I know this."

She looks down at our joined hands. "I think I know what you are going to say, Nick, and I guess you're probably right, but I can't do it again. I can't . . ." Her voice trails off. I press a kiss to her forehead.

"I know. Leave it to me, *da*?" I kiss along the side of her face and down her neck.

"*Da*," she sighs. I love it when she speaks Russian to me, even if it is only one word at a time.

"Let us not talk of this anymore," I say. "I want your mouth forming only one word."

"What's that? Food?" She teases me.

"No, *Nick*. Or *more*."

"How about *now*?"

"I like that word."

I proceed to love her right there.

The next morning, I leave before she awakens. I still can only sleep a few hours a night. My body needs no more than that. Her father will not come willingly, and I have prepared a syringe of curare so that I can place him in the vehicle and take him with me. I am glad Daisy is asleep so she cannot see that I have drugged and disabled her father like this. It is for his own good, but it is hard to watch.

"Father Miller," I explain as I carry him to the sedan that I've rented for this purpose. "I am taking you to him, the man who killed your woman. I know that you are afraid, but once you have seen his death, peace will come to you. It is a mercy. I promise."

His eyes lose some of their wild fear, but he is still not convinced. I do not know if he is as strong as Daisy.

The drive into Minneapolis is short, and we wait in the car until the curare wears off.

"He is in there?" Father Miller gestures toward the run-down, three-story house.

"Yes, he lives in the basement. He steals money for his drug habit. Sometimes he deals, but more often he is using it. When we go in, you must not touch anything inside. Many diseased people have been here."

The sound of Father's heavy breathing fills the car, and for a minute, I fear he might have a heart attack or a stroke. Then this would all be for naught. I wonder if I could even return home to Daisy. But, no, I have watched Father for a month now and spoken with him. He burns with a fever to avenge his woman. He just has never had the means before now.

His hands tremble as they reach for the door, and I see where Daisy gets her strength. I witness superhuman effort as he steps outside of the car, the first step he has taken outdoors in years. Later, I will probably wish I had brought Daisy, just so she could see this.

Exiting the car, I lead the way inside, slowly but confidently. Down the dirty exterior stairs and up to a green door with peeling paint. The lock is easily disengaged. "For safety," I say to Father as I pull my handgun out of my shoulder holster. I motion him backward and then open the door. There is no danger. Our man is not yet awake.

I check the living room, kitchen, closet, and bathroom before facing the closed door at the end of the hallway. I presume it is the bedroom. Pressing a finger to my lips, I motion for Father to step out of the line of fire. He does. He is still trembling, but his courage is admirable.

When I open the bedroom door, I call out a warning. "Mr. Black, a delivery is here for you."

"No goddamn Black here," a voice inside mumbles.

"We will not leave until you come out," I call.

"I told you I wouldn't have the money until Saturday."

Mr. Black must believe we are the dealers. I am ready to wait patiently for Mr. Black to exit, but Father is not. He grabs the gun from my hand and charges into the room.

I hear a yelp and see Mr. Black huddled against the wall with his sheets up around his neck. "Who the fuck are you?" But then recognition sets in, and Mr. Black stupidly begins to laugh. "Holy fuck. You're the old man whose wife I offed when I was fourteen. Stupid bitch wouldn't give me her fucking purse."

Those were the last words he says.

Father raises his arm and empties the magazine into Mr. Black's body. His finger keeps pulling the trigger, almost reflexively. All you can hear in the room is his harsh breathing and the empty click of the chamber cocking and releasing.

Reaching over, I pull the gun from his hands. "It's over, Father. Let us go."

Father turns to me, and his eyes are red and full of tears. "I wish I could kill him a million times." His voice breaks and his body collapses into mine. The sorrow and pain in his voice rends at me. I refuse to imagine what madness I would be driven to if I lost Daisy.

I pat him on the shoulder, though I am bad at comforting. "Now you can be free."

"Thank you, Nick," he tells me, and he breaks down into more sobs.

With a little effort, I return Father to the car and drive us home. He wants to be alone for a while.

Daisy asks me only one question upon my return home. "Is it done?"

I nod, and we never speak of it again.

That spring we find Daisy an apartment in the city. Daisy's father is making slow progress. He will sit on his porch and sometimes he will even walk the perimeter of the house. I've installed a security system for him and Daisy, and I hope one day he will be able to leave the property altogether. But Daisy feels comfortable starting a new life here.

I discover the entire building is for sale and arrange for the purchase of it. I will tell Daisy this later. We can move in later that week. Daisy is anxious to move, so I take her to furniture stores to pick out items for our home. I like to say that frequently—before Daisy, I never had a home.

"Daisy, I like this chair. We should buy it for home."

"Daisy, when we are home, will you make me those potato pancakes?"

And at night, "Daisy, the walls of our home are brick. You can scream as loud as you want."

When the week has passed and we get our keys, Daisy presents me with a keychain. It has two keys—one for my Ducati and one for our home. The movers have come to deliver the bed. It is a massive wooden thing.

"I think you could sleep a family in it," Daisy muses as the four delivery men struggle to carry the mattress into our third-floor loft.

I hope that means she is interested in a family with me.

That night, we sit on the floor with candles all around us. None of the furniture Daisy and I have ordered will be here until the following day. The one overhead light is too bright. There is much to fix in this building. It will give me something to do.

"I bought this building," I confess to Daisy.

"Did you?" She laughs with delight. Her eyes are dancing. Maybe it is just the candlelight. Nonetheless, she looks lovely. I can barely taste the takeout Chinese we are eating. It could be nothing more than fiery peppers, and I wouldn't care. All I can do is stare at her.

Later, I lay her down upon the bed and love her sweetly. Her cries of pleasure fill the loft as I sink between her legs and love her, first with my tongue and then with my cock. As we lie sweaty and breathless in the aftermath, I wonder at the marvel my life has become. And then I allow sleep to overtake me, and there, in my dreams, I take Daisy again and again and again.

DAISY

Nick's last hit is done.

I caress his chest as he comes to bed that night. We are in our new, enormous bed in our apartment. Our apartment *building*, I correct myself. I have no idea what we will do with all these apartments, but I like the idea of it. Perhaps we will set aside an apartment for my father, in case he wants to live closer to us and sell the farm. He can even bring his new dog with him. Perhaps we'll set aside an apartment for Regan.

Just in case.

It's been months, and there has been no further word from Daniel about Regan. We only know that she's safe, but she hasn't returned home. I feel so guilty for my poor, beautiful friend whose only crime was that she had been my roommate. She doesn't deserve whatever fate has befallen her, and it keeps me up at night, worrying about her.

I don't tell Nick that I have nightmares about Regan. I suspect he knows this. My Nick has enough to worry about. There are some nights that he feels me out by telling me stories, determined to find the one that will turn me away. Tonight was one such night. "Did I ever tell you," he said to me over takeout, "about the German priest I did a job on in Berlin?"

He told me about him over dinner. The priest was a pedophile and laundering money out of the coffers of the church. He'd come to the attention of someone higher up in Russian mob circles, one of the rare Catholics in the system. He'd gone down almost immediately, though Nick tells me the man begged for his life the entire time.

Nick did not spare it.

I listened to the story without comment, knowing why Nick

feels compelled to tell me these awful things about his past. I know he thinks he's not worthy of my love. I know this, and I never judge.

Nick was made into a creature of the *Bratva* system, a cold, emotionless killer who murders for money and thinks nothing of it.

Or so he'd have me believe. But my Nick, my *Nikolai*—he is not cold. He is not emotionless. And he thinks of his victims as he lies down to sleep next to me.

I can feel the tension in his big body as he pulls me against him in the darkness. It's nights like this, when he holds me so, so close, that I know he's tormented inside.

And it's on nights like this that I can show him just how much I care.

My hand strokes over his chest, over the motto there. *Death is a mercy.* "Do you still believe this?" I ask him.

His hand brushes over mine, caressing it, and then he presses my palm against his heart. "I think, for first time in my life, I am not sure."

This is an answer that pleases me. Nick has lived with absolutes for so long that I enjoy his uncertainty. It means his worldview is changing. It means that he's not entirely the creature that they made him to be.

I slide my hand out from his and caress his nipple, teasing the peak. I want to play with his body. "Are you tired?" I ask, and there is a husky tremor in my voice that has nothing to do with sleepiness.

His chuckle in the dark is soft. "Why do you ask?"

"I was thinking we could try out our new bed." I bite my lip and slide my hand down the flat planes of his stomach toward his cock. God, I love sex with Nick. It's always a mixture of rough intensity and infinite gentleness, and each time, it's like the first all over again.

"You are not tired?"

He's always so concerned about me. Like I am some fragile flower. Today was an exhausting day because of the move into our apartment, but I feel invigorated now that we are here, in our bed.

We are starting our new life together.

I want to start it right. So I slide my hand to his cock and caress the bulge there. He's already erect. My Nick needs no more than a hint of encouragement, and he's ready for sex. It makes me feel incredibly desirable to know that I can bring him to an intense erection with little more than a word or two. "I'm not tired," I tell him, and I add, "It seems like you're not very tired, either."

And I lean in and nip gently at the skin on his chest.

He groans, holding me closer to him. I know he loves it when I touch him. I move my mouth over his pectoral, kissing at the skin there, and then I graze my lips over his nipple.

I feel his body jolt in response, and then he's flipping me onto my back in the bed, taking control. "If my Daisy wants pleasure," he says, and his voice is a low, thickly accented thrum, "I will give it to her."

Excitement flares through me, and I wiggle with anticipation under him. I'm disappointed that it's so dark in the new apartment. I want to see his lean, tattooed body looming over mine. My hands reach for him, and I trail them along his skin even as he moves over me and begins to hike my sleep shirt up over my torso. A second later, cool air kisses my breasts, and then his mouth is on them, hot and hungry.

I gasp at the sensation of his teeth scraping at my nipples, followed by his tongue as he soothes away the sting. Nick loves my breasts, though they're not impressive by any means. He loves everything about me. He tongues my nipples into hard peaks, leaving me gasping and moaning his name. My nails dig into his shoulders because I know he loves that—hints of roughness mixed with the tenderness.

"My Daisy," he groans, and he begins to kiss a trail down my belly. "Beautiful, precious, wondrous Daisy. I will never tire of your taste."

His sexy words make my pulse flutter hard, and my legs part in anticipation of what comes next.

Nick slides further down, until I can feel his hot breath on the V of my sex. This is one of his favorite things—to lick my pussy until I have at least one orgasm, sometimes two. Sometimes more. One night, he wanted to see how many times he could make me come, and he licked me until I was so tender that the merest flick of his tongue sent orgasmic shockwaves through my body. I walked funny for the next day.

He was very pleased with himself, then. He likes to make me mindless with passion. Like it is a reward.

I don't want endless hours of sexual teasing tonight, though. I want Nick inside me, his flesh pushing into mine. I want that rough, wild joining of our bodies, and I want it now. So I dig my nails in harder to let him know I am impatient.

"Mmm," he says in that husky voice. "Are you wet for me, *dasha*? I think I must taste and find out."

Surely he knows how wet I am right now? I can feel the slickness between my thighs as I squirm with anticipation, his breath heating me between my legs. But then his mouth dips, and I feel his tongue stroke against my clit.

All the breath shudders out of me. A sound escapes me, high and keening. I'll never get used to the sensation. Never.

Nor do I want to. It feels more intense, more magical every time.

Nick murmurs something in Russian, and then he's licking

me harder, swiping his tongue from clit down to my cunt. He licks and sucks at my flesh until I am whimpering with need, the orgasm building in intensity. It's never quiet, easy, routine sex with Nick. It's always fireworks and explosions. I love that he's able to tease me so easily, and that he takes such pleasure in it.

My hips raise as his mouth works me toward my first orgasm of the night. I arch into his mouth as he sucks on my clit, reaching for that pleasure. My fingers dig in to his scalp as I hold his head there, in just the right spot. "Oh, Nikolai," I rasp. "Oh, yes! Nikolai!"

He loves it when I say his full name. I hear his feral growl, and then he tongues me even more swiftly, with even more intensity.

I shatter, just as he intends, and I'm crying out his name as I climax from his mouth alone.

Then he's moving over me, his big body sliding over mine. I feel him fit his hips between my own, feel the press of his cock against my sex. I'm so ready for him that even though I just came, I want more. When his mouth presses to mine, I greedily suck on the tongue that slides between my lips, letting him know just how hungry I am for him.

"My Daisy," he says, his lips moving against my mouth. Then he sinks in to the hilt, spearing himself within me.

I gasp at the pleasure that radiates from his cock buried deep inside me, and I wrap my arms around his neck. I hold him close as he pumps furiously between my legs, bringing me to another shattering orgasm in mere minutes.

His follows close behind, and I hear him groan my name as he comes. I feel him quake, feel his come inside me. There are no condoms separating us; I'm on the pill . . . for now. When we're ready, we'll move forward, and I'll be Daisy Anders, wife to Nick

Anders. And we'll have children. But for now, I must go slow with my Nick. He's so new to being loved at all that I want to enjoy this time between just us.

Nick collapses on top of me, his weight delicious, skin sticky with sweat. I stroke and pet his skin, knowing that he loves nothing more than being touched after sex. I wrap my legs around his and cling to him, like a spider monkey, because I love the weight of his body pressing into my own.

He rolls onto his side, but I don't let go; I simply burrow closer to him. "I love you, Nikolai." I say this every day, but I think he needs to hear it as often as possible.

His arms tighten around me. "Daisy," he murmurs. "My sweet, wonderful Daisy. I love you more than life itself." His hand smooths my hair, and I nuzzle his neck. I love this cuddling after sex. I'm so glad Nick isn't one of those men that rolls over and goes to sleep.

Tonight, though, he's pensive. He continues to stroke my hair for long minutes, silent. Eventually, though, he asks, "Do you regret your life with me, Daisy? With my stained hands? It is because of me you have killed a man. I have taken your innocence in all ways." He sounds sad.

"Never," I tell him fiercely. It is the truth. "It is because of you that I am free, Nick. That my father is free from fear." I lean in and kiss his beloved mouth. "It is because of you that I love and am loved in return."

"You are too good, my Daisy." His voice is thick with emotion. "How did I ever find myself so lucky as to have one such as you in my life?"

"We were made for each other," I tell him, and I press my cheek against his heart. "Don't you think? It's like our lives had to happen the way they did so we could find each other at that precise moment in time. You never would have found me if you weren't a hit man working on that last hit. I never would have met you if you weren't. How can I regret these things?" I kiss the motto on his chest. "It's what brought us together."

He hugs me tighter.

Someday, my Nick will believe what I tell him. Until then, I'm content to cuddle in his arms and repeat my words of love over and over until they finally sink in and he realizes how much I adore him.

We're both patient people, Nick and I. We know how to wait, and there's pleasure in the waiting.

So I press my unmarked body closer to my lover's tattooed one, and I kiss his skin until he rolls me onto my back once more. We make love until the daylight shines through the open windows.

And then we sleep. Together.

If you wish to receive an email when the next book in the Hitman series is released, text BOOKNEWS to 66866. By texting BOOKNEWS from your mobile number, you agree to receive text messages requesting your email address and confirming your wish to receive an email about the next book. Your consent is not a condition of purchase. Standard messaging and data costs may apply.

ACKNOWLEDGMENTS

Special thanks to Lisa and Milasy from the Rock Stars of Romance for their unflagging support and encouragement. We've had such a great time working together.

To our early readers: Daphne, Heather, Louise, Lisa, Melissa, and Michelle. Your insight was invaluable.

To Angie at Angie's Dreamy Reads, Natasha at Natasha is a Book Junkie, and Lisa and Milasy at the Rock Stars of Romance, thank you for hosting our excerpt tour. Special thanks also to the Mistresses at SM Book Obsessions for their "on target" giveaway.

Thank you to all of the bloggers who participated in our blog tour and/or reviewed our book: Sammie's Book Club; Book Drunk Blog; BestSellers & BestStellars; Miss Construed's Reviews; MrsLeif's; Two Fangs About It; Romance Rewind; Reading Books Like a Boss; We Like It Big Book Blog; About That Story; Margay Leah Justice; Book Lovin' Mamas; A Love Affair with Books; Miss Me Passionate; Love Between the Sheets; Starbucks & Books Obsession; Escape Into a Book; Whirlwindbooks; Mary Elizabeth's Crazy Book Obsession; Book Drunk Blog; Booze, Bookz, and Bad Boyz; The Flirty Reader; Eskimo Princess Book Reviews; The To Be Read List; Ripe For Reader; T and A After Dark; Fike's Book Blog; Book Breath Babe;

Shh Moms Reading; Hesperia Loves Books; The Book Blog; Once Upon A Dream Books (formerly known as Life Becomes Me); Dirty Girl Romance; Sassy Girl Books; Must Read Books or Die; All Romance Reviews; A Little Bit Tart, A Little Bit Sweet; Rumpled Sheets Blog; Read This—Hear That; Love N. Books; Biblio Belles; Xscape From Reality With A Book; I Love Lady Porn; Bound By Books; Scandalous Book Blog; Random Musesomy; I Read Indie; Room With Books; 2 Bookaholics; Cruising Susan Reviews; Who You Callin' A Book Whore?; Dirty Books Dirty Boys; Perusing Princesses; The Romance Evangelist; SMIBookClub; Mean Girls Luv Books; random jendsmit; As the Pages Turn; Rookie Romance; Sugar and Spice Book Reviews; Paranormal Romance and Authors That Rock; Alphas, Authors & Books Oh My; Susan Sager; Books, Coffee and Wine; I ♥ Bookie Nookie Reviews; Sarah's Bookshelf; The Biblio-Files: Confessions of a Book Whore; Chapter Break; Made for You Book Reviews; My Daily Romance; First Class Books; Jess's Book Blog; Books Unhinged; Sizzling Pages; Three Chicks and Their Books; Louisa's Reviews; and Books Over Boys.

To all the reviewers who've left reviews and readers who've read our book, we will never be able to give enough thanks.

Read on for a special preview of

LAST **BREATH**

Available March 2015 from Berkley Books!

DANIEL

She's a biter. That's the warning given when I point to the blonde with the glazed green eyes in Senhor Gomes's book of whores. He shakes his head and says that he has access to dozens of others that are better and all willing to engage in whatever perverse activity I want. He brags that there isn't a sick sex act I can think of that Gomes can't fulfill. I like home cooking, I tell him. A Texan in Rio sees a lot of beautiful Brazilian women, but sometimes you want a little star-spangled banner in the rotation.

He nods as if this makes sense to him, but I think it's the money that I'm flashing that he understands. We walk up to the second floor and down a narrow hall toward the back, a windowless part of this brick-and-metal building. I can't call it a home or even a brothel. It's a dingy place where men with deep perversions but shallow wallets can get their rocks off.

I don't want to have sex here, I've explained to Gomes. I have a thing against hellholes and having sex in them. I wave around a lot of cash, and Gomes nods and asks no more questions.

We're a strange parade—Gomes, me, and some house mom trailing behind. He stops at the second-to-last door and removes a key.

I've seen pictures of Regan Porter before, and not in Gomes's look book, but nothing prepares me for her full-fledged, magazine-quality beauty. She hasn't been eating well; her delicate bones are beginning to look sharp in places—at her shoulders, ribs, and hips. But there's no denying her breathtaking looks. Her blond hair is damp, and small strands stick to her perfect skull. Her oval face, with its pink cheekbones and lush lips, and eyebrows that look like wings, stands out like a piece of fine china at a flea market. Though she's thin, there's a delicious curviness in the slope of her side as it dips into the waist and flares back out to form a cuppable roundness at the hip. And those endlessly long legs.

Shit. I close my eyes and swallow. No decent man would be standing here thinking about those legs wrapped around his waist. But then again, I'm not decent. I'm no longer army sniper, Special Forces Daniel Hays who may have once been lauded as a hero for killing insurgents in Afghanistan. Now I'm Daniel Hays, mercenary who kills people for money and spends all his spare time in brothels and flesh dens like this one. Decency is a word I don't even know the meaning of anymore.

It's been too long since I've had a woman. That's my only excuse. That and I'm becoming the monster that I'm hunting. I focus on the bruises on her knees that are scraped red and raw from time on the floor, and the manacle around her ankle. Any feelings of arousal are jettisoned by the obvious signs of abuse.

Glancing sharply at Gomes, I wonder how he's come to possess a beauty like Regan Porter. Gomes is a small-time flesh peddler, stuck up here in the slums, with a house full of females—half of which are missing their teeth or are too old or too broken.

He usually gets what the market calls secondhand goods, the girls that no other house wants. But Regan Porter is gorgeous, and while she looks a little run-down, she's still model beautiful with big pink lips and wide green eyes.

"Nice tits." I smirk for Gomes's sake, and her shudder of disgust only feeds into my growing belief that I'm as dirty as the flesh trader beside me. The dark edges of the world that I now inhabit are seeping into my skin like an oil slick covering an ocean. I shouldn't want to touch her. And if I have to fuck her in front of Gomes to get her out of here—I don't even let myself finish that thought.

There's still life in her eyes. If she's biting and spitting out acerbic insults, there's spirit left in her, and I don't want to be the one to snuff out that last flame. Her eyes convey her hate, and if she had a knife, I'd be sliced from my throat to my belly. I stare back, not because she's fucking beautiful, but because she's still standing. I'm not sure I would've been as strong. I don't know if she sees my admiration or whether she can only interpret varying degrees of lust and degradation, but she sees something. An invisible string spools out between us, and her eyes widen when it hits her like an electrical shock.

For months I've swum in a pool of blood and death and ugly deeds, and to hold on to my sanity and maybe my soul, I've told myself that saving these doves balances the scale. For every life I take, if I save one then it's all a wash in the end. Don't think it's tallied that way at St. Peter's gate, but that's the lie I tell myself so I can sleep at night and look at myself in the mirror the next day. Regan Porter will either be part of my attempt at salvation or the bloody stone that etches out the words *He Failed* on my headstone.

"She looks like a live one," I say to Gomes, playing up my role as the asshole merc who's just been paid for some godforsaken deed and needs to plow his victory lap into some unwilling broad.

He squints at Regan, tallying up her worth. She's valuable now because I'm willing to pay so much for her, and Gomes doesn't really understand why. "Twenty-five thousand could buy you a harem. Her pussy isn't lined with gold. Let me hook you up with someone different," Gomes whines.

Don't know why he wants to hold on to her so bad, but I can see that he's torn between wanting my money and wanting to keep Regan in the whorehouse.

"I prefer to eat domestic," I say. Gomes doesn't really expect a response, or at least he shouldn't. Buying and selling human flesh requires some discretion, even here in Brazil, where prostitution is legal but houses like these aren't. Gomes and I stare at each other while the bangles on the dirty American flag bikini tinkle in the background. *Don't draw attention to yourself*, I silently command the girl.

The urge to beat Gomes until his own mama won't recognize him washes over me in a red, violent haze. My fist in his mouth and the heel of my boot crushing his dick would be phenomenal. I've been in and out of these houses of horror for the last eighteen months looking for my sister. She went on her first and only spring break trip and never came back. I was in Delta Force, playing sniper, when I got the news. I arrived home to find my mother distraught and my dad . . . fuck, I'll never forget the look on his face. Dad was a hardened rancher who'd held on to his family legacy by the repeated sacrifice of his blood to the land. He'd seen shit and done shit, but the loss of his baby girl had hollowed him out. His eyes looked empty as if the news had sucked his insides dry.

I stayed one night and in the early morning hours of the next day, he walked me out to my truck and told me not to come home until I'd found her. And I haven't found her and I haven't been home. There won't be anything to go back to unless I bring her home.

In the months since my sister was kidnapped from Cancun, I've rescued hundreds of girls either in the sex trade or headed for sale. They've been grateful, traumatized, and tearful. I've never once encountered a mouthy one. Not until Regan. She looks like she might bite off my hand if I try to reach for her.

It took me nearly two months to find her after she was sold from Russia. And that snaps me back. Killing Gomes in a black rage isn't going to keep Regan safe or help me find my sister.

Gesturing toward Regan, I try to get him to speed up this transaction. "We're done talking now. Get me a coat for her. I can't take her outside in that getup. Shit."

Gomes leans out the door and yells to someone to get Regan a coat. *"Depressa! Vai-me buscar um casaco."*

I cross my arms, looking like I'm seconds away from walking on this deal, when really I have my fingers close to the guns inside my coat. I could shoot Gomes right now, and I kind of want to, but hasty decisions like that would only hurt my situation. I learned that early on. You can kill a Gomes, but a dozen others like him will rise up from the sewer like an army of rats. If you want to stop something like this, you have to find the source of the rats and cut off the damn head and then cauterize it. But I'll be back for Gomes. I won't be able to sleep at night until I know the only hole he's plundering is the asshole of a demon in the underworld.

The house mom appears at the door and hands Gomes a tissue-thin jacket that won't even cover the tops of Regan's thighs. I rip the thing out of Gomes's hands. He's not touching her again.

"Let's go, sweet cheeks," I command, snapping my fingers toward Regan. She lets out a low, feral growl. I want to laugh in Gomes's face at this—that she's withstood his treatment—but I can't let any approval for her show. Gomes gives a jerk of his head and the house mom scuttles over to unlock the chains around her ankle. As the iron falls away, I see that the skin is scabbed all over. I'm surprised it's not infected. Suddenly the contents of my stomach are at the back of my mouth, and I scrub my hand over my lips to disguise my reaction. I want to throw a blanket over her, shoot everyone, and carry her away.

This is such a goddamned travesty. My tone is sharp and angry. "Put this on." I throw it to her and she catches it almost reflexively, but she's slow as molasses putting on the coat, as if she's weighing whether I'm worse than the devil she knows. Gomes motions for the house mom to hurry Regan up, but I put up a hand to stay the house mom's actions. Regan doesn't want to be touched by anyone. You can read that aversion in every line of her body, which is why I threw the coat to her. I don't need a fight from her. And truthfully I feel sorry for her. God, she is barely a woman—around the same age as my sister, who was twenty when she was taken. Regan is twenty-two or so, Nick had told me. Nick, who sent me here to retrieve her.

"I don't got all day." I point to my wristwatch. It's a reward, I've told people, for killing some family who had the nerve to tell me no. Half the time a badass reputation gets you out of tight spots better than two guns and a dozen magazines. Although I'd take those, too. I glance over and Regan is still taking her sweet time. "You can either stay here chained to a wall or come with me."

It's no kind of alternative, but I'm banking on the fact that she's currently thinking about a million ways she can escape me once she's outside of this place. She gives a little nod, not really to me, but acknowledging some decision she's made in her mind. I step out and walk away, pretending like I don't care for a minute if she follows. Gomes doesn't move but instead exchanges sharp words with the house mom in Portuguese, thinking, I guess, that I won't understand him. But I do. The ability to pick up different languages and quickly is almost a requirement of being part of Delta Force, and I've spent time in both Portugal and Brazil.

"*Faz com que ela veste o casaco!*" says Gomes, ordering the house mom to help Regan put on the jacket.

"*Eu não posso. Ela vai me arranhar,*" the house mom responds. The house mom refuses, fearing that Regan will scratch her. Regan's a terror even chained to the wall. Her fierceness is metal as fuck, and that almost cranks my chain as much as her legs. Some of the girls I've taken from these places are so broken that they don't see anything but their abuse anymore. Some fall back into the business, working on their own or as part of someone's stable, because they can't function normally. Although what the hell is normal, I have no goddamned idea anymore.

A shuffling sound occurs behind me, and I pause. The steps are light, so they don't belong to Gomes or the heavier house mom.

"You aren't going to like owning me," Regan hisses quietly at my back. If I really were an angry john with a taste for home, I'd backhand her, but my response isn't one of anger but of resignation. I want to shake some fucking sense into her and beg her to make it easier for both of us for one hot second. Instead I grunt because deep down, part of me wants to show her how wrong she is. In different circumstances, if we were alone in a dark corner of some bar back home, I'd back her right up to the wall and tell her that not only would she like being owned by me, but she'd fucking beg for it.

But we're not alone. She's not some college girl slumming it in a hole-in-the-wall outside of Fort Benning, so I don't back her into a corner. I don't slip my leg between her golden thighs, and I don't start sucking on the tender skin at the base of her neck. I don't even turn around to look at her, and I guess this makes her even angrier. "I bite and I don't cry and I'll vomit and pee all over you."

Jesus Hermione Christ. This girl has balls of freaking steel. "Can't wait, baby doll," I say, trotting sideways down the narrow stairs. And for all her threats, Regan is close behind me. I can hear Gomes and the house mom making up the end. I can see the front door and our potential freedom beyond.

"You still want this whore?" Gomes calls out. "I have so many others. This one's too much trouble for you."

I laugh, a sour sound so Gomes knows I'm not really amused. "You took my money, Gomes. I'm not into international pussy, so I'm taking this girl and you're going to be happy with the quarter I dropped for her."

We're at the front door now, and Regan has stopped hissing insults at me because she's stunned into silence by the prospect of escape. "How long you think you will keep her?"

Turning to face Gomes, I place my hand on the door. Down here in the entrance, it's actually more dangerous. Gomes has guards at the door, inside and out. He's having trouble processing that I don't want to fuck in his little shithouse.

"You think I'm paying a quarter for her and that I'm going to just trot her back after an evening?" From Gomes's frown, it's clear that he thinks she is coming back tomorrow. I shake my head. For the money that I've given him, he should've assumed that Regan would be fucked until she's dead. "She'll be back when I'm good and ready to return her. I didn't pay that kind of coin for one night."

"What will you do with her?"

"What do you care?" I ask impatiently. Regan is shivering beneath the jacket, the bangles beating a faster rhythm. Her feet are probably cold on the red clay tiles. Outside she'll be warmer, though, and as soon as we're out of the *favelas*, I'll get her some shoes.

Gomes looks a little ill. "I need her back."

I shake my head. "You let me worry about the disposal of this one. You should worry about the fact you've been spreading the tales about your wares into some dangerous places. Places where *Polícia Federal* might have to take notice. Don't be a shithead and ruin it for the rest of us." *And by the rest of us, I mean you, asswipe.*

I look at the two hired muscles standing inside the front room, which serves as Gomes's office and showroom. It's got a deep red carpet that has stains all over it. I don't know whether it's come or blood, but I'm glad I was wearing shoes when I made that transaction with Gomes thirty minutes earlier. With my hand on the doorknob, I give everyone a leveling gaze. "We're done here."

Gomes looks at his goons and then at me. There's something about me Gomes doesn't like, or maybe it's because he thinks he's losing a valuable piece of property. Second thoughts are all over his face, and I ruck up my suit coat on the side so I can have ready access to my gun, just in case. The goons move toward the door of Gomes's front room and the tension becomes heavier, like dense smog descending over the slums. I calculate my next course of action. Gomes does not look armed. He's wearing a thin cotton Panama shirt and linen pants, wrinkled and splattered with liquid around the ankles. The cotton would reveal any hidden guns at his waist or back. He could have an ankle piece, but I'm a good enough shot that he'd be dead by the time he bent over. I dismiss the house mom. The two muscled guys are my only worries. The entryway is narrow, like the stairs, and we are packed into the foyer like little sardines in a tin can. If a firefight breaks out here, we are all toast. I know Regan doesn't want to be touched, but I need to signal her, somehow, to get behind me.

"I worry about you in the *favela*," Gomes says. He waves his hand and one of the goons steps forward. "Ricardo will escort you out, to be sure that you get back to your hotel safely."

Or he'll shoot me in the back and take your blond American prize back to the stable. No, not happening, but I'm anxious to get out of the house. Ricardo can be taken down once we are outside. No doubt there are several other thugs along the way that Ricardo intends to meet up with, but we have way better odds outside.

"Whatever," I answer and then throw open the door, hard. It hits Ricardo in the nose and he curses. Behind me I hear a muffled snort. *Good girl*, I think, and then I walk outside with Regan close on my heels.